CRITICAL ACCLAIM FOR HAROLD SCHECHTER'S
MASTERFUL HISTORICAL NOVEL

NEVERMORE

"Authentic.... Engaging.... Schechter manages at once to be faithful to Poe's voice, and to poke gentle fun at it—to swing breezily between parody and homage."

—*The Baltimore Sun*

"Schechter . . . recounts the legendary author's brush with real-life homicide as one of Poe's own protagonists would—with morbid, scientific rapture . . . plenty of suspense and nicely integrated background details."

—*Publishers Weekly*

"[A] tantalizing tale full of tongue twisters and terror...."

—*Booklist*

"Caleb Carr and Tom Holland are going to have some competition for turf in the land of historical literary crime fiction."

—*The Boston Book Review*

"Schechter does a good job of re-creating Poe's phantas-magoric style."

—*San Antonio Express News*

"Wonderful. . . . I highly recommend *NEVERMORE*. I had more fun with this book than any I have read in a long time."

—*Denver Rocky Mountain News*

"A real page-turner. . . . Deftly re-creates 1830s Baltimore and brings Poe to life.... [Poe] makes an engaging sleuth."

—*Richmond Times Dispatch*

Books by Harold Schechter

The A–Z Encyclopedia of Serial Killers
  (with David Everitt)
Bestial
Depraved
Deranged
Deviant
Outcry
Nevermore

Published by POCKET BOOKS

NEVERMORE

HAROLD SCHECHTER

POCKET BOOKS
New York   London   Toronto   Sydney   Singapore

This book is a work of fiction. Names, characters, places and incidents are products of the author's imagination or are used fictitiously. Any resemblance to actual events or locales or persons, living or dead, is entirely coincidental.

 POCKET BOOKS, a division of Simon & Schuster Inc.
1230 Avenue of the Americas, New York, NY 10020

Copyright © 1999 by Harold Schechter

Originally published in hardcover in 1999 by Pocket Books

ISBN: 0-671-79856-1

First Pocket Books paperback printing January 2000

10 9 8 7 6 5 4 3 2 1

POCKET and colophon are registered trademarks of Simon & Schuster Inc.

Cover art by Tom Hallman

Printed in the U.S.A.

In loving remembrance of

CELIA WASSERMAN SCHECHTER

HISTORICAL NOTE

In March 1834 the Philadelphia publishers Carey & Hart brought out *A Narrative of the Life of David Crockett of the State of Tennessee*, the only authorized autobiography of the legendary pioneer. The book—recounting Crockett's colorful life from his early backwoods exploits to his political battles in the House of Representatives—became an immediate bestseller, transforming its author into a national celebrity, a homespun symbol of America's rugged frontier spirit.

Shortly after the appearance of his life story, Crockett—a savvy self-promoter—embarked on a major publicity tour. Setting out from Washington, D.C., he travelled throughout the Northeast, attracting admiring crowds wherever he went. His itinerary included stops in Philadelphia, New York, Boston, and Baltimore.

For all its commercial success, Crockett's autobiography did not win universal praise. A particularly scathing notice appeared in the *Southern Literary*

Messenger—a distinguished magazine of the day—whose reviewer denounced the book for its "vulgarity."

As it happened, the author of this pan was residing in Baltimore at the very time of Crockett's visit. Living in financially straitened circumstances with his aunt, Maria Clemm, and her twelve-year-old daughter, Virginia, this brilliant young writer was struggling to establish himself as a literary figure. Before long his savagely critical reviews would win him a widespread reputation as the country's most controversial critic—the "tomahawk man" of American letters.

His name was Edgar Allan Poe.

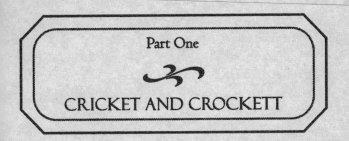

Part One

CRICKET AND CROCKETT

CHAPTER 1

During the whole of a dull, dark, and dreary day, when the clouds hung oppressively low in the sky, I had been sitting alone in my chamber, poring over a medical treatise of singular interest and merit. Its author was the eminent Doctor M. Valdemar of Leipzig, whose earlier volume, *The Recrudescence of Leprosy and Its Causation*, had done much to divest that grave affliction of the aura of preternatural dread that has surrounded its sufferers throughout the ages. In one remarkable stroke, Valdemar had succeeded in elevating the study of this ancient scourge—so long steeped in primitive superstition—to the heights of pure *science*.

Valdemar's latest treatise, which had so absorbed my attention throughout that dismal afternoon in the latter week of April, was offered in the same spirit of enlightened rationalism. Its subject was, if conceivable, even more repugnant to refined sensibilities than the bodily disfigurements produced by infectious *leprosis*. Indeed, it was a subject of such extreme morbidity that—even in the hands of one as averse to mere *sensationalism* as

Valdemar—it resounded more of the ghastly themes of the Gothic than the concerns of medical philosophy.

The volume, prominently displayed in the window of a venerable bookseller on Lexington Street, had caught my eye a few days earlier. Even more than the name of its distinguished author, it was the title of the book, gold-stamped on green leather, that had riveted my attention: *Inhumation Before Death, and How It May Be Prevented.* Here, indeed, was a matter worthy of the most rigorous scientific investigation. For all the imagined terrors that vex the tranquillity of the human soul, surely none can parallel the contemplation of that awful eventuality to which Valdemar had addressed himself in his newest book. I mean, of course, the grim—the ghastly—the unspeakable— possibility of *premature burial!*

Personal affairs of more than usual urgency had delayed my perusal of this remarkable volume. At last, with sufficient time at my disposal, I had sequestered myself behind the closed door of my *sanctum*, where, by the sombre yellow light of my table lamp, I had devoted the better part of the day to the intense scrutiny of Valdemar's treatise.

Applying the prodigious erudition that is the hall-mark of his genius, Valdemar had produced a veritable *encyclopædia* of knowledge concerning this most awful of subjects. His chapter headings alone gave ample indication of the enormous breadth of his undertaking: "Cataleptic Sleep and Other Causes of Premature Burial," "The Signs of Death," "The Dangers of

Hasty Embalmment," "Cremation as a Preventive of Premature Burial," "Resuscitation from Apparent Death," and "Suspended Animation after Small-Pox," among many others. It is scarcely necessary to state that the wealth of useful—nay, indispensable—knowledge embodied in these pages more than justified the somewhat exorbitant cost of the volume.

Still, the all-compelling interest of the book did not derive solely, or even primarily, from the practical information it contained. Rather, it stemmed from the many documented cases Valdemar had assembled from medical reports throughout the world: the all-too-numerous instances of wretched fellow-creatures whose fate it had been to suffer the supreme torments of *living interment*. Indeed, though Valdemar's prose style (in his scrupulous efforts to avoid any taint of the lurid) verged, at moments, on the dryly pedantic, the mere recitation of these cases was sufficiently chilling to provoke in the reader an empathic response of the highest intensity.

At least, so it proved with me.

One particular instance, cited from the *Chirurgical Journal* of London, had transfixed me with horror. This was the case of a young English gentleman who had fallen victim to an anomalous disorder—a cataleptic state of such profound immobility that even his physicians mistook it for death. Accordingly, he was placed in his coffin and consigned to the family plot. Some hours later, the sexton heard an unearthly gibbering issuing from the ground. The gravedigger was summoned; the casket uncovered; the lid prised open.

Within the box lay the young man, cackling wildly, his black hair bleached completely white by fear!

When, by slow degrees, he recovered the power of speech, he described the agonies of his experience. Though seemingly insensate, he had retained his auditory faculties throughout his ordeal. Thus, he had listened—with an acuity born of absolute terror—to every sound that attended his intombment: the closing of the casket; the clatter of the hearse; the grieving of his loved ones; the sickening fall of shovelled soil upon his coffin lid. And yet, in consequence of his paralysis, he had been unable, by either sound or motion, to alert those around him to the extremity of his condition—until, set loose by his utter desperation, a torrent of maddened shrieks had vomited forth from the very pit of his fear-harrowed soul.

Something about this story so impressed itself upon my imagination that, as I sat there lost in contemplation, I gradually fell into a kind of waking reverie—or rather, nightmare. I lost track of time. My familiar surroundings—the small, shadowy chamber with its meagre furnishings and black-curtained window—appeared to dissolve. Darkness embraced me. I felt myself enveloped by the suffocating closeness of the grave.

No longer was I merely *ruminating* upon the agonies of premature burial; I was *experiencing* them as vividly as if my own still-living body had been laid, all unwittingly, in the tomb. I could *feel, hear,* and *sense* every particular of that dread calamity: the unendurable oppression of the lungs—the clinging of the death garments—the rigid embrace of the coffin—the methodical thudding of the gravedigger's shovel—the unseen but palpable presence of the Conqueror Worm.

A scream of the purest anguish arose in my throat. I opened my terror-parched lips, praying that my cries would save me from the ineffable torments of my predicament.

Before I could summon this agonized yell (an act which would unquestionably have alarmed the entire neighborhood and occasioned me a great deal of embarrassment), a dim awareness of my true situation broke into my overwrought fancy. Suddenly, I realized that the noise I had mistaken for gravedigging was in reality the muffled thud of some unknown caller, pounding on the front door of my residence. Or rather, I should say, of the residence I shared with my beloved Aunt Maria and her angelic daughter, my darling little cousin Virginia.

I pulled out my pocket handkerchief and, with a deep groan of relief, wiped away the moisture that my all-too-vivid fantasy had wrung from my brow. Laying aside Valdemar's treatise, I cocked an ear towards the front of the house. I could discern the distinctive tread of my sainted "Muddy" (for so, in tribute to her maternal devotion, I fondly referred to my aunt) as she hastened to answer the knocking. Dimly, I could hear her interrogative tone as she greeted the visitor.

An instant later, striding footsteps echoed in the corridor, succeeded by a sharp, determined rapping upon my chamber door.

Shaking off the horror which, even then, retained a lingering hold on my spirit, I bade the caller enter. My door swung in upon its hinges and a tall, broad-shouldered figure stood silhouetted within the frame. He posed there for a moment, critically surveying my quarters before delivering a statement of such stentorian quality that it smote upon my ears like the discharge of a cannon. The *content* of his remark was no less surprising than its volume.

"Well I'll be jiggered if it ain't as glum as a bearcave in here," he boomed.

So startling was this comment that, as if by reflex, I swivelled in my chair and parted the heavy curtains obscuring the window behind me. Owing to the lateness of the hour (which was rapidly approaching dinnertime), as well as the sullenness of the weather, only a modicum of daylight was admitted by my action. Still, this illumination, added to that of my table lamp, proved sufficient for me to take stock of my visitor.

He cut an imposing figure. Though his height fell several inches short of six feet, he appeared to be a man of nearly Herculean stature: an effect that was in large part due to his erect, indeed military, carriage, as well as to the exceptional span of his shoulders and chest. His full head of thick, black hair framed a visage of equally striking character. There was something in his features—the piercing blue eyes, hawklike nose, and prominent chin—that spoke of boundless interior strength and resolution. To this must be added a vague yet palpable air of natural *bonhomie*. Perhaps his most noticeable characteristic, however, was his robust complexion, which attested to a life of rugged outdoor pursuits.

This latter impression was heightened by his clothing; for though his garments were of the most presentable cut and fashion—high-collared coat, gray-striped pantaloons, stiff shirtfront and cerulean cravat—he seemed strangely constricted in this formal attire, as though he were more accustomed to the loose-fitting garb of the yeoman or hunter.

My inspection of this singular individual—who had yet to trouble himself with the nicety of an introduction—lasted no more than a few seconds. Determined to learn his identity without further delay, I parted my lips and made ready to speak. Before I could give voice to my question, however, he withdrew a folded sheet of paper from his side pocket and opened it with a flourish.

"I reckon I had best say why I'm here, for I see that you are set to bust like an airthquake with curiosity," he declared in his unmistakable backwoods "drawl." There was something strangely familiar in his manner of speech, as though I had heard his voice before. Where I had encountered it, however, remained a mystery, for it was indisputably the case that I had never laid eyes on him before.

"Mighty poor light in here for a feller to read by," he muttered, turning his paper this way and that.

Focussing my attention on this item, I now perceived that it was a printed page which had been detached from a book or periodical. Its tattered right edge offered conspicuous proof that it had been care-lessly—even violently—removed from its source.

Having finally settled on a position, my visitor began to read in a manner which suggested that, though not entirely foreign to him, this activity was by no means habitual. His halting pronunciation, how-ever, in no way impeded the *forcefulness* of his delivery, which was enlivened by his colorful interjections.

"'—*Moreover, we find this work cens . . . cens-u-rable*'—consarn it, but that's a jawbreaker!—'*for the frequent vul-garity of its language*—'"

As I sat there listening, my bemusement at his per-formance rapidly turned into astonishment, for it did not take me long to recognize that he was reading from a work of my own!—a review that I had lately con-tributed to Mr. Thomas White's enterprising new jour-nal, the *Southern Literary Messenger*.

A realization began to dawn within me. At that moment, however, I was distracted from my thoughts by a lively commotion outside my window, as though from a congregation of chattering schoolboys. Though their words were indistinct, there was no mistaking their tone of excited incredulity.

In the meantime, my visitor continued with his reading. " *If the author wishes to make himself a laughingstock, that is his affair. We see no reason, however, why the public should support him in this undertaking, and we would regard ourselves as remiss if we did not warn the unwary away from such fiddle-faddle.*'"

With this sharp, though by no means undeserved, admonition, my review ended—and with it the stranger's recitation. Looking up from the page, he crushed it into a ball and dropped it unceremoniously onto my writing table.

"Well, sir," he said, placing his hands upon his hips and regarding me with a challenging air. "I don't suppose you'll deny that them disfavorable words was written by you."

"I would not under any circumstances disavow my opinions," I coolly replied. "I do, however, insist that you offer an explanation for this remarkable intrusion."

"Why, if you ain't figgered that out yet, I don't suppose you're as all-fired smart as your fancy speechifyin' would have folks believe."

This retort so piqued my anger that—in spite of his superior physique (to say nothing of the debilitating influence which Valdemar's study had exerted on my overstrung nerves)—I half rose from my seat, prepared to forcibly eject the impudent stranger from my chamber.

At that very instant, however, I heard the patter of approaching feet. Suddenly a tiny figure burst into the room. I recognized him at once as Jimmy Johnston, the youngest son of the merchant whose family occupied the residence adjacent to my own. In his wake followed a half-dozen of his playmates. They crowded into the doorway while little Jimmy gazed upward, his expression suffused with such undisguised wonder that he might have been beholding one of Nature's marvels: the snowcapped peaks of the mighty Rocky Mountains, for example, or the roaring cataracts of Niagara.

"Is it . . . is it really you?" the awestruck boy finally managed to stutter.

Emitting a laugh that seemed to originate in the depths of his capacious chest, the stranger leaned down and placed a hand on the shoulder of the gaping lad.

"Right you are, young 'un. I'll be shot if you ain't a dang sight quicker than some other folks hereabouts."

Drawing himself up to his full height, he threw his head back and exclaimed, "I am Colonel David Crockett for a fact. Half-horse, half-alligator, with a little touch of the snapping turtle thrown in. I can shoot straighter, run faster, dive deeper, fight harder— and *write better*—than any man in the whole country."

Then, turning his gaze directly at me, he grinned with a ferocious glee. "And I'm here to skin the infernal hide off'n any lowdown *cricket* who claims different."

CHAPTER 2

A tense hush—similar to those intervals of electrical *stillness* that separate the resoundings of a thunderstorm—fell upon the room. Though only of the briefest duration, it afforded me a moment to muster my thoughts.

That the figure looming before me was indeed the celebrated Colonel Crockett was a fact I had already surmised. Who other than this personage would have taken such evident offense at my critique of his published *memoir?*—a book almost entirely devoid of either literary merit or narrative interest. A tiresome chronicle of Crockett's feats as hunter, fighter, and frontier orator, this volume conveyed an impression of its author as little more than an unlettered ruffian, whose proudest achievement was the slaughter of four dozen members of the species *Ursus americanus* in a single month.

And yet, the defects of this book had by no means diminished its appeal to the vast and vulgar reading public. Thus, Crockett's autobiography was to be found in quantity among the stock of every bookseller in the country, while works of infinitely greater value languished in total obscurity—a circumstance that could hardly fail to chafe at the heart of any serious writer compelled to pursue his high calling under harsh pecuniary conditions.

I hasten to add that, while my own situation was badly straitened, I had in no way permitted personal sentiment to color my opinions. Adhering to the most rigorous standards, my review had been utterly untainted with those envious feelings to which a less objective critic may have naturally succumbed.

At all events, it was not the unwarranted success of Crockett's book which now engaged my attention but rather the derisive remark which its author had just directed at me. By implication at least, he had likened me to a common insect—a "lowdown cricket," in his quaint phraseology. This gibe, I immediately saw, was a somewhat comical linguistic corruption—though whether a deliberate pun or a crude mispronunciation I would not have ventured to say.

Sitting erect in my chair, I unblinkingly met Crockett's impudent gaze. "I see that you have taken umbrage at my assessment of your autobiographical narrative, Colonel Crockett," said I. "That, I suppose, is the natural response of any writer whose efforts fail to elicit the esteem of those who render judgment. If the purpose of your visit is to discover the aesthetic principles upon which my opinion was based, I will be happy to accommodate you."

Here I paused briefly so as to emphasize my point. "On my part, however, I must first demand that you explain your characterization of me as a *cricket*, a creature only slightly removed in unsightliness from that most odious of pests, the domestic cockroach. Perhaps, as I suspect, you intended to say *critic?*"

My visitor's brow wrinkled in evident befuddlement as I spoke. When I had finished, he puckered his lips and exhaled a soundless whistle.

"I'll be hanged if you don't sound like a gilt-edged, hand-tooled, seven-dollar Friendship's Offering," he said. "Just listenin' to you spout off makes a feller's brain feel as wrung out as yesterday's laundry. As for me, I may not know all them highfalutin' words, but I say what I mean. Call yerself a *critic* if you like, but to my way o' thinkin', you and your kind is nothin' but a bunch o' varminous *crickets*—useless little critters that ain't got nothin' better to do than pester other folks with a lot of bothersome noise."

This insult, unendurable in itself, was rendered even more galling by the burst of hilarity it elicited from Crockett's juvenile admirers. Indignation flared within my breast. I arose from my chair, stepped to the front of my writing table, and stationed myself directly before the audacious frontiersman. Standing in such close proximity to him, I was struck anew by the aura of raw physical power which seemed to emanate from his person like an effusion of *eau de cologne*. Drawing myself up to my full height, I addressed him thusly:

"Perhaps the contemplative surroundings in which you presently find me have created the impression of a nature unsuited to manly exertions. If so, you have badly misjudged me. I am the proud offshoot of a race long-steeped in military traditions. The Marquis de Lafayette himself paid public homage to the heroic service performed by my grandfather, General David Poe, in the cause of American freedom. As for myself, my records in the United States Army and the military academy at West Point stand as eloquent testimony to my mettle. While it is true that pugnacity is somewhat foreign to my temperament, I will not shun a fight when my honor is involved. Indeed, I may say of myself, as the Immortal Bard has the melancholy Dane say, that 'though I am not splenetive and rash, yet have I something in me dangerous which let thy wisdom fear!'"

This salvo produced a most remarkable effect upon Crockett, whose eyes appeared to acquire a dull glaze as I spoke, as if the sheer force of my oratory had staggered him. He looked at me open-mouthed for a long moment before shaking his head and replying: "I don't reckon I know of no immortal bird nor any melancholy dame. Here's what I *do* know, Cricket. Someone saw that review of yourn and sent it to me in an envelope. Whoever done it was too yaller to set down his name, but I got my suspicions.

"Now, you may not know it, shut away here in this hen-coop of yourn, but I got me a passel o' inimies in the guv'ment these days who're jest lookin' for any way to make me look foolish. The Great Man hisself is tryin' to see to it that I don't get re-elected on account of he can't bring me to heel, try as he might. But Davy Crockett is no man's man 'cept his own. I will never fetch and carry at the whistle of Andy Jackson nor anyone else.

"Now, that there review of yourn is just the sort o' shot-and-powder my inimies are hopin' will bring me down. Callin' me a buffoon and an ignoramus and whatnot. So here's what I got to say to *you*, Cricket: You speak prime, all right. Why, when it comes to dealin' words, I can't cut and shuffle with you nohow. But that book of mine is as true and honest as I knowed how to make it. It may be poor on grammar and spellin'. But while you was learnin' how to dot your *i*'s and cross your *t*'s, I was fighting injuns in the Creek War alongside Ol' Hickory hisself, afore he got so all-fired high and mighty."

The sincerity of this utterance could not be doubted, though its point had so far eluded me. I propounded to Crockett the question of why he had troubled to seek me out.

"Why, that's as plain as the curls on a buffalo's hide," he replied. "I expect you to write out an apology and see that it gets printed in that high-toned magazine."

"Impossible!" I cried. "Your request would compel me to violate the most sacred principles of my profession. The critic, like the poet, must set aside every consideration other than an absolute and unwavering fidelity to the immutable laws of artistic truth."

"Dang your hide, Cricket!" Crockett exclaimed. "Can't you *never* say a straight word?"

"Here is my word, Colonel Crockett. I cannot—*will* not—do as you request."

Crockett's cheeks ballooned outward. He blew out a long sigh, shrugged his massive shoulders, and said: "Then I don't suppose there's no way around it. You and me must fight, Cricket."

At this pronouncement, a joyous exclamation arose from Crockett's juvenile audience as if from a single throat. "Fight!" they cried. "Mr. Poe and Davy Crockett are going to have a fight!"

Patting the air with both hands, Crockett silenced the boys. "No, no, young 'uns. I don't mean to tussle with a man in his own home. That ain't Davy Crockett's style."

Turning his intense gaze back at me, he said, "Cricket, I'm givin' you 'til tomorrow morning to chaw on this matter. You'll find me stayin' at Mrs. Macready's boardin' house over yonder on Howard Street. I'll expect to see you there afore breakfast time with your answer. It's either an apology or an old-fashioned knock-down-and-drag-out fight atween you 'n' me."

Thus far I had tolerated Crockett's brazen behavior out of that ingrained sense of courtesy endemic to the well-bred Southerner. To be so insultingly addressed within the precincts of my own dwelling place, however, was a provocation I could no longer endure. Throwing back my shoulders, I replied to

Crockett's bullying ultimatum with the only answer it deserved: I screwed my lips into a withering sneer.

Pretending to ignore me, Crockett reached inside his vest pocket and consulted his timepiece. "By crackers! If I don't high-tail it out of here, I'm goin' to miss that supper that the young Whigs is throwin' me over to Barnum's Hotel."

"But Davy," a childish voice protested. It was that of little Jimmy Johnston. "You ain't told us none of your adventures."

Crockett emitted an indulgent chuckle. "Tell you what, lad. Why don't you and the rest of your chums stroll with me for a spell and I'll treat you to a by-gum slam-whanger of a story."

"Hurray!" came the answering shout.

"Let me see now," Crockett commenced, stroking his clean-shaven chin. "You boys ever hear 'bout the time I saved the whole livin' airth from scorchifyin' destruction by wringin' the tail off of Halley's comet?"

He cast me a farewell look that seemed to say, "I will see you in the morning, Mr. Cricket." Then, with his small band of rapt listeners in tow, he swivelled on his heels and departed through my wide-flung chamber door.

CHAPTER 3

Sleep failed to descend upon me that night. Still brooding upon Crockett's ultimatum and the insufferable manner of its delivery, I lay awake in the gloom of my bedchamber, listening to the tempest which raged beyond the walls of my abode. The dense clouds which had darkened the heavens all day had let loose their fury at nightfall. In the intensity of its violence, the storm appeared to be the visible expression of my own inner turbulence, as if to confirm the philosophy of those so-called Transcendental thinkers, who regard the multifarious *phenomena* of Nature as the outward manifestation of the human soul.

That Crockett and I must come to blows was certain. The effrontery of his demand, to say nothing of the impertinence of his manner, precluded a less sanguinary resolution of our differences. It should not be supposed, however, that the agitations of my spirit were occasioned by mere *personal* concern—no, not though the prospect of hand-to-hand battle with a notorious frontier "brawler" was intrinsically daunting. The savagery of the backwoods combatant is both well known and widely deplored. Disdaining the rules of fair play which govern *les affaires d'honneur* in all civilized nations, these ruffians will, in the fury of battle, resort to the most barbaric tricks, not excluding eye-gouging, nose-biting, and other acts of bodily and facial mutilation. I myself once witnessed a bloody "free-for-all" between two burly Kentuckians which left the forearm of one contestant so savagely bitten that a surgeon was required to perform an immediate amputation.

That Crockett was capable of such bloodthirsty conduct was a matter not merely of public record but of positive pride to him. His autobiographical narrative was replete with accounts of his violent exploits. Here was a being who measured his worldly accomplishments in terms of slaughtered bears, slain "wildcats," and scalped Indians, and whose favorite rifle was so dear to his heart that he had bestowed upon it the fond, feminine cognomen of "Betsy."

Still, for all his backwoods braggadocio, I was not unduly alarmed at the idea of engaging with Crockett, who had, after all, passed a considerable portion of his recent life in the refining atmosphere of our nation's political capital—a *milieu* which had undoubtedly exerted a somewhat softening influence upon his native ferocity.

Moreover, despite our disparate sizes, I felt confident in my ability to contest with even so formidable an opponent as Crockett. Like all men of *talent* (I will not call it *genius*, for such a designation, however accurate, must be left for others to apply), I have always provoked the envy of lesser mortals, who have vented their resentment in frequent libelous attacks upon my character. As those who truly know my character will attest, I have never permitted such insults to go unpunished, no matter how powerful the foe. I have thus been compelled on repeated occasions to deploy my pugilistic skills in the service of my Honor and bestow upon some blackguard the chastisement of a well-deserved drubbing.

No. It was not, as I have stated, a craven fear of personal injury that so preyed upon my spirit as to render sleep an impossibility—cowardice being as foreign to my nature as pusillanimity is to the panther's. Rather, it was my ardent solicitude for those two beloved creatures most precious to my heart: my ever-devoted "Muddy", and her darling daughter, Virginia. Cognizant of the degree to which their felicity depended upon my own well-being, I could not fail to suffer the sharpest pangs of apprehension at the prospect of occasioning them so much dismay. The very mention of my impending encounter with Crockett would be sufficient, I knew, to induce within their bosoms the gravest tremors of alarm. And yet to withhold the truth seemed equally deplorable, given the holy atmosphere of uttermost trust and intimacy within which our three commingled souls abided. To confess or to prevaricate—this was the dilemma which had driven my thoughts into a tumult of agonized irresolution.

Thus the dreary hours dragged by—oh, at what a torturous pace!—while, before my weary eyes, a radiant vision materialized in the tomb-like darkness of my bed-chamber. The luminous apparition of my loved ones shimmered in the all-pervading gloom with the distinct and vivid brilliance of an opium-dream. I gazed upon the plain yet pleasing countenance of my Aunty Maria, whom——even more than the sweet, long-departed being who first gave me life——I adored as my own truest *mother*. Alongside that humble visage drifted the gentle linea-ments of my dear little cousin Virginia, towards whom I felt all the fervor of devotion that a brother might direct towards his own darling sister. Indeed, the intensity of my feeling for this ethereal creature was such that I could not conceive of a life bereft of her heavenly presence. Thus, I was determined to bind her even more endur-ingly to my heart through the sacred knot of matrimony. Practical considerations, however, necessitated a tempo-rary deferral of this plan, since——having only recently commemorated the twelfth anniversary of her birth—— she had yet to arrive at that age which, from time immemorial, has signified the threshold of nubility.

As I sat erect upon my bed, contemplating the life-like *phantasma* that swam so thrillingly before my sleep-less eyes, a subtle yet marked transformation began to overtake the features of my angelic Virginia. Gradually, and yet with a grim ineluctability, the vibrant hue of her faultless skin was replaced with a wan and lurid tincture. Her lips, so ripe with the first bloomings of youth, became withered and drawn——her plump cheeks grew waxy and sunken——and a lustreless pall overspread her large, liquid eyes——those cerulean orbs that, only moments before, had shone with the pure light of heaven. My own eyes widened to their fullest extent. I gaped—with what unspeakable horror I can scarcely convey—at the dread metamorphosis taking place before me as the glorious vision of my beloved Virginia—my cousin, soul-sister, and intended bride—was inexorably transfigured into the hideous spectre of a pale and ghastly corpse!

A quivering moan filled my ears, as dire as the lamentation of a lost, tormented soul. I stared about wildly, seeking the source of this fearful sound, before realizing that it had issued from my own tremulous lips. In that interval, the cadaverous vision flickered like a guttering candle-flame—then vanished as though snuffed by the damp night-draft that whispered through the apertures of my window frame.

My racing heart grew calmer by degrees as I pondered on the grim apparition that had visited me. What did it portend? Only a single interpretation presented itself. I would not—*could* not—reveal my coming encounter to my loved ones. The knowledge that I was to expose myself to the threat of physical danger would smite their dear hearts like a death-blow. I must face my trial *alone*.

Rising hurriedly from my bed, I groped my way into my study and seated myself at my writing table. Within my chest I felt the sudden swelling of that profound, poetical sentiment that can only be likened to the feeling of the paramour whose beloved has recently perished in the excruciating throes of consumption (for what occur-

rence can inspire such solemn yet lyrical emotions as the
tragic death of a beautiful young woman?). Illuminating
my oil lamp, I took quill in hand and gave vent to my
overbrimming passions in a song whose fervent tones
accurately reflected the adoration I harbored for my darling Virginia. The verses, to which I afterwards prefixed
the title "To My Darling Sissy," ran thus:

When, at the blessed hour of your birth,
The seraphs came with wings full-pluméd
To place your soul upon the earth,
As did those Kings their gifts perfuméd
Deliver to that humble manger—
So has your love made me a stranger
To terror and to loneliness.
And for *that* gift I thee do bless.

Now is my heart with love so laden
That it would sacrifice its life
If you, who, though still child-maiden,
Refused to join with me as wife—
Though I must wait with patient mien
Until your years have reached *thirteen*,
Which age (*pace* the superstitious)
Shall bring my heart the joy it wishes.

Your hyacinth hair and liquid eyes
Possess my heart and haunt my dreams.
Your face becalms me when I rise
From nightmares that evoke my screams.

And thus our lives are intertwined
Like heart-veins dark-incarnadined.
You shall be bride—I shall be groom—
Until Death seals us in the tomb.

By the time this composition was completed, the tempest had abated. Night had given way to dawn, and the first watery rays of daylight were leaking through the translucent panes of my window. Returning to my bedchamber, I made my way to the washstand and, after performing my ritual ablutions, dressed in my customary garb—black frockcoat, black waistcoat, black trousers, black cravat.

Regarding my face in my shaving-glass, I took note of the doleful alterations which that dreary night of disquietude had wrought upon my features. Suffusing my complexion was a dull yet distinctly unwholesome pallor. Dark lines extended downward from my nostrils, past the corners of my mouth, to the border of my chin. Beneath each of my eyes depended a large, fleshy pouch whose livid tint appeared all the more striking in contrast to the singularly *anaemic* coloration of my skin. My eyes themselves possessed an anomalous tincture, the pale orbs mottled by a fine, crimson webwork of ruptured capillaries.

Notwithstanding these signs of bodily fatigue and excessive—even morbid—cerebration, there could be seen in the *cast* of my features—in the set of my lips and the expression emanating from my eyes—a marked constancy of purpose. Such a look could not fail to impress my opponent with the realization that he was facing no commonplace foe, but rather a being possessed of the same unyielding spirit displayed, in ancient times, when David defeated the Philistine champion Goliath, or when Leonidas, warrior-king of the Spartans, made his celebrated stand at Thermopylae.

Emerging from my bedchamber, I could hear, issuing from our little kitchen, the comforting sounds of my tireless Muddy, who arose at every daybreak to attend, with religious regularity, to her matinal chores. A welcoming warmth radiated from the cooking stove upon whose surface stood a pan of simmering water. Approaching Muddy from behind, I clutched her fondly by the shoulders, at which gesture she gave a little jump and emitted a sharp gasp.

"Oh, Eddie," she said, turning to face me, one hand clutching at the bosom of her housedress. "You gave me quite a start."

"Where is Virginia?" I inquired after planting a filial kiss upon my aunt's ruddy cheek.

"Still abed."

"She sleeps like the dead," I remarked with a heartfelt sigh. "It is the repose of the innocent."

Muddy's broad brow wrinkled as she inspected my countenance. "My gracious, Eddie, but you do look peaked. Another bad night?"

I acknowledged the accuracy of her observation with a melancholy nod. "Slumber—that blessed but fickle benefactress—withheld her sweet nepenthe from my soul."

She regarded me for a long moment before inquiring, "Do I take that to mean 'yes'?"

"That is, indeed, the signification I intended."

She patted my cheek. "Poor, troubled boy," she commiserated. "I cannot help but believe that you would sleep more soundly if you spent less time locked up in that stuffy room, brooding on death and premature burial and whatnot. Perhaps you should try writing something . . . *cheerier*. Why, look at that delightful poem by Mr. Longfellow, 'The Village Smithy.' Surely you could compose something equally charming if you would only put your mind to it."

The earnest, if misguided, simplicity of my dear, well-meaning Muddy elicited from my lips a soft, indulgent laugh—whose tone, however, was not untinged with a rueful awareness that the man of creative *genius* must ever be misunderstood, even by those most sympathetic to his strivings.

"Oh Muddy!" I exclaimed. "Can I not make you see? The true artist must endeavor to give shape to the teeming *phantasmagoria* of the soul—to those swirling shapes and shrouded forms that spring, like a hideous throng of netherworld-demons, from the dark inner reaches of his own harrowed heart and anguished brain!"

Muddy's eyes blinked several times as she stared at me wordlessly. "Perhaps a nice cup of tea might help," she said at last.

As I sat at our table, imbibing the fragrant brew which Muddy had dispensed, my vitals felt suffused with an invigorating heat, as though the fire which burned in the belly of the cookstove now blazed within the depths of my own bowels.

Draining my cup, I sprang from the seat and clutched Muddy to my breast. "I must depart on a matter of the utmost urgency," I cried. "Your potion has inflamed me to the core."

"Oh my," she replied, placing the fingertips of one hand to her lips. "Perhaps you should have allowed it to cool."

Her dear miscomprehension brought a burst of hilarity from my throat. Striding across the kitchen, I paused at the doorway and faced her. "I cannot state for a certainty at which hour I will return," I exclaimed. "But rest assured that, when next you behold me, I will have acquitted myself in a manner befitting a *Poe!*"

"Don't forget your hat, dear," replied the ever-devoted woman. "We may be in for some more weather."

And indeed, though the rains had abated, the sky remained shrouded in gray. Grim, leaden clouds seemed to press down upon the very rooftops of the city. In contrast to the previous evening, however, the unrelieved *gloom* of the atmosphere found no inner counterpart in my own spiritual condition. Perhaps it was due to the warming aftereffects of Muddy's salubrious beverage, or perhaps it was a consequence of her own inspiriting love. I could not say. It was nevertheless the case that I felt infused with a fiery determination——prepared to teach the vaunting Crockett a lesson in etiquette that would not, at any time soon, fade from his consciousness.

Alas, this buoyant mood was not destined to persist. For as I strode along the puddled street, a shrill, unearthly *yowl* sent shivers of terror coursing through every fibre of my being. I froze in mid-stride, paralyzed with fright. At that instant, a feline of the tom-cat variety flung itself from the gap between the two houses on my right. Its coat was of the blackest midnight hue—and as it darted specter-like across my intended path, my heart quailed—and quavered—and sickened—from a sudden violent *spasm* of superstitious dread!

CHAPTER 4

The establishment at which Crockett was lodging was operated by Mrs. Elmira Macready, an elderly widow known to me solely by name—although her deceased husband had been a personage of such lofty repute in our city that, without ever having set eyes upon him, I knew something of his remarkable history. One of Baltimore's most prosperous merchants, Junius Macready was renowned not merely for the magnitude of his fortune but for the singularly enlightened uses to which he had applied it. Entirely free of the philistinism so characteristic of his class, he had been a lifelong devotee of the arts, whose passionate dedication to the elevation of public taste was reflected in his repeated deeds of munificent yet unobtrusive patronage.

In his later years, however, this worthy gentleman had suffered business reversals of such awful severity that they had cost him the bulk of his fortune. The blow proved equally calamitous to his health, and he had died within months of his financial ruin, leaving his elderly widow in sadly degraded circumstances. Compelled to divest herself of virtually all of her worldly possessions—not excluding the stately manse in which she and her husband had passed the long, happy years of their marriage—she had moved into the modest house on Howard Street that was her sole remaining inheritance and managed to subsist by providing rooms to boarders.

Among the many cultural enterprises to which Junius Macready had devoted himself during the height of his prosperity was the ownership and management of the now-defunct Majestick Theatre on Albermarle Street. This splendid auditorium (since converted into a tobacco warehouse) still stands as a sacred shrine within the precincts of my heart, having been the site of a triumphant performance by the beautiful, ill-fated woman to whose existence I owed the gift of my own. I refer, of course, to my sweet, long-departed mother, the actress Eliza Poe, who shuffled off her mortal coil at the all-too-tender age of twenty-four, less than three years following my birth. To this very day, one of my most treasured possessions is a yellowed clipping from the *Baltimore Daily Gazette*, lauding her brilliant characterization of Lydia Languish in Sheridan's *The Rivals*.

Having passed Mrs. Macready's boarding house during my numerous perambulations about the city, I knew it to be located in a tranquil neighborhood, remote from the bustle of the city's main commercial district. This fact, combined with the earliness of the hour—

which had not yet reached eight—caused me to believe that Howard Street would be largely, if not entirely, deserted when I arrived. It was to my great surprise, therefore, that, as I rounded the corner, I immediately perceived a considerable crowd gathered directly in front of the hostelry—as though the public had been notified of my pending encounter with Crockett, and an audience had assembled to witness the proceedings!

How like Crockett it was, I reflected, to convert a private affair into a vulgar spectacle—much as he had transformed himself from an obscure backwoodsman into the self-proclaimed "King of the Wild Frontier." For Crockett's genius—if we may employ the term so loosely—resided less in his capacities as a *statesman* (a *rôle* for which he had displayed only meagre aptitude) than in his natural gifts as a *showman*. His appetite for celebrity— to say nothing of his willingness to cater to the crude tastes of the masses—appeared limitless. I need scarcely add that—for all of his pretensions to authorial dignity—such an appetite was in direct contradistinction to the character of the true man of literature, whose glory derives in no small measure from his readiness, not merely to struggle in solitude with the demands of his art, but to endure—often throughout the course of a lengthy career—the utter indifference, if not outright scorn, of a dull and incomprehending public.

The sight of the crowd gathered before the boarding house so offended my sense of propriety that I felt a sudden impulse to forgo the entire affair and return to my chambers at once, Crockett's insolent challenge unanswered. By then, however, I was near enough to my destination to perceive an anomalous look upon the faces of many of the individuals, who displayed none of the excited eagerness one might expect in the circumstances, but rather a distinct appearance of uneasiness, even distress. Stepping closer, I managed to distinguish a few anxiously muttered words emanating from their midst: *"Murder . . . Butchery . . . Poor woman!"*

My curiosity piqued, I approached the individual most proximate to me—a stout, bewhiskered gentleman standing at the edge of the crowd—and inquired as to the cause of the gathering.

"Why, haven't you heard?" he replied. "A most horrible crime has been perpetrated on these premises."

"Crime!" I exclaimed. "Of what nature?"

"Foul murder," he replied. "The poor widow Macready herself—slaughtered like a lamb in her own bedchamber!"

I gasped in horror at this revelation. "And who was the culprit?"

"That is a mystery as yet unresolved. Even at this moment, officers of the police are gathered within, investigating the monstrous deed."

"Yes," interjected the handsome matron beside him, clutching a knitted shawl to her capacious bosom. "They are being assisted by none other than Colonel Davy Crockett, who—as good fortune would have it—has been lodging in this very establishment during his current visit to our city."

"Why with Davy's help, the police are certain to apprehend the killer in no time." The source of this observation was a young gentleman whose fastidious, if not foppish, attire—so strikingly inapt at that unseasonable hour—endowed him with the unmistakable aura of the *dandy*.

"If such an emotion were possible," the bewhiskered gentleman proclaimed, "I would almost feel a measure of pity for the murderer. For if Davy gets his hands upon him, there will be the need for neither judge nor executioner."

"You speak truly, friend," observed the "dandy." "Why, do you recall the ferocious manner in which Davy subdued Ephraim Packer's notorious gang of Mississippi river pirates, as reported in last month's number of *Crockett's Almanac?*"

"Recall it!" retorted the other. "Only yesterday, I was regaling my wife with the colorful particulars of that astonishing episode. She was transported with admiration as I recounted how Davy, though partly disabled by a pistol-shot inflicted by Packer's cowardly lieutenant, Wicket Finney, defeated the latter in a savage bout of mortal combat."

"To say nothing of Davy's daring when, armed only with his hunting knife 'Big Butcher,' he dispatched no less than six of the murderous cutthroats."

As the two men continued to rehearse the details of Crockett's putative adventure—whose manifest improbability seemed in no wise to tax the credulity of the wonderstruck pair—my attention detached itself from their conversation and turned to the shocking intelligence of which I had just been apprised. That a cold-blooded murder had occurred on these very premises appeared nothing short of uncanny—the terrible fulfillment of the dark premonition that had gripped me when the black cat crossed my path. Surely something more than mere coincidence was involved in this awful circumstance! A dark fatality seemed to be at work, drawing me with the obscure yet inexorable pull of *necessity* into a situation whose outcome I could neither evade nor foresee.

Abandoning myself to the dim, if undeniable, forces of *destiny*, I proceeded to make my way towards the entranceway of the house. "I beg your pardon," I proclaimed as I advanced through the assemblage. "I am here on a matter of urgent business with Colonel Crockett."

My invocation of the idolatrized frontiersman had the desired effect. The crowd parted before me with awed murmurs of respect. A moment later, I ascended the wooden portico and passed across the threshold so recently traversed by that ghastly visitor whose unanticipated calling is, of all earthly misfortunes, the object of the deepest mortal dread. I refer, of course, to that grim intruder—sudden, violent *Death!*

The interior of the house was likewise full of people, many of whom—judging by their negligent state of dress—were lodgers who had been roused from their apartments by the untimely disturbance. Indeed, more than a few of them were standing about in their nightclothes, their faces taut with anxiety and dismay. I pressed my way through the crowd toward the far end of the main corridor, where, before an open doorway, a sombre group had gathered in a knot, straining to peer within.

"Allow me to pass, if you please. I must see Colonel Crockett." By this expedient I soon reached the portal in question and entered that chamber of gloom.

A trio of police officers occupied the center of the apartment, engaged in an urgent consultation. Beside them stood Crockett, looking much the same as he had the previous afternoon, albeit a good deal more dishevelled—as though his ceremonial dinner had degenerated into a night of bibulous revelry. As I stepped inside the apartment, he glanced in my direction, his dark eyes dilating with surprise.

"Cricket!" he exclaimed in evident befuddlement. "What in tarnation . . . ?" Suddenly, a gleam of recognition suffused his features. "Why I'll be hanged if I didn't plumb forgit about our little app'intment in all this-here hullabaloo."

One of the police officers, a portly fellow with a prodigious moustache, turned a curious gaze upon me. "Is this gentleman a friend of yours, Colonel Crockett?"

"Not by a danged sight, Captain," Crockett replied. Then, casting me a solemn look, he said: "I'm afeard our set-to will have to wait for a spell, Cricket. Thar's some mighty bad business that needs taking care of first." And with that he cocked his head sharply towards the bed which stood against the far wall of the chamber and whose presence I had only dimly noted in the few moments since I had arrived upon the scene.

A gasp of utmost horror escaped my lips as I stared with disbelieving eyes at the ghastly figure lying prone upon the mattress. It was the body of an elderly woman with her throat so frightfully cut that the head was nearly detached from the body. The look upon the victim's face—the bulging eyes—the gaping mouth— offered vivid evidence of the unspeakable terror she had suffered in her final moments. The body itself was dreadfully mutilated—so much so as to scarcely retain any semblance of humanity. Thickly clotted blood was everywhere—soaking the bedclothes—bespattering her limbs—even staining the wall above the bedstead. Never had I beheld a spectacle so dire—so hideous— so profoundly *appalling*.

My brain began to reel from the stupefying sight. I stretched out my hand and placed it against the nearest wall in order to steady myself. Here, I reflected dully, is the gruesome confirmation of an all-too-dismal truth: that nothing in the realm of supernatural terror—not the doings of demons nor the depredations of ghouls—can surpass the atrocities visited regularly by *men* upon their fellow-beings.

As if in reply to this thought, the frontiersman— who had been observing my reaction from several feet away—grimly remarked: "Cricket, I've seen things that would curdle the blood of the divvil hisself, but this here beats all. Why, the savagest redskin wouldn't have dealt so unmercifully with that poor old widder-lady."

I opened my mouth to respond, but fear had so depleted my tongue of moisture that I could not effect the simple act of vocalization. "Who . . . ?" I managed to stammer at last. "How . . . ?"

"All of us is wonderin' the same," Crockett remarked, expelling a rueful sigh. "The nifarious deed was found by the chambermaid when she come to rouse Mrs. Macready at daybreak, and that's the only fact we know for a cartainty. Poor gal is upstairs right now, prosterated with grief."

It is an anomaly of our nature that, while our finer sensibilities may recoil from scenes of dire tragedy, there is something deep within our souls that is drawn, with an irresistible attraction, to the *morbid*—the *fearful*—the *ghastly*. Thus, even as Crockett spoke, my gaze was transfixed by the hideous spectacle across the room. I stared at the horribly mutilated corpse with an intensity in which fascination and repulsion were equally commingled. The savage wound which bisected the poor victim's throat had been inflicted with such violence that the blood from her severed jugular vein had (or so it appeared at first glance) sprayed upward as though from a fountain. Above her head, the dark, clotting fluid stained the wall in stripes, blotches, and streaks, creating a macabre pattern which—as I scrutinized it more narrowly—began to assume a singular design in my perception.

"Cricket," said the frontiersman. "I reckon it's time for you to high-tail it back home and leave this business to men that can handle it. You'n me will have to settle our account some other day, after—"

"They are letters," I exclaimed, cutting him off in mid-declaration.

"What?" Crockett ejaculated. His interrogative was echoed by the police officers, who demanded an elaboration of my extraordinary observation.

"Gentlemen," I stated. "Look closely at the seemingly random stain above the bedstead. You will discover that the blood has been deliberately, if hastily, applied in the form of a *word*. Someone has written a message."

Gasping in amazement, the three officers hurried across the room and bent to the wall. A moment later, the moustachioed captain reassumed his upright posture, looked at Crockett, and said: "Well, I'll be damned. He's right."

"How do you cipher it, Captain?" Crockett asked.

"Hard to say," the other replied, turning to face me. "Perhaps Mr. . . . ?"

"Poe," I said, bowing slightly. "Edgar Poe."

The captain replied with a courteous nod. "Perhaps Mr. Poe will oblige us by inspecting the clue he has so cleverly noted and offering his opinion."

"I will be gratified to assist in whatever way possible," I replied and approached the victim's bed.

Avoiding the gruesome spectacle which lay upon the mattress, I focussed my attention upon the bloody notation on the wall. "The printing, as one would expect given the means by which it was accomplished, is irregular in the extreme. Nevertheless," I declared, "the first two letters are readily discerned to be *N* and *E*."

As I made this pronouncement, the captain extracted a small notebook and a stubby lead pencil from his coat pocket and copied the letters onto a blank page.

"The third letter," I continued, "is somewhat more obscure, although it appears to be a capital *U.* This is followed by another *E,* then by a letter which may possibly be another *N.* Its slovenly condition, however, makes it impossible for me to identify it as such with absolute certainty."

"N-E-U-E-N?" said the captain, reading aloud from his notebook.

With that, there came a sudden outburst from the doorway. "Neuendorf!" cried a female voice.

The five of us within the room—Crockett, the police captain, his two subordinates, and I—turned as one man toward the source of this unexpected and mysterious exclamation. There, at the head of the onlookers, stood a slender young woman, who—to judge by her state of careless *dishabille*—was evidently a lodger unceremoniously prodded from her sleep by the morning's commotion. The stricken cast of her features, no less than the pallid hue of her skin, offered ample evidence of her extreme emotional distress.

"Come ag'in?" inquired Crockett of the young lady.

"Neuendorf," she repeated, her voice quavering with agitation. "Hans Neuendorf. That must be his name upon the wall."

"And precisely who is this individual?" inquired

the captain, rapidly inscribing the name inside his notebook.

"A reliable handyman when sober, but a bully and ruffian when under the influence of alcohol," she responded. "Mrs. Macready employed him on occasion because he worked so cheaply and she, poor woman, has been so burdened with financial care since the death of her husband. Last week, however, the two of them became embroiled in a bitter argument over a sum of money he insisted that she owed him for an earlier job. I was reposing in my chamber next door, recovering from a sick headache, when I overheard their altercation. When Mrs. Macready refused to accede to his claim, he threatened to return and 'get what was coming to him.' Judging from the uneven quality of his speech at the time, I assumed that he was drunk, so I did not take his threat seriously—nor did Mrs. Macready. But now . . ." And here the poor creature's voice became so unsteady that she could no longer continue. Burying her face in her hands, she dissolved into helpless tears.

"Can you tell us," the police captain inquired softly but urgently, "where we can find this Neuendorf?"

Suddenly, the young officer standing beside him spoke up. "I believe I know the man, Captain Russell."

"Yes?" the latter said sharply, swivelling towards his subordinate.

"He is a 'tough customer,' all right. Lives in a run-down shanty on the harbor. Not more than one year ago, I had occasion to arrest him on a charge of drunken assault. He did not submit without a fight.

Indeed, it took four of us, including Sergeant Calhoun—who, as you know, is an individual of no inconsiderable size—to subdue him."

While this exchange was taking place between the two officers, I turned back to the wall and resumed my inspection of the bloody letters. Crockett, observing me in this endeavor, addressed me thusly: "What do *you* say, Cricket? Think them letters spell out this-here Neuendorf's name?"

"So far as I can determine," I replied, "there are four additional letters following the ones I have already deciphered. Owing to its indistinct condition, the first is almost entirely illegible. The next two, however, are unmistakably *O* and *R*. And the final letter, although also badly smudged, may indeed be an *F*."

"Why if that don't prove it," Crockett declared, "then I'm a Dutchman."

Captain Russell slapped his notebook shut. "Think of it, gentlemen," he observed in sombre tones. "Even as she lay there, so grievously wounded, the poor victim must have inscribed her killer's name upon the wall, using her own dying blood as ink!"

Thus far I had managed, by keeping my attention riveted upon the wall above the bed, to avoid a too-close view of the gruesome corpse which sprawled only inches away from me. Now, I forced myself to look directly at the victim's hideously mangled throat. The ghastly sight caused my own throat to clench up, as though it had been seized by an iron grip. A few moments went by before I recovered my power of speech. "I marvel, Captain

Russell," I opined, "that an elderly woman who has suffered a wound of such severity could accomplish the act which you have just described."

"Mr. Poe," he replied, "at moments of mortal crisis, even the frailest of people is often capable of feats that would seem, under ordinary circumstances, to be almost superhuman."

"That's the gospel truth, Captain," Crockett averred. "I recollect the time when my mate, Georgie Webster, got hisself shot so full of arrows during a raid on a Cherokee village that he looked like a goldang porky-pine. Even so, he managed to bring down *and* scalp no less'n six of the unhuman savages afore he succumbed to his fearful injuries."

"Mr. Poe," said Captain Russell, extending his right hand, which I clasped in my own. "I am obliged to you for the assistance you have rendered. Your keen powers of observation have proved instrumental in helping us resolve this mystery. Officer Carlton," he continued, addressing the young officer who had reported his own earlier *contretemps* with Neuendorf. "I would like you to remain here and stand watch over the *corpus delicti* until the coroner arrives. In the meantime, Colonel Crockett, Sergeant Donegan, and I will proceed to the harbor and attempt to locate and apprehend the suspect."

"Yes sir," replied Carlton.

Taking a step in my direction, Crockett clapped me on the shoulder. "Cricket, you've acquitted yourself handsome, and that's a fact. Maybe you ain't so all-fired useless as it seems."

"Your gracious words are precisely the sort of courtesy one would expect of you, Colonel Crockett," I answered dryly.

"Thankee," Crockett replied. Then, addressing the portly leader of the police contingent, he declared: "Captain, let's make tracks to the harbor and take care of that low-down, no-account furriner. My dander is up and I'm feelin' mighty wrathy."

And with that, Crockett and the two police officers exited from the chamber and disappeared among the throng that continued to mill outside the door.

For several moments following their departure, I remained standing in the center of the room, lost in contemplation. Though gratified by my undoubted contribution to the apparent solution of the crime, I could not free myself of certain deep and persistent misgivings. That the dying widow could have managed, in her extremity, to record her killer's name in blood seemed difficult, if not impossible, to credit, despite the contrary belief of Crockett and Captain Russell.

All at once, I was struck by a notion.

Stepping back to the wall once again, I peered more narrowly at the letters. Next, I looked downward and scrutinized the fingertips of the victim's blood-dabbled hands, which lay, palm upward, at either side of her head, as though raised in a gesture of horror. My excitement was intensifying with every passing second.

Turning hastily towards the doorway, I discovered that the young woman who had identified Neuendorf had not yet departed the scene. Hurrying to her side, I quickly ascertained that she was intimately acquainted with the murdered landlady, having resided at the boarding house for almost one year. I put an urgent query to the distraught young woman, which she answered without hesitation. Her response confirmed the conjecture that had taken root in my mind. Suspicion blossomed into certitude.

Pushing my way through the crowd, I emerged from the boarding house and hastened toward the harbor.

CHAPTER 5

In tribute to its splendid architectural features—
its ornate churches—its imposing mercantile exchange—its patriotic monuments to the heroes of the
Revolution—the city of Baltimore was widely identified as "The Athens of America," a denomination
which infused the hearts of its citizens with a profound and justifiable pride. But for all its many graces,
Baltimore, like all the world's great cities, encompassed
neighborhoods of a sordid, even sinister, character—
home to the more degraded members of its population. And it was through just such a mean and squalid
quarter that my path now led, as I made my way
towards the bay.

In contrast to the pleasing breadth and uniformity
of the city's main thoroughfares, the streets of this
woebegone district were excessively irregular—as
twisted and cramped as the byways of Dante's nether-
world. Miserable wooden dwellings lined the narrow,
filthy lanes. Aside from a small band of ragged
urchins—who, armed with sharpened sticks, were glee-

fully prodding at the carcass of a skeletal dray horse that lay stiffly where it had expired in the mud—few inhabitants of this district were to be seen. Here and there, however, I could discern a shadowy figure lurking in the doorway of a hovel—some poor, fallen wretch, sunk into a state of hopeless degradation through a combination of worldly misfortune and, no doubt, innate liability to vice.

Inspired by the urgency of my errand, I was already progressing at a rapid pace. Now, in my eagerness to flee the gloom—the dreariness—the sheer oppressive *misery* of this dismal neighborhood, I accelerated my stride and, within moments, found myself within view of the harbor.

I paused for a moment to take in the scene. Tall-masted ships floated upon the gently undulating surface of the bay; while, overhead, raucous gulls swooped and wheeled against the dull, leaden sky. A chill wind blew from the water, carrying upon it that brackish, yet strangely exhilarating, aroma that never failed to fill me with the keenest longing for those wild adventures incident to the life of the seaman—the sublime thrill of the maelström—the intoxicating sensations of the gale—the ecstasies of suffering known exclusively by those who have undergone the extremities of shipwreck!

Recalling my thoughts from these maritime fancies and concentrating my faculties on the purpose at hand, I cast my gaze about and quickly discovered the destination I was seeking. Not more than fifty yards away, at the near end of a jutting dock, stood a miserable wooden shack, its weather-beaten exterior hung with nets, lobster traps, and other *accoutrements* of the fisherman's trade. At the doorway of this unassuming structure, I could clearly ascertain the figure of the brawny frontiersman, standing (or rather, *posing*) with his chest thrust out and arms akimbo. The moustachioed Captain Russell and his subordinate, Sergeant Donegan, were visible immediately to the rear of Crockett, as though sheltering themselves behind the barrier of his formidable physique.

Surrounding Crockett and the officers was a crowd of such considerable magnitude that, in the entire vicinity of the dock, there was scarcely enough space for a single additional spectator. Judging by their dress, I could see that a significant portion of this crowd consisted of perfectly reputable citizens: many of them, no doubt, the same men and women who had congregated outside the boarding house and who—eagerly anticipating a display of Crockett's fabled martial prowess—had followed him here to the abode of the putative killer. Other members of the throng, however, appeared to be individuals of a far less respectable character—undoubtedly denizens of the adjoining neighborhood, who had attached themselves to Crockett's procession as it passed through their grim and desolate streets.

My assumption regarding the unsavory nature of this latter class of onlookers was quickly borne out as, perceiving that there was but little time to lose, I hastened towards the dockside and endeavored to push my way through the mob—only to find myself impeded by a veritable wall of shabbily attired ruffians who comprised the outer perimeter of the crowd.

"Pardon me," I proclaimed, after attempting, without success, to insinuate myself between two of these coarsely dressed individuals. "But I am engaged on a mission of the utmost importance, and must urge you to move aside. The intelligence I intend to convey may help avert a needless and potentially disastrous confrontation."

Neither this appeal, however, nor my redoubled effort to squeeze through the narrow space separating this particular duo had any discernible effect. Indeed, the two men—who remained standing with their backs in my direction—appeared to be as oblivious of my presence as a pair of American bison to the operations of those parasitical members of the avian clan that subsist by pecking insects from the former's thickly matted humps.

My patience having been stretched to the snapping point, I reached up a hand and sharply tapped the nearer of the two on the shoulder of his frayed and filthy overcoat, whose execrable condition was such that, at the touch of my fingertips, a small puff of dust arose from the fabric. This gesture finally drew the attention of the wretchedly clad fellow. Slowly swivelling in my direction, he peered down at me with a face that—both in its individual features and overall cast— seemed expressly designed as the living illustration of the colorfully descriptive vulgarism, "plug ugly."

From the deplorable condition of his sullied complexion, stubbled jaw, and stringy, dun-colored hair, it was sadly evident that an inordinate period had elapsed since he had last availed himself of soap, scissors, razor, or comb. His eyebrows were of a more than wonted shagginess, growing together at the bridge of his nose, so as to form a thick excrescence of hair that bore an unsettling resemblance to a member of that singularly repellent variety of arthropod commonly known as the *centipede*.

From the shadowy recesses of his ocular indentations, two red-tinged orbs regarded me with an expression in which malice, ignorance, and low cunning commingled in equal measure. His misshapen nose— the evident by-product of numerous violent altercations—was further disfigured by its mottled, bulbous tip, whose webwork of ruptured capillaries gave eloquent, if unsightly, testimony of his propensity for alcoholic over-indulgence.

Like countless numbers of his countrymen, he was—as the foully bespattered condition of his shirt-front made only too evident—addicted to the odious practice of "chewing and spitting." Even now, his lips moved in a leisurely, ruminative manner, reminiscent of the mastications of a bovine. The cheek that retained his quid of tobacco was so severely distended that he might have been suffering from a case of infectious mumps.

As I studied the features of this altogether unsavory individual, an expression of coarse amusement slowly overspread his countenance. Forming his lips into an exaggerated pucker, he drew back his head and—snapping it forward with a suddenness that caught me completely unawares—expectorated a glob of vile, brown-colored liquid, which landed with an audible splat only inches from the toes of my shoes.

The crudity of this gesture—to say nothing of the flagrant contempt it conveyed—was not to be endured; and, indeed, under less exigent circumstances, nothing could have prevented me from administering a severe physical chastisement to the lout, in spite of his formidable size (which approximated that of the biblical behemoth invoked in the story of Job). As it was, I was forced to satisfy myself with a sharp verbal rebuke.

"Though your churlish manner," I declared, fixing him with a baneful glare, "no less than the coarseness of your mien, gives more than sufficient indication of your ungentlemanly breeding, I do not, at present, have the leisure to provide you with the lesson in civility that you so richly deserve. My errand concerning Colonel Crockett is of far too pressing a nature to permit of such a procedure."

The ferocity of this admonition not only reduced its object to a stupefied silence but drew the attention of several of his neighbors, who turned to regard me with an expression of undisguised wonderment.

"What the *hell* did he say?" exclaimed one of these bystanders to the ill-bred wretch who was the object of my reproof.

"Damned if I know," replied the latter. "Somethin' 'bout Crockett."

"So you're a friend of Crockett, eh?" said the former, favoring me with an evil grin that disclosed a gaping hole originally occupied by his upper incisors. "Well, that's one sumbitch who's gonna wisht he never left Tennessee. Struttin' around here like he's cock of the roost. Well, ol' Hansie'll learn him. He'll carve that peckerwood up like a Christmas goose."

Before I could formulate a reply to this distasteful pronouncement, an excited din arose from the front of the crowd.

"The fun's about to commence, boys!" exclaimed the toothless individual, as he and his fellows turned back towards the source of the uproar.

Perceiving that I was too late to avert an encounter between Crockett and Mrs. Macready's ostensible assassin—and that, in any event, my efforts to squeeze through the tightly packed crowd were certain to fail—I resigned myself, for the moment, to the *rôle* of spectactor. From my present position at the rear of the throng, however, I could see little more than the crudely shingled roof of Neuendorf's shanty and the very top of Crockett's head.

Quickly gazing about in search of a more favorable vantage point, I spotted, not more than several yards away, a heterogeneous medley of boxes, barrels, casks, and kegs—the recently unloaded cargo of a newly arrived merchant vessel. One particular pile of wooden crates rose to a height of nearly ten feet.

Employing the superior agility which, from the earliest days of my youth, had permitted me to excel in sundry feats of athletic prowess, I hurried to the side of this imposing stack and began to climb. Within moments, I was seated on the lid of the uppermost crate, a situation which afforded me an unobstructed view over the heads of the crowd.

Though I could now perceive them clearly, my ability to *hear* Crockett and his two companions—who were engaged in a heated consultation—was limited by the distance which separated me from the three men. From the gestures of Captain Russell, however—as well as from the few muted words I was able to discern by straining my auditory faculties to the utmost—I inferred that he was urging Crockett to hold back until further reinforcements could arrive. Crockett, however—as I could see both from the emphatic shakings of his head and the resolute set of his features—was in no humor to comply.

Turning back towards the tightly sealed door of the shanty, Crockett began to declaim in a voice whose sheer, far-projecting *sonority* would have been the envy of the fabled Athenian orator, Demosthenes. Obviously intended for the benefit of his audience—as much as for the unseen antagonist to whom it was presumably addressed—the frontiersman's vociferous speech carried easily to the farthest reaches of the crowd.

"Hans Neuendorf!" he shouted. "Give yourself up, and you'll be shown more mercy than ever you showed that poor old widder-lady! If you don't, why Davy Crockett'll come in there and fetch you out quicker'n hell can scorch a feather!"

A long moment passed during which the frontiersman's resounding ultimatum received no reply. Then, a booming male voice issued from the interior of the shack. Though somewhat muffled by the wooden enclosure, the words were of sufficient volume to be heard by everyone present, especially since a profound and intensely *charged* silence had fallen over the expectant crowd.

"I don't know nuthin' 'bout no widder-lady," called the still-invisible Neuendorf from the sanctuary of his tumbledown abode. Though his tone was emphatic, his slurred and irregular enunciation suggested that— even at that unseasonable hour——the speaker had already indulged in alcoholic consumption to the point of near inebriation.

"One thing I *do* know," he continued. "You set one toe over my doorsill, and I'll give you first-rate hell, you big-mouthed son-of-a-bitch. I ain't afraid of you, nor any man."

Expanding his chest to its fullest extent, Crockett threw back his head and roared, "Why, you infarnal varmint! You *best* be afeard! I am David Crockett——sired by an airthquake, half-brother to the alligator, and a near relation to the small-pox on my mother's side! I can out-wrassle a panther, tote a steamboat on my back, and play rough-and-tumble with a lion. I'm a rip-roarer, I tell you. My daddy can lick any man in Tennessee, and I can lick my daddy. I can walk like an ox, run like a fox, swim like an eel, fight like the devil——and swallow a whippersnapper like you whole without chokin'!"

And with that, he clenched his hands into a pair of enormous fists and beat a fierce tattoo on his swollen chest.

Though Crockett's peroration—so characteristic of that ritual boasting associated with the backwoods "screamer"—drew an appreciative roar from his assembled admirers, it made little apparent impression on Neuendorf.

"Far as I'm concerned, you ain't nuthin' but a low-down, meddlin' hound-dog," cried the latter from within his abode. "I ain't no murderer, Crockett. But I ain't no coward, neither. You want me, I reckon you'll just have to come in here and git me. And if that ain't to your likin'—why, you can just kiss my sister's black cat's ass!"

At this insolent, indeed profane, retort, a gasp rose from the crowd. From my perch atop the packing crates, I could see a flush of the most intense outrage suffuse the frontiersman's countenance. Flinging off his coat, he hurled it to the ground, let out a cry akin to the blood-curdling "war-whoop" of the savage Comanche, and—lowering one massive shoulder—projected himself with all the force and ferocity of a maddened bull at the shanty's flimsy door, which gave way with a splintering crash.

As the enraged frontiersman disappeared inside the shack, a tumultuous cheer burst from the crowd, as though from a single, exultant throat. Whistles, whoops, and cries of "Go get 'im, Davy!" and "Give 'im hell, Colonel!" issued from the lips of Crockett's excited followers; while other, markedly coarser voices bellowed, "Tear the egg-suckin' bastard to pieces, Hansie!" and "Rip his friggin' head off!"

Transpiring as it was within the confines of

Neuendorf's cramped habitation—whose single, narrow window was boarded up against the inclement weather that had prevailed for the past several days—the battle was inaccessible to the sight of the crowd. But its ferocity was evident from the frightful sounds that continually emerged from the shanty: the splintering of wood—the shattering of crockery—the savage thud of fist against flesh—the furious cries—the bitter curses. The little building itself began to quiver and quake—so violently that it seemed as if its very walls might collapse from the frenzy of the combat.

Suddenly, a fearful shriek exploded from the interior of the dwelling. There was the sickening sound of a final, brutal blow, followed by a grunt—muted but still audible—of grim satisfaction. Then nought but a complete and ominous *silence.*

An awful hush fell upon the scene. Not a single member of the multitudinous crowd seemed capable of the act of respiration. A long, agonized moment passed, as the entire throng stood as immobile as stone, every eye remaining fixed on the front of the shanty. All at once, a hand emerged and gripped the frame of the door—and a large, wildly dishevelled figure staggered out into the open air, clutching a dripping knife.

A few feet away from my observation post, a well-dressed matron emitted a shriek, then collapsed into her companion's arms at the sight of this tattered—this bleeding—this ravaged apparition.

It was the severely contused and lacerated, but seemingly victorious, figure of—*Hans Neuendorf!*

CHAPTER 6

It might be supposed that—in light of the hostility that existed between Crockett and myself—his ignominious defeat under such highly public circumstances would have infused me with the keenest satisfaction. But such was not the case. So inwardly certain had I been of Crockett's inevitable triumph that the sight of his wounded but still-ambulatory opponent struck me with the shock of a galvanic battery. My brain reeled. Dizziness overcame me. My hands, grasping the box-lid on either side of my body, began to tremble. Only the reflexive tightening of my fingers, which convulsively clutched at the raised wooden edge of the crate, prevented me from tumbling off my perch.

To be sure, the intense agitation I experienced at my first glimpse of Neuendorf was due in no small degree to the disquieting, indeed horrific, appearance of this singular being. Even from a distance, I was struck by the sheer, the overpowering *ferocity* of the man. He was not tall—certainly not more than five feet six inches high. But his limbs were of the most unsettling mold. His hands, especially, were so excessively thick, broad, and overgrown with coarse, matted hair as hardly to retain a human shape. His exceptionally long arms— as well as his strong, if somewhat stubby, legs—were bowed to the point of deformity, endowing him with a distinctly *simian* quality. His head was equally grotesque, being of enormous size and entirely bald.

Add to these inherently repulsive features the disfiguring effects of his violent confrontation with Crockett—his torn and bloody clothing—his bruised and swollen face—his partially detached left ear, which dangled by a ribbon of flesh from the side of his head—and it will readily be discerned why the sight of this appalling individual smote upon my soul with such unnerving force.

Nor was I the only person there to be thus affected. Standing in close proximity to the doorway of the shack, Crockett's cohorts—Captain Russell and Sergeant Donegan—appeared to have been reduced to a state of stupefied paralysis by the outcome of the contest. As Neuendorf took another halting step in their direction, the two police officers finally roused themselves from their daze and reached for the handles of the wooden "billy clubs" that protruded from their thick leather belts.

The weapons, however, proved to be superfluous. Even before the two law men could extract the "billies" from their belts, Neuendorf staggered to a halt, raised both hands to the sky, and—letting out a roar of agonized protest not unlike the death-bellow of a mortally wounded bull moose—collapsed face forward onto the ground!

At this wholly unanticipated turn, the crowd emitted a single, protracted gasp of the utmost wonderment and confusion. In the hush that ensued, a sound like the heavy tread of boot soles upon floorboards issued from the shack. Then the sound grew more pronounced—a looming figure filled the doorway—and out into the wan and pallid daylight stepped Crockett himself, looking (apart from a blood-stained perforation on the upper part of his left shirt-sleeve) hardly the worse for wear!

Gazing about at the sea of astonished faces that confronted him, Crockett—whose own countenance wore a look of consummate satisfaction—expelled a laugh compounded equally of amusement and surprise.

"Well, I'll be shot, kilt, and shoved into the ground without benefit of clargy!" he exclaimed. "You folks didn't reckon that ol' Davy Crockett had got whupped by the likes o' this no-account critter?" And here, he motioned with his chin toward the insensible form that lay outstretched at his feet.

"We did indeed," cried Captain Russell. "That conclusion—though nearly impossible to credit—seemed unavoidable when you failed to emerge from Neuendorf's lair."

"Why, shucks," answered Crockett. "My duds got a trifle disarranged while I was subduin' that varmint, and I just tarried inside for a spell to tidy myself up."

At that instant, a low quavering moan escaped

from the throat of Neuendorf, who stirred slightly on the ground.

Drawing back one booted foot, Crockett delivered a ferocious kick to the right temple of his prostrate adversary, who gave a fluttering groan and subsided again into oblivion. Stooping, Crockett reached for Neuendorf's massive right hand, which continued to clutch the long-bladed knife. Prying open the latter's fingers and removing the weapon, Crockett straightened up again and ceremoniously presented the savage-looking implement to the police official.

"Captain," Crockett announced. "If this here pig-sticker ain't the same knife that kilt poor ol' Mrs. Macready, I wish I may be kicked to death by grass-hoppers!"

Then, turning toward the crowd, he placed his hands on his hips and spoke thusly: "Ladies and gentlemen! You kin head on home now and rest easy, knowin' that—thanks to the brave efforts of yore local constables, along with some humble assistance from yourn truly—the fair city of Baltimore has got nothin' more to fear from this-here low-down, yeller-bellied reptile, whose days of goin' around slaughterin' helpless widders in their beds is plumb *over!*"

This pronouncement achieved the effect which the canny frontiersman had no doubt intended. A jubilant roar erupted from the crowd, a dozen hats were hurled high into the air, and Crockett found himself besieged by admirers, several of whom proceeded to hoist the visibly delighted champion upon their shoulders.

Not every member of the assemblage, however, shared in the general mood of exultation. As I swiftly descended from my post atop the packing crates, a number of the less savory-looking spectators turned and began to depart from the harbor. Among them were the two ill-mannered wretches I had encountered upon my arrival, whose faces wore a look of the deepest disappointment, and who muttered dark imprecations against Crockett as they skulked from the scene.

In consequence of the shifting movement——as well as the partial dispersal——of the crowd, I was now able to make my way toward my objective. Within moments, I found myself standing in close proximity to Crockett, who had been set back down upon his feet and was presently basking in the attention of an attractive young female, arrayed in a richly embroidered muslin dress that did little to obscure the outlines of her womanly physique. From the revealing, if not flagrant, cut of this garment——as well as from her unashamed frankness of manner——I was forced to conclude that, in spite of her evident youthfulness, she was already a thoroughgoing adept in the devious arts of the *coquette*.

"My gracious," she exclaimed in a soft, breathless voice as she laid a plump white hand upon Crockett's rent and bloodied shirt-sleeve. "Your poor arm! Why, that nasty creature has inflicted the most *grievous* wound upon you, Colonel Crockett!"

"This li'l ol' scratch?" the frontiersman guffawed. "Why, I've received skeeter bites that galled me worse. Though I do confess it riles me a mite to have my best shirt tore up so egrejisly." And here, a look of genuine regret crossed his face as he contemplated the badly frayed hole which Neueundorf's blade had produced in the fabric of his garment.

"Why, if you aren't the bravest, strongest man I ever did see," sighed the young woman, clasping her hands beneath her chin and gazing up into Crockett's face with undisguised adoration. "The way you just *stormed* right in there, so fearless and bold. But however did you manage to defeat that awful brute? I'll just *perish* with disappointment unless I hear every last, itty-bitty detail!"

Such a fervent appeal, emanating from the lips of so seductive a creature, would have proven difficult to resist, even for a being less susceptible of flattery than Crockett. Before he could comply with this request, however, and embark on a lengthy—if not exhaustive—disquisition, I took a step forward and planted myself squarely within his line of vision.

"Why, I'll be jiggered!" he exclaimed. "Here's the feller what sniffed out the varmint in the first place!" Taking a stride in my direction, he encircled my shoulders with one muscular arm and drew me several feet apart from the cluster of admirers who had pressed in upon him in anticipation of his impending recitation. Though by nature discomfited, if not actively repulsed, by such gestures of close physical intimacy— particularly from one who was little more than a stranger—I had no choice but to submit to the frontiersman's familiarities.

"Cricket," said he, placing his face only inches away from my left ear and lowering his normally stentorian voice to a volume scarcely louder than a whisper. "When word o' this li'l set-to gets into the newspapers and the public hears about how Davy Crockett single-handedly whupped that nifarious scoundrel, why, my enemies back in Washington City will be fit to be tied! You done me a service, Cricket—there ain't no two ways about it. So I'm all fer callin' it quits atween us. What d'ye say?"

And with that he took a step back and thrust out his right hand in the time-honored gesture of manly reconciliation.

For a moment, I stood paralyzed with irresolution. To withhold from Crockett the intelligence I had come to transmit, no matter how unwelcome it would inevitably prove to the hearer, represented a violation of my own lifelong commitment to the sacred cause of absolute *truth*. But at the same time, I could not help but believe that my tidings would have little immediate effect beyond antagonizing the frontiersman, who would undoubtedly perceive my intervention as a deliberate, if not willfully malicious, attempt to detract from his moment of glory. My brain spun with confusion as I desperately sought a means of resolving this agonizing—this intolerable—this seemingly insurmountable *quandary!*

At that instant, I grew cognizant of a flurry of motion occurring at the very margin of my sight, several yards to the left of where I stood. Casting a rapid glance in the direction of the disturbance, I saw that Neuendorf had regained consciousness and—having pulled himself to his knees—was contending with Captain Russell and Sergeant Donegan, who were attempting to draw his arms behind his back and secure them with a pair of iron manacles. So prodigious was Neuendorf's strength that, under ordinary circumstances, he might have easily resisted this *manoeuvre*. But—still groggy from the punishment he had received at Crockett's hands—he proved, in the end, unequal to the combined exertions of the two officers; who, after a brief, violent struggle, finally succeeded in affixing the shackles to his wrists.

Dragging Neuendorf to his feet, the policemen prepared to escort their captive to the city jail, while, all around, the gathered onlookers—their visages contorted into furious masks of indignation and scorn— assailed the prisoner with catcalls of "Beast!"— "Monster!"—"Murderous reprobate!"

My course became instantly clear. "Colonel Crockett," I declared, redirecting my gaze at the frontiersman, "I accept your gesture in the propitiatory spirit in which it is offered, having no wish to prolong the unhappy state of affairs that has existed between us ever since your abrupt and audacious intrusion into the holy precincts of my domicile. Let me only add that, in view of your clearly demonstrated propensity for impetuous behavior—as well as the nature of the mission upon which I am presently embarked—I pray that circumstances will not once again propel us into so strained, so *inimical* a relationship."

With that, I extended my own right hand, which Crockett immediately enveloped in a firm, not to say bone-crushing, grasp. "Cricket," he said with a soft, chuckling laugh in whose rippling undercurrent I could not help but detect a note of amused condescension. "If you ain't a world-champeen gumbeater, I'll be skinned alive with the blunt edge of a Bowie knife. Take ol' Davy Crockett's word fer it—you've plumb missed yer callin'. Why, with your amazin' talent for highfalutin' palaver, you should be runnin' for Congress!"

Then, favoring me with a hearty wink and a companionable slap on the shoulder that—owing entirely to the unexpectedness of the gesture—sent me staggering a few steps, he spun on his heels and returned to his auditors, who were waiting in a veritable agony of impatience for Crockett to regale them with the facts of his most recent triumph.

Recovering my balance with the sure-footed agility typically associated with the species *Felis domestica*, I quickly made my way to the side of Captain Russell, who, positioned directly behind Neuendorf, was employing his "billy club" in the manner of a prod. The scowling captive, however, could not be budged.

At the sight of my person, the captain momentarily suspended his efforts and gave me an acknowledging nod. "Ah, Mr. Poe," he exclaimed. "I am pleased that you have arrived in time to witness the arrest of this scoundrel"—and here, he administered a vicious poke with the tip of his "billy" to the area of the prisoner's dorso-lumbar vertebrae. "Without your help, his identity might yet be unknown to us."

At these words, Neuendorf swivelled his massive head in my direction and fixed me with a baleful stare. It was a look of such pure, such *overpowering* malice that my entire frame shuddered with dread.

Doing my best to ignore the glowering captive, I addressed the police captain thusly: "It is precisely the question of the killer's identity that has brought me here, Captain Russell. I have something urgent to impart that may shed vital new light on the case."

Frowning in perplexity, Russell replied: "Needless to say, I am most curious to hear this information of yours, Mr. Poe. But our conference must be postponed until my prisoner is conveyed safely to jail."

No sooner had he uttered these words than a gruff, deep-voiced command—"Stand aside, if you please!"—emanated from the midst of the remaining onlookers. An instant later, the crowd split in two and a half-dozen police officers, led by a sturdy fellow with ruddy-hued cheeks, emerged—or rather burst—into view.

"Captain Russell," he exclaimed somewhat breathlessly as he drew to a halt directly before his superior. "We came hurrying just as soon as we received news of the appalling crime." He cast a contemptuous look at Neuendorf. "I see that you have already managed to apprehend the perpetrator."

"Thanks to none other than Colonel Davy Crockett," replied Captain Russell, indicating the frontiersman, who was holding forth in the most animated fashion to his throng of wide-eyed admirers. Situated several yards away, I could clearly overhear Crockett's intensely vivid recitation: "... That's when the murderin' divvil grabbed hold of my hair," he declaimed, accompanying his tale with a variety of histrionic gestures. "He yanked me towards him, then give me a butt in the head that near blinded me, for the varmint's skull is as hard as an iron pot. But I managed to pull loose from his infarnal grip and give him a real sockdolager straight to the snout. That riled him so bad that he run his fingers right up my nostrils. So we wrassled and jerked and clawed for a while, 'til I made a lunge and caught hold of his ear with my teeth. ..."

In the meanwhile, Russell continued to confer with the new arrival. After a final word, the captain turned aside and faced me again, while the ruddy-faced officer and his cohorts formed a circle around Neuendorf. Then, grabbing the latter by his pinioned arms, the policemen half-led, half-dragged the captive from the scene, while the remaining spectators pelted him with a final barrage of invective.

"Well, Mr. Poe," said Captain Russell when the contingent of officers, with the prisoner in their midst, had disappeared from view. "Now that I have placed Neuendorf in the custody of my men, I am at liberty to hear these mysterious tidings of yours. Pray tell me what is so urgent. I confess that my curiosity has been piqued."

Apart from Crockett's rapt circle of auditors, most

of the crowd had dispersed by this point. A handful of loiterers, however, continued to mill about the scene, casting curious looks at the captain and myself.

"Perhaps it were best," I suggested, with a meaningful glance at these bystanders, "if our interview took place in a somewhat more secluded location. The information I possess is intended solely for your ears."

Acknowledging the validity of my concern, Captain Russell led me in a circuit to the rear of Neuendorf's shanty and, from thence, out onto the dock. We stopped at a point halfway along the length of the pier, sufficiently far from the shore to ensure our privacy—our only audience being a dark-winged seagull perched upon one of the massive wooden piles that rose at intervals from the dark depths of the water.

"Well, Mr. Poe ...?" inquired the officer with an anticipatory look.

Shivering slightly in the chill breeze that wafted from the bay, I cleared my throat and announced, "Captain Russell, I have compelling reason to believe that the man you have placed under arrest may not, in truth, be the culprit."

The captain raised his eyebrows. "You surprise me, sir!" he exclaimed. "Having observed the brute at close hand, how can you question his incorrigible nature? Or," he added, patting his side with one hand, "his fearsome facility with *this?*"

Glancing down, I saw that the knife which Crockett had confiscated from Neuendorf and presented to Captain Russell was thrust through the latter's wide leather belt. It was, in truth, a ferocious-looking implement, with a carved, stag-horn handle and long, serrated blade.

"Of Neuendorf's violent capacities I have not the slightest doubt," I replied. "My conclusion, however, is based, not on his *potential* for homicidal behavior, but on the incontrovertible facts of pure, empirical evidence!"

"Evidence?" echoed the captain, his brow furrowing.

"I refer to the bloody message on the wall above the bed of the unfortunate victim."

"But you, Mr. Poe, were the one who so ingeniously perceived the villain's name in the gruesome inscription which I and my associates mistook for nothing more than a stain!"

Here, I held up one finger. "Not precisely. As you may recall, I was able to identify five of the letters without difficulty. Four of them, however—or nearly *half*—were applied in such a slovenly manner as to be, at the very least, *ambiguous*, if not wholly indecipherable."

Frowning, Captain Russell tugged on one end of his luxuriant moustache. "Do you mean to suggest," he inquired after a momentary pause, "that the dying woman inscribed a different name on the wall?"

I fixed him with a look of the greatest intensity. "I mean to suggest something whose implications are even more startling."

"And what exactly is that, Mr. Poe?"

"That the mysterious word—or, more precisely, *graffito*—was not written by Mrs. Macready at all!"

The look on Captain Russell's face in response to my pronouncement resembled nothing so much as the stunned expression of a steer that, preliminary to its slaughter, has just been dealt a hammer-blow to the skull. His eyes gaped—his jaw dropped—and he appeared to have lost the power of speech. A long moment passed before he finally exclaimed, "And what is the basis for this extraordinary assertion?"

"As in all matters pertaining to deductive reasoning," I replied with a smile, "my conclusion is based on a close observation of the *physical* evidence, coupled with a forceful exertion of the *analytical* faculties."

As the captain continued to regard me with a look of awed incomprehension, I proceeded thusly: "Assume, for the sake of our discussion, that the dying landlady, in spite of the appalling severity of her wounds, had somehow managed to drag herself into an upright position and inscribe, with her blood-dabbled fingers, the identity of her slayer on the wall above her bed. Since no apparent injuries had been inflicted on *either* of her arms, it is only natural to assume that, in performing this act, she would have relied on the hand she customarily employed for writing.

"Now, following your departure from the boarding house in the company of Colonel Crockett, I continued to examine the sanguinary markings which I had detected on the wall. I observed that each of the letters slanted distinctly to the *right*—a circumstance that could only occur if the landlady herself were *right-handed*. Gazing more closely at her hands, I noticed the very remarkable fact that—though her palms, wrists, and forearms had been bedabbled with the gushings from her neck wound—her fingers themselves were entirely free of blood. This, in itself, strongly suggested that the landlady was not the source of the mysterious message, which had unmistakably been applied with the unknown author's *fingertips*. To confirm my inference, I sought out a bystander intimately acquainted with Mrs. Macready. In response to my query, this young woman informed me that, in the exercise of every manipulative skill—from sewing and needlepoint to *writing*—Mrs. Macready was *left-handed!*"

I waited for a moment to let the import of my discovery sink in. Following a protracted pause during which his expression underwent a most striking change, from utter bafflement to burgeoning doubt to unmitigated skepticism, Captain Russell shook his head and declared, "Well, Mr. Poe, this is most intriguing, indeed. I must confess, however, that your so-called empirical evidence seems excessively slight when measured against the overwhelming proof of Neuendorf's savage nature. I refer not merely to the man's intimidating—nay, terrifying—demeanor, but also to the vicious threats he is reported to have made against Mrs. Macready. To say nothing of the furious resistance he offered when confronted with the prospect of arrest."

"I concede that Neuendorf is a being of singularly unprepossessing aspect," I replied. "But surely we cannot judge the man's culpability by his grim, even ghastly, appearance. As for his threats, while unquestionably deplorable, they scarcely constitute 'overwhelming proof' of his guilt. Nor does his fierce opposition to Colonel Crockett, which may, indeed, be interpreted in the very opposite light—to wit, as the indignant defiance of an innocent man."

"Until that innocence is established beyond the shadow of a doubt," the captain said stubbornly, "I will persist in regarding him as the most plausible suspect in this case—with all due respect to your ingenious suppositions, Mr. Poe!"

However lamentable, such obstinacy on the part of a mere *functionary* like Captain Russell was only to be expected. I was in the process of formulating a reply when my attention was distracted by the resounding *clump* of bootsoles upon the wooden planks of the dock. Gazing in the direction of the noise, I saw Colonel Crockett advancing towards us in long, purposeful strides. At his side, her right arm linked with his left, was the brazen young woman to whose simperings the frontiersman had quite clearly succumbed.

"Why, Cricket," he called out, "have you drug Captain Russell all the way out onto this-here jutty jest so you kin chaw his ear off?"

This impertinent salutation deserved, at the very least, a *stinging* riposte. Before I could deliver one, however, the captain let out a chuckle and exclaimed, "Our friend Mr. Poe is not chewing my ears off at all, Colonel Crockett. He is, however, *filling* them with speculations of a most dubious order."

"I reckoned as much," laughed Crockett, coming to a halt directly before us. Draped across his left arm was the jacket he had discarded prior to his battle with Neuendorf. The injury he had received to the upper part of that limb was now bound with an embroidered lace handkerchief whose owner, I surmised, was the personage presently clinging to his opposite arm.

"Captain," said Crockett, extending his meaty right hand, "I come to bid you good-bye. My friend Miss Mule Lady here—"

"Mull*any*," interjected the young woman with a sweet, if somewhat brittle, smile.

"Miss *Mullany* has kindly offered to show me the sights o' yore fair city. I'm jest *bustin'* to visit Mr. Peale's museum and see them splendaciously presarved Egyptian mummies I've heard tell about!"

After exchanging a hearty handshake with the police officer and bidding the two of us a final farewell, the frontiersman and his escort strolled away. A moment later, Captain Russell—after conveying, once more, his deepest gratitude and appreciation—began to follow in the direction of the receding couple.

Before he had progressed more than a few paces, however, he paused and turned to face me. "One thing more, Mr. Poe," he said. "If the bloody markings above Mrs. Macready's bed did not form the name 'Neuendorf,' then what, pray tell, *did* they spell?"

"That, indeed, is a most pertinent question," I replied. "Unfortunately, I cannot, as of the present moment, answer it with any degree of certitude."

"I see," muttered the captain in a vaguely *smirking* tone, as though to say, "I thought as much." Then, with a polite tip of his hat, he swivelled on his heels and sauntered away.

I was now left alone on the pier. My feelings, as I stood there contemplating the events of the morning, can scarcely be described—so wildly *confused*, so intensely *contradictory*, were the emotions which possessed my soul. That I alone had perceived a deliberate pattern of denotation in the seemingly random markings left upon the wall of the murder scene was, on the one hand, a source of the keenest satisfaction. But my failure to persuade the police captain that the horribly butchered victim could not, under any circumstance, have been the author of this communication filled me with a sense of the bitterest frustration.

All at once, my heart was seized with a far different—and infinitely more *unnerving*—sensation. I was not, after all, alone on the dock! Someone—or something—was situated directly at my rear, scrutinizing me with an intensity so *fierce*, so *palpable*, that I could *feel* its gaze upon my back.

My heart quailed—an icy chill ran through my frame—a sense of insufferable anxiety oppressed me. Who—or *what*—was the unseen presence lurking at my back?

Slowly—torturously—I turned to face my unknown observer—then froze and gave a startled gasp at the sight of the great, dark-winged seagull eying me from atop the massive wooden pile!

An instant later—still fixing me with a look of almost *preternatural* intelligence—it opened wide its beak and emitted a shrill and ominous cry, as though endeavoring to communicate a deliberate meaning. What that meaning might be, I could not begin to conceive. But as I stood upon the windswept dock, staring at the grim, ungainly, ghastly fowl, every fibre of my being was suddenly suffused with a sense of the deepest and most dire *foreboding!*

CHAPTER 7

That evening, following a modest but nutritive repast of brown bread and bean porridge prepared by my ever-devoted Muddy, I retired to our little parlor and seated myself before the beneficent warmth of the fireplace, seeking to dispel the ague-like chill that had taken such a tenacious hold on both my body and spirit. The hours which had elapsed since the unprecedented events of the morning had been among the most dreary and difficult of my existence.

My wonted routine had been utterly disrupted, all efforts at literary creation having been rendered thoroughly impossible by the teeming *phantasma* that swirled within my overstimulated brain. How could my imaginative faculties operate under such intensely unsettling conditions? How could the sources of artistic inspiration assert themselves when my mind was *thus* overwhelmed with images so turbulent and fearful?—visions of the horribly slaughtered landlady—of the suspected assailant, so simian-like in appearance as to resemble a hideous Borneo ourang-outang—and of the grim, and ghastly, and ominous fowl that eyed me with such strange, if inscrutable, meaning?

Since literary exertion was out of the question, I had passed the better part of the afternoon attempting to resolve the mystery posed to me in parting by Captain Russell—to wit, if the bloody markings left at the murder scene did not spell out the name "Neuendorf," what, then, *were* they meant to signify?

My efforts at deciphering the message, however, had come to nought—in large part, I felt sure, because the agitations of the morning had so worked upon my brain as to render largely ineffectual my powers of cogitation. Now, as I stared into the wavering glow of the fireplace, it suddenly came to me that what I needed was a far more *methodical* approach than mere contemplation.

Rising from my seat, I hastened to my study, removed a sharpened lead pencil from the drawer of my writing table, and on a blank sheet, boldly printed the letters that I had positively identified, leaving the remaining spaces blank. The resulting inscription looked like this:

$$N E \_\_ E \_\_\_ O R \_\_$$

I then carried the paper and pencil back into the parlor and resumed my place before the crackling hearth.

Holding the paper before me, I mentally inserted the letter "A" into the first blank space. My plan was to proceed, in a systematic fashion, through the entire alphabet—one letter at a time—and see what words suggested themselves.

The first two products of this experiment— "NEAE_ _OR_" and "NEBE_ _OR_" —yielded nothing. The third letter, however, produced "NECE_ _OR_." Immediately, the word "Neces-sary" sprang to mind—a possibility that depended on my having misread the letter "a" as an "o."

While I felt reasonably confident that I had not committed such an error, I could not be *absolutely* cer-tain. I therefore inscribed the word "necessary"—fol-lowed by a small question-mark—at the top of the paper, and returned to my procedure.

So intent was I on this enterprise that I quickly became oblivious of my surroundings. As a result, I was wholly unaware that someone else had crept stealthily into the room and tip-toed up behind me. All at once, my vision was shrouded in absolute black-ness as a pair of dainty little hands slipped themselves around my eyes!

"Guess who!" trilled an angelic voice close by my left ear.

Owing entirely to the sheer *unexpectedness* of this intrusion, I half-started from my seat with a stifled shriek. It took only an instant, however, for me to grasp the reality of the situation. Settling back onto my chair, I sat panting for a moment, waiting for my racing heart to resume its normal rhythm.

"Let me see," I finally breathed when the moisture

had returned to my terror-parched mouth. "Could it be the fabled Helen, whose face, as the poet Marlowe wrote, 'launched a thousand ships/And burnt the top-less towers of Ilium'?"

"No, silly!" came the giggling response.

"Hmmm," I muttered, tapping a forefinger against my lips. "Might it possibly be the legendary Queen Guinevere, whose beauty brought low the noblest realm in Christendom?"

"No!" squealed the delighted voice behind me.

"Well, then," I sighed in a tone of exaggerated defeat. "I am at a loss to say just *who* it may be."

"It's me, Eddie!" exclaimed the cherubic being whose identity I had, of course, perceived from the very start of her delightful *charade*. Removing her hands from my face, she skipped around to the front of my chair. "Your dearest little Virginia!"

I emitted a chuckle and gazed fondly at the darling maiden whose features never failed to infuse my bosom with the deepest sentiments of tenderness and joy. Though of a somewhat diminutive stature for her twelve and a half years, there was an almost palpable air of vibrant health and youthful vivacity about her person—qualities that seemed particularly evident in the bewitching plumpness of her cheeks, arms, and torso. Her countenance was transfixing in each of its separate aspects—in the mischievous twinkle of her cerulean eyes—in the surpassing delicacy of her rosy little mouth—in the charming uptilt of her tiny nose—and in the lustrous texture of her dark brown hair, which she wore in that endearingly artless style commonly known as "pig-tails."

As she stood before me—swaying her dear little body from side to side with her hands clasped behind her back—her gaze suddenly alighted upon the sheet of paper that lay across my lap. "What's that, Eddie?" she inquired in her soft, slightly lisping voice. "A puzzle?"

"Of a sort," I replied with an indulgent smile.

"Oooh, goody!" she exclaimed. "Let me see." And with that, she took a quick step in my direction and snatched the paper from my lap.

"No, no, dearest Sissy," I exclaimed, reaching out a hand. "Please return it forthwith. Though my present occupation might appear, to your innocent eyes, to be little more than a mere *pastime*, I am, in fact, engaged in a matter of the gravest urgency, relating to the circumstances of which I have already apprised you." Over dinner, I had recounted to both Sissy and Muddy the dramatic events of the day—omitting only those gruesome details whose recitation would have achieved no other effect than to unsettle the tender sensibilities of my dear ones.

My appeal, however, made little impression on the darling child. "Come and get it, if you want it!" she squealed, backing away from me with the sheet concealed behind her.

"Please, Sissy," I implored. "Under ordinary circumstances, I would eagerly welcome this diversion. But it has been a most difficult, most *fatiguing* day for your poor Eddie. My present state of nervous debility does not permit me to enter into the frolicsome spirit of your proposal."

The fervency of this plea could not be resisted. Forming her lips into a charming little pout, she took several steps forward and thrust the paper at me. "Here. Take it. You're no fun at *all!*" she exclaimed, stamping one foot on the floor in the most captivating manner imaginable.

I placed one hand over my eyes. "Do not chastise me so, Sissy," I sighed. "I am already sorely taxed with weariness and frustration."

Her voice suddenly brightening, the darling maiden cried out, "Want me to sing you a song?"

It was evident that my undertaking would have to be postponed for an indefinite period. "Yes," I said with a relenting smile. "I would enjoy that very much."

"Goody!" she cried, clapping her hands excitedly. "You just sit there and shut your eyes and I will sing you one of your favorites. Guess which!"

I spent a moment in silent rumination before venturing, " 'The Hangman's Tree'?"

"Uh-uh," she replied.

" 'The Unquiet Grave'?"

"No."

" 'Barbara Allen'?"

"Yes!" she exclaimed. Then—as I settled back in my seat with my eyelids shuttered—she cleared her throat and began to trill, in a voice whose surpassing beauty might have induced envious pangs in a seraph:

"In Scarlet Town where I was born,
There was a fair maid dwelling,
Made every youth cry 'Well a-day,'
And her name was Barb'ra Allen.

" 'Twas in the merry month of May,
All the flowers blooming,
Young William Grove on his deathbed lay
For the love of Barb'ra Allen.

"He sent a servant unto her
In the town where she was dwelling.
'Come, Miss, O Miss to my master dying
If your name be Barb'ra Allen!'

"Slowly, slowly she got up,
And to his bedside going,
She drew the curtain to one side
And said, 'Young man, you're dying.'

"He stretched one pale hand to her
As though he would to touch her.
She hopped and skipped across the floor.
'Young man,' says she, 'I won't have you.

" 'Remember, 'member in the town,
'Twas in the tavern drinking,
You drank a health to the ladies all
But you slighted Barb'ra Allen.'

"He turned his face toward the wall,
His back upon his darling.
'I know I shall see you no more,
So good-bye, Barb'ra Allen.'

"As she was going to her home,
She heard the church bell tolling.
She looked to the east and looked to the west,
And saw the funeral coming.

"'Oh hand me down that corpse of clay
That I may look upon it.
I might have saved that young man's life,
If I had done my duty.

"'Oh mother, mother, make my bed
Oh make it long and narrow.
Sweet William died for me today,
I shall die for him tomorrow.'

"Sweet William died on a Saturday night,
And Barb'ra Allen on a Sunday.
The old lady died for the love of them both,
She died on Easter morning."

As I listened, with eyes still sealed, to the ravishing strains of this grave and stately ballad, a mysterious image began to rise up like a ghostly *revenant* from the shadowy depths of my overwrought brain. At first, this strange yet tantalizing shape was too dimly indistinct—

too faint and faraway—for me to recognize. But as the melodious voice of my dearest Virginia continued to trill, the shape appeared to draw closer—its features grow clearer—until a radiant female countenance shone brightly before my wonderstruck mind's eye.

Though I had not set eyes on its *living* counterpart since my earliest childhood, the face that now loomed before me was as familiar to me as my own, for I had contemplated its *painted* likeness a thousand—nay, *ten* thousand—times in the course of my existence. It was the visage of my blessed mother, the celebrated actress Eliza Poe, known to me solely through a delicately wrought miniature that was, of all my earthly possessions, by far the most precious.

What—I sat there wondering—had so suddenly evoked the resplendent image of my long-deceased mother at this very moment? After briefly reflecting on this matter, I was forced to conclude that there was something in the nature of Virginia's performance that had called the heart-piercing vision to mind. Perhaps, I surmised, my dear, lamented mother—whose musical, as well as histrionic gifts, had brought her acclamation from critics and theatre-lovers throughout the country—used to lull me to sleep in her arms with this very melody during that all-too-brief period when I had enjoyed, for the only time in my poor, troubled existence, the unutterable bliss of her sweet, maternal presence.

Whatever the reason for the sudden appearance of this ravishing vision, its effect upon my overstrung nerves was both instantaneous and wrenching. Moisture welled behind my eyelids, and a racking sob rose up from the innermost depths of my sorrow-fraught bosom. In the meantime, Virginia continued with her song:

"Sweet William was buried in one graveyard,
Barb'ra Allen in another;
A rose grew on Sweet William's grave
And a brier on Barb'ra Allen's.

"They grew and they grew to the steeple top,
And there they grew no higher;
And there they tied in a true lover's knot,
The rose clung to—"

All at once, I became aware that Virginia's song had broken off. My tear-dampened lids fluttered open. "Why, Sissy," I sniffled, extracting a handkerchief from the pocket of my trousers and employing it to dab the moisture from my eyes, cheeks, and nose. "What has caused you to cease in so abrupt and surprising a manner?"

Gazing at the object of my query, I perceived that she was staring in a most quizzical fashion at a spot somewhere to the rear of my left shoulder. Swivelling in my seat, I was surprised to see Muddy posed at the threshold of the parlor. Her plain yet (to my eyes) intensely pleasing visage wore a look of barely suppressed excitement, akin to that of a messenger bearing news of an exceedingly *thrilling* nature.

"Sorry to interrupt, Eddie dear," the good woman declared, "but there is a visitor here—a most *distinguished* visitor, if I may say—to see you."

Given the untimeliness of the hour—which was already well past eight o'clock—this pronouncement was startling indeed. No sooner had it issued from her lips than she moved to one side, whereupon the mysterious caller—who had, until that moment, remained invisible behind her—stepped boldly forth into the room. I need hardly describe the intense pang of dismay that smote my heart at the sight of this unwelcome being, whose earlier farewell to me I had gratefully—though, as it now appeared, prematurely—viewed as *permanent*.

It was none other than Colonel Crockett!

CHAPTER 8

H e was attired in his customary garments, with
the addition of a wide-brimmed, high-crowned
black felt hat which——in a rare concession to the precepts of civilized behavior——he had evidently doffed
upon entering our premises and was now clutching in
one hand.

Stuffing my tear-dampened handkerchief into the
breast pocket of my frockcoat, I rose from my chair
and offered him a civil, if less than wholehearted,
greeting.

"Cricket," he replied, "I'm right sorry to come
bullin' my way into yer home at such an uncivilized
hour. But there's been a heap of bad doings, and I'm
plumb eager for you 'n' me to have a pow-wow." Then,
with a nod towards Virginia, he added, "That was
awful purty singin', young miss. If you don't warble as
sweet as a bluebird in a cottonwood tree, why, I'm an
injun."

"Thank you!" chirped Virginia, favoring the
intruder with the prettiest curtsy imaginable. Then, in

a voice so sweetly ingenuous that it might have emanated from an angel, she inquired, "Are you really the famous Colonel Crockett—the same one that Eddie was saying such terrible things about at dinnertime?"

"I am the genu-wine, blowed-in-the-glass article, there ain't no buts about it," the frontiersman acknowledged with a low-throated chuckle. "And hearin' that Cricket's been castin' dispersions on me don't exactly come as no surprise. There ain't much love lost atwixt us, that's for a certainty. But"—and here, he turned to regard me with a look of solemn intensity—"I'm hopin' him 'n' me can bury the hatchet. There's some mighty bad business that needs attendin' to—and there ain't no time to waste."

"The 'business' to which you allude," I retorted, "must be urgent indeed if it has impelled you, once again, to disrupt in so precipitate a manner the tranquillity of our domestic *milieu*."

"It is for a fact, Cricket," came the somber reply.

At this moment, Muddy—who had been gazing at our visitor with (it pains me to say) a most *irksome* look of admiration on her countenance—stepped forward and extended one hand in Virginia's direction. "Come, dear," she said. "Let us leave Eddie and Colonel Crockett to their affairs."

"Okay!" chirped the darling maiden. Skipping across the floor, she grasped her mother's hand, whereupon the two angelic creatures exited the room. Just before they vanished over the threshold, however, Virginia turned to look at Crockett. "I hope you will come again soon," she exclaimed, "and I will sing another song for you!"

"You can depend on it, gal," replied Crockett.

By now, the logs in the fireplace had been reduced to a mound of glimmering embers. The parlor, though still comfortably warm, was half-hidden in shadow. Stepping to the oil lamp that sat on a small, claw-footed tea-table in the center of the room, I raised the glass chimney and ignited the wick with a sulfur match. Then——still clutching the paper sheet upon which I had inscribed the enigmatical letters——I returned to my place and gestured towards the high-backed elbow-chair facing me.

Settling into this seat, the frontiersman crossed one leg over the other and rested his felt hat upon the peak of his knee. "That's a right purty gal you got there, Cricket. Why, I had no idea you was a daddy."

I could feel a hot flush of indignation suffuse my entire countenance. "You have entirely misapprehended the nature of the relationship that exists between Virginia and myself," I declared. "She is not *my* daughter, but rather that of the good woman in whose company she has just now departed, my aunt Maria Clemm. Virginia is, in short, my *cousin*——though it is my fervent prayer that, before another year has passed, she will consent to be my wife!"

At this pronouncement, the frontiersman regarded me with an expression of slightly stupefied wonderment. He stared at me wordlessly before expelling a low, barely audible whistle. "If that don't beat all," he muttered beneath his breath. "Well," he continued after a momentary pause, "it ain't your family circumstances that I come here to discuss, Cricket—though I will confess that the whole situation sounds a mite *peculiar*. But as I say, that ain't none o' Davy Crockett's business."

"And what precisely *is* this business of yours, Colonel Crockett?" I inquired. "For an individual engaged in a mission of such purported urgency, you are, if I may say so, proceeding at a most *dilatory* pace."

"It's that infarnal miscreant, Neuendorf," sighed Crockett. "It appears that he ain't the killer after all." In the warm glow of the lamplight, I could not help but discern that his customary expression of inordinate self-confidence had been replaced by one of self-doubt.

"On what evidence," I exclaimed, "is your assertion based?"

"On the fact that he warn't even in town last night when Mrs. Macready got herself kilt. He's been gone for near a week. A dozen folks has come forward to swear oaths to it. The pestiferous varmint was off workin' on a fishin' vessel that only just sailed back into port at daybreak this mornin'."

This revelation produced a most singular response within my bosom: a not unpleasurable feeling of vindication, followed at once by an intense throb of dismay.

As though possessed of a preternatural faculty that permitted him access to my innermost thoughts, the frontiersman declared, "Aye, Cricket, it's a mighty plaguesome state of affairs, and no mistake. For if that

devilish rascal Neuendorf ain't guilty, then the butch-
erous killer is still walkin' the streets."

A long moment passed while I digested this intelligence. "The situation you have described," I said at
last, "while certainly distressing, is nothing less than
what I had already surmised. Indeed, immediately
prior to your unanticipated arrival, I was endeavoring
to decipher the mysterious word left at the crime
scene, under the conviction that it did not, in fact,
spell out Neuendorf's name." And here I held up the
sheet of paper upon which the mysterious notation
was transcribed.

"Why, that's just what brung me here tonight,
Cricket! After the police was forced to set Neuendorf
free, Captain Russell come to see me and told me all
about your little palaver this morning. Thinks I—
'There's more to this-here Cricket feller than meets the
eye!'"

"I am, of course, deeply touched by your heartfelt
encomium," I replied with more than a hint of *wryness*
in my tone. "But as to the precise purpose of your
visit," I continued, "I must confess that I remain in the
dark."

"That's easily answered. I'm here to lay out a
proposition—that you 'n' me hook up together! Why,
with that rattlin' good head of yourn and my own—if
I may say—*uncommon* endowments, I reckon we'll catch
that low-down murderer quicker'n a blind horse can
bump into a fence post!"

So startling was Crockett's proposal that, for a

moment, I was rendered utterly incapable of speech. "Am I to understand," I inquired at last, "that you are suggesting a partnership between us?"

"You have struck the nail bang on the head, Cricket."

Another moment passed as I struggled to digest this extraordinary development. "And what of the police? Surely it is the responsibility of duly appointed law officers, and not of private citizens, to engage in the pursuit and apprehension of notorious criminals."

Plucking his wide-brimmed hat from his knee, Crockett uncrossed his leg and leaned forward in his chair. "No disrespect meant to Captain Russell and his boys, but I don't take much stock in 'em, Cricket. They ain't no different from any other constabulary I ever struck—so saddled with doin' things accordin' to the book that they move as slow as cold molasses in January. And anyways," he added with a grin, "I ain't no private citizen. I am a real sure-enough U. S. congressman!"

"So you are," I replied, arranging my features into an expression that—while falling short of a *smirk*— nonetheless conveyed a fair degree of skepticism. "Indeed, at the risk of wrongfully impugning your motives, I cannot help suspecting that they are not wholly untainted with considerations of a *political* nature."

This observation elicited a singular response in the normally buoyant frontiersman. Far from offending him, it appeared to plunge him into a mood of solemn introspection. His smile faded, his brow contracted, and—casting his gaze downward—he nodded in a slow, reflective manner. When, after the passage of several silent moments, he opened his mouth to speak, it was in a tone of unwonted gravity. "You ain't entirely uncorrect, Cricket," he conceded. "Catchin' the heinous miscreant that kilt poor ol' Mrs. Macready sure won't do me no harm come election day, I won't deny it."

Suddenly, his countenance underwent another striking transformation, his sombre expression turning into one of fierce resolution. "But you've plumb missed the mark if you reckon that's the only reason I'm set on runnin' the varmint to ground," he asserted. "You seed with your own two eyes what he done to that poor ol' widder-lady. Why, it's enough to make a man's bristles stand up stiff as the thorns on a honey-locust tree. If you reckon I'm about to set still and not stir a finger while that unhuman devil's on the loose— well then, Cricket, all's I can say is, you have sadly misjudged Davy Crockett's character!"

Much to my astonishment, I found myself reacting with a real, if somewhat *grudging*, respect to this impassioned declaration. While not entirely dispelling my doubts as to the purity of Crockett's motives, such spirited words could not help but strike a responsive chord within the breast of any but the most hopelessly *phlegmatic* male. As Crockett had correctly observed, I had indeed been witness to the full horrors of the atrocity. They had inflamed within my bosom, no less than in *his*, a fervent desire to see the perpetrator brought to justice. To assist in that enterprise would be a source of the most profound personal satisfaction.

Moreover, by accepting his proposal, I would be able to show the cocksure frontiersman, once and for all, that—owing to the inherent superiority of intellect over brawn—the man of exceptional *mental* capacities will always perform at a higher level of distinction than one endowed with mere *physical* prowess. I hasten to add that feelings of mere *personal* rivalry with Crockett played no part in my calculations—such petty emotions being wholly alien to my character.

"Well, Cricket, what d'ye say?" urged Crockett as I continued to deliberate on the matter.

Straightening up in my chair, I regarded the frontiersman with a look of the most solemn and purposeful *intensity*. "Colonel Crockett," I declared, "having given your proposition the careful consideration it so manifestly deserves, I have reached the conclusion that it is, indeed, my sacred duty—as a *man* no less than a citizen—to assist, in whatever way possible, in the resolution of this dreadful mystery. As a result, I have decided to respond in the affirmative."

Raising one hand to the level of his shoulder, the irrepressible frontiersman let out a delighted whoop and delivered a resounding slap to his right knee. "By jings, Cricket, them's the very words I was hopin' to hear! Why, you 'n' me'll capture that pestiferous varmint afore you can say 'Jack Robinson'!"

So *infectious* was Crockett's enthusiasm that I could not help responding with an indulgent half-smile—

which, however, rapidly faded from my countenance as I was struck with a troublesome thought. "But surely, Colonel Crockett, you must have weighty obligations elsewhere that require your immediate attention. While I hesitate to question your optimistic conviction, it is possible that this matter may not, in fact, be resolved quite as expeditiously as you believe."

"It's true as preachin', Cricket—there's more folks'n you can shake a stick at that's clammerin' after me. Why, the Big-Whigs of Boston was fixin' to throw me a riproarious dinner at the Tremont House the day after next. But that little shindig'll just have to wait for a spell. No sir," he insisted with an emphatic shake of the head. "I don't aim to stir from this fair city of yourn 'til the culprit has been brung to justice."

"Well, Colonel Crockett," I replied, "should this affair require more time than you anticipate, you will at least have the privilege of spending it in Baltimore, which, as you say, is truly one of the fairest—as well as one of the most *progressive*—municipalities in the land." Then, cocking an eyebrow, I added, "I assume that your newfound acquaintance of this morning has already introduced you to some of its many attractions."

"You mean Maryanne Mullany?" said the frontiersman with a distinctly *rakish* grin. "Why, that sweet li'l gal was what I'd call downright *hospitable*. Yessir, she showed me a sight or two that had my eyes bulgin' out as big as a bullfrog's."

"I have no doubt," I replied dryly. "And which of these marvels, if I may inquire, were you most taken by?"

"Lemme see," he reflected, stroking his square, smooth-shaven chin. "There was that splendiferous cathedral that ain't like nothin' I ever seed. And the Holliday Street The-ayter. And that dazzlin' big buildin' over yonder on Gay Street."

"Ah yes," I said. "The New Export-Import Mercantile Association Building—one of the most imposing commercial structures in Baltimore."

"That's the one—she's a dilly, all right. And then there was that huge-acious statue of George Washington that I've heard tell so much about. It's a corker, and no mistake. Course, I don't entirely cotton to seein' *any* man—not even a United States President—stuck way high up on a pedestal that way. It don't hardly seem right. Though I don't s'ppose the one we got now would have any objections to bein' treated in such a manner. Hell, ol' Andy Jackson already acts so high 'n' mighty that . . . why, Cricket, what in tarnation has come over you?"

Though I was, at that instant, entirely unconscious of my facial expression, it must have been of a most remarkable character to have brought the frontiersman's soliloquy to such an abrupt halt. But however singular my *aspect*, it could only have been a faint representation of the exceedingly *agitated* sensations that were swirling within my bosom.

"What the devil's the matter, Cricket?" repeated the frontiersman.

"Of course!" I exclaimed, staring down at the sheet of paper in my lap. "It is not *one* word but *two!*"

Rising swiftly from his place, Crockett stepped behind my chair and peered over my shoulder. "Slow down, Cricket," he said. "You're movin' a mite fast for me."

"The letters above Mrs. Macready's bed! I have been proceeding under the assumption that they formed a *single* word. But let us suppose that there were, in fact, *two*. In view of the intensely feverish circumstances under which he was undoubtedly operating, the author of the cryptic message—who, as I continue to believe, was the *perpetrator* of the deed and not the unfortunate victim—may easily have omitted the space between them, thus running the words *together*."

"I still ain't altogether followin' you, Cricket."

"Look!" I exclaimed. Taking my pencil, I quickly filled in the four blank spaces with the characters "W," "X," "P," and "T," thus producing the following lexical formation:

NEWEXPORT

"Why, what in tarnation does it signify, Cricket? I can't cipher it nohow."

"New Export!"

"You mean like that building I seed this morning—the whaddayacallit?"

"Precisely! The New Export-Import Mercantile Association Building. Indeed, it was your allusion to it a moment ago that gave rise to my deduction."

"But what in blue blazes does that buildin' have t'do with poor ol' Mrs. Macready?" inquired the frontiersman in a tone of deep perplexity.

"Indeed, Colonel Crockett," I replied as the frontiersman walked back to the elbow chair and reseated himself upon it. "*That*—to quote the immortal Bard of Avon—is the question. As for the *answer*—while I am at a loss to propound a *definitive* reply, I can, at the very least, offer an educated *surmise*."

"Go ahead, Cricket. I am all ears."

"The connection relates to Mrs. Macready's late husband, Junius—for much of his life one of Baltimore's most prominent citizens. In his latter years, this gentleman suffered grievous reversals which led to his near-total financial ruin and, ultimately, to his rapid physical decline and unseasonable death. The precise details of this catastrophe are, of course, unknown to me. But at the time of its occurrence, rumors abounded that his fall had been expedited, if not wholly *effected*, through a bitter feud with members of another venerable Baltimore family, the Ashers, whose fortune also underwent a considerable diminution through their monomaniacal pursuit of their *vendetta* against Macready. Indeed, far more than their wealth was affected, since the patriarch of the family, Samuel Asher—like his hated adversary Junius Macready—was left a broken man. He, too, perished soon afterwards, leaving as his only heirs a pair of notoriously reclusive—and, according to repute, wildly eccentric—adult children."

"But where in thunderation does that buildin' enter into it, Cricket?"

Here, I leaned forward in my seat and fixed the

frontiersman with a firm, unwavering gaze. "According to newspaper accounts published at the time of Macready's demise," I replied, "the precipitating cause of the enmity between this gentleman and the Ashers involved the edifice in question, in whose extravagantly costly construction the two had been major investors."

For several moments, the frontiersman sat frowning in silence, tugging pensively at his lower lip. "And you figger," he inquired at last, "that these-here Asher children might've had a hand in Mrs. Macready's killin'?"

"Given their apparently justified reputation for anomalous, if not highly *abnormal*, behavior—as well as the poisonous rancor that has, for many years, infected the relationship between the two parties—such a possibility is not wholly beyond question."

"Well, then," said Crockett, rising purposefully to his feet. "Our path is plain as shootin'. We must commence by payin' them Asher folks a little visit. Whereabouts will we find 'em, Cricket?"

"They continue to reside in their ancestral home, a once-splendid but now exceedingly dilapidated manse located in a remote area of the countryside, approximately twenty miles north of the city."

Settling his wide-brimmed hat on his head, the frontiersman said: "Well then, Cricket, you'n me'd best get us some shut-eye. Come morning, I will hire us a couple of mounts at a livery stable and fetch you first thing after breakfast."

"Your suggestion seems eminently reasonable,"

said I, rising from my seat. "Allow me to show you to the door."

Preceding the frontiersman out of the parlor and down the narrow hallway, I escorted him to the front door. Pausing at its threshold, I turned to him and said, "There is one final matter, Colonel Crockett. While fully committed to this enterprise, I must insist on a single stipulation."

His brow knitted in evident perplexity.

"From this point forward," I explained, "I wish to be called by my actual cognomen. I can—I *will*—no longer tolerate your repeated denomination of me as a member of that vexatious order of *orthoptera* known scientifically as *Gryllus domesticus*."

For several moments, the frontiersman simply regarded me with a look of open-mouthed wonderment, as though stunned into an awed silence by the sheer *vehemence* of my declaration. At last, his face brightened and a broad grin spread slowly over his countenance. "Why, it took me a minute to cipher your meanin'," he chuckled. "But I am happy to oblige, Cr—er, Poe!" Then, as if to ratify our new understanding, he extended his powerful right hand.

I shook it politely. Then, with a parting farewell, he threw open the door, stepped into the fog-shrouded night, and took leave of me until the morrow.

CHAPTER 9

My efforts to heed the parting advice proffered by the frontiersman—that, in his quaint phraseology, I "get some shut-eye"—met with only meagre success. My slumbers were fitful in the extreme: sporadic periods of vexed and restless sleep, interrupted by long, dreary hours of wakefulness. Like an injured man who picks compulsively at a scabbed-over wound, my harried brain could not cease from dwelling on the dismaying events of the day just past—or from speculating on the difficulties and perils still to come.

Foremost among the subjects of these latter speculations were the two individuals that Crockett and I proposed to visit on the morrow. What little knowledge I possessed of Roger and Marilynne Asher derived largely from hearsay, for I had never so much as set eyes on either member of this notoriously reclusive pair. I knew that—as unmarried siblings who had already passed well into the middle years of their allotted spans—the two represented the ultimate termination of the eminent Asher line, whose family name would utterly perish with their own inevitable extinction. I knew further that—while their widely reported proclivity for erratic and even *bizarre* behavior had earned them a reputation as difficult, if not exceedingly *disagreeable*, human beings—their personal failings were at least partly offset by a deeply ingrained sense of civic obligation, which manifested itself in repeated deeds of munificent patronage, particularly in the realm of cultural pursuits. As a result, their family name could be found on opera houses, musical academies, and theatres throughout the city, including the glorious Asher Playhouse on Fayette Street.

Indeed, in their dedication to the cultural life of their native city, the Ashers—somewhat ironically—shared a close, common bond with their family's archenemy, the late Junius Macready, who had likewise been, in the heyday of his fortunes, an unstintingly generous supporter of the theatrical arts in Baltimore.

As I lay, head enpillowed, in the darkness of my bedroom, I was suddenly struck by the realization that a distant and indirect, but nonetheless *real*, connection existed between the Ashers, the Macreadys, and myself. The common thread that united me, however tenuously, to the others was our shared affinity with the still-nascent world of American theatre, of which my own angelic mother, Eliza Poe, had been, during her all-too-brief existence, one of the shining ornaments.

I threw back my bedclothes and rose from the mattress with a groan; then—barefooted and clad only in my nightdress—made my way slowly through the tomb-like darkness of my chamber and into my study. Seating myself at my writing table, I struck a match and enkindled my oil lamp, which cast a dull circle of light over the crowded surface of the table.

My work space—like that of every true *littérateur*—was fairly blanketed with a wild miscellany of books, writing implements, loose sheets of blank paper, and thick piles of manuscript pages. Balanced atop one of these piles—where it served as an exceedingly convenient paper weight—was a small casket-shaped box of antique mahogany. Extending both of my hands across the table, I removed this object from its perch and placed it directly before me.

This box had been in my possession for many years, having been bestowed upon me—in one of his rare acts of generosity—by my recently deceased guardian, the churlish Richmond merchant John Allan. It was an exceedingly handsome object of rare and elegant design, its smooth, highly polished lid secured by a miniature lock of the most delicate workmanship. Sliding open the middle drawer of my writing table, I reached inside and extracted a tiny brass key on a slender chain. Then—carefully inserting the key into the corresponding hole in the lock-plate of the little box—I opened the latter and slowly raised the lid.

Since receiving it as a gift on my sixteenth birthday, I had employed the box as a sort of "treasure chest"— a receptacle for those articles and documents most significant to me. Among its other contents, it contained the sparse mementoes—all the more precious to me for their pitiable *meagreness*——of my mother's tragically brief life and aborted career: a handbill from a production of David Garrick's *Miss in Her Teens,* in which she played the ingenue *rôle* of sixteen-year-old Biddy Belair; a miniature portrait of her as the doomed, grievously wronged Desdemona; and several yellowing newspaper reviews of her performances in the plays *Time Tells a Tale, The Provoked Husband, The Belle's Stratagem,* and sundry of Shakespeare's timeless tragedies.

Removing these fragile notices from the interior of the box, I laid them out carefully before me and began to peruse them. It did not take me long to discover what I was searching for.

It appeared in a lengthy review of a production of *King Lear,* mounted at Baltimore's renowned Front Street Theatre in the fall of 1807. After paying glowing tribute to my mother's "heart-wrenching portrayal" of the martyred Cordelia, the article made note of the various local luminaries who had been present for the opening-night performance. "The audience, which filled every available seat in the splendid auditorium, comprised some of Baltimore's most eminent citizens," the reviewer had written. "Among those in attendance, who greeted Miss Poe at the conclusion of the play with a thunderous ovation, were Chief Justice Stephenson Archer of the Court of Appeals; Mr. Septimus J. Claypoole, proprietor of the *Baltimore Daily Advertiser;* Dr. and Mrs. Jared Parkhurst; Mr. and Mrs. Junius Macready; Mrs. Josiah Nicodemus, widow of the renowed ship's captain; and Mr. Samuel Ogden Asher."

Here, indeed, was proof of the strange, if not *portentous*, connection that I had been struck by while lying in bed! I say "portentous," for the juxtaposition, within this decades-old theatrical review, of the Poe family name with those of the Ashers and Macreadys struck me as a veritable portent of the events now unfolding.

For several minutes, I sat motionless at the table, attempting to envision that long-ago evening when my mother's thrilling portrayal of Lear's doomed, saintly daughter brought the city's most *jaded* audience to its feet in a wild display of clamorous approbation. Gradually, however, an enormous lethargy—akin to the inertia that invariably follows the delirious excitement of an opium-dream—began to steal over me. My eyelids felt as heavy as lead, and from the bottommost depths of my being there issued a resounding *yawn*.

Locking away the relics of my mother's tragically abbreviated life, I restored the casket-shaped box to its place. So intense was the fatigue that had settled upon me that the simple prospect of rising from my seat, crossing the room, and returning to bed seemed unutterably dreary. Extinguishing the oil lamp, I folded my arms upon the tabletop, rested my drooping head upon them, and fell into a profound and instantaneous sleep.

I cannot say what roused me, beyond a dim but gnawing awareness—operating even in my unconscious state—that the morning had dawned. I awoke from an unsettling dream in which a small but undaunted figure struggled to save a maiden from the clutches of a vile king. Leaping from my chair, I crossed rapidly to the window, and drew back the curtains. Though a thick blanket of clouds continued to darken the sky, it was clear that the day was already several hours old. Returning to my bedchamber, I quickly performed my matinal ablutions, threw on my clothes, and hurried out to the kitchen.

I entered the little room to find my aunt in the act of laying out a breakfast of buttered and toasted bread, sorghum molasses, and tea.

"Why, good morning, Eddie," the dear woman exclaimed as I stepped up beside her and planted a fond, filial osculation upon her cheek. "I was just about to knock on your door. I am so pleased that you have finally managed to sleep until a decent hour."

"And what precisely *is* the hour?" I inquired as I seated myself at the table, unfolded my napkin, and tucked it into the collar of my shirt.

"Nearly eight-thirty," she replied, lowering herself into the chair beside me.

This intelligence produced a tremor of alarm which—like the electrical shock from a galvanic battery—coursed through every fibre of my being. The day was even more advanced than I had realized! Snatching up a slice of toast, I spooned a dollop of syrup upon its surface, hastily bit off a mouthful, and washed it down with a great, gulping swallow of the steaming beverage.

"Oh, Eddie," clucked Muddy as she regarded me with a look of intense maternal solicitude. "Do not wolf your food down so, or you will give yourself a terrible case of dyspepsia. You know how sensitive your stomach is."

"To savor the pleasures of my morning repast is—alas!—a luxury I cannot afford, for I am anticipating the imminent—if not *momentary*—arrival of Colonel Crockett."

"Oh?" said Muddy with an inquiring look.

Though I had apprised both my aunt and cousin of the previous day's dire occurrences, I had somewhat concealed from them (as I have already indicated) the full extent of my own involvement, for fear of causing them undue anxiety on my behalf. The same motive now impelled me to persist in my course of dissimulation. I casually explained that I had agreed to serve as a kind of guide for Colonel Crockett, who had expressed an interest in viewing some of the famously picturesque sights of the Maryland countryside.

"Why, that sounds very pleasant, Eddie," she replied. "I take it, then, that you have patched things up with Colonel Crockett."

"We have indeed achieved, if not a lasting reconciliation, then at least a temporary *rapprochement*."

"I am delighted to hear it," she said, smiling broadly.

"In any event, dearest Muddy," I continued, "you should not expect me home until quite late. Indeed, my arrival may well be delayed until well past the *witching hour*, so please do not feel obliged to remain awake until my return."

At that instant, a sharp rapping upon the front door of our domicile announced my companion's arrival.

"Finish your tea, dear," said Muddy, rising from her place. "I will go answer."

As the good woman bustled from the kitchen, I quickly imbibed the remainder of the invigorating brew. Then, plucking the napkin from my shirt collar, I rose from my seat and repaired directly to my bedroom. Judging from the dismal aspect of the sky, I could see that there would be no immediate respite from the dispiriting weather that, for the past several days, had held our fair city in so *chill* and oppressive a sway. I removed my hat and cloak from their respective wall-hooks and hurried from the room.

As I approached the open front door, I saw Muddy posed at the threshold conversing with Crockett, who was standing just outside our doorway beside a handsome pair of steeds—one a bay, the other a strawberry roan. Both sets of reins were clutched in his gloved right hand.

"Mornin', pard," he exclaimed when he saw me. "I was just tellin' your Aunty Clemm here not to fret if we ain't returned by sundown, seein' as how we got us a considerable sight of country to cover afore we reach that Ash—"

Standing directly to the rear of Muddy—and thus safely out of her sight—I shook my head vigorously at Crockett. The frontiersman's eyes widened slightly in surprise, then flickered with a glint of recognition as the meaning of my gesture dawned on him.

"—afore we reach, uh, that place we're headin' to," he concluded.

Donning my hat and cloak, I made my way past my aunt and out onto the quiet street, whereupon the frontiersman held out the reins of the bay. Grasping these, I placed my left foot in the stirrup and mounted the equine in one motion.

"I am sorry the weather isn't nicer for your trip," said Muddy to us both.

"Ain't as bad as all that, Mizz Clemm," said Crockett as he swung himself onto his steed. "I been out huntin' when the day was so miserable cold that the very sunrise froze fast as it was tryin' to dawn! Why, this-here day is as splendid as a sunny mornin' in June by comparison. Speakin' o' which—you tell Miz Virginny that ol' Davy Crockett is looking forward to hearin' her sing ag'in. Hang me up for bear-meat if that li'l gal's voice ain't as sweet as a canary-bird's."

"I will tell her you said so," Muddy said with a broad, beaming smile

"And tell her for *me*," I declared, "that this cheerless spring morn has been rendered even more dismal, since I must now pass an entire day without a glimpse of her fair countenance!"

"I certainly will, dear," said Muddy. Then, with a little wave of her hand, she bade us farewell and—as we reined our steeds around and headed off along Amity Street—called out a parting valediction:

"Have fun, boys!"

* * *

The possibility of meaningful discourse with my companion was, at first, entirely precluded by the reactions he provoked as we made our way towards the northernmost reaches of the city. On every thoroughfare along which we passed, he was instantly recognized by pedestrians and travellers alike, who hailed him with shouts of "Up and at 'em, Davy!," "Hurrah for Crockett!," and other such fervent salutations. The beaming frontiersman acknowledged each of these greetings with a wave of his hat and an ebullient "Thank'ee, good citizen!"; while I rode silently beside him, a reluctant Panza to his irrepressible knight-errant.

It was not until we had left the city behind us that an opportunity finally arose for us to talk. It was Crockett who initiated our discussion by inquiring about my urgent interruption of his conversation with Muddy.

"I declare, Poe," he exclaimed, "but I near about busted my noggin tryin' to figger out what in tarnation you was signallin' for. Why, your head was shakin' like a man with the Saint Vitals dance."

I explained that my actions had been prompted by the concern I harbored for my Aunt Maria, from whom I was determined to keep the particulars of my involvement in the present enterprise. "My behavior," I added, "was thus the natural expression of the solicitude I possess for my aunt—a being towards whom I feel all the tenderness and gratitude of a son."

Crockett cocked his head to peer at me as we trotted abreast of each other along the rutted path that wound into the luxuriant countryside.

"And what became of your nat'ral mother, Poe?—
for I take it that the poor woman is no longer among
the living."

I acknowledged the accuracy of this observation with
a melancholy sigh. "A glorious star whose intense, if transitory, brilliance gave boundless delight to all who gazed
upon it, my mother—the celebrated thespian Eliza
Poe—perished of the consumption at the tender age of
twenty-four, when I was little more than an infant."

My companion clucked his tongue in sympathy.
"And your father?"

At the mere allusion to my male progenitor, I
could feel my heart stiffen with rage. "Though loath
to violate any of the ten sacred precepts of the
Decalogue, I am powerless to contemplate that
deplorable being—for I will not honor him with the
designation of *man*—without succumbing to the most
vituperative thoughts." I paused for a moment until I
had regained sufficient control of my emotions to
continue. "He, too, was an actor—though of such a
mediocre stamp as to incur the unreserved scorn of
audiences and critics alike. I know nothing more about
him, for—in an act of almost inhuman cruelty—he
utterly abandoned my doomed, sainted mother less
than one year following my birth."

"Why the varminous miscreant!" Crockett said in
shocked indignation. "Hanging ain't good enough for
a serpent such as that!"

"Perhaps, indeed, that is the fate which eventually
befell the unprincipled wretch. For he vanished as

though into thin air, and has never been seen or heard from again."

We rode in sombre, ruminative silence for a moment. "Well, Poe," the frontiersman observed at last, "you was dealt a mighty bad hand for a young 'un, and no mistake. It is monstrous hard to be an orphan in this world."

"Harder than is easily imaginable by those who have not suffered such a calamity," said I. For several moments, I was incapable of further speech, as I inwardly decried the evil fate which had not only deprived me of a mother's affections but had subsequently thrust me into the heartless care of a harsh and unfeeling guardian.

At length, having regained a measure of self-composure, I continued thusly: "It is solely through the goodness of my aunt's unstinting heart that I have known, for the first time in my ill-starred existence, the sweetest of all earthly blessings—unconditional *mother-love!*"

"Them's mighty fine sentiments, Poe," Crockett said with an approving nod. "But there ain't no cause for your Aunty Clemm to fret. Why, so long as Davy Crockett's around, you'll be as safe as a baby possum tucked inside its mama's pouch—even if that pestiferous rascal Neuendorf *does* come a-huntin' for you, like he swore."

So startled was I by this latter observation that I involuntarily jerked on the reins of my horse, causing him to rear slightly and nearly throw me into the little stream that Crockett and I were in the process of fording. Quickly regaining control of the steed, I proceeded onto the opposite bank, then turned to my companion. "Neuendorf? For what possible reason would he have made such a threat—when it was I who endeavored to persuade the police that the bloody markings at the murder scene did *not,* in fact, spell out his name?"

We had come to a halt on a grassy slope beside a stand of willows. Resting one forearm on the pommel of his saddle, Crockett leaned forward and gently stroked the neck of his steed with his opposite hand. "Why, reason don't enter into it, Poe—not with a varmint such as that. He somehow took it into his head that, if it warn't for you, me 'n' him would've never locked horns in the first place. Leastways, that's what Cap'n Russell has informed me. Now, he's goin' around swearin' that he'll use your skin for a razor strop and cut out my heart and cook it for stewmeat."

With an inward shudder, I recalled the savage, long-bladed knife that Neuendorf had wielded so furiously in his encounter with the frontiersman.

"Well, I'll be shot if you ain't gone white as an eggshell!" exclaimed Crockett. "You ain't *worried* about that no-account varmint?" Sitting straight in his saddle, he reached out a hand and gave me a resounding slap on the shoulder. "Why, I hope he *does* come a-lookin' for us. I will settle his hash quicker'n an alligator can chew a puppy!"

Contemplating the distance that still lay before us—an extensive stretch of wild, uninhabited country whose every hillock, tree-grove, and ravine might serve as the ideal location for an ambuscade—I observed: "I must confess to feeling somewhat perplexed that—knowing of Neuendorf's vicious threats, to say nothing of his savage, implacable nature—you did not consider it prudent to carry a weapon, Colonel Crockett."

"Weapon!" he replied with a booming laugh. "Why, if my two bare hands ain't enough to dispatch that infarnal critter, I wish I may be choked with a saw-log." Then, with a cluck of his tongue and a tug of his reins, he directed his steed back onto the trail, while—urging my bay forward—I quickly drew up alongside him.

Directly overhead, a deep-pitched rumble emanated from the grim, lowering clouds. Smiling broadly at the sound, Crockett raised his right hand nearly to the level of his shoulder, delivered an exuberant slap to his thigh, and loudly proclaimed: "Just listen to it sing, Poe! Folks may crow all they want about the roar of Niagara or the growlin' of the sea—but give me a splendacious peal o' stormbrewed thunder and your other nat'ral music is no more than a penny whistle is to a church organ! By the Great Bein' Above, a reg'lar roarin' thunder-clap is the greatest treat in all o' creation! Just give me one touch o' this sort o' nat'ral music afore I go to sleep, and I wake feelin' so full o' glory that I could hug the Mississippi, bust a big rock with my hands, and feel powerful enough to do the duty of an entire sawmill!"

Then, casting a sideways glance in my direction, he said: "Why Poe, did I ever tell you about the time I tried to cure myself o' a monstraciously bad gut-ache by swallerin' a thunderbolt? No? Well, it happened way back in the spring o' 1816, not too long after me an'

Ol' Hick'ry got done subduin' the Creek injuns durin' the Redstick War. Anyways, I awoke feelin' a mite poorlyish that mornin'. So I says to myself, 'Davy . . .'"

As we continued our journey northward, trotting abreast of each other, Crockett proceeded to regale me with his colorful narrative—of whose details, however, I remained largely oblivious; for my attention was firmly riveted, not on his outrageous "tall tale," but on the gloomy, surrounding landscape, whose seemingly innocuous features—hills and dales, outcroppings and thickets—were suddenly imbued with the grim—the fearful—the *daunting*—prospect of hidden, lurking *peril!*

CHAPTER 10

I passed the remainder of our journey in a condition of extreme unease, while, trotting alongside me, the voluble frontiersman poured out a torrent of his extravagant—and seemingly inexhaustible—narratives. Though apparently intended as high-spirited *divertissements*, these tales—involving his savage encounters with Indians, panthers, alligators, wolves, and monstrously proportioned members of the ursine family—had the very opposite effect, serving not to mitigate but rather to *exacerbate* my already acute state of nervous irritation.

It might be supposed, then, that—as we emerged from a dense grove of pines in the late afternoon and caught sight of our destination directly before us—I would have responded with a sense of the keenest gratitude and relief. Such, however, was not the case. I know not how it was, but at my very first glimpse of the venerable Asher manse, my heart was suffused with the most profound and insufferable *gloom!*

What was it, I wondered—as our horses approached the dark, looming edifice—what was it that so unnerved me in the contemplation of the House of Asher? For—aside from a general air of dilapidation and neglect—there was nothing which I could immediately perceive about the building to account for its grim—its sorrowful—its singularly *oppressive*—effect upon my soul.

As the frontiersman and I reined our steeds to a halt before the massive front door, I looked upon the external features of the building—upon the bleak, discolored walls—upon the vacant, eye-like windows—upon the minute fungi that hung in a tangled webwork from the eaves—with an utter depression of spirit that I can compare to no earthly sensation more properly than to the afterdream of the reveller upon opium. The mere sight of the building filled my soul with an indescribably disquieting sensation—a species of intense nervous agitation bordering on dread!

"Mossy-lookin' ol' place, ain't it?" said Crockett, dismounting from his steed and lashing the reins to a once-ornate but now badly corroded hitching post. Gazing up at the building with a look of disapprobation, he shook his head and muttered, "Why, if *I* was to live in such grandiferous style, I reckon I'd take a heap better care o' my diggin's than these-here Asher folks!"

As I climbed down from my steed and led it to the hitching post, Crockett approached the front door. "What in tarnation——?" I heard him exclaim. Stepping to his side, I saw that his attention was riveted on the heavy, iron knocker affixed to the center of the door. This object was of a most singular design, wrought into the shape of a rearing centaur whose brutish face wore an expression of utter, wanton carnality. Clutched in the creature's arms was a swooning maiden, garbed in such an exceedingly immodest fashion that——I blush to pen the words——the contours of her bosom were revealed in the most flagrant manner imaginable!

"These Ashers," said Crockett as he continued to gape at the door-knocker with an expression in which rapt fascination and shocked indignation seemed equally commingled. "They ain't Froggies by any chance?"

"To the best of my knowledge," I replied, "the family is of English descent."

"Well," muttered Crockett, "I'll be hanged if I ever struck anything like it!" Then, grasping the elaborately wrought knocker, he pounded it repeatedly against the iron plate.

Crockett's action was followed by a silence so prolonged that I was gripped with a dispiriting thought. Perhaps the inhabitants had ventured forth from their dwelling, and our journey had been for naught! At length, the frontiersman reached up for the knocker and, once again, announced our presence with a series of loud, insistent rappings——but to no more effect than before.

I had just turned to my companion and was on the brink of articulating my suspicion when I became cognizant of a series of distinctive noises from within the house: the shuffling of feet——the sliding of a bolt—— the creaking of hinges. The door opened to a width of several inches, barely permitting me to perceive a singularly pallid visage peering out at us from the gloomy interior of the dwelling.

"What do you want?" demanded a voice that sounded as rusty and ill-accustomed to use as the door hinges.

"Good afternoon," I replied in a tone of the utmost civility. "We wish to speak to the master of the house, Mr. Roger Asher."

"Impossible!" cried the anaemic-faced individual. "He does not care to speak to you or anyone! Go away!" And with these intensely disagreeable words, he commenced to shut the door.

Before he could achieve this goal, however, Crockett extended a hand and, placing it flush against the door, prevented it from closing.

"Not so fast," he exclaimed. "Me 'n' my friend have done a sight o' travellin' to git here, and we ain't of a mind to be treated in such an uncourteous style."

"But you are not welcome here!" the other protested.

"That is as it may be. But Davy Crockett don't cotton to such rudeness. It gets me hotter'n a curling tongs to be dealt with so *perempterously!*"

This fervent pronouncement appeared to give the pallid fellow pause. "Colonel David Crockett?" he inquired after a moment. "Of the state of Tennessee?"

"The one 'n' only," replied the frontiersman. "And this here's my pard, Mr. Edgar Poe o' Baltimore."

"Poe," said the other in a musing tone. "That

name, too, is not wholly unfamiliar to me." Following another brief interval during which he appeared to be engaged in a furious inner debate, he exhaled a sigh of resignation, took one step backward from the entranceway, and threw the door open to its widest extent. "Perhaps I have been overly precipitous. Come, gentlemen—enter. Hurry! Hurry! The air is abominably cold and damp, and I do not wish to be exposed to such a pernicious draft!"

In response to these proddings, Crockett and I quickly crossed the threshold into that mansion of gloom, whereupon the pallid gentleman—who, I had already surmised, was none other than the proprietor himself, Mr. Roger Asher—immediately slammed the door shut behind us.

"This way, gentlemen," said the singular individual as he preceded us down a long, shadowy corridor. Its lofty walls were hung with dark, tattered draperies whose rich (if badly moth-eaten) fabric was wrought with a fantastic network of arabesque figures and wild, filigreed designs.

Ushering us into a vast and gloomy drawing room, our cadaverous host gestured towards two massive, ebony chairs that rested on a frayed carpet of Saxony material before a glowing fireplace. Doffing my hat and travelling cloak, I lowered myself into one of these furnishings, while Crockett settled into its mate. Asher, in the meantime, stepped to the fireplace to stir the smoldering embers with a poker—thus affording me an opportunity to glance about the great, dismal chamber.

Its dimensions measured, according to my estimate, no less than thirty by twenty-five feet. The floorboards were of ancient oak, darkened nearly to blackness with age; the ceiling—likewise of a gloomy-looking oak—was lofty, vaulted, and elaborately fretted with the wildest and most grotesque specimens of a semi-Gothic, semi-Druidical style.

The wall opposing the doorway through which we had entered was dominated by a tall, crimson-paned window, framed by voluminous curtains, also of a distinct, if somewhat faded, crimson hue. Feeble gleams of scarlet light made their way through the trellised panes and served to render sufficiently distinct the more prominent objects surrounding me. My eyes, however, struggled in vain to reach the remoter corners of the chamber, which were steeped in shadow and which appeared to be occupied by a pair of motionless sentinels. These latter—so I subsequently discovered—were complete, if somewhat rusty, suits of *medieval* armor that had belonged to the Asher family for many generations. One of these figures stood at rigid attention, a ferocious-looking battle-ax, or *halberd*, clutched in its gauntleted right hand. The other had been arranged in a particularly *warlike* posture, its knees flexed, its hands grasping a long-handled pike that was pointed directly forward, as though the figure were poised for an attack.

The general furniture of the room was profuse, antique, and—like the chairs upon which Crockett and I were seated—comfortless in the extreme. In short, the entire chamber created a distinct impression of musty, decaying grandeur—of former opulence and grace now deteriorated into stern, grim, and irredeemable *shabbiness.*

Asher himself created a similar impression: that of a being raised in an atmosphere of luxury and refinement who had—through those reversals of fortune so sadly endemic to our human lot—been reduced to a life of extreme and even *abject* degradation. Tall, gaunt, and exceedingly unwholesome in appearance, he was garbed in a once-fashionable—though long-obsolete—style: threadbare knee breeches, a yellow-stained linen shirt with ruffled front, and a dusty swallow-tailed coat with badly frayed cuffs.

His age was nearly impossible to determine, though I inferred—from the little I knew of his family history—that he could not be much older than two-score-and-five. But so bloodless—so wan—so dreadfully *wizened*—was his countenance that he might have been a personage of sixty or eighty—or, indeed, an embalmed and exsanguinated corpse that had somehow regained the power of animation. Beneath the white and vellum-like surface of his visage, the facial bones protruded with an almost skeletal sharpness and clarity. His thinning, fine-textured hair hung in limp, greasy strands to the level of his shoulders, and was of such an inordinate *blondness* as to appear almost white. Beneath his broad, jutting brow, his sunken eyes shone with a strange, slightly hysterical lustre; and when he spoke, a set of moldering, peculiarly sharp and rodent-like teeth were visible behind his pale and flaking lips.

Most disconcerting of all, however, were the incessant movements of his delicate, long-fingered hands, which rubbed each other in a constant *scrubbing* motion, not unlike the grotesquely fastidious gestures of the *Musca domestica*, or common housefly.

"So," croaked this singular individual as he turned his attention on my companion. "You are the celebrated Colonel David Crockett."

"I am for a fact," the latter replied. "And who might you be, if it ain't too bold to ask?"

"Roger Asher—at your service," said the other with a slight bow, confirming the identity I had already deduced. Straightening up again, he scrutinized the seated frontiersman with a long, appraising look in which I perceived more than a hint of amused curiosity and condescension.

"Were my *dear* sister, Marilynne, not so severely indisposed, she would be most honored—indeed, most *thrilled*—to meet you, Colonel Crockett," said Asher in a tone that conveyed the same inexplicably *derisive* attitude as his expression. "For—of the few remaining pleasures available to her—the reading of your most remarkable, most *unbelievable* adventures, as reported in the monthly almanacs published in your name, is by far the foremost."

"Why, that speaks mighty well o' the lady!" Crocket exclaimed. "And I hope that I may yet have the pleasure to meet your poor, ailin' sister afore me 'n' my friend is obliged to depart."

"That is doubtful, very doubtful," Asher replied

with a distinctly exaggerated, indeed *histrionic*, sigh. "I am afraid that dear Marilynne has long been suffering from a severe, if somewhat obscure, malady that may shortly result in her untimely demise." This melancholy statement was delivered with a most anomalous expression—a slight but unmistakable smile of grim satisfaction, as though the impending dissolution of his sibling were a consummation not entirely to be dreaded.

"Why, I'm plumb sorry to hear it," Crockett remarked.

Rubbing his hands with the avidity of a glutton who has just had a platter of rare and delectable *viands* set before him on the dining table, Asher replied, "No, no, Colonel Crockett! There is no need for sorrow. All of us must endure our going hence, even as our coming hither. And there are worse—yes, infinitely, *unimaginably* worse—things than mere *death!*"

"Why, that's as true as gospel," rejoined Crockett. "I recollect one time back in the canebrake country when a mate o' mine by the name o' Ephraim Wadlow poked his rifle into an ol' holler log to rouse out a great fat coon that was hidin' there, and a whole nest o' yeller jackets cum roarin' out at him like a pack o' savagerous redskins on the warpath. Now, Ephraim——"

Before my companion could proceed, I loudly cleared my throat in an effort to prevent yet another of his tiresome disquisitions, as well as to attract the attention of Asher who had thus far entirely—and with decided incivility—ignored my presence. As the latter swivelled to gaze down upon me with one pale eyebrow cocked, I boldly declared: "I infer from your evident recognition of my name, Mr. Asher, that you are as familiar with my own accomplishments as you are with Colonel Crockett's."

"Why, no, not at all," Asher replied with perfect *nonchalance.* "Up until now, your existence has been wholly unknown to me. With the name of *Poe,* however, I have long been familiar, for there was a most gifted actress of that name whom my late father—a man of rare discernment and taste—greatly admired, and whom I myself once had the honor of seeing in a memorable performance of Garrick's *Miss in Her Teens.*"

"You refer to my dear mother, Eliza Poe," said I, struggling to subdue my chagrin at Asher's blithe unawareness of my own identity. Such, I mused, were the indignities that must ever be endured by the man of true artistic talent, whose rarefied achievements are inevitably overshadowed by the coarse endeavors of those lesser beings who, like Crockett, cater solely to the crude sensibilities of the masses.

"I see!" exclaimed Asher. "And what became of the lady?"

"Dead," I replied in sorrow-choked voice. "Lo, these many years."

Nodding grimly—as though my statement had only confirmed him in a bitter supposition—Asher declared: "But this, you see, is the *perverse* nature of life: that the good, the graceful, the gifted—those with power to bring light and joy to the world—are cruelly snatched from our midst in the very flower of their youth; while others"—and here, his countenance assumed an expression of the most profound resentment and distaste—"who do nothing but make each day a *hell* for those nearest to them, cling to their existence with a monstrous *tenacity!*"

This impassioned outburst left our frail and sickly host visibly shaken. For a moment, he seemed to totter on his feet—eyes shut tight—sunken chest heaving—gaunt frame quavering as though from the sudden onset of the Spanish *influenza*. Several moments elapsed before his inner tumult subsided. His eyelids fluttered open and his lips drew back into a mirthless smile that—while seemingly intended to convey a courteous hospitality—had all the warmth of a corpse's grotesque *rictus*.

"So, gentlemen," said he, "to what do I owe the honor of this unlooked-for visitation?"

I parted my lips to reply. Before I could produce a sound, a faint but startling cry—as ghastly as the supplications of a lost, tormented soul—drifted from the bowels of the house. My mouth grew instantly dry—the blood congealed in my veins—and my throat closed as tight as though an assassin's garrote had been jerked around my neck, rendering me utterly incapable of speech!

Wearily shaking his head, Asher exhaled a soft, defeated sigh and said: "There she goes again. Forgive me, gentlemen—my sister beckons. She is, I fear, a most demanding, indeed a most *tyrannical*, patient. But what choice do I have? I am her sole source of comfort. It is I alone who can minister to her needs—no matter how burdensome, how onerous, how monstrously excessive they may be! But not for very much longer—oh, no! For the portion of life that remains to her is meagre indeed."

In delivering himself of this extraordinary speech, our host had once again wrought himself up into a state of near-hysterical agitation. His bony hands trembled, his gaping eyes gleamed, and froths of spittle formed in the corners of his mouth.

"Please, gentlemen," he gasped. "Make yourselves at home." Then—as another shrill, unearthly cry wafted from the inner reaches of the house—he swivelled on his heels and bolted from the drawing room.

"Queer sort o' feller," Crockett mused, staring after our departed host.

"Indeed," I replied. "Though whether his eccentricities are of the sort that might result in murder remains to be determined."

"Well," said Crockett, slapping his thighs and pushing himself to his feet, "why don't you 'n' me have a look-see around while we got us the chance." Pointing his chin at a three-branched candelabrum that stood on a small, marble-topped table at my elbow, he added: "Grab that candlestick, Poe, and let's have us some light."

I rose from my seat. Sitting on the tabletop beside the candelabrum was a tarnished silver cup holding several wooden matches. Employing one of these to light the three half-consumed tapers that protruded from the candelabrum, I lifted the latter by its stem and carried it over to Crockett, who had stepped near the fireplace and was staring in deep perplexity at a large, gold-framed canvas that hung above the mantel.

"What in blue blazes do you make o' *this?*" exclaimed the frontiersman as I came up beside him.

I raised the candelabrum so as to shed additional illumination on the canvas. It was indeed a most shocking, a most *lurid* composition. The painting depicted a turbanned emperor languidly reclining in his boudoir, while, all about him, a bevy of voluptuous (and entirely unclothed!) young women—evidently the members of his private *seraglio*—were being savagely slaughtered by a crew of knife-wielding assassins. Besides the state of shameless undress in which the women were depicted, what endowed this work with its singularly dismaying—if not *obscene*—quality was the expression of serene satisfaction on the face of the potentate as he watched the ghastly bloodshed taking place around him.

"Unless I am mistaken," I observed, "I believe this to be a copy—and one which has been executed with a fair degree of technical proficiency—of the well-known painting *The Death of Sardanapalus*, by the famed French artist Eugène Delacroix."

"French artist, eh? I should've known some danged foreigner was behind it! I declare, Poe—if this ain't the *undecentest* thing I ever clapped eyes on, then I wish I may be fried in bear grease. Why, it ain't hardly fit to be hung in a sportin' house!"

We continued to circulate about the chamber, scrutinizing Asher's imposing collection of oils, whose subjects—brazen odalisques, Saturnalian revels, pagan rituals of the most shocking and unbridled nature—provoked a continuous stream of outraged protests from the indignant frontiersman.

"Dad fetch it," he declared at last, "but these-here pictures are the beatenest thing I ever seen! What kind o' folks would want such wickedness hangin' in their parlor? You mark me, Poe—this Asher feller may put on his high-tone airs, but he ain't nothin' but a dad-blamed rapscallion!"

At this point in our investigations, we had come to a massive bookcase that stood against one wall of the chamber. Examining the rows of dusty, antique volumes that lined the shelves, I was forcibly struck by the degree to which they conformed—in their exceedingly anomalous subject matter—to the unhallowed paintings that constituted Asher's art collection. Among the many rare and curious editions that filled the towering bookcase, I recognized such grotesque, even *sinister,* works as the *Belphegor* of Machiavelli; the *Subterranean Voyage of Nicholas Klimm* by Holberg; the *Chiromancy* of Robert Flud; the *Malleus Malificarum* of Jakob Sprenger and Heinrich Kramer; Robert Scot's *Demonogly;* the *Practica Inquisitionis Heretice Pravitatis* of Bernadus Guidonis; and—perhaps most remarkable of all—a small octavo edition of the *Virgliæ Mortuorum secundum Chorum Ecclesiæ Maguntinæ*.

As I inspected the titles of this astonishing library,

my eyes fell upon a strangely familiar book, gold-stamped and bound in rich, green leather. Emitting a cry of surprise, I reached out and snatched the volume from its place.

"What's the matter, Poe?" Crockett exclaimed.

"Look!" I cried. "It is a copy of the very work that I was in the process of perusing when you first arrived at my domicile several days ago to confront me with your astonishing and ill-considered ultimatum!"

Taking the book from my hands, Crockett opened the cover, his face assuming a most singular expression of bafflement and wonder as he scrutinized the title page.

"*In-hu-mation Afore Death,*" he read. He glanced up at me. "What the devil does it signify, Poe?"

"It is a treatise about the awful—the ghastly—the unspeakable—calamity of *premature burial!*"

"Premature burial!" Crockett exclaimed. "You mean plantin' a feller six foot under afore he's even given up the ghost?"

A tremor of horror ran through my frame. "That, indeed, is the dire, the *appalling* circumstance denoted by the phrase," I replied. "Of all the horrors that may be visited upon mortals, it is the one whose mere *contemplation* is most assured to fill our souls with unendurable anxiety and overpowering *dread!*"

"It's a corker, all right," Crockett conceded. "Poe, there ain't *nuthin'* 'bout this Asher feller that sits right with me."

Clapping the volume shut, he thrust it back into

my hands; whereupon I restored it to its place on the shelf. As I turned back towards Crockett, I perceived by the glow of my candelabrum that he was frowning at something that lay just beyond the limits of the massive bookcase. Following his gaze, I saw that it was directed at a small recess or *nook* which, until that moment, had been obscured by the pervading gloom of the chamber.

It was not, however, the recess itself that had riveted the frontiersman's attention but the object it contained. This appeared to be some sort of glass-fronted cabinet or display case, standing chest-high and supported by an elaborately carved wooden base. From our present vantage point, we could not identify its contents—though there seemed to be but a single, shadowy object enclosed behind its glass-fronted door.

The frontiersman, who was standing to my left, turned his head to look at me. In the flickering glow of the tapers, his face had the lurid cast of a carnival mask.

"I got me a funny feelin' 'bout that thing," he said grimly, gesturing in the direction of the cabinet.

I drew a deep, somewhat tremulous breath. "I share in your misgivings. Perhaps we should resume our seats. Our host is bound to return momentarily."

"That's a right smart idea, Poe," said Crockett. "But I aim to have a look at that-there whatnot first." And having made this pronouncement, he quickly strode towards the little nook, stooped before the cabinet, peered inside—and let out a startled cry!

"Fetch me that candlestick!" he exclaimed, motioning to me with a frantic, beckoning wave.

Obeying—albeit reluctantly—the frontiersman's command, I stepped to his side and bent before the cabinet, holding the candelabrum close to the glass. All at once, I felt myself tottering on the verge of insensibility. Raising the candelabrum—which I had nearly let slip from my hand—I held the tapers close to the glass and stared in an agony of horrified incredulity at the unspeakable object within.

It was the upper half of a naked—and partially dissected—female cadaver, severed at the waist. One entire side of this poor victim's face, neck, and torso had been peeled away to expose the underlying flesh— the raw, striated muscles, viscous membranes, sinuous veins, and glistening tissues. By some inexplicable means, however, the corpse had been so perfectly preserved that it possessed an almost uncannily lifelike, even *animate*, quality!

I turned to gape at my companion, whose own face wore a look of stunned incomprehension. Our shared, premonitory suspicion had just been confirmed in the most appalling way imaginable.

We had stumbled into the lair of a madman!

CHAPTER 11

Had my very life hung upon the movement of a limb or the utterance of a syllable, I could have neither stirred nor spoken—so *paralyzed* had I been rendered by the fearful sight before me. Even the boisterous frontiersman had been startled, for once, into an appalled and absolute *silence*. Crouched before the cabinet, we stared aghast at its grisly contents, utterly oblivious of the rest of our surroundings—until a voice behind us said:

"So, you have discovered the gem of my collection!"

So abrupt, so unexpected were these words that my reaction could not have been more violent had a hired assassin snuck up behind me and discharged a pistol at my back. Emitting a startled cry, I lost my hold upon the heavy candelabrum and let it fly from my hand; while Crockett swiftly spun around to face the unseen speaker. As he did so, he caught sight of the airborne candelabrum and—shooting out a hand—snatched it by the stem.

"Good heavens!" cried Roger Asher—for it was,

indeed, that singular being who had come up behind us in so stealthy a manner. "Are you all right, Mr. Poe?"

A moment passed before I was fully capable of speech. "Fine, quite fine," I said at last, extracting my pocket handkerchief and using it to dab away the moisture that had sprung to my brow and upper lip. "Your abrupt and unanticipated observation merely caught me unawares."

"Well, *I* ain't so all-fired *fine*," Crockett proclaimed.

Raising one eyebrow, Asher turned to regard the frontiersman. "And what is the matter, Colonel Crockett?"

"*This* here's the matter," the frontiersman replied—and with that, he thrust the candelabrum close to the glass-fronted case, illuminating the appalling object within.

"Ah yes," smiled Asher, rubbing his long, pale hands together as though attempting to cleanse them of a stain visible only to himself. "Magnificent, is she not?"

"Magnificent!" Crockett cried, nearly sputtering with indignation. "Why, in all my born days, I ain't never set eyes on nuthin' that were half so horrificacious!"

For a moment, Asher simply stared at him in wordless surprise. Then a burst of hilarity issued from his throat. "I see! I see!" he said when his laughter had finally subsided. "You take her for the real thing. Ah well. It is a tribute to the genius of the great Fontana!"

"Fontana?" I exclaimed. "Do you mean the renowned Florentine naturalist?"

Turning in my direction, Asher gazed at me with an approving look. "My compliments, Mr. Poe. I perceive that you are a man of rare erudition."

I acknowledged this commendation with a little bow.

"You are correct," Asher continued. "The *objet* displayed within this cabinet is, indeed, an original product of the esteemed abbot's *atelier.*"

"The steamed abbot's *what?*" Crockett ejaculated.

"His studio," said I to Crockett as I turned to gaze again at the cabinet—not, this time, with the sense of unutterable horror with which I had formerly contemplated its contents, but with a sentiment of the purest admiration—astonishment—even *awe.*

"This is not," I continued, "the fiendishly mutilated body of an actual female, as you and I mistakenly believed. Rather, it is—so we may infer from Mr. Asher's assertion—a wax sculpture of uncanny realism, crafted under the direction of the celebrated eighteenth-century cleric, Abbot Felice Fontana of Florence, Italy, whose world-famous shop produced anatomical specimens for use by the medical specialists of his day. So stunningly detailed, so exquisitely rendered were these models that no less a personage than Emperor Joseph II of Austria, after making a pilgrimage to Florence to view Fontana's creations, bestowed a knighthood upon him and commissioned him with the execution of nearly twelve hundred pieces!"

"Good land!" Crockett exclaimed. "You mean to tell me that this-here piece o' gruesomeness ain't nuthin' but a hunk o' beeswax?"

Asher emitted a low-throated chuckle. "It is indeed, Colonel Crockett—though only in the sense that the *David* of Michelangelo Buonarroti is nothing more than a 'hunk of' Carrara marble."

"Well, I'll be jiggered," muttered Crockett as he squinted through the glass front of the display cabinet.

"But how," I inquired, "did you come to be in possession of such a treasure?"

The question elicited a tremulous sigh from our pallid host. "There was a time, Mr. Poe, when no indulgence was beyond my pecuniary means. But that," he added in a musing voice, "was in a day long past—before utter, irredeemable ruin descended upon the once-proud house of Asher." For a moment, he seemed to become oblivious of his surroundings, his eyes assuming a wistfully meditative and *faraway* look.

Suddenly, he bestirred himself from this melancholy reverie and focussed his attention once again on our presence. "Come, gentlemen," he said with somewhat strained cordiality. "My sister is resting soundly. Oh yes. Very soundly indeed. Allow me to offer you some small refreshment. You must be famished after your long journey."

"Now you're talkin'!" Crockett declared. "Why, I am so all-fired hungry, I could eat a whole bushel o' bear-steaks, salted with hail storm and peppered with buckshot!"

"I fear that I cannot offer you anything quite so substantial." Asher smiled. "But what pitiful fare I possess, you are more than welcome to share. And as we dine, you can tell me, at long last, what has brought you to my doorstep."

Turning on his heels, he began to lead us from the cavernous chamber. Before he had proceeded more than a step or two, however, he paused—swivelled—and extended one long, bony hand in Crockett's direction.

"Allow me to relieve you of that light, Colonel," said he. "Though your hands are, I am sure, a great deal steadier than those of your friend, I would feel more confident if the candelabrum were in my own. My abode, as you may perceive, is full of old and exceedingly *combustible* furnishings. It would take very little to ignite a blaze and turn the entire house into an inferno."

And then, with an odd, rueful smile, he added: "Or rather, even *more* of an inferno than it already is to those of us doomed to inhabit it."

Asher's characterization of his culinary offerings as "pitiful" proved to be—not the customary, self-deprecating protestation that etiquette demands of a dinner host—but strict and wholly warranted truth. Guiding us by candlelight through the shadowy corridors and cavernous chambers of his vast and sprawling mansion, our pale and wraithlike host ushered us into a gloomy, low-ceilinged kitchen, where, within a smoky fireplace, a large iron cauldron sat upon a bed of glowing coals, sending forth thick and exceedingly *malodorous* fumes. As Crockett and I seated ourselves at an ancient, benchlike table that occupied the center of the room, Asher bustled about the kitchen, fetching pewter bowls and tarnished utensils, which he set before us, along with heavy glass tumblers and a dark, dusty decanter of wine.

"What else?" he wondered aloud, while rubbing his hands in his characteristic gesture. "Ah, yes!" He hurried across the room to a sideboard that stood in the shadows; whereupon we heard him exclaim, "Shoo! Shoo!" This ejaculation was instantly followed by the frantic *scrabbling* sound of dispersing rodents. Seconds later, he returned with a wooden platter that held the remnants of a dark, crusty loaf, pocked with dozens of miniature teethmarks.

"Now," Asher said, setting the bread down upon the table. "For the *pièce de résistance.*"

As our host stepped over to the fireplace, Crockett directed an interrogatory look at me across the table and whispered, "For the *what?*"

"The main dish," I explained in language suitable to the frontiersman's understanding. Reaching for the decanter, I carefully filled each of our glasses nearly to the top, then set the receptacle back upon the table.

Moments later, our host returned with a large ceramic crock out of which protruded the handle of a tarnished silver ladle. Grasping the ladle in one hand, he used it to fill each of our bowls with a bubbling portion of some pungent, viscous mixture, evidently of that variety commonly known in the South as a

gumbo. The appearance, texture, and aroma of this con-
coction were so wholly unappetizing that—in spite of
the audible rumblings issuing from my abdominal
region—I could scarcely bring myself to sample it.
Only the dictates of civilized etiquette compelled me
to spoon a modicum into my mouth. In no way to my
surprise, its taste turned out to be in utter conformity
with its other attributes—which is to say, repellent in
the extreme.

Its vileness, however, seemed in no wise to deter
the appetite of the frontiersman, who proceeded to
empty his bowl with avidity.

As for myself, I could not tolerate more than a few
tastes of the loathsome pottage, which I managed to
consume only by washing each separate spoonful down
with a mouthful of the decanted beverage. This latter
proved to be a very passable, indeed quite exceptional,
Amontillado sherry.

Stimulated by the bracing effects of this fluid, I
commenced—at Asher's prompting—to recount the
ostensible reason for our visit, setting forth a story
which Crockett and I had devised during our journey
from the city. According to this tale, Crockett—as
part of his campaign against the political machina-
tions of President Jackson—was taking advantage of
his current tour to secure the financial support of the
most prominent and well-to-do citizens in each of the
cities that he was visiting.

"But am I not correct in believing, Colonel Crockett,
that you yourself are a protégé and onetime comrade-in-

arms of our *glorious leader?*" The bitterly ironical tone with which Asher pronounced the latter phrase made his own political sympathies sufficiently clear.

"True enough," said the frontiersman, tearing off a portion of the rodent-gnawed loaf and using it to mop up the vestiges of soup that clung to the inner surfaces of his bowl. "But me an' Ol' Hick'ry have come to a parting o' the ways. I still admire the man and am proud to have fought alongside him. But it now appears that I am expected to bow to his policies, no matter at what cost to my conscience. And that just ain't my style. Nossir—Davy Crockett ain't the kind to sneeze when another man takes snuff."

"A commendable sentiment," said Asher. "But I am afraid, Colonel Crockett, that if you have travelled out here in the hope that I might offer some pecuniary support for your campaign, you have made the journey in vain." Letting his spoon fall into his emptied bowl with a clatter, Asher shut his eyes and passed one trembling hand over his brow, as though afflicted with a sudden headache. "Do you imagine, sir, that I live in such straitened—such *hellish*—circumstances by choice?" After a brief pause, he opened his eyes again and gazed at Crockett with a look of surpassing bitterness. "However prominent the Asher name remains, the fortune upon which its reputation was founded exists no more!"

By this time, I had drained my tumbler of its contents and was in the process of replenishing it from the decanter. Though my extreme sensitivity to alcoholic stimulation led me—under ordinary circumstances—to maintain a rigorous *temperance*, I could scarcely refrain from indulging in Asher's excellent vintage, whose beneficent warmth had already served to quell much of the inner agitation induced in me by the trying events of that long, fatiguing, and exceedingly debilitating day. Imbibing another large swallow of the sherry, I felt my entire being infused with a sense of such profound contentment that the glum, oppressive kitchen—with its cobwebbed roof beams and crimson-eyed rodents peering out from the shadowy corners—began to assume a most pleasing, snug, and even *homelike* aspect in my perception.

"If I may be so *bold*," I said at last, speaking very slowly and deliberately. "I am most curious to learn the details of your family's misfortunes, having heard certain rumors over the years in regard to the matter."

Asher responded with a dismissive wave of the hand. "I do not wish to discuss it. Suffice it to say that the calamity was brought about by the Machiavellian dealings of a scoundrel named Macready."

"Macready?" Crocket said in a tone of exaggerated *ingenuousness*. "Like that poor landlady that was so savagerously murdered in her boarding house on Howard Street?"

Asher, who had just taken a sip from his tumbler, appeared so startled by these words that he nearly expectorated the liquid from his mouth. "Murdered!" he gasped. "When?"

"Just two days past," said Crockett. "On Wednesday."

"How very bizarre!" said our host. "I myself was

not far from Howard Street that day, having escorted my poor sister Marilynne to the home of the eminent Dr. Balderston for a consultation on her rapidly worsening condition."

At this casual admission—which established Asher's presence in the city at the very time of the killing—Crockett and I exchanged a meaningful look.

"And who was responsible for the deed?" Asher continued.

"Danged if *I* know," Crockett replied with a shrug.

For a moment, Asher sat in silent meditation. At length, in a voice so muted that he appeared to be reflecting aloud, he said: "Then that is the end of the detested line. Good! Good! But how strange that it should happen *now*, when I myself dream of—" Before he could finish articulating this enigmatic thought, he gave his head a rapid shake, as though rousing himself from a reverie.

"Enough of these morbid musings!" he exclaimed in a tone of somewhat strained and hollow-sounding conviviality. Reaching for the wine decanter, he replenished all three of our glasses, then lifted his own in a toast. "To your health, gentlemen!"

Raising his tumbler to his lips, he threw back his head and drained his drink in a single swallow.

I myself had imbibed a considerable quantity of the Amontillado by then, and was staring with rapt intensity at the silver candelabrum, whose three glowing tapers seemed to float before my eyes like a trio of ravishing, golden-tressed *faeries* garbed in robes of gossamer white. So transfixed was I by this radiant vision that only gradually did it dawn upon my consciousness that my host was endeavoring to communicate with me.

"Excuse me?" said I, my words sounding strangely slurred to my ears.

"I was inquiring as to your profession, Mr. Poe. I am still ignorant of the line of work you pursue."

"Pursue?" said I, quaffing another mouthful of the wine. "I pursue the most rare—most *elusive*—prize of all: Ideal Beauty!"

"Indeed!" said Asher in a tone that carried a subtle, if unmistakable, note of *wry* amusement. "And with what weapons do you stalk this precious quarry?"

"I wield only one," I grandly declared. "My quill!"

"I see!" he exclaimed. "So you are a writer!"

I acknowledged the accuracy of this observation with a little bow.

"And what exactly is it that you write?"

"Tales—poems—"

"And the orneriest book reviews this side o' thunderation!" Crockett interjected.

"Splendid!" cried Asher, ignoring Crockett's remark. "Our country is in desperate need of poets."

"Hear! Hear!" I exclaimed, as I placed my hands upon the edge of the table and began to push myself to my feet. "Let us drink to the Muse Erato, Goddess of the lyric!"

Unfortunately, I had underestimated the unmanning effects which Asher's intoxicating beverage had already produced upon my nervous system. As I attempted to rise—preparatory to delivering my toast—my feet became entangled in the legs of my stool and I found myself sprawled upon my back, staring upwards at the heavy wooden ceiling beams, which appeared to be rotating at a most alarming rate of speed.

As though from a considerable distance, I could hear the voice of my eccentric host exclaim: "Oh dear!"

As I vainly attempted to elevate myself from the floor—which appeared to be *rocking* in a most singular manner, not unlike the deck of a storm-tossed vessel—I became aware that Crockett had risen from his seat and was looming directly above me, one hand outstretched in my direction. "Grab ahold, ol' hoss. I reckon you've had a mite too much to drink."

I reached up and clasped the frontiersman's hand, whereupon he drew me upright with a single, forceful *tug*. Regarding me with a look of intense solicitude, our host asked if I had sustained any hurt.

"None whatsoever," I assured him. "Indeed, I am feeling quite *energetic*, and am most eager to commence our journey homeward."

"I will not hear of it," Asher declared. "I insist that you both remain here tonight as my guests. Come." Rising from his place, he took hold of the three-branched candelabrum and motioned us to follow him from the room.

"C'mon, ol' hoss," said Crockett, clutching me by one elbow. "Lemme help you navigate."

Submitting myself to the frontiersman's assistance, I allowed him to lead me from the kitchen and through the intricate passageways and cavernous chambers of the great, gloomy manse—our pallid host preceding us by several paces, his glowing candelabrum held aloft. My faculties of perception—so *acute* under ordinary circumstances—had been reduced to a state of such alcohol-induced *bleariness* that I was able to form only a vague and general impression of my surroundings: of the heavy, sombre tapestries—the dark, massive furnishings—the phantasmagoric armorial trophies—and the atmosphere of stern, deep, and irredeemable *gloom* that hung over and pervaded all.

After what seemed to be an interminable period, I found myself ascending—with the aid of the frontiersman—a long, steep, and twisting stairway. Then I was escorted along a dark and narrow corridor, whose walls were lined with countless antique portraits in the fantastic style of the sixteenth-century visionary Domenico Theotocopuli. At last, our host came to a halt before a heavy, carved door, into whose lock he inserted a key from an iron ring which he extracted from his coat pocket. Then the door was flung open, and I felt myself being led across the threshold and into a musty-smelling chamber, whose central feature was a large canopied bed that occupied the middle of the room.

While Crockett helped me struggle out of my frockcoat, Asher stepped to the head of the four-poster and enkindled an agate lamp that stood upon a small, oval bed-table. Then, turning towards me with a little bow, he bade me good-night and walked briskly from the room.

Crockett steered me towards the bed, whereupon I seated myself on the edge of the mattress, crossed one leg over the other, and began to remove my boots in preparation for retiring. As I struggled with the laces, my companion took a quick glance over his shoulder—as though to ascertain that Asher had, in fact, departed—then leaned close to me and said, in a voice that was scarcely louder than a whisper: "You had best hit the hay, Poe, for that liquor has made you downright obfusticated. I aim to do me some more jawin' with ol' Asher and see what I can pry out o' him, for I am plumb mistrustful of that rascal. If he ain't nuttier'n a squirrel in an acorn patch, I wish I may be hanged!" Patting me on the shoulder, he said, "See you in the mornin', pard"—then turned and hurried from the room.

Abandoning my efforts to undo my boot-laces—which appeared to have been knotted with such diabolical cunning that they might have been tied by King Gordius himself—I extinguished the bed lamp and collapsed backwards onto my pillow. To my great surprise and consternation, however, the beneficent god Somnus did not immediately hold out to me his cup of sweet nepenthe. Recumbent upon the great canopied bed, I lay open-eyed in the unfamiliar darkness, while—all about me—a profusion of bizarre and lurid apparitions seemed to swirl madly about in mid-air, as though engaged in the delirious revelry of a wild and unrestrained *masque*.

At length, these riotous spectres merged into the no less vivid phantasms of *dream*. I sank into a fitful slumber. How long I remained in this unconscious state, I cannot say with precision. I am certain of only one thing—that, at some later point in that harrowing night, I awoke from my sleep with a stifled gasp of horror—possessed by the sudden and absolute conviction that I was no longer alone in the chamber!

At first I was too frightened to employ my vision. Motionlessly, I lay with my eyes closed tight, attempting to persuade myself that I was merely *imagining* the presence of another being in the room. At length, I forced my shuttered lids apart. How shall I attempt to convey the utter—the *inexpressible*—terror that gripped me at the confirmation of my awful apprehension?

A dark and ominous figure loomed at the foot of my bed. Biting my lower lip to prevent myself from crying aloud, I lay there in an *agony* of mortal dread. Perhaps, thought I, the figure was merely another airy, alcohol-induced chimera. But no! It was far too *real*— far too *substantial*—to be an illusion. Besides, though my head throbbed with pain, I could tell that I had largely recovered from the effects of my intemperance and was once again in full possession of my senses!

For what seemed like an eternity (though it could not have been longer than a few moments) I remained rigidly immobile, hardly daring to breathe. Neither Asher nor Crockett had thought to draw the draperies of the single window in the room; and now, through the unobstructed panes, a flood of moonlight came spilling inside—the cloud-covered sky having evidently cleared up at long last. As my vision grew adapted to the luminary conditions of the chamber, I could see with increasing clarity that the intruder was—a woman!

Perspiration burst from every pore of my body, and stood in icy beads upon my forehead. All at once, the dark figure began to move—or, rather, *float*—toward the head of my bed. Closer and closer it drew, until it seemed to hover directly above me. It bent nearer to my pillow, until I could feel its soft breath upon my face. At that instant, its own countenance was illuminated by the in-flooding moonlight, and I gazed up at its features with a feeling of utter disbelief and incomprehension.

A numbness—an iciness of feeling—pervaded my frame. I gasped for breath. My breast heaved—my brain reeled—and my whole spirit was possessed with a vague yet intolerable anguish.

With a wild cry of terror, I half-started from my pillow—then fell backwards and lapsed into a swoon!

CHAPTER 12

How long I remained in my terror-induced swoon I am unable to say. I can only recall a period of utter oblivion, followed by a long—unsettling—and uncannily *vivid* dream which gradually took shape within the depths of my mind. I was alone on a desolate tropical isle, where the scorching sun beat down with merciless intensity. All at once, I became aware of a strange noise: a low, ominous *rumble* that grew steadily louder, building to a thunderous *crescendo*. Glancing around in wonderment and fright, I perceived—in the near distance—the cone of a mountainous volcano, out of whose flattened apex there suddenly erupted a thick column of glowing sparks, followed by a fountain of seething red lava. The ground beneath my feet began to tremble, then shake with all the violence of a cataclysmic earthquake. My whole body began to vibrate in tune with this explosive display of nature's fury. Suddenly, from out of the subterranean depths of the volcano, a great booming voice—like that of a pagan deity—began to issue stern and occult commandments.

It was only then that I became aware that I was partially *awake*. My dream was not a dream at all! The sweltering heat was *real*. So, too, was the violent shaking of my frame. And the voice—whose timbre and inflection I now recognized as peculiarly familiar—was addressing me in loud and insistent words:

"Poe! Wake up! The goldamned house is afire!"

My eyes shot open. A few feet away, I could perceive the face of Colonel Crockett. His skin was slick with perspiration—his dark locks matted and dishevelled—his features wrought into an expression of grim urgency. My senses were still sufficiently bedazed that a few moments elapsed before I became fully conscious of several anomalous circumstances—the lurid, flickering illumination by which I was able to discern Crockett's face in the darkness of the room—the acrid smoke which stung my eyes and assaulted my nostrils—the crackling sound emanating from just outside the room. Only then did the full—the fearful—the blood-chilling—truth smite my awareness like a thunderbolt.

We were in the midst of a roaring conflagration!

I bolted upright and leapt from the bed. Waving for me to follow, Crockett raced to the doorway of the bedchamber, calling over his shoulder: "Hump it, Poe, or we'll be fried to a cinder!"

Eyes tearing, throat burning, I dashed from the room on Crockett's heels and followed him down the long, smoke-filled corridor—only to find, as we approached the landing, that our escape was obstructed by a wavering column of flame that was marching inexorably up the stairwell. Quickly glancing about him, Crockett spotted the closed door of what appeared to be another bedchamber a few feet from where we stood. Leaping to the door, he twisted the knob—then ejaculated a curse.

"Locked!" he cried. Taking one step backwards, he raised his right boot to the door, and—with a single, mighty kick—sent it crashing inward on its hinges. Disappearing inside, he re-emerged a moment later with a bedsheet in his hands.

"It's shinny down or die, Poe," said he, looking at me with a savage grin as he tied one corner of the bedsheet to the carved, wooden balustrade and tossed the rest over the side. Clambering over the railing, he gathered the sheet between his hands—forming it into a kind of rope or cable—then slid down this makeshift *life-line* until he reached its bottommost extent, whereupon he dropped the remaining distance to the floor and landed nimbly on his feet.

"C'mon, Poe!" he called to me from below, cupping his hands to his mouth so as to be heard above the roar of the inferno. "There ain't nothin' to it!"

Fear driving the blood in torrents upon my heart, I repeated the exact procedure I had seen Crockett perform so successfully. Bestraddling the railing, I clutched the sheet with sweat-soaked hands, then half climbed, half slid down the length of the linen. For a moment, I dangled in mid-air, my feet waving wildly. Then—closing my eyes and muttering a silent prayer—I released my hold on the linen and plummeted downward. My feet hit the floor with a thud—I bounced once—and ended up prostrate on my stomach, slightly stunned though otherwise unhurt. Almost instantly, a powerful hand reached down, clutched me by one arm, and yanked me to my feet.

"No time for dilly-dallyin', Poe. This way!"

So sharp, so suffocatingly *dense* was the smoke—so fierce and searing the heat—that it was all I could do to keep pace with the frontiersman as he swiftly made his way through the blazing passageways of the house. Choking, coughing, half-blinded by the rivulets of perspiration that streamed from my forehead and into my eyes, I stumbled along at his heels, while, all around us, the conflagration raged in unmitigated fury.

Following my companion through an arched doorway, I found myself back in the great cavernous drawing room, which was now a scene of blinding—of *blazing*—destruction. The heavy, ancient draperies had been turned into fiery sheets. The art works constituting Asher's prized collection of paintings were ablaze in their gilded frames. The antique furnishings, including the chairs that Crockett and I had occupied earlier in the evening, had become little more than kindling to feed the insatiable appetite of the fire. Even the carved oaken ceiling had been transformed into a dome of roaring flame.

For the first time, Crockett seemed at a loss. With eyes that blazed as intensely as the surrounding conflagration, he peered through the main doorway of the drawing room, which opened into the corridor that led to the front of the house. Following his gaze, I perceived that the entire corridor was now completely obstructed by what appeared to be a solid mass of flame.

"Trapped!" he cried. "Like a pair o' coons inside a holler stump!" Frantically, he looked about for another point of egress, while—seeking some relief for my heat-seared lungs—I turned my face upward like a drowning man in desperate search of oxygen.

At that instant, through a swirling cloud of smoke, I perceived a sight which—despite the intensity of the heat—immediately caused my blood to turn cold. Directly above my head hung an enormous wheel-shaped chandelier which depended from a massive braided cord, as thick—under normal circumstances—as the anchor-rope of a whaling vessel. By this point, however, the rope had been so eaten away by the fire that it had been reduced to the apparent thickness of a boot-lace! As I stared upward, as though transfixed by this petrifying sight, the remaining strands of the rope sizzled—snapped—and the great, circular chandelier came crashing downward towards my person!

Frozen with terror, I would certainly have been utterly obliterated—crushed like a beetle of the genus *scarabæus* under the bootheel of a heedless pedestrian. But in the next instant, I was struck, not from above, but from the side—by a large hurtling object that knocked me off my feet just as the falling chandelier plunged to the floor with a thunderous crash!

It was the frontiersman, who—having spotted my

perilous situation—had thrown himself at my immobilized form and saved me from certain destruction!

"Dad fetch it, Poe," he gasped, raising himself to his knees, "but you are a tolerable sight o' trou—"

Before he could complete this remark, his attention appeared to be riveted by something several yards away from where I lay. Raising myself to one elbow, I followed his glance and saw at once the ghastly sight that had captured his notice.

It was the lifeless body of our host, suspended directly in front of the more warlike of the two armored figures, the one brandishing an outthrust pike. Asher had been impaled on this fearsome weapon, whose long, spear-like tip had penetrated his breast and emerged, blood-caked, from between his shoulder blades. He hung there like a discarded marionette, arms adroop, knees buckled, head lolling forward.

"Stuck like a worm on a fishhook," said Crockett. "He's a goner, Poe—an' you 'n' me will be, too, unless we can figger out some way outta—" Gazing hurriedly about him, he suddenly exclaimed, "By God—*that'll* do!"

Looking to see what had elicited this reaction, I perceived that Crockett was staring at the wooden display case containing the priceless anatomical model from the studio of the legendary Abbot Fontana. This article of furniture had thus far escaped the flames—though the intensity of the ambient heat had cracked its front panel of glass, behind which the flayed and partially dissected wax torso had begun to melt like a grotesque, anthropomorphic candle.

Springing to his feet, Crockett dashed to the cabinet; then stooped, threw his arms about its sides, and—with a grunt so loud that it could be heard above the crackling of the flames—raised it to the height of his chest. The muscular cords of his neck bulged with exertion as he carried the cabinet several yards away to the tall, Gothic window (whose voluminous curtains were now little more than twin sheets of flame) and heaved it through the crimson panes, which shattered outward with a splintering crash.

"Time to git up 'n' git, Poe!" Crockett called to me—then turned and disappeared through the gaping hole he had created in the glass.

Scrambling to my feet, I hurried across the floor, climbed through the jagged opening in the shattered window and—after pausing for a moment on the exterior ledge—leapt down several yards and landed in the copious bushes that fringed the rear of the house.

Shaking in every limb, I hurriedly extricated myself from the entangling undergrowth, then staggered towards an open field that lay at some distance from the house. I sank to my knees, rolled onto my back, and lay spread-eagled in the grass, staring upwards at the blackness of the heavens, where shimmering stars commingled with the fiery embers that floated skyward from the blazing house.

Several moments elapsed before I was able to draw myself up into a sitting position. Employing my loose-hanging shirttail as a kind of towel, I wiped the moisture from my stinging eyes and looked about for

Crockett. At first, I could see him nowhere. Gradually, however, I became cognizant of a sound drifting above the roar and crackle of the inferno. It was a hoarse male voice, emanating from a point somewhere off to my left. As I strained my ears to listen, I perceived that the voice was repeatedly shouting, "Miz Asher! Miz Asher!"

Rising with a groan to my feet, I made my way in the direction of the sound until, in the unholy crimson glow of the fire, I spotted the frontiersman. Moving as close to the house as the scorching heat would allow, he was circumambulating the premises, hands cupped to his mouth, calling out the name of Asher's sister in the evident hope of finding her still alive. Even at a glance, however, I could determine that his efforts were futile. By now, the once-stately manse was little more than an enormous furnace. Billowing clouds of smoke poured through every ruptured window; tall flames shot upward from the roof and danced along the ramparts. It was inconceivable that anyone trapped within those blistering walls could yet be alive.

Hurrying up beside the frontiersman, I laid one hand upon his shoulder. "It is no use, Colonel Crockett," said I in a voice loud enough to be heard above the noise of the conflagration. "Unless, like ourselves, the mistress of the house has somehow managed to escape, we must forgo the hope of saving her."

Crockett turned to me with a look of weary resignation. "I reckon you are right, Poe," he sighed, dropping his hands to his sides. "C'mon!"

With the frontiersman in the lead, we bent our steps to the front of the house, where we discovered—not entirely to our surprise—that our horses, in their instinctive terror of the flames, had managed to tear their reins free of the hitching post and were nowhere in sight. By that point, the extreme, the unprecedented strains of that seemingly endless night of misery and peril had begun to exact their inevitable toll. Overcome with both physical and mental exhaustion, I sank to the ground beneath a towering tree, resting my back upon the gnarled trunk. Crockett—whose exertions had, at the very least, equalled my own—lowered himself beside me. For several moments we sat side by side in utter silence, transfixed by the scene of cataclysmic destruction taking place before our eyes.

At length, I turned my head toward my companion and asked: "In heaven's name, what happened, Colonel Crockett?"

He opened his mouth to reply but was seized by a paroxysm of coughing. Finally, he shook his head and replied: "Blamed if I know. After you went to roost, me 'n' Asher headed back to the kitchen and commenced to palaverin' some more. We was hittin' his jug at a tolerable pace, too. After a spell, ol' Asher said he'd best go see how his sister was farin'. I was feelin' a mite drowsy by then, so I put my head down on my arms and figgered I'd get me a little shut-eye 'til Asher came back. Next thing I know, I'm wide awake and the whole damn house is burnin' like a canebrake afire."

At that instant, a thunderous noise—like the roar

of a thousand demons—smote upon our ears. Swivelling our heads in the direction of the fearsome sound, we saw the blazing roof collapse inward with an ear-splitting crash. An enormous geyser of smoke and flame and fiery cinders erupted into the sky—a fierce blast of scorching air blew the massive front door from its hinges—the ramparts toppled—the very earth beneath our bodies trembled—and the stately and venerable house of Asher was no more!

Part Two

SHADOW

CHAPTER 13

With the tedious particulars of our journey homeward, the reader need not be concerned. Suffice it to say that, when the sun finally ascended over the smoldering ruins of the once-proud house of Asher, Crockett and I——having remained seated on the ground with our backs propped against the tree——rose stiffly to our feet and commenced what promised to be an exceedingly *arduous* trek in the direction of the city.

We had proceeded only a short distance, however, when the fickle goddess Fortuna——who had, until that moment, appeared to revel in our discomfiture——unexpectedly took sympathy for our plight. Rounding a bend, the frontiersman and I were overjoyed to spy our horses grazing contentedly on a gentle, grassy slope. Had I not felt fatigued to the point of near-paralysis, I might have broken into a rapturous dance of celebration at the mere sight of the beasts. Mounting our steeds, we promptly reined them in a southerly direction and headed towards the city at a gentle walk.

So *benumbed* was I by exhaustion that I passed the entirety of our journey in a condition akin to that of the chronic somnambulist. I recall only the jouncing motion of my steed—the beneficent warmth of the day—and the droning voice of the irrepressible frontiersman, who (in spite of his own utter lack of sleep) poured forth a more-or-less continuous soliloquy, of whose content I remained, in my stupefied state, mercifully oblivious.

My next memories are of arriving, after a seemingly interminable period, at the doorway of my domicile on Howard Street—of dismounting from my steed and staggering through the front door—of the distressed exclamations of my dearest Muddy and Sissy as they led me to my chamber and helped me to bed.

Then all was silence—and stillness—and the blessed darkness of oblivion.

I slept like the dead. But for all their profundity, my slumbers offered me little, if any, relief from the agonies I had endured during my recent misadventure. My dreams were of the most dismaying, the most *harrowing* variety, in which a pale and wraithlike figure pursued me through the labyrinthine passageways of a gloomy, Gothic manse, while—faintly visible in the background—a slender, dark-haired female with indistinct features floated ghostlike through the shadows.

I awoke not with a start but by slow degrees, my consciousness reviving in small, incremental stages. Unclosing my eyes, I remained, for several moments, in a state of extreme mental confusion, uncertain as to my whereabouts. Only gradually did the realization dawn upon me that I was safe in my bedroom and that, seated beside me—wringing her hands as she gazed down at my face with a look of ineffable solicitude— was my own dearest Muddy!

"Oh, Eddie!" she exclaimed in a tremulous voice. "Thank heavens that you are finally awake!"

As my bleary vision cleared, I perceived, by the attenuated quality of the daylight outside my window, that the afternoon was already well advanced. Upon inquiring as to the time, I was very much surprised to learn that I had been asleep for nearly sixteen consecu- tive hours—a circumstance that naturally accounted for the intense sensation of hunger of which I quickly became conscious.

As though endowed with a preternatural faculty that enabled her to read my very thoughts, Muddy immediately declared: "Poor boy, you must be fam- ished!" When I acknowledged the accuracy of this observation with a small, affirmative whimper, she promptly rose from her seat and bustled from the room, returning a short time later with a bowl from which wafted the indescribably delicious aroma of chicken *consommé*. After helping me to sit upright with my back propped against several pillows, she perched at my side on the mattress while I ate.

Thanks to the salubrious effects of Muddy's invigorating broth, my spirits were soon restored to such an extent that—in response to her queries—I was able to provide her with a detailed, if suitably modified, account of my recent ordeal. In conformity with my earlier, well-intentioned prevarication, I explained that—having travelled through the countryside until late in the afternoon—Colonel Crockett and I had taken refuge from the threatening weather in the imposing Asher residence, whose master had kindly invited us to partake of dinner. The remainder of my story adhered closely to the truth, though I revealed nothing of my deplorable intemperance, or of my subsequent encounter with the strange, spectral female in the darkness of my room—an incident which I had also refrained from mentioning to Crockett.

I had just completed the last spoonful of broth when Sissy appeared in my room and—after taking the place of Muddy (who bustled off to begin her dinner preparations)—spent the next several hours at my bedside, beguiling me with her extensive, if not inexhaustible, repertoire of ballads, songs, humorous anecdotes, and riddles.

By the time dusk approached, my eagerness to escape from my bed had reached the point of near desperation. At my insistence, Sissy had finally taken a respite and joined Muddy in the kitchen for supper. Donning my dressing gown, I made my way into my study, seated myself at my writing table, and enkindled the lamp. No sooner had I done so, however, than

Muddy re-appeared at my door and announced that Colonel Crockett had arrived and was eager to see me.

"Please bid him enter forthwith," I replied.

Moments later, he strode into the chamber, appearing as ruddy and robust as though he had just enjoyed an invigorating outdoor stroll. He was garbed in his customary high-collared coat and gray-striped trousers. In one hand, he clutched the brim of his black felt hat; in the other, a newspaper folded in quarters.

"Evenin', pard," he exclaimed. "I am powerful glad to see you up 'n' around. Your Aunty Clemm says that if you warn't quite dead since you come home, you was actin' mighty nigh it."

I made a casually dismissive gesture with one hand. "Her unwavering concern for my well-being has led my dearest Muddy to exaggerate the severity of my condition. While it is true that I have remained largely confined to my bedchamber since our return, I have done so almost entirely for the purpose of maintaining that precious seclusion so conducive to exertions of a contemplative nature—my primary interest having been to meditate on the significance of our recent ordeal."

"Well, when it comes to meditatin', you are a regular rip-hummer, all right," said Crockett with a chuckle.

After moving a straight-backed chair close to my writing table, Crockett turned it around so that its slatted back faced in my direction—then straddled the seat as though it were a saddle and rested his folded forearms upon the headpiece.

"It don't take long to curry a short horse, Poe, so I'll get right to the particulars. Now that this Macready business has been settled up, I'm fixin' to move on."

I made no effort to conceal my surprise, openly conveying it in both my voice and facial expression. "But what makes you so certain that the matter has been, as you put it, 'settled up'?"

"Why, there ain't no *buts* about it, Poe! It's plain as preachin'! Asher kilt that poor ol' landlady to git vengeance on the Macreadys for ruining his life. Once he seen that you 'n' me was onto him, he knew the jig was up an' made up his mind to end it all by burnin' up the whole kit 'n' kaboodle—himself, his house, that pestiferous sister o' his, and you 'n' me into the bargain!"

"But how, then, do you account for the hideous manner of Asher's death?"

"That's easily explained," the frontiersman replied. "Once that blaze got roaring hot, he must've decided that bein' roasted alive warn't such a prime idea after all. So he high-tailed it for the front door. But in all the smoke an' gen'ral confustification, he ran smack-dab into that skewer an' ended up like a gigged bullfrog."

"And you are absolutely confident of this *analysis*?"

"Blamed if I ain't. That's how the police calculate it, too."

"Ah—then you have already communicated your theory with the authorities."

"You know me, Poe. I ain't one for dilly-dallyin'. 'Be sure you're right, then go ahead!'—that's Davy Crockett's motto." Extending one hand across the table, he proffered me the newspaper. "Here. Take a gander."

Frowning, I unfolded the paper and held it close to the lamplight. It proved to be that morning's edition of the *Baltimore Chronicle*. Immediately, my gaze lighted upon a bold headline occupying several columns on the front page:

SHOCKING TRAGEDY!

ASHER HOME DESTROYED BY CONFLAGRATION!

Roger Asher and Sister Perish in Blaze!
*Thrilling Tale of Escape Related
by Colonel David Crockett*

Perusing the article—whose author had evidently derived much of his information directly from Crockett—I soon encountered the passage to which the latter had been alluding. It read as follows:

> As to the cause of the devastating blaze, an explanation was proffered to police by the celebrated frontier scout, author, and congressman, Colonel David Crockett of Tennessee, who, as fate would have it, was present at the Asher home at the time of the tragedy. In

an interview with Police Captain Horace Russell, Colonel Crockett—who has been a visitor to our city for several days—intimated that a connection may well have existed between Mr. Roger Asher and the recent, ghastly murder of Mrs. Elmira Macready—the widow of the late Junius Macready, who had reputedly been embroiled in a singularly bitter feud with Mr. Asher's deceased father, Samuel, over business dealings involving the New Export-Import Mercantile Association.

"Pitch me naked into a briar patch if that Asher feller didn't butcher that poor ol' landlady in her bed, then start the fire hisself to escape bein' hung," Colonel Crockett is quoted as having said. "Tell the good folks o' Baltimore that Davy Crockett says they can rest easy—for the varminous murderer o' Mrs. Macready is now roastin' in flames a monstrous sight hotter than the ones that burned up his house!"

Neatly re-folding the newspaper into quarto size, I passed it back to the frontiersman and regarded him silently for a moment before saying: "With the *plausibility* of your interpretation I have no dispute. Nevertheless, I cannot entirely share in your sense of absolute *conviction.*" Here, I hesitated for a moment, silently engaged in an internal debate over the advisability of revealing to Crockett the particulars of my extraordinary nocturnal visitation in the hours preceding the outbreak of the fire.

At length—having reached a decision—I inhaled deeply and remarked: "There is one additional piece of information of which I have not yet apprised you, Colonel Crockett. Of its possible significance I myself remain in considerable doubt—though it may well have a direct bearing on the events which subsequently transpired."

His brow furrowed in perplexity, Crockett said: "Great guns, Poe! You got me feelin' exactly like Moses when the candle went out—plumb in the dark!"

Placing my arms upon the surface of the writing table, I leaned forward and proceeded to describe my encounter with the mysterious female figure who had appeared so unexpectedly in my chamber on the night of the fire. I elected, however, to make no mention of her extraordinary countenance, whose features had struck me as so startling, so *uncanny*, that—in my subsequent ruminations on the episode—I had come to doubt the reliability of my own perceptions.

Crockett took several moments to assimilate this singular narrative, all the while regarding me with narrowed eyes. At length, he shook his head and exclaimed: "Dad fetch it, Poe, but that don't change nuthin'! What you seen was more'n likely that ailin' sister o' Asher's, who drug herself from her sickbed an' wandered into your room by mistake. Or maybe it warn't nuthin' but your own imagination. I'll be scalped with a jackknife if you weren't downright obflusticated from all that liquor."

"Conceivably so," I acknowledged. "Indeed, I myself have considered both of these possibilities."

"No sir," said Crockett, rising to his feet. "There ain't no doubt in my mind." Settling his broad-brimmed hat onto his head, he thrust out his right hand and said, "Put 'er there, pard, for I will be leavin' town presently."

At that instant, from the threshold of my chamber, there emanated the distinct sound of a delicate foot stamping emphatically upon the floorboards. "But you *can't!*" sang out a sweet, mellifluous voice in a tone of endearing protestation. "You *promised!*"

I directed my gaze at the source of this ejaculation, while Crockett swivelled to look in the identical direction. There, in the doorway of my room, stood my darling Virginia, her arms folded across her chest, her countenance arranged into an expression of the most charming petulance imaginable.

"Evenin', Miz Virginny," Crockett said, immediately doffing his hat again and favoring her with a small bow.

"You said that you would come and hear me *sing!*" my angelic cousin and wife-to-be retorted.

"Why, I plumb forgot," Crockett conceded.

"How about *now?*" Virginia cried with enchanting impetuosity.

Extracting a watch from his pocket, Crocket consulted the time for a moment before snapping the lid shut. "I'm afeard that ain't so convenient," he said in an apologetic tone. "I got me an app'intment with a lady friend, and blamed if I ain't already a mite tardy." For a moment, he mused in silence. Then, addressing Sissy, he said: "Tell you what. I ain't fixin' to shove off 'til the mornin' after next. If it's agreeable with your mama, why, I'll come by for a farewell supper tomorrow night and we'll have us a regular jamboree."

"Oh, goody!" exclaimed Virginia, clapping her hands as she bounced up and down on the balls of her feet.

"That set all right with you, Poe?" Crockett inquired, turning in my direction.

In truth, the frontiersman's proposal filled me with sentiments of a less than enthusiastic nature. Nevertheless, I saw no way to demur without violating every precept of my deeply inbred sense of Southern hospitality.

"Perfectly," I replied. "And I am certain that dear Muddy will likewise be delighted."

"Well, that settles it," said Crockett with a broad smile as he replaced his hat atop his head. Bidding me good-night, he strode to the doorway and departed—though not before assuring Virginia that he was "keen as mustard" to hear her sing on the morrow.

The following morning, I resolved to devote the entire day to my professional duties in regard to Mr. Thomas White's admirable new publishing venture, the *Southern*

Literary Messenger. I rejoiced at the prospect of thus returning to my work. The unparalleled events of the past week had resulted in my complete, if unavoidable, neglect of those responsibilities upon which my very livelihood—and, along with it, the material well-being of my loved ones—depended.

Immediately following my morning repast, I therefore retired to my study with the intention of examining the sizable stack of books which Mr. White had recently sent me for the purpose of reviewing. Plucking the topmost volume from this pile, I quickly discovered that it was nothing more than one of the myriad of wretchedly inferior sentimental novels that had been flooding the American marketplace in recent years. To peruse the book and compose a suitably scathing review occupied my efforts until noontime, at which point I interrupted my labors to enjoy a modest lunch.

Following this midday refreshment, I resumed my labors. Knowing the current, lamentable state of the American literary scene, I fully expected the next book on the stack to be as deplorable as the first. To my surprise, however, the volume turned out to be, not a work of fiction at all, but a scientific study whose title instantly riveted my attention: *Curious Beliefs and Peculiar Customs among the Savage Peoples of Melanesia, Being an Inquiry into the Operations of the Primitive Mentality, along with an Enlightened Scientific Consideration of Certain Notable Superstitious Conceptions and Ritualistic Practices.* Its author was a German scholar, unknown to me until that moment, named Maelzel.

True to its title, this volume proved to be replete with information of such surpassing interest and curiosity that it could not fail to make the deepest impression upon my imagination. From its opening section—which dealt with the ghastly, the abhorrent, the *unthinkable* practice of human cannibalism—each succeeding chapter was more startling than the one preceding it. Before I had perused more than a few pages, my attention was so thoroughly engrossed in this remarkable volume that I became wholly oblivious of my surroundings.

Of all the subjects treated by the author, however, the one which exerted the strongest grip upon my imagination had to do with the widespread superstitious belief in the sinister essence—and autonomous *tendencies*—of the human *shadow*. According to Maelzel, the native islanders of the South Pacific universally held it to be true that the shadows cast by their physical bodies were the visible manifestations of their innermost souls. Among the tribesmen of Fiji, for example, the word for shadow—*yalo-yalo*—was but a duplication of the word for the soul: *yalo.* Thus, to these savages, every man possesses a mysterious, even *daemonic,* double or alter ego that operates as the physical projection, or *embodiment,* of the evil impulses reigning in his heart. According to their beliefs, moreover, this shadowy *doppelgänger* actually has the power to separate itself into an independent entity while its owner is asleep and act out those dark and violent impulses on the latter's behalf!

As I continued to peruse this remarkable tome, I

gradually became aware of an emphatic pounding upon the front door of my dwelling. I remained where I was, fully expecting either Muddy or Sissy to respond to the importunate summons. Several moments elapsed before I recalled that—when Muddy had brought me my midday repast—she had informed me of her intention to take Virginia on a marketing expedition to procure dinner provisions. Quickly glancing at my clock, I was startled to see that the time was already close to 4:30 P.M.! Of such all-absorbing interest was Maelzel's singular work that the better part of the afternoon had elapsed while I was engrossed in its pages.

Assuming that the caller was Colonel Crockett, arrived—albeit somewhat earlier than I had anticipated—for dinner, I arose from my place and hurriedly made my way to the front door. Throwing it open, I was amazed to discover, not the frontiersman, but a personage I had not anticipated seeing again—Police Captain Russell!

I invited him inside, whereupon he stepped over the threshold, doffed his hat, and said: "I apologize for this sudden intrusion, Mr. Poe, but a matter of extreme, if puzzling, significance has arisen. I would be very much obliged if you would accompany me to the scene of this mystifying development."

"Indeed," I replied, "this is a most unexpected turn. But what in heaven's name has occurred?"

"Something that bears directly upon the homicide of Mrs. Macready and calls into serious question the guilt of her presumed killer, the late Mr. Roger Asher."

Far from taking me by surprise, this statement only served to confirm my nagging suspicions; for—in contrast to the frontiersman's sense of absolute certainty—my own belief in Asher's culpability had been tempered by grave and appreciable doubts.

"I have no objection to your proposal, Captain Russell," I declared, "and indeed welcome every opportunity to assist. I am, however, expecting the momentary arrival of Colonel Crockett, who has been invited here as a guest for dinner."

"He will not be coming" was the captain's surprising reply.

This pronouncement elicited a sharp twinge of apprehension in the depths of my bosom. "Has some mishap befallen him?"

"Oh, no! Not at all," the captain hastened to assure me. "But when apprised of this recent development, I immediately sent word to the colonel, who is even now awaiting us at the scene."

"But what precisely is it that you have discovered?" I cried, my curiosity having been raised to the highest imaginable pitch.

"Something distressing," came the portentous reply. "Something very distressing indeed."

CHAPTER 14

Before leaving, I took the time to compose a note to Muddy, informing her that a crisis had arisen which would require the presence of both myself and Colonel Crockett. Had she not already completed her errands, she should refrain from purchasing any provisions of a *perishable* nature, since it seemed likely that this sudden and wholly unforeseen occurrence would necessitate a deferral of our dinner plans.

Next, I sought out little Jimmy Johnston—the same lad who had displayed such uncontained admiration for the frontiersman when the latter first appeared at my dwelling—and (with the inducement of a copper penny) prevailed upon him to repair to Lexington Street, where Muddy and Sissy had gone to do their marketing, and deliver the note.

I then fetched my frockcoat and departed with Captain Russell, who remained mute on the purpose of his mission—though its *urgency* was clearly betokened in the tautness of his visage and the grim determination of his stride.

Our destination proved to be a squat, markedly dilapidated building of faded red brick on a street lined with dwellings of a similarly shabby nature. Gathered in front of this edifice was an assemblage of perhaps two dozen men and women, whose general air of titillated interest put me in mind of the similar, if considerably more substantial, crowd that had collected outside Mrs. Macready's boarding house.

At my first glimpse of this gathering, I experienced a pang of the keenest apprehension. Though Captain Russell had steadfastly withheld any information about our destination—saying only that he wished me to view the scene with my perceptions unbiased by any preconceived notions—I could not fail to surmise that I was being escorted to the *locale* of yet another atrocity. Now, the sight of the morbidly curious crowd—so reminiscent of the one I had encountered on that fateful morning exactly one week earlier—only lent strength to this supposition.

With Captain Russell in the lead, we pushed our way through these milling by-standers, entered the building, and found ourselves inside a small, dark, exceedingly cramped entrance hall. Immediately, my sense of olfaction was assaulted by odors of the most disagreeable variety—a noisome combination of stale cooking smells, pervasive mildew, and human *excreta*, along with a subtle yet unmistakable undercurrent of organic putrefaction.

Peering down the dark, narrow corridor that extended from the entrance hall, I perceived a dull, yellow glow emanating from what was evidently an open dooway.

"This way," said Captain Russell.

I followed the Captain down the murky, malodorous hallway and stepped into the chamber. Immediately, my eyes lit upon the imposing figure of the frontiersman, who was standing at the opposite end of the room, conferring in muted tones with a young policeman whom I instantly recognized as Officer Carlton. So engrossed were these two in their conversation that—for several moments after Captain Russell and I made our entrance—they remained oblivious of our presence, thus affording me an opportunity to peruse the surroundings.

The room was both eloquent—and *redolent*—of the most extreme, the most *dire*, poverty, neglect, and degradation. Its furnishings consisted solely of a broken-down bureau of deal, whose drawers were missing all but one or two of their small, wooden knobs; a table and chair of equally *shoddy* construction; and an old bedstead upon whose execrable mattress lay a frayed, moth-eaten, and badly rumpled coverlet. The jaundice-yellow wallpaper was ancient, water-stained, and peeling. At the foot of the bed stood an unemptied chamber pot—the source of much of the rank, miasmic atmosphere that suffused the quarters. Contributing to this *foetor* was the smell emanating from the table, whose surface was littered with the vestiges of various meals—the decaying fragments of a catfish; the partially gnawed *disjecta membra* of a chicken;

a beef bone to which waxy gobbets of congealed fat continued to cling. Of the hordes of vermin swarming brazenly over these loathsome remnants, I shall spare the reader a description.

And yet, for all of these extreme—nearly unbearable—signs of squalor and misery, the room also contained evidence that its inhabitant was a being not entirely devoid of intellectual substance or cultivation. In every corner of the little chamber stood a towering pile of yellowing newspapers and magazines; while scattered here and there—around the floor—upon the bureau top—beneath the bedstead—were dozens of dusty, leather-bound volumes.

By this point, both Crockett and his young interlocutor had become aware of our presence. Swivelling to face me, the frontiersman folded his arms across his chest and declared: "Well, it took you long enough to git here, Poe. I judge you warn't exactly *itchin'* to find out how wrong you was!"

So unanticipated—so *bewildering*—was this statement that my mouth literally dropped open in confusion. "I am at a complete loss to comprehend your meaning, Colonel Crockett," I said after a moment. "*Wrong* in what regard?"

"Why, about that Asher feller bein' the one that killed poor ol' Mrs. Macready."

This observation rendered me nearly as thunderstricken as his previous one. "But it was you, not I, who leapt to that conclusion!"

"Why, only on account of you bein' so blamed sure

that them goldanged letters spelled out *New Export*."

I was formulating an indignant retort to this out-rageous accusation when Captain Russell interceded. "Gentlemen, gentlemen," he said, raising both hands and patting the air in a conciliatory gesture. "There is little to be gained from such mutual recriminations. My intention in summoning you here was not to pro-voke a confrontation but—on the contrary—to secure your cooperation in helping to resolve this new and most *distressing* development."

His countenance assuming a deeply *chastened* expression, the frontiersman declared: "Why, you are right as rain, Cap'n. I wish I may be shot if this busi-ness ain't riled me up hotter'n a copperhead in July." Turning towards me, he thrust out his right hand and said: "Put 'er there, pard. I'm plumb sorry for behavin' in such an ornery style. You 'n' me is in this together for the long haul!"

"I accept your gesture of contrition with the gen-erosity of spirit it so clearly deserves," I answered as I clasped his outstretched hand.

"So," said Crockett, after releasing my hand from his grip. "How do you cipher the situation, Poe?"

"I would be better able to reply to your query had I the slightest conception as to what the situation *is*," I replied.

"Why, Cap'n," exclaimed Crockett. "Ain't you told Poe what's took place here?"

"Permit me to do so without further delay," said Captain Russell as he turned to address me. "This poor—indeed, pitiable—dwelling, Mr. Poe, is the apartment of an elderly gentleman named Alexander Montague, who has lived alone for many years since the death of his wife. According to his nearest neighbor—a most kind-hearted woman named Purviance— Montague suffers from both a debilitating case of atrophic arthritis and an extreme deterioration of vision which has rendered him nearly blind. As a result, he has been compelled, for many years, to rely on the good offices of Mrs. Purviance, who—for the mere pittance he is able to pay her—comes by each day around noontime to attend to certain of his most basic needs."

"Like emptyin' that there piss-pot," Crockett interjected, thrusting a thumb toward the article in question.

"Precisely so," said Captain Russell. "Upon making her customary visit earlier today," he continued, "Mrs. Purviance was amazed to find that Montague— who rarely, if ever, ventures from his bedchamber— was not present in the room. This in itself was a most unaccountable circumstance. It was not, however, until she looked in the parlor that she made the discovery which sent her hurrying to my office in alarm."

"To what discovery do you refer, Captain?" I inquired with a frown.

"Ain't you set eyes on it yet?" asked Crockett in surprise.

"I have viewed no other portion of this apartment than the room in which we are presently standing."

"Why, no wonder you was so all-fired dumb-founded when I laid into you in such a cantankerous style," Crockett exclaimed. "Come on!" Grabbing the oil lamp that stood on the table, he led me from the room and across the little hallway, with Captain Russell and his subordinate bringing up the rear.

We entered a low, narrow doorway and found ourselves inside a small, sparsely furnished parlor whose general condition was every bit as deplorable as that of the bedchamber. Without pausing, Crockett stepped to the opposite side of the room and, standing beside a tattered and exceptionally *rickety*-looking sofa, raised the lamp so as to illuminate the wall directly above this woebegone piece of furniture.

So stained and moldy was the wallpaper that, for a moment, I could not discern precisely what the frontiersman intended me to see. It was not until I stepped to his side and peered closely at the spot he was indicating that my eyes widened in startled recognition.

Inscribed upon the wall were nine bloody letters, unmistakably produced by the same hand that had left the inscrutable message over the bed of the butchered landlady. Only this time—because its author had evidently exerted greater care in his handiwork—every individual character was meticulously shaped.

What the message *referred to* I could not immediately say. But as to its *denotation* there was no ambiguity. The letters did not constitute the name "Neuendorf." Nor—I now saw clearly—did they form the words "New Export."

What they spelled was "NEVERMORE."

CHAPTER 15

One conundrum, at least, had thus been resolved: the signification of the sanguinary message left at the scene of the landlady's murder. This revelation, however, brought us no closer to an ultimate solution of the case, whose mysteries had only been deepened by the newest developments. What did the inscription "NEVER-MORE" *mean?* Who was its author? And what had become of the aged, nearly sightless, and severely incapacitated being in whose parlor this singular——this *sinister*——communication had now been discovered?

That Alexander Montague had become the latest victim of the same unknown *maniac* who had perpetrated such unspeakable atrocities upon Elmira Macready seemed beyond dispute. No reasonable observer could fail to conclude that the enigmatic word defacing the parlor wall had been printed with the old man's life's blood. And yet, in contrast to the landlady, whose fearfully butchered body had been displayed with such stark—such *obscene*—visibility, there was no discernible sign, in the present case, of a *corpus delicti*. The old man's body had evidently been removed from the premises by the killer—for what grotesque, what *ghastly* reason, it was impossible to conceive.

For approximately the next half-hour, our little party—Captain Russell, Officer Carlton, Colonel Crockett, and I—remained inside the parlor, conducting an exhaustive search of the cramped and wretchedly appointed room. In spite of its thoroughness, however, this investigation failed to turn up the slightest clue as to either the fate or the whereabouts of the missing man. We then crossed back to the opposite side of the hallway and embarked on a similarly meticulous examination of the bedchamber. Our efforts here proved equally fruitless.

Focussing his attention on the bedstead, Colonel Crockett did discover, on the underside of a bedraggled feather pillow, a discoloration of reddish-brown hue that appeared to be dried blood. This mark, however, was of no greater size than might have resulted from a common nosebleed. In general, moreover, the bedclothes and mattress were so foully besmirched with every variety of matter—from the vestiges of numberless foodstuffs to the evidence of human incontinence—that the precise nature of any individual stain was nearly impossible to determine.

His visage contorted into an expression of extreme distaste, the frontiersman let the fetid pillow drop back upon the mattress, then exhaled a deep sigh of exasperation. "Damned if this ain't the queerest business I ever struck!" he declared. "Who exactly *was* this Montague feller, anyways?"

Captain Russell, who was in the process of picking through the scant belongings in the topmost drawer of the rickety bureau, cast a glance over his right shoulder and replied: "As of yet, we have been able to ascertain very little information about the man. His life——at least during the time that he has occupied these quarters—— has been, as the result of his manifold infirmities, reclusive in the extreme. Is that not the case, Officer Carlton?"

"Aye, sir," replied the latter, who was kneeling by the fireplace and employing a poker to sift through the hearth, as though the heap of dead ashes might hold a clue to the vanished man's fate. "That's the impression I've gathered."

While my companions had busied themselves in the above-mentioned ways, I had bent my efforts to a meticulous scrutiny of the many dusty tomes scattered about the room. Now, as I stood in one corner of the chamber with a heavy volume open in my hands, I looked up from its pages and announced: "Of one fact, gentlemen, we may at least be certain. Mr. Alexander Montague may be fairly described as a man of both formidable learning and keen discernment in matters pertaining to literature."

"And how do you reckon *that?*" inquired Crockett.

"My conclusion is based on a scrupulous examination of the books which appear to constitute the bulk of Montague's personal belongings and which consist, in large part, of expensive, if rather poorly maintained, editions of the great English dramatists, including Marlowe, Dryden, and, of course, the immortal Shakespeare. Here in my hands, for example, I have a rare eighteenth-century collection of Jacobean melodramas, including John Ford's *The Broken Heart* and *The White Devil, or Vittoria Corombona* of Webster.

"To be sure," I continued, "the mere *ownership* of such books may, in certain cases, be proof of nothing beyond intellectual pretension." (In stressing this latter point, I had in my mind my late guardian, the boorish merchant John Allan, whose personal library was stocked to the point of *ostentation* with the most costly volumes of classic works—though he himself rarely spent time perusing anything more weighty than a ledger-book.) "Almost without exception, however, the volumes in this room are filled with handwritten annotations, whose author I take to be Montague. These copious marginal comments clearly bespeak a sensibility deeply attuned to the complex intellectual and moral *themes*—no less than to the sublime aesthetic *pleasures*—of the material."

"A most ingenious observation, Mr. Poe," declared Captain Russell.

"Thank you," I replied. Clapping shut the volume in my hands, I restored it to its place upon the bureau-top; then—stepping to one of the many piles of old newspapers ranged around the periphery of the chamber—I removed the uppermost copy from the pile. It was, I saw at a glance, a copy of the *Baltimore Daily Advertiser*, dated October 21, 1809. So fragile—so desiccated with age—was this publication that, as I raised it towards the lamplight, its edges disintegrated in a shower of powdery, yellow dust. Almost at once, the entire area of my frontal sinus cavity was seized with an overpowering *itch*. I struggled to subdue this tormenting sensation—but to no avail. Throwing back my head, I drew in a series of sharp, increasingly loud inhalations which culminated in the discharge of a thunderous sneeze.

"Great guns!" cried the frontiersman. "What an earsplitter!"

I was in the act of extracting my pocket handkerchief when a second sneeze, equal in both force and volume to the first, erupted from my nasal passages.

With a sympathetic cluck of the tongue, Captain Russell exclaimed: "I fear that you may be contracting a nasty *catarrh*, Mr. Poe."

"It is merely a reaction to the intensely unwholesome atmosphere of this room," I replied, sniffling.

"It's mighty ripe in here, for a certainty," said Colonel Crockett.

By now, my eyes had begun to water profusely. Laying down the crumbling newspaper, I declared: "Gentlemen, I fear that there is something in the insalubrious air of this chamber to which my respiratory system is, in the highest degree, *susceptible*. I think it best, therefore, to return to my abode, where I can employ my energies to better advantage by ruminating in undisturbed solitude on the manifold mysteries that now confront us."

Stepping before me, Captain Russell shook my hand and solemnly declared: "Your assistance in this grave and troubling affair is deeply appreciated, Mr. Poe."

I acknowledged this tribute with a little bow.

"And tell them two purty gals of yourn," said Colonel Crockett, "that I'm right sorry about missing tonight's shindig. If they ain't undisposed to the notion, I'll be there tomorrow—come hell or high water!"

"I take it, then," said I to the frontiersman, "that you have decided to postpone your departure."

"I reckon so."

"But what of your commitments elsewhere?"

"Why, Poe," answered Crockett, planting his fists on his hips, "I guess you ain't heard. There are some things that Davy Crockett ain't *never* been known to walk away from: a fight, a friend in need—and unfinished business!"

My intention was to return directly to my dwelling, where—shut off from the distractions of the world— I could focus the full power of my *ratiocinative* faculties on the mysteries at hand. But to defer my cerebrations until I reached my abode proved an impossibility. No sooner had I emerged into the darkening streets than my overstimulated brain began to revolve the numerous facets of the baffling case.

If it established nothing else, the bizarre disappearance of Alexander Montague—accompanied as it was by the inscrutable message "Nevermore"—proved conclusively that Roger Asher had been innocent of the murder of Elmira Macready. The hand that had left the bloody writing on the latter's bedroom wall was unmistakably the same one responsible for the inscription on Montague's parlor. And that hand could not possibly have belonged to Roger Asher, who had perished so horribly prior to the old man's disappearance.

To be sure, the fact that Asher was not the slayer of Mrs. Macready did not *necessarily* signify that no connection existed between his death, the murder of the landlady, and the subsequent disappearance of Alexander Montague. But what this link might be remained utterly obscure—particularly in the absence of any substantive information about the life or background of the vanished man.

My own perusal of the publications scattered throughout the latter's bedroom had convinced me only that Montague had been a singularly literate individual—at least in the epoch preceding the deterioration of his eyesight. It had evidently been many years since he had indulged in the habit of reading. The handwritten marginalia I had discovered in his books were faded with age; and the issue of the *Baltimore Daily Advertiser* I had been examining was no less than a quarter-century old. The exceedingly brittle condition of the other newspapers in the room suggested that they were of equally antique vintage. Why Montague had bothered to preserve these worthless *gazettes* was yet another enigma in a case already replete with them. Perhaps the answer was no more mysterious than the extreme and unaccountable reluctance—characteristic of a certain class of individuals—to discard possessions of even the most trivial and transitory value.

I had been vaguely aware, since being apprised of the missing man's identity, that his cognomen possessed a strangely familiar ring. Try as I might, however, I could not conceive of the circumstances under which I might have previously encountered it. In an attempt to prod my memory, I now began to repeat his name silently as I bent my steps homeward—*Alexander Montague, Alexander Montague.* But to no avail.

So engrossed was I in this effort that I had been paying scant attention to my surroundings. All at once, a piercing breeze—infused with a pungent blend of maritime aromas—drifted from the harbor; and I realized with a start that I was passing close to the abject neighborhood where, just one week earlier, Colonel Crockett had engaged in his memorable battle with the redoubtable Hans Neuendorf.

This recollection induced a tremor of *dread* that coursed through every particle of my being. The unparalleled events of the past several days, beginning with my arrival at the house of Asher, had driven all thoughts of Neuendorf from my mind. Now, the vivid recollection of that fierce and implacable ruffian—and of the dire threats that he had reportedly levelled against my person—came rushing back upon my consciousness. My heart quailed—my limbs grew cold—my bosom heaved with the sudden onset of insufferable anxiety!

By now, darkness had fallen. The streets—which had been teeming with wayfarers just several hours earlier—were largely devoid of human presence. Accelerating my pace, I plunged headlong down the deserted thoroughfares—the devious by-ways, the narrow, crooked lanes. All at once, as I rounded a corner, I was seized by an absolute—and wholly *alarming*—conviction: I was being followed!

Readers of an inherently *skeptical* bent may suspect that this belief was merely a product of my intensely agitated state of mind—of the profound apprehension induced within me by my sudden recollection of the menacing ruffian who had promised, according to Crockett, to "use my skin for a razor strop." Certainly, such tricks of fancy are among the most commonly known of all phenomena of a merely *delusional* nature. In the present instance, however, nothing could be further from the case. So powerful—so *palpable*—was my sense of being *stalked* that it could only have sprung from those innate and primitive instincts which continue to operate deep within the souls of even the most highly civilized of modern men—instincts designed by a protective Nature to alert us to the presence of imminent, mortal *peril!*

A single backwards glance would have sufficed to confirm—or refute—my conviction. But I did not dare to slacken my pace, even for the instant that such an action would have required. Onward I rushed, making at full speed for Amity Street, while my unseen pursuer followed upon my heels—so close as to cause the hairs on the nape of my neck to bristle with terror!

All at once, I saw my destination directly ahead of me. With rasping breath and pounding heart, I accelerated my pace and reached—with what delirious relief I can scarcely express!—the threshold of my dwelling. Clutching the doorknob with one trembling hand, I stopped—whirled around—and let out a gasp of astonishment and incomprehension.

Apart from a scrawny and bedraggled dog that was trotting along the paving stones and pausing intermittently to sniff at the curb, the street behind me was utterly deserted. I strained my eyes to peer into the darkness that lay beyond the compass of the flickering street lamp. But my phantom pursuer was nowhere to be seen.

CHAPTER 16

Quickly entering my abode, I secured the latch, then made my way towards the warm, intensely *welcoming* glow that emanated from the kitchen doorway. At the threshold, I paused for an instant to savor the bewitching atmosphere of snug domesticity that permeated the humble scene.

At the small, circular table sat Muddy and Sissy. Before them lay the vestiges of their simple evening meal, which——to judge from the morsels that littered their plates——had consisted of cheese, salt beef, and brown bread. As I gazed in silent adoration at the two angelic creatures, Muddy became suddenly aware of my presence and, clasping her hands to her bosom, exclaimed: "Oh, Eddie! Thank goodness! I have been so dreadfully worried!"

Stepping across the room, I sank into the chair directly across from the saintly woman and gazed lovingly at her plain yet beguiling countenance.

"Be assured, darling Muddy, that——while somewhat fatigued from the unparalleled events of this most trying, most *distressing* day—your Eddie is, in all other respects, entirely well."

I next turned my gaze upon Sissy and communicated Crockett's message. "He is most eager to hear you sing, and has vowed to be here, come"——here, I felt it apt, for Sissy's benefit, to modify the frontiersman's coarse vernacular—"come Hades or high water."

"Hurray!" exclaimed my angel. "I will go practice right now!" And with this declaration, she sprang to her feet and disappeared from the kitchen. Seconds later, the heart-piercing strains of that noble ballad "The Unconstant Lover"——rendered in Sissy's ethereal voice——could be heard issuing from the parlor.

For a moment, Muddy and I listened in rapt silence. Then, turning to me with a look of intense maternal solicitude, the dear woman said: "Eddie, is everything all right? I have started to feel that you are keeping something from your Muddy."

"Clearly," I replied, "nothing can exceed, in terms of sheer *discernment*, the perspicacious power of a sympathetic heart. Your loving intuition has not misled you, dearest Muddy. Nevertheless, I must persist in my present course of unwonted, if well-intentioned, secrecy. To apprise you of the truth would not, by any means, diminish your anxiety on my acount."

"Whatever you think best, dear," Muddy sighed, reaching across the table and patting my right hand with her own. "But I hope that you will be careful!"

Fervently, I raised her chapped and reddened, yet inexpressibly *precious*, hand to my lips and covered it with devotional kisses. "Oh, Muddy!" I exclaimed, my voice cracking with emotion. "You are as dear to me as the doomed, long-departed woman who first brought me into this world. Indeed, even *dearer*; for—while she was but the mother of *myself*—you are mother to one who means more to me than my own *life!*" And with this heartfelt testimonial, I turned my head in the direction of the parlor, where Sissy had embarked on a surpassingly *melodic* rendition of the popular ditty "There's a Star that Shines for Thee."

"Her voice is like the angel Israfel's," I sighed, "whose glorious hymn—so legend has it—made the very moon blush with love." I listened until Sissy's performance came to an end. Then, placing my palms upon the table-edge, I pushed myself to my feet and declared: "I must retire to my study. There is a matter that demands my urgent attention."

"Shall I fix you a nice cheese sandwich and bring it to your room?" inquired Muddy.

My stomach—which had been deprived of the least morsel of food since the morning—responded to this offer with a ravenous growl. Assuring Muddy that nothing could afford me keener pleasure, I took temporary leave of the dear-hearted woman and repaired directly to my *sanctum*, where—after enkindling the lamp that sat upon my writing table—I settled down to think.

So manifold were the mysteries now confronting me that, at first, their sheer *profusion* rendered me incapable of systematic analysis. It quickly became evident that I could best achieve my purpose by selecting a *single* enigma and focussing the entirety of my attention upon it. I decided to commence with the bloody word "Nevermore"—and, with this end in view, I dipped my quill into the inkpot and inscribed the inscrutable message on a blank sheet of paper.

Propping my elbows on the tabletop, I rested my chin in my hands and stared down at the paper. The melancholy tone and sinister connotations of the word were sufficiently clear. But what could it possibly *mean?* Did it signify a threat—or the fulfillment of one? Did it refer to a secret in the lives of the *victims*—or was it an allusion to something known solely to the perpetrator? Try as I might, I could not conjure up a single association that might shed light upon the mystery.

At this point, Muddy rapped upon my chamber door and—in response to my summons—entered with a platter and teacup in her hands. Setting these items directly before me on the writing table, she bestowed a fond maternal kiss upon the top of my head, then tiptoed from the room. No sooner had she departed than I snatched up the sandwich and greedily devoured it, washing down each delicious mouthful with a gulp of the invigorating brew. Feeling much restored by this simple yet savory repast, I decided to abandon my efforts at interpreting the mysterious word and turn instead to the tantalizingly familiar name of the vanished, elderly recluse. Brushing a sprinkling of bread crumbs from the paper, I lifted my quill and, directly below the word "Nevermore," inscribed "Alexander Montague."

The nagging sense that I knew this name from somewhere had grown into a near-certainty. Keeping my gaze fixed upon the appellation, I began to review within my mind every conceivable *context*—professional—personal—familial—in which I might have encountered it. After fifteen full minutes of this effort, however, I was no closer to a solution than I had been at the start.

In making her egress from my room, Muddy had inadvertently left the door slightly ajar. Now—as I continued to stare at the paper, cudgelling my brain—I became dimly aware of a singularly *poignant* melody drifting from the parlor. Pricking up my ears, I listened more attentively to the mellifluous sound. It was the honeyed voice of my darling Sissy, performing a song that possessed a particular—indeed, an exceedingly personal—significance to me.

The song was "Nobody Coming to Marry Me" —a tune that my dear, departed mother, Eliza Poe, had performed as a regular part of her theatrical *repertoire*. Indeed, so closely associated was she with this simple yet heart-piercing ballad that it came to be regarded, by admiring audiences everywhere, as her professional "signature." Many years had elapsed since I had heard its touching lyrics and captivating melody. Now, leaning my weary head back on the crest of my chair, I closed my eyes and let the sweet, affecting music suffuse my soul:

"Come blind, come lame, come cripple,
Come someone and take me away!

> For 'tis O! what will become of me,
> O! what shall I do?
> Nobody coming to marry me,
> Nobody coming to woo!"

All at once, I was struck with a thunderous realization. My eyes gaped—my mouth fell open—and I sat bolt upright in my chair. Half-rising from the seat, I reached across my writing desk and, with trembling hands, snatched the small, casket-shaped mahogany chest from its perch atop my manuscript pile. Extracting the little brass key from the middle drawer of my desk, I hurriedly unlocked the chest and rummaged through its contents until I found the item I was seeking—the yellowed newspaper clipping from 1807 which described my mother's memorable performance as Cordelia at Baltimore's Front Street Theatre and listed the names of the more notable citizens who had been in attendance on that long-ago night.

A single glance at this review confirmed the realization that had hit me while listening to Sissy's ravishing song. I now knew precisely who Alexander Montague was, for his name appeared prominently in the clipping—not as one of my mother's fellow-thespians, nor as a member of the eminent and enthusiastic crowd who had so wildly cheered her performance.

Alexander Montague had been the *author* of the piece!

So intense was the emotion excited in me by this discovery that I can scarcely convey my reaction in mere *words*. Leaping to my feet, I began to pace rapidly around the center of the room, while my brain reeled with a multitude of tumultuous thoughts.

Several days earlier, during my initial examination of this review, I had been struck with a sense of its *portentous* significance. This intuition had now been confirmed with the uttermost force. That the sinister sequence of events which had commenced with the landlady's murder was connected, in some still-unaccountable way, to the world of American theatredom could no longer be doubted. But what could that connection conceivably *be?* What reference did it bear to the bloody word "Nevermore"? And how, if at all, did the slaying of Elmira Macready, the death of Roger Asher, and the disappearance of Alexander Montague relate—through my own mother's distant yet nonetheless tangible association with these individuals—to *me?*

I halted in my track and considered my alternatives. Only one course of action seemed appropriate. I must communicate my discovery to the authorities without delay. Though my heart did not rejoice at the prospect of venturing forth again into the darkness of the city, I felt it my duty as both a citizen and a *man* to subdue my misgivings and proceed forthwith to the police.

Nothing, however, was to be gained by sharing my intentions with Muddy. Extinguishing my table lamp, I swiftly crossed the room, slipped into the hallway, shut the door softly behind me, and stole silently towards the front of the house.

Even before reaching the entranceway, however, I was struck with another thought. If—as seemed possible—the mystery in which I was now so deeply embroiled bore some still-unknown relationship to my own departed mother, it might prove wise of me to undertake my own *personal* investigation of Montague's premises before alerting the police. I felt motivated, too, by my strange—deepening—and intensely *unnerving*—conviction that, at the heart of the mystery, lay a fearful secret that I alone was fated, if not *doomed*, to confront!

Stepping out into the street, I buttoned my frock-coat, thrust my hands into its side pockets, and hurried away in the direction of Alexander Montague's dwelling.

CHAPTER 17

Having no wish to repeat the unnerving experience I had endured earlier in the evening, I decided to follow a less deserted, if somewhat more *circuitous*, route to Montague's dwelling. Twenty minutes later, I arrived safely at my destination. I had counted on finding the front door to the squat, shabby building unlatched, and—trying the knob—was confirmed in my expectation. As I stepped into the entranceway, however, I was startled to discern a dull yellow glow emanating from the doorway of the bedchamber at the far end of the cramped, noisome corridor.

For a moment, I remained frozen in place, my mind in a ferment as I sought to account for this anomalous and wholly unforeseen development. Was it possible, I wondered, that either Captain Russell or his subordinate, Officer Carlton, was still within the apartment, pursuing the investigation? In an effort to test this hypothesis, I cleared my throat and loudly inquired: "Hello? Is someone there?"

The sound of my voice echoed hollowly in the

dark, vault-like corridor before fading into utter silence. After the lapse of several seconds, I called out again. Once more, my interrogative cry elicited no response.

Evidently, the apartment was devoid of any human presence but my own. Only one conclusion suggested itself: whoever had been the last to depart from Montague's dwelling had neglected to extinguish the oil lamp.

"Surely," I whispered to myself, "this must be the explanation. Only this, and nothing more."

Even so, I could not rid myself of the singular conviction—which had, by then, taken firm hold of my spirit—that I was not entirely alone in the apartment. Cupping a hand behind my left ear, I swivelled my head in the direction of the bedchamber and strained my auditory faculty to the utmost. I could detect no other sound, however, besides a faint, uncertain rustling, as though from the gentle stirrings of a window curtain.

I heaved a sigh of relief. Clearly, the inordinately *unsettling* events of the past several days had so wrought upon my nerves that I had begun to perceive perils where none existed.

Having thus reassured myself, I made my way toward the dimly lit doorway, the floorboards creaking noisily in the tomb-like silence of the corridor. As I neared the bedchamber, however, my heart was once again seized by a sudden, sickening *qualm* of superstitious dread.

Drawing to a halt several feet from the doorway, I paused to reconsider the wisdom of my present course of action. Perhaps I had behaved too precipitously in choosing to return to Montague's apartment without first apprising the police of my recent discovery. For a moment, I gave serious thought to abandoning my enterprise and repairing, instead, to the headquarters of Captain Russell. Before I could act on this impulse, however, a monitory voice within my head reminded me of the well-founded basis for my original decision: to wit, the strange, thus-far-inexplicable—but none-theless verifiable—connection between the victims of the still-unknown madman and my own sainted mother!

Manfully subduing the spasm of unease which had momentarily gripped me, I traversed the remaining distance to the doorway of the bedchamber, and—after drawing a deep breath—boldly stepped across the threshold.

A single glance assured me that there was no one in the room. It was now unmistakably clear that I had merely imagined the lurking presence of another human being. Releasing my breath in a long sigh of relief, I stood in the center of the floor and slowly gazed around.

The condition of the chamber was different in certain notable regards from the way it had been several hours earlier, when I had last viewed it. A number of these changes were distinctly for the better. Some-one—perhaps the neighbor woman Mrs. Purviance, who habitually performed such menial services for the incapacitated tenant—had evidently been enlisted to dispose of the more objectionable *detritus*. The loathsome, vermin-infested food scraps had been removed from the table, and the noisome receptacle at the side of the bed had been emptied of its excessively disagreeable contents.

The window, too, had been opened several inches, evidently for the purpose of ventilation: a circumstance which accounted, not only for the improved atmosphere of the room, but also for the gentle movements of the moth-eaten window-curtains, whose faint rustlings I had detected from the hallway.

In spite of these alterations, however, the overall ambience of the room was, if anything, even more deplorable than it had been previously. In their concerted effort to uncover some clue as to the missing man's whereabouts, the trio of investigators—Captain Russell, Officer Carlton, and Colonel Crockett—had left the chamber in a state of near-shambles. The bureau drawers had been ransacked—the bedclothes virtually shredded—the piled newspapers scattered everywhere across the floor.

Given the apparent thoroughness of the search which my associates had conducted, I felt somewhat at a loss as to how to proceed with my own investigation. This state of uncertainty, however, lasted but a moment. Bending down, I retrieved one of the old, brittle newspapers that lay close to my feet. I then straightened up, and—holding my breath (so as to avoid inhaling any of the dust-like particles of disintegrating paper which had precipitated my earlier fit of uncontrolled *sternutation*)—I quickly leafed through the fragile pages of this twenty-year-old gazette.

Within seconds, I had come upon a piece by Alexander Montague dealing with the acoustical deficiencies of the then newly constructed Holliday Street Theatre. The discovery of this article served to account for the otherwise baffling collection of moldering newspapers stored within the room. It was clear that Montague had meticulously preserved a copy of each of the issues to which he had contributed a review.

That one or another of these writings might contain a clue to the mysteries associated with the bloody word "Nevermore" seemed at least remotely plausible to me. The sheer *number* of newspapers littering the room, however, made the prospect of pursuing this line of investigation excessively daunting. In any event, there was no possibility at all of my engaging in such an onerous undertaking at the moment. Carefully refolding the newspaper, I laid it on the tabletop and cast my eye about the dimly illuminated room.

Immediately, my gaze lighted upon the leather-bound volume of Jacobean drama which lay atop the bureau, in precisely the same position I had left it when forced to flee the noxious confines of the room several hours earlier. Although I had looked through this volume with reasonable care, it now struck me that some additional information might be gleaned from a more scrupulous perusal of its pages—as well as from a closer examination of the numerous other books belonging to Montague. With this end in view, I made for the bureau. I had taken only one or two steps, however, when I was brought to a sudden—and startled—halt.

A muffled scrape, like the sound of another person moving stealthily across the floorboards, had issued from a spot somewhere close behind me!

So unexpected—so utterly *alarming*—was this noise that I felt my heart cease to beat and my limbs grow as rigid as the sculpted appendages of the celebrated *Hermes* by the Greek master Praxiteles. Not daring to move—to breathe—or indeed, to so much as blink an eye—I listened in an extremity of terrified suspense. But though I remained in this state of frozen attentiveness for several agonizingly protracted minutes, I could detect no repetition of the sound.

Very gradually—oh, with what slow, *exquisite* caution I can scarcely convey!—I forced myself to turn around and face the unknown entity whose steps I had heard so distinctly. But in the dull illumination provided by the oil lamp, I saw that there was nothing behind me: only the empty room—and the darkened corridor—and the gloomy doorway of the little parlor directly across from the bedchamber.

A mirthless chuckle escaped from my lips, as I chided myself for the inordinate violence of my reaction. "To have experienced such intense trepidation at what *must* have been a mere household rodent, scampering over the floor," I said aloud. "Surely, Eddie, you have been beside yourself this day!"

As a result of the fresh draft of night air issuing through the partially open window, the temperature inside the bedchamber was cool to the point of chilliness. Even so, the sudden fright I had just endured had caused my brow to bead with perspiration. Desiring to dry my forehead, I reached into my trouser pocket for my handkerchief. As I extracted this article, a coin fell from my pocket and, striking the floor, rolled underneath the bed.

In view of my lamentable pecuniary circumstances, I could scarcely afford to sacrifice a coin of even the most trivial denomination. Getting to my knees, I peered into the shadows beneath the bedstead. The illumination issuing from the oil lamp that stood upon the dining table, however, was insufficiently bright to permit me to penetrate the darkness. Standing erect, I stepped to the table, clasped the lamp by its base, carried it back to the bedside and—reverting to my kneeling position—made a renewed effort to locate the errant coin.

I now had a clear, well-illuminated, and unobstructed view. The coin, however, was nowhere to be seen. As I slowly moved the lamp to and fro, surveying the entire area beneath the bedstead, I perceived a possible explanation for this surprising circumstance. One of the floorboards was partially raised, as though it had come loose from the surrounding planks, thus creating a noticeable gap into which the rolling coin might easily have disappeared.

This minor structural irregularity was perfectly in

keeping with the generally dilapidated state of the apartment. Nevertheless, there was something about the sight of this partially dislodged floorboard that sent a sudden, premonitory chill coursing through my frame. I had no doubt that Colonel Crockett and the others had made the most thorough examination imaginable of the little dwelling. Montague's bed-chamber had clearly been searched from ceiling to floor. There was one place, however, where my fellow investigators had, I felt sure, *not* thought to look:

The area *below* the floor!

A sudden paroxysm of inexpressible anxiety seized my heart as I scrambled to my feet. Already my hands were perspiring so copiously that—after setting the lamp back upon the tabletop—I took a moment to dry my palms against the legs of my trousers. Then, returning to the bed, I clasped it by its underframe and, with a grunt of effort, dragged it towards the cen-ter of the room until the loosened board was fully exposed.

For several moments, I merely stared down at the planking, while—within my heaving bosom—a turbu-lent battle raged. On one side were those inner promptings urging me to flee to the headquarters of the police and notify Captain Russell at once. On the other was an equally powerful impulse—born of both intense curiosity and a deeply ingrained sense of per-sonal duty—to complete my investigatory mission by confronting whatever unknown mystery lay concealed beneath the floor.

At length, I could procrastinate no longer. With a wild cry of desperate resolution, I stooped to the board, and—wedging my quaking fingers beneath its upraised edges—tore it from its place.

Immediately, a foul, fetid odor wafted up from the hollow space beneath the floor. My heart quailed—my limbs quaked—and a cry of delirious horror escaped from my terror-parched mouth, as I looked down upon the inexpressibly *awful* sight that smote my gaping eyes. Dropping the plank, I stumbled backwards, trembling convulsively in every fibre.

At that instant, directly behind me, I heard a distinct *susurration* and felt a warm exhalation of breath on the back of my neck, which caused each separate nape-hair to bristle and stand erect!

A shriek of the purest terror issued from my throat as I whirled around. There, standing only inches away, was a sight even more stupefying in its way than the ghastly thing I had just glimpsed beneath the floor.

It was she: the same dreamlike—no! *nightmarish*—figure who had appeared before my disbelieving eyes in the gloomy chamber of Roger Asher's ill-fated abode.

I screamed again. Then darkness washed over my vision—I felt the strength drain from my limbs—and all conscious sensations were swallowed up in a mad rushing descent of my soul into the blackness of utter oblivion!

My submerged consciousness returned—not suddenly, like the luckless sailor who, having plunged overboard, bursts from the briny depths, crying madly for help; nor by slow degrees, like those near-amphibious divers of South Sea isles who, after plundering the priceless oyster beds, drift lazily back to the sunlight, pearly treasures in hand——but rather by fits and starts, like an exhausted swimmer who alternately sinks and struggles again to the surface, until, through sheer heroic effort, he fights his way safely to shore.

As I lay prostrate on the floor of the chamber, there first came to my insensate soul a dim awareness of motion and sound——the tumultuous motion of my heart and, in my ears, the sound of its beating. Then a pause in which my mind reverted to blankness. Then again sound, and motion, and *touch*——a tingling sensation, pervading my frame. Then the mere consciousness of existence, without thought. Then thought—— and a shuddering recollection of the horrors I had so recently endured. Then a lapse into insensibility. Then a rushing revival of soul and, with it, a sudden awareness that I was not alone in the room!

My eyes fluttered open and, as my clouded vision began to clear, I discerned a shadowy countenance hovering directly above my own. At that instant, a familiar voice——whose stentorious tone had never before sounded so welcome to my ears——boomed out:

"Over here, Cap'n! He's stirrin' at last!"

I blinked my eyes several times, until my ocular faculty had regained its former clarity and focus, and found myself staring up into the visage of Colonel Crockett, who was regarding me with an expression in which concern and relief appeared equally commingled.

"By jings, Poe," he declared. "I was commencin' to fear that you warn't *never* going to come 'round."

At that instant, Captain Russell bustled over and, stooping beside me, exclaimed: "I am exceedingly glad to see you awake, Mr. Poe."

With a groan of exertion, I elevated the upper portion of my torso and, supporting myself on my elbows, gazed around. A trio of policemen, among whom I recognized Officer Carlton, were conversing together in hushed, solemn tones as they huddled around the opening in the floor, which appeared to have been enlarged by the removal of several additional planks.

"Are you able to stand?" inquired Captain Russell.

"I believe so," I responded, rising first to my knees and then—somewhat unsteadily—to my feet.

"Here," said the frontiersman, clasping me by one arm. "Lemme give you a hand, ol' hoss."

Standing erect, I suddenly became aware of an acute, throbbing ache, originating at the rear of my cranium. Reaching one hand behind my head, I felt a small but decidedly protuberant lump of such exquisite tenderness that, at the merest touch of my fingertips, a searing shaft of pain—like a flaming arrow propelled from the bow of an Apache warrior—shot through my head, causing me to wince in agony.

"You are looking a mite poorly, Poe," said Crockett.

"I appear to have struck the back of my head

against the floor, thus inducing a swollen knot, or edema, of considerable sensitivity."

"Them goose-eggs'll smart like the dickens, all right," commiserated the frontiersman. "But what in blue blazes *happened*, Poe? Last time we saw you, you were shovin' off for home."

"Yes," added Captain Russell. "I have been wondering the same."

Having had no opportunity—in the few moments that had elapsed since I emerged from my swoon—to formulate a plausible explanation for my presence in Montague's apartment, I frantically cast about for a stratagem that would gain me a measure of time. A sudden spasm of pain at the posterior region of my cranium provided me with the solution. I opened my mouth as though to respond to Crockett's query—then, emitting a pitiful groan, I clutched my head, closed my eyes, and tottered slightly on my feet.

Taking me by one arm to steady me, Crockett said: "Maybe you oughta set a spell, Poe, before you try talking."

With the frontiersman's assistance, I made my way to the rickety chair that stood beside the dining table and—after lowering myself onto the seat—propped one elbow on the tabletop and rested my forehead in my hand. I remained in this attitude for several moments, as though waiting for my dizziness to subside—all the while ruminating busily on the best way to proceed.

To confess the actual, motivating cause of my visit

seemed imprudent in the extreme, since I had yet to ascertain what—if any—association existed between my sainted mother, Eliza, and the recent atrocities that had now befallen no less than *three* individuals whose names appeared in the precious newspaper clipping I kept stored in my casket-shaped "treasure box." My terrifying encounter with the ghastly female spectre— the mere sight of whose countenance had caused my soul to sicken and my brain to reel—only served to reinforce my inclination to provide the police with a carefully tailored version of the truth.

At length—having resolved on a suitable story—I looked up at Crockett and Captain Russell and said: "Forgive me, gentlemen. The shock, both physical and mental, which I have so recently endured has left me somewhat light-headed. In answer to your query: After arriving back home, I found myself overcome with a sense of intense *chagrin*. To have abandoned the investigation merely as the result of a minor disorder of my respiratory functions constituted, I believed, a gross dereliction of my responsibilities.

"I therefore resolved to return forthwith, under the assumption that I would find you still engaged in the search. In this supposition I was mistaken. Discovering—to my surprise—that the apartment was vacant, I determined to continue the examination of the premises on my own. As I pursued this endeavor, something—I cannot recall with any clarity precisely *what*—drew my attention to the space beneath the bed. Moving aside this article of furniture, I immediately noticed a loose plank in the floor and, without hesitation, pried it up with my fingertips. So ghastly—so appalling—so utterly *hideous* was the sight which smote my eyes that I staggered back in an ecstasy of horror, and, slipping upon one of the many old newspapers scattered about, toppled backwards and struck my head upon the floor—evidently with sufficient force to render me absolutely unconscious."

"I see," said Captain Russell, regarding me with a look of peculiar intensity as he tugged meditatively on a corner of his luxuriant moustache. "Well," he sighed after a momentary pause. "It appears, Mr. Poe, that, once again, you have rendered us an inestimable service. Your persistence, ingenuity, and singular powers of both observation and deduction have led to a discovery which had escaped the best efforts of myself and my associates."

I acknowledged this tribute with a gracious nod. "But how," I inquired, "did you come to learn of my presence?"

"It was the neighbor lady," the frontiersman declared. "Mrs.—dang it all, but I've disremembered her name."

"Mrs. Purviance," Captain Russell said to Crockett; then, turning to me, he explained: "Hearing a piercing shriek from these premises—which carried clearly through the kitchen window that we had left open for the pupose of ventilation—the good woman immediately dashed into this apartment from her dwelling next door and found you sprawled upon the floor. In the next instant, she caught sight of the gap in the boards and, peering within, ran to police headquarters in a condition of nearly uncontrolled hysteria."

"Can't hardly blame her for taking on so," said Crockett. "I'm blest if that thing over yonder ain't downright *horrificacious*." And, so saying, he tilted his head in the direction of the three police officers who were, at that moment, in the process of removing the buried horror from its place of concealment beneath the planking.

It was the body of an elderly male, clothed in a frayed, cambric shirt and patched, tattered trousers. Having already glimpsed the thing once, I was better prepared for the sheer ghastliness of its condition. Even so, I took a moment to steel my nerves before focussing my attention on the hideous remains that now lay stretched upon the floor.

That the corpse was that of Alexander Montague seemed incontrovertible. The deplorable state of the clothing—the haggardness of the frame—the sparse, grizzled tufts sprouting from the temples of the otherwise hairless skull—all clearly betokened that the body was that of a pitiably undernourished and indigent old man. Even his most intimate acquaintances, however, would have been unable to identify the deceased from what remained of his *features*—so fearful—so gruesome—so inhumanly *savage*—were the wounds that had been inflicted on the victim's countenance!

The eyes had been gouged from their sockets, leaving a pair of loathsome, blood-encrusted cavities. The nose had been entirely excised, and, in its place, a ragged, roughly triangular hole gaped in the center of the face. As ghastly as these mutilations were, however, they did not compare—in terms of sheer *grotesqueness* —to the awful condition of the mouth, whose corners had been brutally sliced upwards, almost to the level of the ears, endowing the dead man with the leering—the indescribably *macabre*—appearance of a Hallowe'en "Jack-o'-lantern."

In a voice half-choked with revulsion and outrage, Captain Russell observed: "Never, in all my years as an officer of the law, have I been witness to a crime of so bloodthirsty—so *fiendish*—a nature."

"I reckon I ain't neither," Crockett said grimly— then added: "Except only once."

Shooting him a sharp, inquisitive look, Captain Russell asked: "Yes? And when was that?"

The frontiersman folded his arms across his capacious chest, and—turning towards Captain Russell— replied thusly: "Way back in the winter of '14, when I was fighting alongside Ol' Hick'ry in the Redstick Wars. We had us a young feller in our troop—maybe eighteen years of age—by the name of Gibson. Rance Gibson. To look at him, you'd a reckoned he hadn't no more harm in him than a newborn baby lamb. Had curly blond hair as soft as any school-gal's, and eyes as clear and blue as a Tennessee mountain stream. But when the killing commenced, why, them eyes'd blaze like the devil's—and that sweet li'l ol' lamb would turn uglier'n a copperhead in July.

"I recollect one time in particular, when we was heading southwards to join forces with Major Daniel Beasley's company down around Fort Talladega. We were fording the Coosa River when a whole passel of Creek warriors come a-whooping and a-hollering out of the woods like a cloud of Egyptian locusts. Well, me and the boys yanked out our firearms and, in less time than it takes to skin a badger, we had 'em on the run. Chased 'em all the way down to Tallusahatchee, where a couple dozen of the varmints took refuge in an empty log house. Well, we set that house on fire, and every time one of them red devils come running out through the door, we shot 'em down like dogs.

"As we was enjoying this sport, one injun boy— couldn't a been no older than twelve or thirteen— come a-tearin' through the door and got shot just a few feet away from the burning house. His arms and legs was all shattered, and he had fallen so near to the fire that the grease was just a-*stewin'* out of him. But I'll be hanged if he wasn't still alive and doing his damnedest to crawl along the ground. Not a murmur escaped him, neither. So sullen is your redskin when his dander is up that he had sooner die than make a noise or ask for quarters.

"Anyways, I was just taking aim with ol' Betsy to put the boy out of his misery when I saw one of my own men run up to the redskin, fall upon him with a blood-curdling cry, and commence to carve him up with a big ol' huntin' knife. I was plumb dumb-foundered to see such savagerous behavior in a white man. And when I saw just who it *was*, why, you coulda knocked me over with a feather pillow.

"It wasn't none other than that sweet-faced young 'un, Rance Gibson!

"Well, I jumped from my hiding place and come a-running up beside him. Before I could reach him, though, he'd already carved up that redskin boy like a Thanksgiving Day turkey. Sliced off his ears, his nose, and was commencing to work on the fingers when I grabbed him by the wrist and asked just what in tarnation he thought he was doing. He looked at me with a smile so mean that I'll be hanged if it didn't give me the fantods. Said he was collecting some trophies. Said he planned to dry 'em out like beef jerky and wear 'em on a necklace.

"And that's just what he done. Strung 'em on a leather thong and wore 'em 'round his neck."

Here, Crockett breathed a sigh and shook his head slowly, before concluding: "Would a took the injun boy's pecker, too, if I hadn't a stopped him."

By the time Crockett had completed this appalling tale, the stillness in the room was so intense as to be almost palpable. Not only Captain Russell and myself but the three police officers as well—who were huddled around Montague's corpse—stared at the frontiersman in a state of utter—of *awestricken*—silence.

It was Captain Russell who finally spoke. "The atrocities you describe, Colonel Crockett, do indeed sound remarkably similar to the horrors that have been inflicted on the present victim. Is there any possibility that this Gibson fellow, now grown into full manhood, is currently residing in Baltimore, where he has embarked on a career of ghastly murder to satisfy his unnatural blood-lust?"

Crockett gave a mirthless snort through his nose. "'Tain't likely, Cap'n. Wearing that necklace proved to be a mighty poor idea on ol' Rance's part. A couple of weeks after the scrape I just mentioned, me 'n' my troop was ambushed by a party of Creek warriors down around a place called the Horseshoe Bend on the Tallapoosa River. We finally beat 'em back, but ol' Rance was took captive. I guess them injuns didn't cotton to the notion of him wearin' pieces of one of their own kind as a knickknack. By the time me and the boys found ol' Rance, them Creeks had been having their fun with him for a good twenty-four hours."

"I presume he was dead," said Captain Russell.

"Not yet," Crockett replied grimly. "Though he sure-enough wished he *was*. Them infernal varmints had cut a little hole in his belly, yanked out one end of his guts, tied it to a dog, and made the cur run 'round a big wood post 'til Rance's innards was all unwound. And that was just for starters! He was still breathing when we found him, but we soon put him out of his misery."

Several moments elapsed before Captain Russell found his voice. "We must assume, then," he observed somewhat hoarsely, "that the killer of both Alexander Montague and Elmira Macready is a creature of a similar ilk—someone possessed of a profoundly disturbed imagination that is capable of conceiving the most grotesque horrors and morbid acts. Once we locate such a man, we are sure to have found the perpetrator of these unspeakable crimes!"

"I reckon you are right, Cap'n," Crockett replied. "But tracking down such a critter is likely to be trickier than——" All at once, the frontiersman interrupted his statement and, in a deeply solicitous tone, inquired: "You feeling all right, Poe?"

"Fine," I replied—though, in fact, a sudden, sickening wave of dizziness had swept through my brain, causing my head to reel and my vision to darken. Placing one hand over my eyes, I propped my elbow on the tabletop and waited for the vertiginous sensation to pass.

Stepping to my side, the frontiersman gently remarked: "Sorry, pard. I reckon it wasn't good judgment to go on that way about such horribleness." Reaching down one hand, he laid it upon my shoulder and said: "You have done a rattling good day's work, ol' hoss. Let me help you to your feet, and I will fetch you home."

CHAPTER 18

Crockett's proposal to escort me home to Amity Street would, under ordinary circumstances, have been greeted with a polite but firm refusal; for—in spite of the lateness of the hour and the dreary expanse of deserted thoroughfares that lay between Montague's dwelling and my own—I would normally have required no such assistance. My nerves, however, had been so completely unstrung by the dismaying events of the day that I not only acceded to his offer but positively *welcomed* it.

Even with Crockett's companionship, the long march homeward promised to be a wearisome undertaking, given my state of extreme emotional and physical *depletion*. The reader may thus imagine my intense and delighted surprise when—upon emerging with Crockett from Montague's dwelling—I spied a handsome chaise hitched to the wooden post directly in front of the house.

Undoing the reins, the frontiersman climbed into this conveyance and motioned me to assume the seat beside him. "Mr. Potter, the hotel manager, loaned me the use of this-here buggy for as long as I am lodging here in Baltimore," my companion informed me as I settled into my place. "Said he reckoned a man of my station ought to be riding around in style." Then, with a flick of the reins and a cluck of the tongue, Crockett urged the steed forward.

As we proceeded along the moonlit streets towards our destination, the rhythmic motions of the carriage, combined with the hollow clopping of the animal's hooves upon the paving-stones, seemed to lull me into a sort of Mesmeric trance. My eyelids felt weighted with lead—my head drooped—my shoulders slumped—my mouth hung partway open. Sunk into this stuporous state—incapable not merely of speech but, indeed, of coherent thought—I sat dully beside my companion, so utterly oblivious of our progress that I bolted erect with a startled gasp when the chaise suddenly drew to a halt and the frontiersman announced: "Here we are, ol' hoss. You'd best git yourself straight to bed. I'll be shot with a packsaddle if you ain't plumb tuckered out."

With a muttered word of gratitude, I dismounted from the vehicle and made my way towards my front door.

"I will see you and them two purty gals of yours tomorrow evening," Crockett said by way of farewell, as he skillfully maneuvered the carriage around and headed back in the direction from whence we had travelled.

The extremity of my mental fatigue was such that I could make no sense of Crockett's parting words. For what unexplained reason he intended to visit my household on the morrow I neither knew nor cared. My only thought at that moment was of the sweet, unutterably beguiling object that lay just within the walls of my abode. I mean, of course, my *bed*.

Slipping inside my dwelling, I closed the door carefully behind me and paused briefly in the entrance-way. The interior of the house was as silent and dark as the tomb. Evidently, Muddy had remained ignorant of my surreptitious departure from the house after supper. Had my absence been discovered, I would undoubtedly have found her seated at the kitchen table, anxiously awaiting my return.

Making my way down the lightless but utterly familiar hallway towards my bedchamber, I cautiously opened the door and stole inside. The curtains of my window had not been drawn, and moonlight—pale and ghostly— streamed through the unobstructed panes. So profound was my fatigue that the mere prospect of exchanging my garments for a nightshirt plunged my soul into despair. Staggering towards the bed, I collapsed face downward upon the mattress and fell instantly asleep.

To those who—for whatever reason of bodily or emotional suffering—have endured its prolonged deprivation, there is nothing on earth (or in heaven) more devoutly to be desired than sleep. Nowhere is this truth made more wrenchingly evident than in the justly renowned soliloquy of the tormented protagonist of Shakespeare's magnificent (if, perhaps, somewhat imperfectly motivated) tragedy *Macbeth*:

> Methought I heard a voice cry "Sleep no more!
> Macbeth does murder sleep"—the innocent sleep,
> Sleep that knits up the ravelled sleave of care,
> The death of each day's life, sore labor's bath,
> Balm of hurt minds, great nature's second course,
> Chief nourisher in life's feast.

And yet, while few passages in literature possess more of the truly *sublime*, these lines do not take sufficient account of a no less important, though absolutely *contrary*, phenomenon—the degree to which sleep itself may, on occasion, be the source, not of healing, solace, and refreshment, but of the very opposite effects: to wit, nervous agitation, spiritual unease, and even more debilitating exhaustion.

Such, unhappily, was the case with the vexed and tormented slumber I experienced that night. Awakening with a sob from a harrowing dream—in which a chimerical creature with vulture wings, a woman's head, and the body and legs of an arachnid pursued me through a labyrinth of subterranean chambers—I lay prone upon the mattress and stared wildly about my chamber. From the intensity of the daylight suffusing the room, I deduced that the morning was already well advanced, and—consulting my clock—saw to my astonishment that the time was approaching the noon hour!

Dragging myself from my bed, I stood for a moment with throbbing head and reeling brain, like a man attempting to readjust to solid land following a protracted voyage at sea. Eventually my dizziness subsided, and—crossing unsteadily to the washstand which stood at the opposite end of my chamber—I splashed a handful of cold water onto my face before regarding myself in my shaving-mirror.

The debilitating effects of that long and surpassingly *dreary* night were all-too-plainly inscribed upon my countenance. The mere sight of my reflection in the glass—of my pale and haggard complexion—of the purplish sacs depending from beneath my eyes—of the intricate webwork of crimson capillaries defacing the orbs themselves—brought an involuntary gasp of dismay from my lips. Turning from the glass with a shudder of revulsion, I traversed my chamber, flung open the door, and stepped into the hallway.

No sooner had I done so than my finely attuned auditory sense was struck, not by any particular sound, but—on the contrary—by the entire *absence* of acoustical stimuli. An intense, almost preternatural, *hush* seemed to suffuse the atmosphere, suggesting that mine was the only living presence in the dwelling. This impression was quickly confirmed when—upon calling out to both Muddy and Sissy—I received no reply.

Deeply puzzled by this strange, this *unaccountable*, development, I proceeded to the kitchen, where the mystery was immediately resolved. For there, at my place at the table—along with a platter holding several biscuits and a single slice of cured ham—lay a sheet of paper that contained the following message, inscribed in my darling Muddy's neat, if somewhat childlike, hand:

Dearest Eddie,

We have gone to the market to buy the necessaries for tonight's dinner with Colonel Crockett. We left at 11. The door to your bedchamber was still closed and all was silent within. Oh, Eddie! It is so nice that you have finally managed to get a good night's sleep! Here is your breakfast, dear. We will return later.

Your own
Muddy

I now recalled Crockett's solemn vow to come and listen to Sissy's enchanting *repertoire* of ballads. Of course! So *that* was the occasion to which he had been alluding when he took his departure last evening! The extraordinary events of the past twenty-four hours had driven all thoughts of his promised visit from my mind.

The mere prospect of having to play host to the frontiersman caused my heart to sink within my bosom. Few social requirements are more supremely wearying than the effort to maintain a convivial mien when one's soul is weighted down by care. Still, I could see no way to avoid, much less to defer, tonight's *fête*.

So fervently had Sissy been anticipating the affair that I had no other alternative than to resign myself to its inevitable—and all-too-imminent—occurrence.

Fortifying myself with the simple but wholesome breakfast that Muddy had provided, I rose from the table and repaired to my study. I was painfully aware that an inordinate number of days had passed since I had last applied myself to my creative endeavors. I was already long overdue on the delivery of a promised tale of *sensation* for publication in a future number of the *Southern Literary Messenger.* And yet, to endeavor to engage in the act of literary composition seemed, at that moment, entirely futile. The all-too-vivid recollection of the horror I had witnessed on the previous eve—of the butchered old man buried beneath the floorboards of his own home—precluded the possibility of the sort of sustained imaginative effort necessary for artistic production.

It was imperative, moreover, that—until the present crisis was resolved—every modicum of my energy be devoted to its resolution. As long as the unknown perpetrator remained at large, no one in the city was safe from the maniac's knife. There was, I confess, another and more immediately *self-interested* reason for my extreme sense of urgency. My latest encounter with the dark, uncanny female in the gloom of Montague's dwelling had reinforced my conviction that—in some distinct, if still-inexplicable, way—the horrors that had descended upon our fair city were intimately connected with *myself.*

Closing the study door behind me, I crossed to my writing table. As I lowered myself into my seat, my gaze fell upon the yellowed newspaper review of my mother's long-ago performance at the Front Street Theatre. No sooner did I notice this item—which lay precisely where I had left it the previous evening—than I was struck with a singular notion.

Up until that moment, I had scrutinized this article solely with an eye to identifying the various, eminent audience members whose names were mentioned within the text. The thought now occurred to me that a clue to the mystery might reside elsewhere—namely, in the particular *play* that was performed on that memorable evening in 1807. This, as the reader will recall, was Shakespeare's supreme tragedy *King Lear*, in which my mother had won such excited acclaim in the *rôle* of Cordelia, the elderly monarch's doomed, saintly daughter.

Retrieving my well-worn edition of Shakespeare's complete dramatic works from the shelf on which it stood, I reseated myself at my desk and opened the heavy, leather-bound volume to the appropriate place. Within minutes, I was so entirely engrossed in this *towering* (if, perhaps, somewhat overly protracted) masterpiece that I grew entirely oblivious of my surroundings. By the time I arrived at the almost unbearable *dénouement* of the play, my eyes were moist—my bosom had begun to heave—and a thick mucosal lump, or *globus hystericus*, had risen into my throat. The mental image of the anguished old man, cradling the corpse of his grievously wronged, yet ever-devoted, child proved more wrenching than my overtaxed emotions could tolerate (particularly since, within my mind's eye, the lifeless figure draped in the howling king's arms was that of my own deceased mother!). Laying the heavy book aside, I buried my face in my hands and wept.

Eventually my tears subsided. So intense—so utterly irresistible—was the spell cast by Shakespeare's lofty genius that, reaching again for the book, I quickly became immersed in another of his plays—then another—and another. The single interruption occurred when Muddy appeared at my door to inform me that she and Sissy had returned from their expedition. We spent several minutes engaged in pleasant, if largely inconsequential, conversation before I returned to my reading. Thus the hours elapsed until—by the dimming of the daylight seeping in through my study window—I discerned that the afternoon was rapidly advancing and that Colonel Crockett's arrival could not be far off.

It has frequently been observed that the entirety of human experience—all that can be known of nature, the world, and the "poor, bare, forked" beings who inhabit it—is contained within the compass of Shakespeare's unsurpassed works. For this reason, the British poet Coleridge (whose opinions on literary matters, though rarely *original*, are asserted with a singular authority) deservedly describes the Bard as "our *myriad-minded* Shakespeare." And indeed, should I ever find myself aboard an ocean-going vessel whose crew, after engaging in a violent mutiny, horribly butchers the officers and sets the surviving passengers adrift in a meagrely provisioned lifeboat; and should I then be washed ashore upon a tropical isle inhabited solely by savage cannibals, venomous serpents, and blood-thirsty predators—I think that I could *still* find contentment so long as I had, as my constant companion, my leather-bound volume of Shakespeare's unexcelled *oeuvre*.

My examination of *Lear* and the other plays I perused that afternoon only confirmed this impression of the *preternatural* richness of the Bard's inexhaustible imagination. Every aspect of existence seemed present in his work—every degree of baseness and nobility, of sacrifice and betrayal, of love and hatred, of soaring tragedy and coarse, uproarious comedy. Indeed, one thing only appeared to be missing from those pages.

Try as I might, I could not discover a single clue that would shed light on the meaning of the grim and inscrutable word "NEVERMORE."

CHAPTER 19

Among the countless examples of unparalleled wisdom contained within the *corpus* of Shakespeare's plays is the immortal observation put forth by the melancholic Jaques in the pastoral comedy *As You Like It*: "All the world's a stage,/And all the men and women merely players." When one considers the degree to which every human being is compelled, from the era of earliest childhood, to conceal his innermost self behind a mask of conventional propriety, the fundamental truth of this epigram can hardly be contested.

Nevertheless, it is equally the case that certain *exceptional* men and women are more innately suited to play-acting than the rest of humankind. Such, indeed, was my own situation. From the days of my youth—when I had earned the plaudits of my classmates for my performance as Colonel Manly in a school production of Royall Tyler's delightful comedy, *The Contrast*—I have been noted for the plenitude—if not, indeed, the *prodigality*—of my histrionic gifts. That I should have been endowed so abundantly with this skill is, of course, a matter of little surprise, considering the brilliantly talented being who brought me into this world. (That the father who sired me was also engaged in the theatrical trade has little bearing on the matter, since his abilities were of such a notoriously negligible stripe.) To be sure, science has yet to account for the mechanism by which certain traits of character and ability—no less than of physical appearance—are transmitted from one generation to the next. But that our intellectual powers, our aesthetic aptitudes, indeed even our *moral* faculties, spring primarily from heredity—far more than from the circumstances of our upbringing or education—can hardly be doubted.

At all events, my intrinsic capacities in this regard stood me in especially good stead on the evening of Crockett's visit, permitting me to assume a *façade* of polite sociability, even while my soul remained in a state of extreme and tumultuous agitation.

Crockett arrived just at sundown, attired in his customary garb. In one hand he clutched a bouquet of posies; in the other, he held a small, oblong package wrapped in white paper and secured with a length of string.

Standing in the entranceway of our abode, he extended the paper-wrapped bundle towards Muddy, who had arrayed herself for the occasion in her most becoming blue-calico dress. "Blamed if you don't look downright elegant in that get-up, Miz Clemm," he declared. "Here. These sweetmeats are for you."

Then—as Muddy accepted the gift with a

delighted exclamation of gratitude—he held out the bouquet to Sissy. "And I brought these-here flowers for you, Miz Virginny."

Snatching it from his hands, Sissy buried her face in the blossoms, deeply inhaled their aroma, then looked up at Crockett with her face all aglow. "Oooh, thank you, thank you, thank you! They are so *very* beautiful!"

"Not half so much as you, Miz Virginny," replied the frontiersman with a smile.

"Oh, where shall I keep them?" cried Sissy, casting an inquiring look at Muddy.

"Come, dear," said the good woman. "Let us find a nice jar and put them in water." Then—excusing herself with a little curtsy—she turned and led Sissy in the direction of the kitchen.

As my two loved ones bustled down the hallway, Crockett turned in my direction and—after scrutinizing my visage for a moment—said with a frown: "Why, you are looking kind of blue around the gills, Poe."

"The lineaments of distress that you perceive upon my countenance," I replied, "are merely the natural response to the deeply unsettling events of the past several days."

"Why, I can't hardly blame you for that," said Crockett. "Danged if this business ain't left me feelin' downright uneasy myself. Tell you what. Let's me and you have us a pow-wow before I leave, so we can cipher out our next move."

"I endorse your suggestion wholeheartedly," I declared.

"All right, then," said the frontiersman, reaching out a hand and clapping me upon the shoulder. "Now let's go hunt up them two purty gals and have ourselves a *time*. Hang me up for bear-meat if I ain't as hungry as seven wolves tied together by the tail!"

The frontiersman's irrepressible enthusiasm, undiminished even by the grisly horror we had so recently witnessed in the home of Alexander Montague, ensured that the dinner would be an exceptionally lively one—at least from the viewpoint of Muddy and Sissy. As for me, the evening proved even more trying than I had anticipated; for I was compelled—despite my intensely *agitated* mood—to sustain an air of polite attentiveness while Crockett regaled us with endless tales of his heroic and wildly improbable frontier exploits.

Even the most far-fetched of these anecdotes, however—such as his wholly incredible account of capturing an enormous mammal of the species *Procyon lotor* (more commonly known as a *raccoon*) by *grinning* at the creature until it plummeted from its perch on a tree-branch—seemed reasonable in comparison to his concluding story. This outrageous narrative was related as our dinner finally drew to an end, in response to a somewhat impetuous query tendered by my darling Sissy.

Our meal—a simple but savory stew of beef, potatoes, and various seasonal vegetables—having been completed, we were seated 'round the table, enjoying our post-prandial beverages while partaking of the store-bought confections Crockett had purchased. All at once, Sissy, who had been attending to our guest's fantastical narratives with a look of delighted (and, to my eyes, intensely *irksome*) admiration, set her tumbler of milk down upon the table and exclaimed: "Colonel Crockett. You have told us such *wonderful* tales about your adventures! But there is one thing you *haven't* told us. Have you ever been in love?"

"Virginia!" Muddy gasped in consternation, placing the fingers of one hand upon her lips. "What a little nosy-parker you are!"

"No, no, Miz Clemm!" chuckled the frontiersman. "No need for reproving the gal. It's a natural enough question." Then quaffing the remainder of his coffee, he replaced the cup upon its saucer, swivelled in his chair, and gazed at Sissy with a look of utter solemnity upon his countenance. "Yes, Miz Virginny, there was once a gal I loved so bad my heart would rise smack up into my throat and choke me like a cold potato whenever I thought of her."

"Really?" cried Virginia. "And what happened?"

"Why, I couldn't hardly go around feeling so tee-totaciously out-of-sorts all the time," Crockett replied. "So I found a way to cure myself."

"*Cure* yourself?" Virginia exclaimed.

"Yes, ma'am. Through the splendiferous healing powers of *e*-lectricity."

Then, as both Muddy and Sissy gaped at him in wonder, the frontiersman folded his arms across his chest and continued thusly: "You see, a few years back, when I first came to Washington City, I heard-tell about this monstrous smart doctor that had found a way to put *e*-lectricity into glass bottles. And when a feller had the rheumatiz or the Saint Vitals dance or just about anythin' else that was plaguing him, why this ol' doc would just pour some of that *e*-lectricity down that feller's throat, and blamed if it wouldn't cure him as clean as a barked tree!

"So I saw how it was done and determined that whenever anything ailed me, I would try it. Only I didn't give a hoot about the bottles, for I reckoned I could just as well take some *e*-lectricity in the raw as it came shooting from the clouds during a thunderstorm. You see, I had been used to drinkin' out of the Mississippi without a cup, so I figgered I could just as well swallow the lightning straight from the sky.

"Now, as I was saying, along about this time, I fell in love with a gal by the name o' Margaret Botts. Just looking at that little filly made my heart begin to flutter like a duck in a puddle. There was a problem, though. I'll be hanged if that pesky little gal wasn't already hitched to another feller!

"Well, ol' Davy wasn't about to go barking up another man's tree. So I set about to study on the problem, and at last I calculated a solution. I reckoned I would get rid of my passions by swallowin' some *e*-lectricity.

"I knew it had to be done by bringing the lightning right smack against my heart and driving the love clear out of it. So I waited 'til there was a pestiferous thundergust one afternoon. Then I went out into the countryside, and I stood there with my mouth wide open, so that the *e*-lectricity might run down and hit my heart and cure it of love. I stood so for an hour, and then I saw a thunderbolt a-coming, and I dodged my mouth right under it, and—bang!—it went clear down my throat! My land! It was as if a whole tribe of buffaloes was kicking inside my bowels. My heart spun around amongst my insides like a grindstone going by steam, but the lightning went clear through me and tore my trousers clean off as it come out t'other end.

"I had a mighty sore gizzard for two weeks afterward, and my innards was so hot that I used to eat raw vittles and they would be cooked before they got fairly down my throat.

"But that-there *e*-lectricity plumb did the job—for I ain't never felt love since."

While this crude backwoods "yarn"—with its unseemly emphasis on alimentary processes—struck me as entirely unsuitable for the dinner table, it elicited a lively, not to say *intemperate*, display of amusement from both Muddy and Sissy. At length—their hilarity having subsided—our guest sat forward in his chair, delivered a resounding slap to one knee, and declared: "Well now, ladies, I reckon I've done enough jabbering for one night." Turning to gaze directly at Sissy, he said: "Miz Virginny, it would make me happier than a dog with two tails to hear you sing for a spell."

Sissy clapped her hands excitedly. "Goody!" she

cried. "Come!" Then—springing from her seat—she hurried from the kitchen.

Crockett, Muddy, and I rose from the table and proceeded into the parlor, where Sissy had already stationed herself in the center of the room. While Crockett lowered himself into the solitary easy chair positioned by the fireplace, Muddy and I arranged ourselves on the little settee. No sooner had we taken our places than Sissy—her delicate white hands clasped before her bosom and her sweet, seraphic countenance positively *lustrous* with excitement—announced her intention to commence with the engaging ditty, "We're on Our Way to Baltimore." Raising her eyes heavenward, she parted her lips and began to sing:

> "We're on our way to Baltimore,
> With two behind and two before,
> Around, around, around we go,
> Where oats, peas, beans, and barley grow,
> In waiting for somebody!
>
> "'Tis thus the farmer sows his seed,
> Folds his arms and takes his ease,
> Stamps his feet and claps his hands,
> Wheels around and thus he stands,
> In waiting for somebody!"

As the rollicking melody poured from the darling maiden's white and surpassingly *shapely* throat—filling the room with sounds unlike any ever heard by mortal ears in the mere *sublunary* realm—I could feel my extreme agitation of spirit begin to abate. Such was the intensely soothing effect of Sissy's unearthly vocalizations that—however often I had listened in wonder to the wildly melodic rhapsodies that issued from her lips—they never failed to have a deliciously palliative, if not actively *sedative*, effect upon my soul.

No sooner had she completed the ditty than Sissy—after acknowledging our applause with a charming curtsy—embarked upon another song—then another—and another—until it became evident that we were to be treated to her entire musical repertoire. Very gradually—while Crockett clapped his hands and stamped his feet to the rhythm of each separate number—Sissy's ineffable rendition of such standards as "Home, Daughter, Home," "Green Willow," and "The Butcher Boy" induced within my soul a condition not unlike that experienced by the confirmed user of opium who—having indulged to excess in his habitual vice—sinks into a profound, if not entirely disagreeable, trance.

How much time elapsed while I remained in this pleasurably stuporous condition, I am at a loss to say. All at once, I grew cognizant of a sudden cessation of sound. Sissy had stopped singing!

As my inebriated senses began to regain their normal acuity, I perceived that the angelic maiden was standing in an attitude of intense contemplation, her right index finger pressed against her tight-squeezed lips, her pale brow furrowed, her gaze directed downward. At last she shrugged—sighed—and, looking at Crockett, declared: "I can't think of any more songs."

"What about 'The Amsterdam Maid'?" Muddy piped up beside me.

"Oh yes!" Sissy cried delightedly. "I forgot!" Then extending one delicate hand in her mother's direction, she exclaimed: "Come, Muddy. Sing it with me!"

"Goodness, no!" the dear woman cried, rapidly waving one hand back and forth in a gesture of emphatic demurral.

"Go on now, Miz Clemm," the frontiersman urged. "I'd be tickled to hear the two of you singing together."

"We-e-ell," Muddy said in a relenting tone. "All right, then." Rising to her feet, she moved to Sissy's side and placed her arm around her daughter's shoulder. Then—as the two stood gazing fondly at each other—the heaven-sent pair began to perform the rousing old "shanty" in voices of surpassing beauty:

> "In Amsterdam there lived a maid
> And she was mistress of her trade,
> I'll go no more a-roving with you, fair maid.

> "For a-roving, a-roving, since roving's been my ruin,
> I'll go no more a-roving with you, fair maid.

> "Her eyes were like two stars at night,
> And her cheeks they rivalled the roses red,
> I'll go no more a-roving with you, fair maid. . . ."

As the song proceeded, Muddy—who had appeared somewhat constrained at the start—grew increasingly animated, rolling her eyes, tapping one foot, and swaying her body in time to the music. Gazing upon the dear-hearted woman, I could not help but marvel—as I had done on so many previous occasions—at the deep, the *inexplicable* paradox which she embodied. Here was a woman of such profound inward beauty—such sheer, preternatural *goodness*—that her soul seemed utterly unblemished by the merest speck of earthly imperfection. And yet she was related, by the closest ties of kinship, to a being whom I had every reason to detest. I mean, of course, her brother—my natural father—David Poe, Jr., the creature who had abandoned his young wife and infant children in the most heartless fashion conceivable. By what strange, hereditary means could two such contrasting, even *antithetical*, personalities have sprung from the same ancestral roots? It was a mystery all insoluble.

The song ended. While the two performers blushed, beamed, and curtsied, Crockett and I burst into a wild ovation.

"Hurrah!" cheered the frontiersman. "That was prime, and no mistake!"

"Brava!" I cried, rising to my feet. "Rarely have I been privileged to hear such intoxicating, such richly *melodious* sounds!"

All at once, Sissy pointed a dainty forefinger in my direction and exclaimed: "Now it's your turn, Eddie!"

This unforeseen remark startled me into a momentary silence. "I beg your pardon?" I replied at last.

"The gal is right, Poe," Crockett said. "You are the only one among us who hasn't pitched in tonight."

Here was a truly unexpected turn! Had it occurred earlier in the evening, I would surely have resisted. My dismal mood, however, had been considerably brightened by the buoyant duet which my loved ones had just performed. Moreover, I could see that the long and wearying party was rapidly drawing to a close—a prospect that could not fail to infuse my heart with a sense of the keenest satisfaction. In short, for the first time that evening, I was feeling positively *festive*.

"I will be happy to accommodate your request," I said with a smile and a bow. Exchanging places with Muddy and Sissy, I positioned myself in the center of the room, while my loved ones arranged themselves on the settee. For several moments, I stood in silent rumination. At length, I gazed at my auditors and announced: "Ladies and gentleman. For your pleasure and edification, I shall recite one of the most powerful and poignant poems in our language. It was composed in 1586 by a young Englishman named Chidiock Tichborne. A Catholic noble who plotted to replace Queen Elizabeth with a monarch of his own faith, Tichborne was sent to the dreaded Tower of London to await execution for treason. On the night prior to his beheading, he composed a moving letter of farewell to his devoted young wife, Agnes, enclosing the following stanzas. These were later set to music and published in a widely distributed collection of madrigals. The poem, which has come to be known as 'Tichborne's Elegy,' goes thusly."

Placing one hand upon my bosom and raising the other aloft, I directed my gaze towards the ceiling and proceeded to declaim the following verses:

"My prime of youth is but a frost of cares,
My feast of joy is but a dish of pain,
My crop of corn is but a field of tares,
And all my good is but vain hope of gain;
The day is past, and yet I saw no sun,
And now I live, and now my life is done.

"My tale was heard and yet it was not told,
My fruit is fallen and yet my leaves are green,
My youth is spent and yet I am not old,
I saw the world and yet I was not seen;
My thread is cut and yet it is not spun,
And now I live, and now my life is done.

"I sought my death and found it in my womb,
I looked for life and saw it was a shade,
I trod the earth and knew it was my tomb,
And now I die, and now I was but made;
My glass is full, and now my glass is run,
And now I live, and now my life is done."

Having enunciated the final words, I maintained my position for a moment while awaiting the expected ovation. To my surprise, however, my performance was greeted, not by a burst of applause, but by a heavy—protracted—and absolute—silence. Gazing at my auditors, I saw that both Muddy and Sissy were staring at me with expressions that were nothing short of *stricken*.

"Oh, Eddie," cried Sissy. "That was so dreadfully sad! Did you say that Mr. Tichborne was *killed* after writing that poem?"

I nodded. "He was led to the block early the next morning and beheaded."

Sissy gasped and raised a hand to her throat.

"And the poem was written to his wife?" inquired Muddy in a tremulous voice.

"Yes," I answered. "It was included in a letter of farewell that he composed to his beloved soul-mate just hours before he faced the executioner's blade."

"And how old was he when he died?" Muddy asked, her voice cracking slightly.

"A mere twenty-eight."

A silent moment ensued as Muddy and Sissy turned to gaze at each other, their darling features arranged into identical expressions of intense and sorrow-laden *dismay*. All at once, Sissy burst into tears, leapt from the settee, and dashed from the room. Muddy, her own eyes brimming with moisture, quickly rose to her feet and bustled after her sobbing daughter.

Somewhat thunderstruck by the intensity of my loved ones' reaction, I turned to look at Crockett, who was regarding me with a wry expression while shaking his head slowly from side to side. At length, he slapped both hands upon his thighs and pushed himself erect.

"By jings, Poe, but you are a regular barrel of fun," he said as he stepped to my side. Placing his hands upon his hips, he gazed at the doorway through which Muddy and Sissy had fled. "Reckon me and you might as well attend to our business," he said, emitting a sigh. "Looks like this-here party is *over!*"

CHAPTER 20

Ushering Crockett into my *sanctum*, I enkindled the oil lamp that stood upon my writing table; whereupon—reaching into the breast pocket of his high-collared coat—the frontiersman extracted two *panatelas* and extended one towards me.

"Smoke?" he inquired.

Though I had partaken of cigars on certain rare social occasions (such as the farewell dinner given to me by my fellow cadets, following my cunningly contrived discharge from the United States Military Academy at West Point), I had never developed a fondness for the habit—my finely wrought constitution being in no small degree susceptible to the intoxicating influences of tobacco. I therefore declined Crockett's offer with a polite shake of the head.

Returning the proffered cigar to his pocket, Crockett placed the other one between his teeth, bit off the tip, then positioned the head directly over the glowing chimney of the oil lamp. Having ignited it to his satisfaction, he seated himself in the straight-backed chair that faced the writing table, crossed one leg over the other, and—eyes narrowed against the plumes of smoke drifting upwards from his pana-tela—regarded me intently.

As I scrutinized his countenance in turn, I perceived that his expression—which, throughout the evening, had been luminous with pleasure—was now deeply clouded with concern. "Is something the matter, Colonel Crockett?" I inquired. "You appear, of a sudden, to have lapsed into a mood of uncharacteristic solemnity."

Plucking the cigar from his mouth, the frontiersman released a thick plume of smoke into the room. "I didn't want to spoil the party for you and the gals, Poe, so I did my damnedest to shove my worries aside for a spell. But I have been in a mighty black humor since earlier today."

"And what is the cause of your unhappiness?"

"When I got back to the hotel, there was a message from my crony in Washington City, Mr. Thomas Chilton. Seems like my enemies in Congress are fixing to push through Ol' Hick'ry's Injun Bill."

"I assume that you are referring to the government's plan to dispossess the Southwestern tribes of their rightfully deeded territories and remove them to far less favorable tracts west of the Mississippi?" The impassioned debate over this proposal having been extensively reported in the newspapers, I was, of course, familiar with its details.

"That's the one," Crockett said grimly. "Why, if I

don't get re-elected, them redskins will never get a fair shake."

"I must confess, Colonel Crockett," said I, "that—in light of both your youthful exploits in the Creek War and your frequent denigrations of the red man's character—I am excessively surprised at your sympathetic concern for the Indian cause."

"Why, Poe," Crockett exclaimed, "you are plumb mistook about my sentiments. I won't deny that I do not look with favor upon a murderous savage hell-bent on mischief. But I have always been a friend to the Chicksaws and Cherokees and other law-abiding tribes. And besides, our government give the injuns our sacred *word*. A treaty is the highest law of the land. I would rather be an old coon dog belonging to a poor man in the forest than belong to any country that won't do justice for all."

For several moments following this fervent declaration, I sat in silent contemplation of the frontiersman, whose deep-rooted integrity, though sometimes obscured by his overbearing manner, could in no way be doubted. At length, I cleared my throat and declared: "In view of the pressing political matters requiring your attention, it is even more imperative that we accomplish our mission in the most expeditious manner possible."

"Amen to that," Crockett said. "Have you ciphered out the meaning of that pestiferous word yet?"

"Sadly," I said with a heartfelt sigh, "and in spite of my prolonged and strenuous efforts to discover its signification, the answer is no." Here, I folded my hands and rested them upon the tabletop. "There is, however, certain information of which I have yet to apprise you—information which, I have good reason to believe, bears directly upon the fearful mystery in which we two have become so deeply embroiled."

"I am all ears," Crockett said, taking another puff of his long, slender cigar.

I leaned forward in my seat and fixed the frontiersman with a penetrating look. "The story that I related to you and Captain Russell, regarding my motive for returning to Montague's dwelling, was not, strictly speaking, the truth."

"Why, what in blue blazes do you mean?" Crockett said, his brow furrowed with perplexity.

"I mean," I replied, "that I have uncovered a singular—albeit inscrutable—connection among the various personages who have met such ghastly deaths over the course of the past, unparalleled week."

Then, having thus thoroughly engaged the frontiersman's attention, I drew a deep breath and proceeded to apprise him of the circumstance that had sent me rushing back to Montague's dwelling in search of clues—i.e., my discovery that, among my collection of cherished *memorabilia*, was a decades-old newspaper clipping composed by Montague and containing allusions to both the Asher and Macready names.

"That something other than mere *coincidence* is involved in this matter," I asserted, "seems to me a deduction beyond reasonable dispute."

For several moments Crockett sat in silence, chewing ruminatively on his glowing panatela, which protruded from one corner of his mouth. "Well," he drawled at length, "that is most uncommon curious, for a certainty. What in tarnation do you make of it?"

"As of yet," I answered with a sigh, "I have been unable to arrive at a satisfactory explanation. It would appear, however, that—at the heart of the mystery that now confronts us—lies some dark and ominous secret involving the theatrical realm."

"Well, I'll be jiggered!" Crockett exclaimed. "The theatre, eh?" Giving his head a regretful shake, he exhaled a stream of cigar smoke and said: "I'm afraid I can't be of much use to you there, ol' hoss. I ain't never even *been* to the theatre excepting only once, and that was to see Mr. James H. Hackett play-acting in *The Lion of the West* in Washington City."

"There is something else that I have yet to divulge," I declared after a momentary pause. "Something of such a fantastic and inexplicable nature that—in spite of having witnessed it with my own eyes—I can scarcely credit the evidence of my senses."

"Don't keep me guessing," said Crockett, "for I am fit to bust with curiosity."

Fully cognizant of the sheer *implausibility* of the information that I was about to impart, I hesitated briefly before declaring: "There was another person in Montague's apartment. A woman."

A long moment passed while Crockett absorbed this remarkable, this *startling* revelation. "A woman?" he said at last, regarding me with a deeply quizzical expression.

"That is correct. She appeared in Montague's bedroom immediately following my appalling discovery of the old man's horribly mutilated corpse."

Regarding me with an intensely doubtful expression, Crockett declared: "Why, it must've been that neighbor lady, Mrs. Purviance."

I gave my head an emphatic shake. "No. While it is true that I obtained only the briefest glimpse of this person before I lapsed into insensibility, my view of her countenance was sufficiently clear to assure me of her identity. The woman I saw—and here I shall not blame you for reacting with a high degree of skepticism, for I am fully aware that the fact I am about to relate is of the most fantastic and anomalous nature—the woman I saw was the identical being who entered my bedroom on the night of the fatal conflagration at the Asher residence!"

Removing his cigar from his lips, Crockett stared at me silently for a moment. "Damn it, Poe," he exclaimed at last, "but that's the *beatenest* thing I ever heard."

"I concur entirely with your assessment."

"Don't you reckon that what you saw was just a figger of your imagination?" Crockett inquired. "After all, you was mighty shook up after turning up that ol' man's carcass."

An involuntary shudder coursed through my being as I recalled the awful—the *unspeakable*—moment when, staggering backwards from the appalling sight I had just glimpsed beneath the floorboards of Alexander Montague's bedchamber, I heard—then felt—then *saw*—the same uncanny creature I had confronted once before.

"I assure you, Colonel Crockett," I said grimly, "that the figure I observed was as palpably real as you yourself."

Re-inserting his half-smoked panatela between his teeth, the frontiersman chewed on the tip for a moment before inquiring: "Why in tarnation didn't you tell Cap'n Russell none of this?"

"For several reasons," I replied. "First, because of my conviction that the mystery might be more expeditiously resolved by a pair of determined and resourceful individuals, operating independently of the police. As you yourself have noted, the professional law officer—even one who, like Captain Russell, is endowed with unusual *acumen*—is invariably hampered in his efforts by the necessity of adhering to the strict protocols of the law. As a consequence of this constraint, the typical police investigation, no matter how vigorously pursued, tends to proceed at a lamentably dilatory pace. In the present circumstance, such a delay is almost certain to have tragic results, given the possibility—or, rather, *likelihood*—that the perpetrator of these atrocities will continue to commit similar outrages until caught."

"Can't hardly argue with you there," Crockett said.

"There is another consideration, too," I said after

a brief pause, "one which—while imbued with a tincture of self-interest—must nevertheless be acknowledged."

"I'm listening," said Crockett.

"Distinct advantages would accrue to each of us should we manage to resolve this mystery on our own. For you, the favorable publicity that you would inevitably receive could only be of benefit in regard to your political ambitions."

"I'd be lying if I denied it," the frontiersman acknowledged. "And how about you, Poe. What do *you* stand to gain?"

The yellowed newspaper review still lay upon the table. By way of replying to the frontiersman's query, I picked it up, rose from my seat, and—stepping to the opposite side of the table—handed it to Crockett.

"Read this," I said, as he cast me a quizzical glance.

Holding the clipping towards the light, Crockett began to peruse it, squinting through the smoky haze issuing from the smoldering tip of his much-reduced panatela. A moment later, he plucked the cigar from his mouth and—gaping up at me—exclaimed: "Why this here writin' is all about *Eliza* Poe! Ain't that your deceased mother?"

I nodded in the affirmative.

"But what in tarnation does all this dad-blasted business have to do with *her?*"

"That, Colonel Crockett, is precisely what I intend to find out."

* * *

Declaring that he was feeling "dog-tired," Crockett took his leave soon afterwards—though not before we had resolved upon a course of action. From my earlier perusal of the newspaper clipping, I had already determined that, among the eminent Baltimoreans identified in the review, only one now remained alive: Mrs. Henrietta Nicodemus, whose late husband, Josiah, had made a considerable fortune as the owner of a large fleet of merchant vessels, following a singularly adventurous career as the captain of the brig *Grampus.* The aged widow, who remained a prominent figure in Baltimore's flourishing social scene, resided in baronial splendor in one of the city's most fashionable districts. It was this magnificent residence—and the elderly (though still-vital) personage who inhabited it—that the frontiersman and I proposed to visit on the morrow.

After bidding me good-night—and enjoining me to tell Muddy and Sissy that the evening had been a "regular slam-whanger"—Crockett departed. No sooner had I locked the front door behind him than, returning to my study, I began to pace rapidly about the floor, my soul in a state of extreme and unbridled *agitation.*

Throughout the course of our dinner party, I, like Crockett, had managed to keep my anxieties at bay. Now that I was alone—the frontiersman having departed, Muddy and Sissy asleep in their chambers—these forcibly suppressed emotions returned with an overpowering *intensity.* Especially unnerving was the memory of the anomalous female being, whose uncanny countenance (a precise description of which I had deliberately withheld from Crockett) filled me with even greater feelings of foreboding and dread than the fearfully mutilated visage of the murder victim.

All at once, as I circumambulated the floor for the dozenth time, my gaze fell upon the volume that had so riveted my interest when I had discovered it among the books sent to me for review by my employer, Mr. Thomas White. It lay atop a stack of papers on a corner of my writing table, where I had left it the previous afternoon. I refer to the remarkable study by the German scholar Heinrich Maelzel, *Curious Beliefs and Peculiar Customs among the Savage Peoples of Melanesia.*

Seating myself at my desk, I snatched up this volume and quickly searched through its pages until I came upon the passage that had impressed me so forcibly the previous afternoon, during my initial examination of the book. The section in question, which I had underscored in pencil, read as follows:

> Among the myriad superstitions that beset the mind of the Fijiian islander, perhaps none is more striking than his deeply rooted conviction that his shadow is a living entity, possessed of the power to detach itself from its owner and travel abroad on its own mysterious—and not infrequently *sinister*—errands. Such a phenomenon most often occurs in the night-time, when a person is asleep, although

——under certain conditions——the shadow may take temporary leave of its owner even during broad daylight.

Once separated from its owner, this spectral being may assume human shape. According to the beliefs of these savages, such an entity will be a kind of *mirror reflection* of the original: left-handed where the owner is right, cunning where the owner is guileless, etc. (Indeed, it may even appear as a being of the opposite sex.) Thus disguised, it is at liberty to move freely throughout the world, engaging in behavior of the most immoral and even atrocious kind——in bestial violence, implacable vengeance, or vulgar sensuality: behavior which is utterly forbidden to (though perhaps secretly desired by) its owner.

In this way, the shadow can be viewed as the manifestation of those diabolical impulses so deeply buried within the bosom of its owner that even *he* is unaware of their existence. Thus is he able to perpetrate the most hideous deeds, while maintaining a steadfast ignorance of the evil which his own hidden longings have wrought.

The emotional effect elicited in me by this passage can scarcely be formulated in words. As I perused it again in an agony of superstitious terror, I began to quiver in every fibre of my being. Flinging down the heavy volume, I staggered to my feet and retreated to my bedchamber, where I threw myself headlong upon the mattress and endeavored to find refuge in the sweet oblivion of sleep.

But in vain! For no sooner had I shut my eyes than a grim, an *appalling*, vision materialized within my mind, rendering sleep an utter impossibility. It was *she!*—the same ghastly female being whom I had encountered on two separate occasions and whose very existence—I now believed with a certainty that caused the very marrow to chill within my bones—was intimately bound up with my own!

CHAPTER 21

Since the inception of our nation as an autonomous political entity following the War of Independence, the American citizen has always taken the deepest patriotic pride in the *egalitarian* principles upon which his country is founded. The redoubtable Crèvecoeur—in identifying the particular attributes that distinguish our youthful republic from the hidebound societies of the Old World—placed the utmost emphasis on the matter of comparative *wealth*, proclaiming that "the traveller through our districts views not the hostile castle and the haughty mansion, contrasted with the clay-built hut and the miserable cabin. The rich and the poor are not so far removed from each other as they are in Europe."

Like so many beliefs cherished by the multitude, however, this assertion of the relative economic equality permeating our society bears only a tenuous relation to the truth. To be sure, the American system is blessedly free of that privileged, aristocratic order whose preeminence stems from no other cause than the accident of birth. Nonetheless, only the most undiscerning observer could fail to perceive the extreme disparities in circumstance that characterize the classes in America. However *theoretical* our dedication to egalitarian ideals may be, there is quite as much *practical* inequality in the New World as the Old. The magnates of the Exchange do not strut less proudly in Manhattan than in London; nor are their wives and daughters more backward in supporting their pretensions. Man's vanity—and the desire for distinction inherent in our all-too-human nature—simply cannot be altered by any merely political or legislative principle.

Indeed, it may be argued that the commercial essence of the American system renders our society even *less* attractive, in certain notable regards, than the aristocratical nations of Europe. For—however undeserving the nobility may be of the inordinate wealth and power that accrue to it simply by virtue of inheritance—it is nonetheless the case that, historically, men of highborn rank have always served as the primary patrons of the arts; whereas, in our own country, the possessors of wealth are, by and large, those inordinately successful members of the mercantile class devoid of the slightest appreciation of music, painting, or literature. As a result, it is the Philistine who dominates in America; while men of rare talent—I may even say *genius*—in the fields of literary and artistic pursuit are often reduced to the most humble, even desperate, of circumstances.

These reflections were inspired in me by my first, astonished glimpse of the remarkable Nicodemus mansion, tales of whose extravagant architectural features I had often listened to in wonder, though—until that moment—I had never had occasion to observe them at first hand.

In accordance with the arrangements we had made the night before, Colonel Crockett had arrived at Amity Street shortly after breakfast time, driving the handsome chaise so generously furnished to him by his exceedingly *accommodating* host. Climbing onto the seat beside the frontiersman, I had found him in freshly restored spirits, his buoyant mood undamped by the cold and constant drizzle that fell from the overhanging clouds.

Following a journey of some twenty-five minutes through the damp and cheerless streets, we arrived at our destination. Occupying almost the entirety of a city block, the Nicodemus estate was encompassed by a ponderous wall of solid brick. Crouched atop the gateposts of this lofty rampart were two carved, glowering creatures with leonine torsos, vulture wings, heads like those of snarling dragons, and the taloned legs of eagles.

Passing between these exceptionally *fanciful* sculptures—which loomed like the ferocious chimeras that guard the portals of ancient Near-Eastern temples—we proceeded along a curving pathway, canopied by the overspreading branches of many gigantic, gnarled trees, and at length found ourselves in a cobblestoned courtyard, gazing upward at the strange—the grotesque—the wildly *idiosyncratic*—exterior of the fabled house of Nicodemus.

While Crockett climbed down from the carriage and tethered the reins to an elaborately wrought hitching post, I stared in silent wonderment at the *façade* of this singular edifice. Its owner and principal designer, Josiah Nicodemus, had led a life of far-flung maritime adventure in his youth and early manhood, first as a cabin boy, then a common sailor, until—ascending by degrees through the ranks of third, second, and chief mate—he had at length become captain of the whaling vessel *Grampus*. In these various capacities he had voyaged to every part of the globe, viewing at first hand the glory that was Greece—the grandeur that was Rome— the exotic splendor of the East—the savage beauty of darkest Africa—and the paradisaical charm of the Polynesian tropics.

After retiring from the sea, Nicodemus had invested his savings in the shipbuilding trade, eventually achieving a success that surpassed his wildest hopes. Wealthy beyond measure, he had set about to construct a residence that would re-create the combined wonders of all the sights that had so bedazzled his senses in his youth. This singular ambition was realized in the remarkable building that now loomed before me, whose design was characterized by a discordant—if not utterly *bizarre*—juxtaposition of architectural embellishments, from medieval battlements, to Corinthian columns, to Oriental minarets, to the sort of elaborately scrolled buttresses characteristic of the Italian *baroque*—the entire, unparalleled combination giving to the whole an air of Arabian Nights *fantasticalness*, as though the building had sprung full-blown from the teeming reveries of an inordinately imaginative child.

Taken individually, each of these elements displayed a considerable degree of tasteful craftsmanship. I could not help but be impressed, for instance, by the exceedingly fine example of arabesque tilework that covered the *architrave* above the main doorway, and that appeared to be modelled on the glorious mosaics embellishing the fabled tomb of Itimadud-Daula in Agra, India. The sheer profusion and inconsistency of the countless *decora*, however, bespoke a sensibility that was the very opposite of tasteful—i.e., one given to the most vulgar display of garish ostentation. Indeed, thought I as I contemplated the surpassingly gaudy manse, only someone entirely devoid of aesthetic sensitivity would mistake such flamboyance for true elegance and grandeur.

This reflection was confirmed only seconds later when, stepping to my side, my companion glanced upward at the extravagant *façade* and exclaimed: "Well, I'll be jiggered if this-here Nicodemus lady ain't got the bullyest place I ever struck. Makes that ol' Asher house look as low-down as the south end of a north-bound horse."

Curbing my impulse to reply to this observation with a suitably sardonic rejoinder, I ascended the steps and pounded on the wrought-iron knocker. Seconds later, the front door was opened by a stooped and white-haired manservant, who—after giving us a slow, appraising glance—politely inquired as to our business.

"We are here to speak to Mrs. Henrietta Nicodemus about a matter of the utmost importance," I replied. "My name is Mr. Edgar Poe, and this," I added, gesturing towards my companion, "is Colonel Crockett of Tennessee."

The mere mention of the latter's name elicited a singular response from the elderly servitor. His eyes seemed to protrude from their sockets, and his mouth fell open to its fullest extent.

"Colonel Crockett? You mean *Davy* Crockett?"

"The original ripsnorter," said the frontiersman, crossing his arms over his brawny chest.

"Naw," exclaimed the incredulous servant. "Can't be!"

"It's me for a fact," Crockett asserted. "Tough as a hick'ry branch, savage as a meat-axe, and fierce as a Texas tornado."

"Well dog my cats," said the old man with a chuckle. "You two gen'mun wait right here while I go tell Miz Henrietta. Why, she'll be fit to bust when she hears *this*." So saying, he swivelled on his heels and shuffled away with a rapidity that seemed wholly anomalous in one whose grizzled head, wrinkled visage, and shrivelled frame clearly marked him as a septuagenarian.

As the elderly—if still remarkably *spry*—manservant vanished into the extensive interior of the Nicodemus manse, I turned to my companion and dryly remarked: "Your name, Colonel Crockett, appears to be a veritable *open sesame*."

"An open *what?*" he replied with an expression of intense puzzlement.

I proceeded to explicate both the meaning and derivation of the phrase with a concise synopsis of the story of "Ali Baba and the Forty Thieves" as recorded in the celebrated collection of Arabic tales, *The Thousand and One Nights,* a massive, handsomely illustrated volume of which—as translated by the renowned Orientalist, Antoine Galland—had been one of the beloved *divertissements* of my childhood. Before I could provide my companion with anything more than a superficial conception of this work, however, the venerable manservant—still moving with an alacrity that belied his hoary age—reappeared at the doorway and beckoned us inside.

As we proceeded through the many intricate passageways and commodious chambers that formed the ground floor of the manse, I was struck by the unparalleled eccentricity of the decor, which was marked by the same wild—if not *fantastic*—eclecticism that characterized the *façade.* In both the selection and arrangement of the embellishments, the evident design had been to dazzle and astound. Little, if any, attention had been paid to what is technically known as *keeping,* or to the proprieties of nationality. The eye wandered from *objet* to *objet* and rested upon none: neither upon the huge totemic carvings of the untutored inhabitants of Micronesia—nor the mummified felines of the ancient Egyptians, displayed in their ornate sarcophagi—nor the elaborately carved opium pipes of the heathen Chinese. In their sheer variety and *strangeness*, the multitudinous artifacts filling the house reminded me of nothing so much as the collection of rare and exotic curios to be found at the world-renowned Baltimore Museum.

At length, my companion and I were ushered into an enormous apartment, crammed, like the rest of the house, with a bizarre and promiscuous assortment of bibelots: intricately engraved walrus tusks—shells of tropical cocoa-nuts, chiselled into the form of grotesque human faces—taxidermically preserved infant alligators, arranged in whimsical poses—and much, *much* more. A capacious chair, or rather *throne*—whose rosewood arms were carved in the shape of grinning dolphin-heads—occupied one corner of the room. Seated in this imposing piece of furniture was an equally imposing, if rather unsettling, specimen of womanhood, whom I immediately took to be the very personage Crockett and I had come to interview.

She was attired in a handsome dress of dark, plum-colored satin, trimmed with black lace and ornamented with a large cameo brooch. What struck the eye of the observer, however, was not the richness of her garb but the extraordinary dimensions of her *physique.* To put the matter with the greatest sensitivity and tact, Mrs. Henrietta Nicodemus was a being of remarkable *corpulence*, with arms as meaty as a pair of smoked Virginia hams, and a row of double chins that descended like a marble staircase to the snowy vastness of her bosom. That her late husband, whose fortune had been founded in the whaling business, had taken such a woman for his wife seemed entirely apt, since her flesh appeared to be composed of the same cretaceous material to which the former ultimately owed his remarkable success—*viz.* that oil-rich substance commonly known as "blubber."

Notwithstanding her unwieldy size, the widow—whose age was impossible to determine, though she could not have been younger than fifty—proved to be as agile as her wizened manservant; for, upon spying the frontiersman, she heaved her bulk from the seat and came waddling toward him with surprising celerity.

"It *is* you, my dear man!" she cried, gazing up at my companion with her dark, if exceptionally small and rounded eyes, which resembled nothing so much as a pair of plump little raisins embedded in a mound of bread dough. "I did not believe Toby when he said so."

"It's me for a certainty," replied Crockett, gazing inquisitively at the woman. "Though I can't rightly say that I recollect ever meeting you before."

"You never have. And yet, I feel as though I know you as a friend, for I have been positively *enthralled* by your wonderful autobiography. What an adventurous life you have led! And how *thrillingly* you recount it in your book!"

"Why thank you, ma'am," Crockett said with a little bow of the head. "I am right tickled to hear it."

Scrutinizing my companion with a look of undisguised admiration, the widow continued: "You look *precisely* as I imagined you would—though far more fashionably dressed than I would have expected 'The King of the Wild Frontier' to be!"

Emitting a low chuckle, my companion replied: "Them ol' buckskins of mine is the very thing for hunting varmints in. But they just won't *do* when it comes to calling on a purty gal."

A delighted ejaculation—not dissimilar in both volume and pitch to the distinctive cry of the North American whooping crane—erupted from the matron's throat. "You have my express consent to keep talking, Colonel Crockett," she exclaimed. "I could listen to your delightful 'palaver' all day."

Knowing all too well how little encouragement the frontiersman required to embark on one of his interminable disquisitions—and fearing that he might misconstrue the widow's hyperbole for a literal invitation—I hastily cleared my throat in an effort to deflect our hostess' attention away from my companion.

This stratagem proved immediately effective. Casting a curious gaze in my direction, the elderly widow inquired: "But who is this handsome—if exceedingly sombre-looking—young man at your side?"

"Mr. Edgar Poe," I declared with a polite bow. "At your service."

"Poe?" she repeated. "A relation of the late General David Poe?"

"I am proud to be known as his grandson," I declared with an acknowledging nod.

"Then you must also be related to that splendid, though ill-fated, young woman, the late Elizabeth Poe."

"She was," I said in a voice heavily fraught with emotion, "my own darling mother."

Clasping her hands and raising them to her enormous bosom, the widow exclaimed: "Her untimely demise was a great loss to every lover of the theatre."

"It was a tragedy of indescribable magnitude for all who knew her," I tremulously replied.

"But to what do I owe the honor of this visit from two such distinguished gentlemen?" the widow inquired.

"The occasion for our visit," I said, "is, in fact, connected to that bygone era when the American stage was fortunate enough to be graced by the unexcelled performances of my dear, departed mother."

"Really?" said Mrs. Nicodemus in an incredulous tone as she cast an inquisitive gaze back and forth between Crockett and myself. "But that was so many years ago!"

"True enough," Crockett said. "But there just ain't no way of telling when things might turn up again after a considerable spell of time. Why, I once knowed a feller by the name of Cyrus Culpepper that got shot in the posterity during a skirmish with some redskins, and that ball got buried so deep in his flesh that there just warn't no way of digging it out. Well, ol' Cyrus he recovered by and by. Then one day—maybe ten, fifteen years later— he was sitting down to dinner when he felt something queer tickling him deep down in his throat, like as if he had a cherry pit stuck in there. So he coughs, and he spits, and then all of a sudden, something comes shooting out of his mouth and goes sailing clear across the table! It was that ol' lead ball! Danged if it hadn't worked itself up from his bottom clear on into his throat!"

As was so frequently the case with the frontiersman's anecdotes, this one had the effect of reducing me to a state of near-stupefaction. For a moment, I simply stared at him wordlessly. Mrs. Nicodemus, on the other hand, emitted a squeal of delight. "Oh, Colonel Crockett," she exclaimed. "You are—as you yourself would undoubtedly put it—a regular *humdinger.*"

"I am for a fact," Crockett answered with a grin.

"Come, gentlemen," said the elderly widow. "Let us be seated." Turning to her liveried manservant, she added: "Toby, bring some refreshments for our guests."

"Yes, Miz Henrietta," answered the latter. Swivelling on his heels, the grizzled servitor vanished from the room.

As our hostess made her way back to her ponderous throne, Crockett and I settled ourselves into a pair of comfortable armchairs. Immediately to the right of my seat stood an octagonal table, upon whose goldthreaded marble top rested a most remarkable object. It appeared to be a flawless globe of perfectly transparent crystal, supported on a base of polished rosewood. Upon closer inspection, however, the seemingly solid crystal proved to be a hollow glass ball entirely filled with water. An exquisitely rendered miniature *tableau*— representing a quaint Alpine village—was contained within the aqueous interior of the globe, the very bottom of which was blanketed with a sediment of pure white crystals.

"Ah," exclaimed our hostess. "I see that you have noticed one of the true treasures of my collection. Go ahead. Lift it up and give it a little shake."

Complying with the widow's directions, I raised the object in my hands and agitated it gently. Immediately the white crystals began to swirl about the interior of the globe, creating the uncanny effect of a mountain village caught in a fierce, winter blizzard!

"Well, I'll be ding-busted!" Crockett exclaimed delightedly as he observed this extraordinary illusion.

"It is a wonder, is it not?" said the widow. "The captain—my late husband, Josiah Nicodemus—brought it home from one of his many far-flung voyages."

"It is marvelous, indeed," I said, carefully replacing this priceless *objet* on the tabletop.

"Now," said our hostess, folding her white, dimpled hands and resting them on her voluminous lap. "Please apprise me of your mission without further delay. My curiosity can no longer be contained."

Leaning forward in my seat, I gazed intently at the widow and inquired: "Were you acquainted with Mrs. Elmira Macready?"

The sheer unexpectedness of this query rendered the widow momentarily speechless. "Only slightly," she at length replied. "And that was many years ago. Of course, I am aware of the dreadful fate which befell the poor woman, having read the horrid details of her murder in the gazettes." She shook her head slowly from side to side, causing her multiple chins to wobble in a somewhat disconcerting manner. "It is a disgrace that the police have yet to apprehend her killer," she added, clucking her tongue in disgust.

"Why that's the very thing that's brung us here," said Crockett.

A look of utmost astonishment came over the widow's countenance. Her mouth fell open, and her little eyes expanded to the approximate size of the polished onyx beads favored as magical talismans by the native inhabitants of ancient Sumeria. "Why, whatever can you *mean?*" she exclaimed with a gasp.

"Permit me to elucidate," I said. I then proceeded to offer a concise summation of the mysterious and alarming events that had commenced with the killing of Mrs. Macready, omitting only those gruesome details which would have caused my elderly auditor gratuitous dismay. I concluded by inquiring: "Does the word 'Nevermore' suggest any particular meaning to you?"

Arranging her features into a look of intense concentration, she sat silently for several moments before replying: "None that I can think of."

At this disappointing—if not wholly unexpected—reply, I exhaled a protracted sigh.

"I still do not see," said the widow, "how all of this unpleasantness relates to *me*."

"More than twenty-five years ago," I replied, "Shakespeare's magnificent—if occasionally over-wrought—tragedy *King Lear* was mounted here in Baltimore at the Front Street Theatre, with my mother in the *rôle* of the saintly Cordelia. An old, indeed somewhat disintegrating, review of this performance is among my most treasured possessions. In examining this notice, I was astonished to discover that all three of the individuals who have recently met such ghastly— such *unspeakable*—deaths were in attendance on that long-ago evening." Here, I paused for a moment and fixed the widow with a meaningful stare. "You and your late husband were present at the performance as well."

"But surely this is nothing more than sheer coincidence!" the widow exclaimed.

"Maybe so," Crockett said. "But there ain't no harm in playing it safe for a spell."

"Playing it safe?" said Mrs. Nicodemus. "In what way?"

"For one thing," I said, "you must exert inordinate caution in regard to your future visitors. Only those individuals with whom you are most intimately acquainted should be permitted to enter your premises until such time as the perpetrator of these atrocities has been apprehended."

The widow's response to this admonition was surprising in the extreme: she placed the fingers of one white, dimpled hand over her mouth and emitted a soft *chortling* sound, as though I had uttered a singularly amusing witticism.

"What's so all-fired funny?" Crockett inquired.

"Only a few days hence," she replied with a smile, "more than one hundred of my acquaintances shall be present in my home."

"Why, what do you mean?" I exclaimed at this startling pronouncement.

"My annual masked ball takes place on Saturday night."

"Then it must be cancelled," I said emphatically.

"Impossible!" she cried. "The Nicodemus *masque* has taken place each year for more than two decades. Surely you have heard of it."

In truth——though I was unaware of its imminent occurrence——no resident of our city could fail to be cognizant of this celebrated *fête*, which was widely regarded as the highlight of the Baltimore social season.

"But dad-blame it," Crockett exclaimed. "Having a passel of folks wandering around here in masks is the foolishest notion I ever struck! Why, it's just *asking* fer trouble!"

A ruminative expression had come over the widow's countenance as the frontiersman spoke. All at once, it was replaced by a look of delighted realization, as if she had been visited by a sudden insight. Clapping her hands together excitedly, she declared: "I have it!"

"Yes?" I inquired, leaning forward in my seat.

"The two of you must attend the party along with my other guests," she said cheerfully. Then, as the frontiersman and I stared at her in thunderstruck silence, she continued: "Don't you see?——it is the perfect solution! In this way, the event can proceed as planned, while my person will be under your protective scrutiny."

Smiling broadly, she added: "Why, with two such

guardian angels hovering about, surely no harm can befall me!"

Of the remainder of our visit I have little to recount. Toby having fetched a tray of tea-cakes, the frontiersman and I helped ourselves to several of these delicacies, while our hostess—who devoured half a dozen of the pastries before I had disposed of my first—continued to insist that her well-being (if not, indeed, her very survival) depended on our presence at her *masque*. At length, we yielded to her importunities, and—after ascertaining the precise time of the event—we thanked her for her hospitality and took our leave.

Emerging into the courtyard, we discovered that the rain had ceased to fall, although the sky remained sombre and gray. Climbing aboard his conveyance, Crockett and I proceeded in the direction of Amity Street, engaging in desultory conversation along the way. Twenty minutes later, we arrived at our destination. As I dismounted from the carriage, I observed that my companion was gazing curiously at something directly to my rear. Turning my head, I saw that his attention had been caught by a small but conspicuous object resting on the doorstep of my dwelling. It was a package of roughly circular shape, crudely wrapped in brown paper and secured with a length of coarse twine.

"I don't recollect seeing that parcel when I came to fetch you this morning," said Crockett with a frown.

"No," I replied, stepping towards the doorway. "Clearly, it has been delivered since our departure."

Gazing down at the package, I saw at once that I was the intended recipient, my cognomen having been inscribed on the wrapper in heavy, black crayon. Though my family appellation comprised only three letters, the writer had somehow contrived to misspell it, the crayoned address appearing thusly: "*Mr.* E. A. Po, Amity St."

I reached down for the little bundle and took it in my hands. The object enclosed within the paper was heavier than I had anticipated, and of a somewhat pliable consistency. Here and there, the wrapper was defaced with oily, reddish-brown stains. There was something vaguely—though palpably—disagreeable about the parcel that induced an instinctive feeling of repugnance within my bosom.

Shuddering with distaste, I carried the package back to the vehicle, set it down on the seat beside Crockett, and attempted to undo the cord, which had been tied with a devilish ingenuity. As I continued to struggle with the recalcitrant knot, the frontiersman suddenly said: "Let me have a go at her, pard."

Taking the string in both hands, he gave a single, forceful tug—accompanied by an emphatic *grunt*—and snapped the twine in two. The wrapping fell open—the contents of the package lay exposed to view—and I stared down at the strange, the *unaccountable* object before me with a sensation of utter bewilderment and dismay.

"What in Sam Hill—?" muttered the frontiersman.

It was a length of animal hide that had been carefully rolled into a coil. Taking one end of this odious object in his fingers, the frontiersman raised it aloft, causing it to unfurl to its full length of approximately two and a half feet. To judge from the color, texture, and condition of the hide, it had evidently been stripped from the body of a horse suffering from a severe case of the mange. Adding to its intensely *unsavory* appearance were the mucilaginous particles of sinew and fatty tissue clinging to its underside, as though it had been freshly removed from the body of the dead—or dying—beast.

"What do you reckon it means, Poe?" Crockett asked, eyeing the repellent object with a look of extreme aversion.

I was on the brink of replying that I had not the slightest conception of its import when I perceived that, in its overall dimensions, the horsehide strip bore a rough approximation to a leather strop. All at once, I emitted a startled gasp of realization.

"Have you ciphered it out?" asked Crockett, regarding me with narrowed eyes.

"I have indeed deduced the significance of this loathsome object," I replied grimly. "It is a reminder of a threat which you yourself communicated to me during our journey to the ill-fated house of Asher—a message from one who has vowed, as you reported, to 'use my skin for a razor strop.'"

Several moments elapsed while the frontiersman simply stared at me in baffled silence. All at once, his eyes widened—his mouth gaped—and he exclaimed: "You mean that pestiferous varmint, Neuendorf! Why, hang me up for bear-meat, Poe, if you ain't hit the nail plumb on the head!"

CHAPTER 22

It is a phenomenon of our nature that a super-abundance of any experience—whether pleasurable or painful—diminishes the impact of any *single* sensation. Just as a plethora of sensual delights renders any *individual* indulgence less intense, so too does a surfeit of woes reduce the onerous effect of any isolated affliction.

Thus it proved with the odious parcel left on my doorstep by Neuendorf. Had it occurred during a period of extended tranquillity, the unanticipated intrusion of this profoundly disquieting object would almost certainly have plunged me into a state of extreme distress. Arriving as it did, however, at a time of such intense, such *unparalleled* anxiety, I experienced it as merely one more vexation in a long series of unsettling events. Though certainly dismayed by this ghastly reminder of Neuendorf's implacably vindictive temperament, I was too taken up with other, more urgent matters to dwell on it for very long.

The sense of alarm occasioned in me by the reception of this odious article was further assuaged by Crockett. Seated in his chaise with the excoriated strip of hide held aloft in one hand, he had insisted that the entire episode offered irrefutable proof of Neuendorf's fundamentally pusillanimous nature.

"Why, looky here, Poe," he had exclaimed. "If I aimed to skin a feller's carcass, would I bother with such tomfoolery as sending him a chunk of horseflesh? No sir. I'd just show up one morning with my sharpest hunting knife and carve him up quicker than an owl can swallow a rat. You mark me, Poe, this here bit of nastiness don't amount to shucks."

And so saying, he had leaned over the front of the carriage and—with a contemptuous flick of the wrist—flung the vile article into the gutter, where it was instantly set upon and devoured by a pack of roving swine.

Among the many concerns preoccupying my mind in the days following our interview with Mrs. Nicodemus, one of the most pressing had to do with the latter's impending *gala*. Immediately prior to our departure from her home, Mrs. Nicodemus had proposed that—to blend in more fully with her other guests, all of whom would be attending with partners of the opposite sex—Crockett and I each invite a female companion. When, upon returning to my dwelling, I had broached the subject with Virginia, she had responded with the utmost enthusiasm. It quickly occurred to me that Sissy and I could achieve a singularly *vivid* impression by arriving in costumes that embodied a related thematic or pictorial concept, so that—when viewed in conjunction with each other—we would produce the dramatic effect of a *tableau vivant*.

As I sat in my study on the following morning, cudgelling my brains over the still-unknown meaning of "Nevermore," my gaze happened to fall upon a volume of Ovid's *Metamorphosis* in Dryden's excellent (if not consistently felicitous) translation. All at once, I was struck with an inspiration regarding the approaching masquerade. Within moments, I had sought out both Muddy and Sissy and excitedly shared my conception with them. They quickly perceived its charms and gave their eager approbation.

To assemble our costumes was simplicity itself. My own outfit was readily concocted from a few ordinary and easily obtainable household objects—*viz.* a bedsheet, a hammer, and a chisel (the last two articles being loaned to me for the occasion by a neighbor, Mr. Reuben Bourne, who earned his living as a mason). Another bedsheet—artfully stitched together by Muddy in the form of a surpassingly elegant gown of antique Grecian cut—likewise constituted Sissy's principal garb. Her masquerade was completed with the aid of a thick white paste compounded of flour and water and skillfully applied to her face, thus creating the altogether convincing illusion that her lovely visage was composed of hewn, statuary marble.

By such simple, yet ingenious, means my conception was triumphantly realized; so that—when the eve of the gala finally arrived—Sissy and I stood forth as the living incarnations of that fabled antique couple, the sculptor Pygmalion and his exquisite statue, Galatea, whose beauty was such that—overwhelmed with desire for his own creation—the artist offered fervent supplications to the goddess Aphrodite, who answered his prayers by transforming the lovely marble figure into a being of flesh and blood.

At precisely six o'clock on Saturday evening, while Sissy and I stood in the parlor, effecting some final adjustments to our costumes, there came a resounding knock upon the front door of our dwelling: Colonel Crockett had arrived to convey us to the party. This summons was answered by Muddy, who—upon opening the door—gasped so loudly in wonderment that the noise carried clearly from the front hallway to the parlor. Her amazed ejaculation was immediately followed by the tramp of approaching footsteps. Seconds later, the frontiersman loomed before us. Framed in the doorway—with his feet spread wide, his chest thrust forward, and a proud, military elevation of his head—he stood as though posing for our inspection and admiration. And in truth, he cut a striking figure.

In dramatic contrast to his customary attire, he was garbed in a hunting shirt of dressed deerskin, fringed with beads of variegated colors and belted close to his muscular body with a girdle of wampum, through which a gleaming hunting knife had been thrust. Resting upon his head was a raccoon-skin cap, the shaggy tail of which hung suspended from the side and lay draped across the collar of his shirt. His legs were encased in buckskin trousers, gartered to the knees with the sinews of deer; and upon his feet were moccasins fashioned out of scraps of buffalo hide and ornamented, in the Indian style, with porcupine quills. Cradled in one arm was a magnificent Kentucky rifle, its gleaming stock adorned with silver filigree. A pouch and horn, slung crossways over his brawny chest, completed the picturesque costume.

Our inspection of Crockett's colorful garb lasted for nearly a minute—during which time the frontiersman scrutinized us in turn with an expression of intense bemusement. At length, he shook his head slowly and declared: "I been standing here and studying over it, but I'm blessed if I can cipher it *nohow.*"

"To what precisely are you referring?" I inquired.

"I'm referring," he replied, "to why you 'n' Miz Virginny are rigged out in them nightgowns."

Seeking to correct this gross misapprehension, I proceeded to offer a brief, though in all essential respects *comprehensive*, synopsis of the classical myth of whose central protagonists Sissy and I were meant to be the living *simulacra*. "To judge from your own costume, Colonel Crockett," I continued, "I see that you have chosen to attend tonight's *fête* in the guise of a typical wilderness huntsman."

"Typical, my eye!" he exclaimed in a voice ringing with disdain. "You are looking at the most savagerous son of a wildcat there ever was—the original iron-jawed, brass-mounted, copper-bellied King of the Wild Frontier!"

At this resounding declaration, Muddy—who had come up behind our visitor and now stood directly to his rear just beyond the threshold of the parlor—clapped her hands delightedly.

"Well, now," said Crockett, "I reckon we ought to make tracks. Poe, you ain't the only one who's bringing a purty gal to this frolic. I got one waiting outside, and I'll wager she's growin' a mite antsy by now."

Bidding good-night to Muddy—who saw us to the front door, where she bestowed a fond maternal hug upon both Sissy and myself—the three of us emerged into the street. In place of the anticipated chaise there stood an elegant *barouche*, which Crockett's ever-obliging host, Mr. Potter, had placed at the frontiersman's disposal for the evening. A liveried driver occupied the box, while a young woman sat in the rear of the coach. She was garbed in the elaborate costume of a Turkish *sultana*, with the lower half of her face concealed beneath the folds of a diaphanous veil. Even so, I immediately deduced that she was the somewhat brazen individual who had attached herself to the frontiersman following his ferocious battle with Neuendorf, and whose family name, as I recalled, was Mullany.

My conjecture in respect to her identity was confirmed when Crockett introduced his companion by name. As Sissy and I mounted the carriage, Miss Mullany scrutinized us with an expression of undisguised perplexity.

Before I could enlighten her as to the signification

of our costumes, Crockett exclaimed: "Why, they are rigged out as Mr. Pigmalion and his gal."

"I don't believe I am familiar with those individuals," Miss Mullany said amiably as Sissy and I settled into the seats directly across from her.

"Well," said the frontiersman, assuming his place beside his companion, "I can learn you all about 'em in two shakes of a dead lamb's tail."

Then—placing an arm around the exposed white shoulder of the colorfully attired young woman—he embarked on a lively, if somewhat garbled, rendition of the entrancing fable, while the driver maneuvered the coach down Amity Street and in the direction of Mrs. Nicodemus' grand masquerade ball.

CHAPTER 23

Arrived at our destination, our carriage took its place at the end of a long line of conveyances, each of which—as it drew up to the main portal—disgorged a party of gaily, if not *garishly*, costumed revellers, who immediately disappeared into the wide-flung doorway of the manse. At length, it was our turn to disembark. Climbing down from the *barouche*, we followed the stream of chattering, ebullient guests through many deviously winding corridors, until we found ourselves within a vast—sumptuously appointed—and dazzlingly lit—ballroom.

This magnificent hall had been fitted up with every kind of device which could possibly give *éclat* to a masquerade. Dozens of lavish floral arrangements complemented the opulent decor of the room, whose gilded walls, marble floors, and richly embroidered tapestries were thrown into brilliant relief by a series of sconces, each containing a blazing flambeau. Arranged along one wall was a massive table, laden with such an abundance of delectable foodstuffs that it constituted a veritable "groaning-board." There were platters piled high with every species of flesh and fowl—ham, turkey, venison, veal, partridge, chicken, grouse, and wild duck—dishes heaped with oysters, shad, lobster, crab, and trout—bowls replete with cherries, plums, and every variety of luscious fruits—baskets overstuffed with biscuits, breads, and rolls—countless bottles of Claret, Madeira, and Champagne—an enormous ceramic vessel brimming with rum punch—and a plethora of pies, cakes, tarts, and other delicacies so appetizing—so savory—that the mere sight of this tantalizing *cornucopia* resulted in the immediate, uncontrolled excitation of my organs of salivation.

The atmosphere of the ballroom was infused with the perfumed aroma of the many floral bouquets, and filled with the surpassingly mellifluous sounds emanating from the instruments of a group of elegantly garbed musicians, to whose high-spirited melodies a number of the revellers were already dancing a merry quadrille. Everywhere one gazed, the eye was dazzled with the splendor—the color—the sheer ingenious *novelty*—of the various costumes. There were richly dressed courtiers and knavish brigands—picturesque Alsatian peasant girls escorted by grinning harlequins—Parisian damsels chatting gaily with portly monks—pig-tailed dairy maids cavorting with moustachioed pirates. Now a Highland lassie would trip past, arm in arm with a jolly sailor; next a plumed and painted Osage warrior would stroll by in the company of a handsome Tripolitan noblewoman. Hamlet, the

melancholy Dane, engaged in lively repartee with Julius
Caesar; Torquemada stood laughing with King Henry
VIII. Pretty feminine costumes of Poland and Italy
were much in evidence—the former consisting of
bright satin skirts, trimmed with ermine and heavy
bullion fringe; the latter of cherry satin, profusely
adorned with gilt ornaments, small bows, and tassels.

And seated in the midst of all—occupying her
massive throne (which had evidently been transported into the ballroom for this occasion)—was the
hostess herself, Mrs. Henrietta Nicodemus, elaborately coiffed, costumed, and made up to resemble a
(somewhat overfed) facsimile of the beauteous, if ill-
fated, French queen Marie Antoinette.

The vast ballroom, aswirl with so much life, color,
and diversity, offered a singular spectacle, one guaran-
teed to elicit both wonder and admiration in the
observer. Even the most fanciful—the most *fantastical*
—of the costumes, however, did not create the sensation
produced by the appearance of my brawny companion
in his roughhewn, buckskin garb. From the moment of
our entrance, a stir of excitement rippled through the
assembled masqueraders, who paused in their activities
to gape at the frontiersman in undisguised awe. As we
made our way across the floor, I could distinctly hear the
delighted gasps—excited murmurs—and awed ejaculations issuing from the lips of the crowd:

"Look!—It is *him!*—Davy Crockett himself!"—
The King of the Wild Frontier!"

Within moments, we found ourselves standing

before the throne-like chair of Mrs. Nicodemus, who—upon becoming aware of our presence—arose from her seat and regally extended her plump right hand towards the frontiersman, as though offering it for a kiss.

Reaching out and seizing it with his own—far larger—and exceedingly powerful right hand, Crockett gave it an energetic shake. "Evenin', Miz Nicodemus," he drawled. "I wish my rifle may hang fire forever if this ain't a plumb *rip-roarious* shindig. And don't you look as *purty* as a morning glory on a fine, sunshiny day!"

Her inordinately *rotund* face flushing with pleasure, our hostess took several moments to exclaim over Crockett's colorful garb before turning to Miss Mullany, who introduced herself to the widow with an elegant curtsy. Next, the latter directed her attention towards Virginia and myself. After inquiring as to the identity of my companion, she scrutinized our costumes for a moment before observing: "What a delightful choice of masquerades! Do you know, Mr. Poe, that—of all the tales in *The Metamorphoses*—the story of Pygmalion is, by far, my very favorite?"

"Well, split me all to flinders!" Crockett cried. "How in the nation did you cipher it out so quick? That's an uncommon sound head you got on them shoulders of your'n, Miz Nicodemus!"

Perceiving an opportunity to inject a note of levity into the proceedings, I smiled urbanely and remarked: "Which, of course, is more than could be said for poor Marie Antoinette herself, once she fell into the clutches of Monsieur Robespierre and his cohorts."

I had anticipated that my witticism would elicit, if not an outburst of sustained hilarity, then at least a hearty display of appreciative mirth. Contrary to my expectations, however, it was succeeded by an absolute—protracted—and distinctly uncomfortable—*silence.*

I could only infer that—by virtue of its reliance on the rather sophisticated device of historical allusion—my jest had proven to be overly subtle for my auditors. I was on the brink of offering a concise account of the Reign of Terror—by way of illuminating the inherent *drollery* of my remark—when Mrs. Nicodemus turned her gaze on a gentleman who had been standing silently at the side of her throne.

The demeanor of this personage—who was garbed in the costume of a medieval Knight Templar—was exceptional in every regard. Though only of medium height, he possessed a posture so singularly erect that it invested him with an appearance of unusual height—an effect reinforced by the extreme, though by no means unattractive, slenderness of his frame. His finely molded countenance was suffused with an air of aristocratical *hauteur,* while—from his dark, liquid eyes—there emanated a vague though palpable look of barely suppressed *ennui.* Beneath his long, aquiline nose, a jet-black moustache—whose ends were combed and waxed into the shape of two absolutely symmetrical *curlicues*—adorned his upper lip; while his somewhat recessive chin was embellished with a carefully trimmed goatee. His mouth was thin—very pallid—and arranged into a perpetual expression of mild, if distinctly *supercilious,* amusement.

Addressing this individual in an apologetic tone, Mrs. Nicodemus said: "I trust, my dear Count, that Mr. Poe's innocent sally is not a cause for offense."

"I assure you, Madame," he replied with a weary shrug, "we French cannot afford to be sensitive on this account. Even for us, the excesses of *La Terreur*—and most especially, the unfortunate enthusiasm for Docteur Guillotin's ingenious device displayed by certain of our *compatriotes*—are a matter to be treated with scorn." After favoring me with a thin smile, he turned his gaze upon the frontiersman. "So you are the famous Colonel Crockett, *non?*" he inquired, raising one eyebrow.

"Blamed if I ain't. And who might you be?"

"Le Comte de Languedoc," replied the other with a little bow. "At your service."

"The Count," Mrs. Nicodemus explained, "was an old acquaintance of my late husband's. He is here to take a tour of our glorious Western prairies."

"Don't say?" Crockett remarked, scrutinizing the Frenchman through narrowed eyes. "Fixing on seeing the grandiferous sights of nature, eh?"

"*Bien sûr,*" replied the Count. "And, perhaps, to hunt some of your *magnifique* wild buffalo."

This latter remark caused a broad, somewhat satirical, smile to spread across the frontiersman's sun-browned visage. "Buffalo?" he exclaimed. "Why, Count, hunting buffalo ain't no sport for amateurs. When riled, them critters'll turn as ugly as a copperhead in July. I once seen an ol' bull go after a passel of redskins like a whole team of thunderbolts, even though the critter already had so many arrows stuck in him that he looked as thorny as a gol-danged honey locust tree."

"I flatter myself, my *cher* Colonel, that I am not wholly unskilled in matters of the hunt," replied the other. "Though I confess that, in the *métier* of savage pursuits, the American huntsman is, *sans doute*, unsurpassed in the world." The subtly mocking tone in which this latter statement was expressed did not escape the notice even of the frontiersman, who—though normally oblivious of the nuances of *irony*—bristled visibly at the comment.

"I take it," continued the Count, "that the weapon you have clutched so lovingly in your arms is your celebrated rifle, Old—how do you say?—*Bitsy?*"

"*Betsy*," Crockett growled in reply. Then, gazing fondly at his rifle, he declared: "She's my pride and joy, for a certainty."

Taking one step forward, the Count extended his right hand in the direction of the weapon and inquired: "May I?"

After a brief moment of reluctant hesitation, Crockett surrendered the rifle to the Frenchman, who, after hefting it in both hands, raised the stock to his shoulder and peered down the length of the barrel, directing the muzzle towards the far end of the cavernous hallway, where a pair of French windows opened onto a lush, extensive garden.

"Go ahead and cock her, Count," said Crockett. "She ain't loaded."

After making a thorough inspection of the piece—its shining lock and breech; its polished, silver-ornamented stock; and its singularly elongated barrel—the Frenchman observed: *"Vraiment,* it is an imposing—if, perhaps, somewhat cumbersome—firearm."

Snatching it from the latter's hands, Crockett exclaimed: *"Cumbersome?* Why, I'll be shot if that ain't the most chuckleheaded, numskulled—"

"Gentlemen, gentlemen!" cried Mrs. Nicodemus. "Please—this is an evening for gaiety, not discord!"

After casting a final, venomous look at the Frenchman, Crockett turned to the widow and declared: "Danged if you ain't right, Miz Nicodemus. You just go on and attend to your business, and don't fret your purty head about a thing. Me and Poe'll keep our eyes peeled. Why, with us two here, you'll be as safe as a turtle with its head tucked into his shell."

Offering his arm to Miss Mullany and motioning to Virginia and me with a tilt of his head, Crockett said: "C'mon, let's get us some of them fine-looking vittles." Then, leaning towards me and placing his mouth close to my left ear, he added *sotto voce:* "And some of that first-rate liquor, too. That thin-gutted frog-eater has got me feeling hotter than hoss radish!"

Striding towards the banquet-table with his flouncing companion at his side, Crockett secured a large delftware platter and commenced to fill it with a prodigious quantity of viands. Even before he had devoured a single forkful, however, he was surrounded by a group of voluble admirers who eagerly importuned him for a tale.

"Friends, I ain't in no ways undisposed to oblige," he replied. "Just give me a minute to stow away some of this-here grub. Blamed if I ain't hungry enough to eat a whole buffalo and pick my teeth with its horns."

While the frontiersman was thus engaged, Sissy and I—whose costumes had drawn marvelling stares from the other masqueraders as we strolled, arm-in-arm, across the floor—made our way down the length of the table, assisting ourselves to a large variety of refreshments, including—in my case—a brimming cup of rum punch; my thirst having been seriously exacerbated by both the warmth of the room and the nervous tension induced in me by Crockett's near-altercation with the Frenchman. This beverage proving singularly refreshing, I quaffed the entire cupful in a single, protracted gulp and immediately refilled it before continuing to help myself to the assorted delicacies of the extensive *buffet*.

Our platters being fully laden, Sissy and I repaired to one of the many small, circular tables disposed around the periphery of the hall and seated ourselves directly across from one another. Before turning my full attention to my dinner, I took a moment to make a careful survey of the room. Our hostess had left her throne and was moving about the hallway, bestowing bright, effusive greetings upon her friends and acquaintances. Some of the masqueraders were still engaged in a lively dance; others were gathered in laughing, chattering groups of three or four; still others were—like Sissy and myself—seated at tables, partaking of the bounteous meal; while a sizable group was now gathered around Crockett, who was holding forth while devouring great, swollen mouthfuls of food. The entire scene was one of mirth—vivacity—and singularly elevated spirits.

"Ooh, Eddie," sighed Virgina, as she masticated a forkful of mutton. "Isn't this the grandest, most *splendid* party you have ever attended?"

"It is, to be sure," I replied with a smile. "Though the most splendid sight of all is the one upon which I am even now gazing."

Smiling brightly at this tribute, Sissy continued to look about the ballroom, her eyes aglint with excitement. In the meantime, I bent my ears to Crockett's recitation. Being seated only several yards away from the ever-expanding audience surrounding the frontiersman, I could clearly hear his words above the lilting sounds of the music:

"If you haven't heard tell of one Mike Fink," boomed the frontiersman's deep-pitched voice, "I'll learn you something about him, for he was a helliferocious fellow and an almighty fine shot. Mike was a boatman on the Mississippi, but he had him a little cabin at the head of the Cumberland and a horrid handsome wife that loved him the wickedest you ever see. Well, one day I fell in with him in the woods, and he says to me: 'I've got the handsomest wife, and the fastest horse, and the sharpest shootin'-iron in all Kentuck—and if any man dare doubt it, I'll be in his hair quicker than it would take a hurricane to tear through a cornfield.'

"This put my dander up, and I says: 'I've nothin' against your wife, Mike, for it can't be denied that she's a monstrous handsome woman. And I ain't got no horses. But I'm damned if you speak the truth about your rifle, and I'll prove it. Do you see that-there tom-cat hunkered on top of that fence post, about a hundred and fifty yards off? If he ever hears again, I'll be shot if it shan't be without ears.'

"So I blazed away with ol' Betsy, and dang if that ball didn't cut off both the ol' tom's ears and shave the hair clean off his skull, as slick as if I'd done it with a razor. And the critter never stirred nor knew he'd lost his ears 'til he tried to scratch 'em. So I says to Mike . . ."

As the frontiersman continued to regale his admirers with this flagrant, if innocuous, "whopper," a peculiar sense of serenity began to suffuse every fibre of my being. I was, of course, acutely aware that Crockett and I had been invited as *guardians*, not guests. We had been charged with the gravest imaginable responsibility— *viz.* to maintain a tireless watch over our hostess, so as to ensure that no harm befell her in the course of her *fête*. In contradistinction to the other masqueraders, mere *personal* enjoyment was—for us—a subsidiary, if not wholly immaterial, concern.

Nevertheless, so convivial—so pleasing—so surpassingly benign—was the entire atmosphere of the ball that my sense of foreboding had, by slow degrees, begun to evaporate. The perfumed air—the delectable food— the transporting sight of my Sissy's enchanting visage—

all conspired to induce within my bosom a mood of singularly unwonted relaxation and contentment.

All at once, however, I became cognizant of an angry commotion emanating from Crockett's direction. Casting my glance thitherward, I saw that the frontiersman had abruptly broken off his recitation and was engaged in an acrimonious debate with another individual, whose identity was obscured by the surrounding masqueraders. A stab of intense apprehension pierced the innermost core of my bosom. I quickly rose to my feet and—standing upon tip-toe— perceived at once that my premonition was founded on solid fact. The personage with whom Crockett was arguing was none other than the Comte de Languedoc! At that instant, Mrs. Nicodemus could be seen bustling towards the circle of onlookers, who parted to make way for the visibly dismayed hostess. Patting my lips with my linen napkin, I placed it on the table beside my depleted cup of punch, and instructed Sissy to await my return. Then, I hurriedly made my way towards the scene of the clamor, and—following in the wake of Mrs. Nicodemus—soon found myself standing beside the two deeply incensed antagonists.

Clasping her hands to her capacious bosom, Mrs. Nicodemus looked beseechingly from Crockett to the Count, and then back again. "Gentlemen, gentlemen!" she cried. "I am very much distressed at this unseasonable outburst. What in heaven's name has happened?"

"I'm powerful sorry for putting you in a lather, Miz Nicodemus," answered Crockett. "But I'll be

hanged if this-here impudacious scoundrel hasn't riled
me up hotter than blazes."

Mrs. Nicodemus cast a bewildered look at the
Frenchman.

"My offense, *Madame*," said the latter, "was merely
to offer a mild expression of doubt at the Colonel's
insistence that he could—as he put it—'shoot the
tongue out of a crow on the wing at a distance of a
hundred yards!' This inspired him to reply with a most
outrageux slur on my countrymen!"

"Why, it wasn't no part of a slur!" Crockett said
protestingly.

"And what exactly did you say, my dear Colonel?"
asked Mrs. Nicodemus with a sigh.

Crockett gave a shrug of his exceptionally broad
shoulders. "Why, nothing more than the gospel
truth—that your average Froggie knows as much about
firearms as a dead skunk knows about Scripture."

"*Mon Dieu!*" muttered the Count under his breath.
"But this is not to be endured!" Drawing himself up to
his full height, he took one step towards the frontiersman and—uttering his words between tightly clenched
teeth—said: "I shall be happy to disprove this infamous *calomnie* at any time, *mon cher* Colonel."

"How about right here and now, *Monsieur?*" said
Crockett with a sneer, his inimitable pronunciation rendering the final word as "mon-sewer."

"I am at your disposal," the Count replied with a
stiff bow.

"Well, then," said Crockett with a smile of intense

satisfaction, "let's you and me have us a little shooting match."

This statement elicited an enthusiastic huzzah from the lips of the surrounding crowd, whose number, by this point, had grown to encompass virtually the entire population of the ballroom.

"A shooting match?" gasped Mrs. Nicodemus. "Here? Why, that is impossible!"

"Not by a considerable sight," said Crockett. Raising one hand, he pointed his forefinger at the colossal French windows that stood at the opposite end of the ballroom. Behind their immaculately polished glass panes stretched a lush and carefully tended garden, replete with sculptures, fountains, ponds, flowerbeds, and shrubberies; and of such extensive dimensions that it virtually comprised a small park. "We'll just fix up a target in your backyard."

While the crowd voiced its unreserved enthusiasm for Crockett's proposal, Mrs. Nicodemus ruminated in silence for several moments. At length, she exhaled a relenting sigh and declared: "I suppose I must bend to the will of my guests. And I must confess that, to witness a competition between two such excellent marksmen as Davy Crockett and the Comte de Languedoc would be a rare treat."

An exultant cheer arose from the crowd at this pronouncement. "Then let's get the ball rolling!" shouted the frontiersman as he shouldered his firearm. Standing at his side, his distaff companion, Miss Mullany, clapped her hands excitedly and exclaimed:

"Oh! This is just too thrilling for words. I fear I shall simply *perish* from excitement!"

As the exuberant crowd began to make its way towards the opposite end of the ballroom, I hastily stepped up to Crockett and—tugging him by the fringed sleeve of his hunting shirt—drew him aside.

"While I appreciate your sense of indignation at the Frenchman's somewhat supercilious manner," I said in a voice only slightly louder than a whisper, "I cannot help but wonder, Colonel Crockett, if your proposal is entirely well-advised. Our mission, after all, is to maintain a careful and unremitting watch over our hostess. Surely, your contest with the Count can only serve to distract our attention from this overriding purpose."

"Don't you go fretting about it, Poe. Miz Nicodemus'll be standin' right beside me the whole time. You just keep your eyes peeled, while I take care of that pesky furriner. Hell, it'll all be over in less time than it takes to skin a badger." Then—after bestowing a reassuring pat upon my shoulder—he offered his arm to the Mullany woman and strode towards the opposite end of the ballroom, where the entire assembly was gaily streaming through the wide-flung French windows and out into the moonlit garden.

By this point, Virginia had sought me out and was regarding me with bright, *scintillant* eyes. "Ooh, Eddie!" she exclaimed in her seraphic voice. "Imagine! We will actually get to see Colonel Crockett shoot his legendary rifle."

"Come, then, my lovely Galatea," said I. "Let us join the others." Taking her by the arm, I ushered her toward the garden, pausing only briefly to secure another cup of rum punch before proceeding into the surpassingly balmy spring night.

By the time Sissy and I joined the rest of the party, Crockett and his opponent had already agreed upon a site for their competition. This was an extensive and neatly trimmed lawn, encompassed on three sides by a border of privet hedges. In the center of this grassy expanse, at a distance of approximately one hundred yards from its southernmost boundary, stood a gigantic—gnarled—and excessively ancient oak tree. So inordinately bright was the moonlight emanating from the gibbous orb that the entire scene was illuminated with an almost preternatural clarity.

As the party of revellers arranged themselves about the periphery of the lawn, Mrs. Nicodemus issued an order to her elderly manservant, Toby, who hurried back into the mansion, returning several moments later with a deck of playing cards, a hammer, and a nail. Repairing to the oak tree, he extracted a single card from the pack and—with his hammer and nail— affixed it to the center of the trunk at approximately shoulder height. Even in the exceedingly radiant moonlight, however, the markings of the card were impossible to discern at such a great distance. This necessitated another brief delay, while the uncomplaining servitor was dispatched to fetch a flambeau from one of the sconces in the ballroom. Following his return, he was directed to stand beside the oak tree with the torch extended so as to illuminate the playing card, which—it could now be seen—was the ace of spades.

These preliminaries having been accomplished, the contestants made ready to proceed. According to custom, the Comte de Languedoc, as the party who had received the challenge, was entitled to the initial shot.

"Here you go, Count," said Crockett, presenting his rifle to the Frenchman with an exaggerated flourish. "Now, don't forget. The bullet comes out the end with the hole in it."

This sally elicited a paroxysm of mirth from the crowd of costumed spectators and a glare of icy indignation from the Count.

Assuming his attitude with a good deal of studied elegance, the Frenchman slowly raised the rifle to his shoulder—took careful aim—lowered the muzzle—raised it again—repeated the maneuvers—and fired!

The thunderous report of the fabled weapon was followed by a moment of hushed anticipation from the crowd, who fixed its collective gaze upon the elderly manservant as he held the flambeau close to the tree-trunk and peered at the card. A moment later, Toby straightened up, turned towards his mistress (who was standing directly to the right of the two contestants), and—cupping one hand to his mouth—cried: "It's a bull's-eye, sho as preachin'! I'll be ding-busted if that card ain't been drilled clean through the middle!"

This pronouncement drew a sustained round of applause from the spectators, to which the Frenchman responded with a gracious bow of acknowledgment. Then, turning towards Crockett, he thrust the rifle into the latter's hands. "Now, *mon cher* Colonel," he said with a contemptuous sneer, "let us see if you can do better than *that!*"

"Oh, I don't reckon that'll be none too troublesome," Crockett said casually as he unplugged the stoppered tip of his powderhorn with his teeth and proceeded to reload "ol' Betsy." This operation was achieved in short order—whereupon, with barely a glance at the target, he swiftly raised the muzzle and retracted the trigger with an unhesitating squeeze of the forefinger. Thought was scarcely quicker than his aim, and—as the smoke floated above his head—he lowered the breech to the ground, leaned his hand upon the barrel, and peered at the target with an expression of supreme assurance.

Once again, the crowd retained its breath as the elderly manservant held his torch close to the tree. An inordinately protracted period elapsed while he conducted this inspection. At length, his grizzled head shaking with incredulity, he looked up and declared: "I can't hardly believe my own eyes, but Marster Davy has clean missed the target." Then—after making a second examination of the trunk, as if to assure himself that his ocular sense had not deceived him—he turned to us again and exclaimed: "Danged if he ain't missed the whole *tree!*"

An audible gasp of shocked bewilderment arose from the crowd, while the Frenchman threw back his head and emitted a loud, gloating "Haw!"

Crockett, however, seemed entirely unperturbed by this extraordinary—this *unaccountable*—development. "Now, Count," he remarked with a smile, "I ain't saying that ol' Toby's eyes have plumb bamfoozled him. But before you start boasting on your victory, why don't you and me take a little stroll over yonder and have us a look-see for ourselves?"

In an instant, the expression on the Frenchman's attenuated countenance underwent a dramatic transformation, from outright exultation to profound suspicion. His pale brow deeply furrowed, he silently scrutinized Crockett for a moment before replying, "*Bien sûr.*"

With Miss Mullany at his side—"Ol' Betsy" in his arms—and the Comte de Languedoc at his heels—Crockett strode boldly up the center of the lawn towards the great, gnarled tree. Along with Mrs. Nicodemus, Sissy and I followed directly behind; while the throng of masqueraders—venting their excitement in a loud, *buzzing* murmur—swarmed about the tree, male and female alike jostling each other for the most advantageous positions.

Having reached his destination, Crockett drew close to Toby, who continued to stare at the target with an expression of utmost perplexity.

"Step aside, ol' hoss," Crockett commanded the servant; then, turning to the Frenchman, he declared:

"Count, whyn't you take a gander at that-there ace of spades."

Complying with this directive, Languedoc stepped up to the tree and peered closely at the target for a moment before turning to the assemblage and announcing: "As can clearly be seen, there is but a single bullet hole in *la carte!*"

Next, he plucked the card from its retaining nail, revealing the corresponding hole in the bark. Into this he then inserted the long, tapered forefinger of his right hand, as though to demonstrate in the most graphic way conceivable that only a single bullet had penetrated the trunk.

"How far in can you reach that nose-picker of yours, Count?" Crockett inquired.

Frowning with annoyance, Languedoc moved his forefinger ever more deeply into the trunk. All at once—as his slender digit continued to probe the bullet hole—a look of stunned incomprehension began to spread over his countenance.

Perceiving this expression, Crockett grinned broadly and said: "Something wrong, Count?"

"*Ce n'est pas possible!*" gasped the latter.

"Let *me* in there," Crockett said, motioning the Frenchman aside. "And we'll find out just how possible it is!"

As the crowd pressed even closer to the tree, Crockett extracted his hunting knife from his belt and—applying the long, pointed tip to the bullet hole—dug out the contents, which dropped into his open palm, positioned directly against the tree trunk.

"Bring that torch a mite closer, Toby," said Crockett, extending his palm, "so the good folks can see for themselves."

Toby did as directed; whereupon a gasp of the utmost astonishment arose from the crowd. There, in Crockett's hand, lay *two* flattened lead balls, one directly on top of the other. So unprecedented—so sheerly *astonishing*—was this sight that a dead silence, of nearly a minute's duration, elapsed before the spectators could grasp its full significance.

The Count had indeed scored a bull's-eye. Crockett, however, had then performed a feat that was nothing short of miraculous, firing his bullet directly into the hole produced by his competitor's shot!

As Languedoc continued to gape in open-mouthed wonder at the conjoined pair of bullets in Crockett's hand, the crowd erupted in a tumultuous burst of applause. At length, when the cheering had subsided, the Frenchman gazed into Crockett's face with a look of unqualified admiration. Addressing the frontiersman in a deeply respectful—if not *reverential*—voice, he declared: "Never have I seen anything like it. Colonel Crockett, I bow to your superiority. *Vraiment*, fame has not made too great a flourish of trumpets when speaking of your skill as a marksman."

Thrusting out his right hand, Crockett replied: "No hard feelings, Count. You are a mighty good shot yourself—though a monstrous slow one—and I hope

I ain't been guilty of committing a fox paw, as you Frenchies call it, in suggesting otherwise!"

After declaring Colonel Crockett the champion—and congratulating the Count on a feat of marksmanship that, had it been accomplished against any less remarkable opponent, would surely have earned him a victory—Mrs. Nicodemus raised her arms towards the assembled company and invited them to return to the ballroom forthwith and resume the festivities. This proposal was heartily endorsed by everyone present, and—with much laughter and merry conversation—the picturesque revellers proceeded indoors, while the orchestra—which had suspended its performance for the duration of the contest—struck up a lively gavotte.

The hours that ensued were ones of unrelieved revelry and mirth. To the wildly melodious sounds of the orchestra, the gay masqueraders swirled about the ballroom like a host of writhing phantasms. Around and around they spun, taking hue from the many-colored tapestries and the blazing flambeaux, and causing the rollicking—the *delirious*—music to seem as the echo of their own ecstatic steps.

In the midst of this revelry, I was careful to maintain a scrupulous watch over our hostess. That no untoward happenstance was likely to occur—that our fears for Mrs. Nicodemus' safety were utterly without a basis in reality—had become abundantly clear. Nevertheless—in strict accordance with the obligation I was there to fulfill—I made certain to keep the corpulent widow more-or-less continuously within my view. Crockett, too, while freely engaging in the festivities, made every effort to position himself in relatively close proximity to our hostess as she circulated around the ballroom. Thus, it remained possible for us to discharge our duty while simultaneously indulging in the pleasures of the ball.

Though opportunities to exercise my talent had, in recent years, been exceedingly scarce, I was, in truth, a dancer of considerable virtuosity, my terpsichorean skills having been perfected in the grand salons of my Richmond youth. Now, transported by the infectious spirit of the occasion, I took my angelic Sissy into my arms and whirled her about the floor in giddy, enraptured revolutions, pausing only occasionally to refresh myself with another—and still another—cup of the singularly *invigorating* punch.

How much time elapsed in this frolicsome manner, I cannot say with any sense of accuracy. At length, however, I became aware of an overpowering need for a respite. A sudden sense of the deepest fatigue had suffused every fibre of my being. Drawing Sissy to the periphery of the dance floor, I communicated my desire for a brief *interregnum*. The angelic child, whose own appetite for merrymaking seemed limitless, responded with a charming petulance, stamping her foot and exclaiming: "Oooh, Eddie. You are always spoiling my fun!"

Her adorable denunciation was interrupted by the timely appearance of Colonel Crockett. "Miz Virginny," he declared, "I'd be tickled if you'd oblige me with a spin around the floor."

This invitation elicited a delighted exclamation of assent from Sissy, who immediately slipped one hand through the crook of the frontiersman's proffered right arm. Before leading her onto the dance floor, Crockett turned to me and declared, "Well, Poe, I don't reckon there is much to be afeard of tonight."

"Indeed," I replied, "our apprehensions regarding the security of our hostess appear to have been groundless."

Arranging her features into an endearingly *querulous* look, Sissy suddenly exclaimed, "Why have you stopped to talk to Eddie, Colonel Crockett? I thought we were going to *dance*." Then, with an insistent tug on the frontiersman's arm, she drew him onto the floor, where the two of them were quickly lost amidst the swirling throng of waltzers.

Glancing around the ballroom, I saw our hostess standing off to one side, safely surrounded by a veritable *retinue* of jovial friends. I thus felt myself at liberty to enjoy a brief interval of repose. As I cast my gaze about the ballroom, searching for a place to take my ease, I grew cognizant of an anomalous sensation. Not only the dancers, but the entire hall and all of its appurtenances appeared to be revolving at a dizzying rate of speed. I was forced to conclude that—in succumbing to the intensely convivial spirit of the occasion—I had indulged in an excess of punch, and was now suffering from a marked, though by no means incapacitating, case of inebriation.

Having noticed a capacious elbow-chair situated

in a far corner of the room, I bent my steps in the direction of this inviting article of furniture. Unfortunately, the Fiend Intemperance (as is ever his wont) had so wrought upon my powers of locomotion that I found it impossible to wend my way across the floor without colliding into a surprising number of my fellow masqueraders, several of whom responded most ungraciously—with sharp, reproachful looks and muttered imprecations.

Having no wish to render myself a nuisance, I resolved to leave the ballroom entirely for a brief interval and seek out a more secluded place to rest. Accordingly, I proceeded (albeit somewhat unsteadily) to the nearest place of egress, and at once found myself in a long—dimly lit—and exceptionally lofty corridor, lined on both sides with glass-fronted cabinets, containing countless additional specimens of the late Captain Nicodemus' unparalleled collection of exotic *bibelots*.

At length, after much (erratic) walking, I perceived a shaft of golden light in the gloom up ahead. This, I soon discovered, was issuing from a partially opened door. Approaching the latter, I opened it to its fullest extent with a gentle shove of my hands, and found myself gazing into a vast, lavishly appointed *boudoir*, belonging—I inferred from its contents—to Mrs. Nicodemus herself.

The room was brilliantly lit by a series of wall-mounted gas-jets, a mode of illumination so recently introduced to our fair city—and as of yet so inordinately costly—that I had never before witnessed it first-hand. Needless to say, I was transfixed by the sight of this marvelous innovation. Of even *more* compelling interest to me at that moment, however, was the enormous four-poster bed that occupied the center of the room, and whose broad, deep, and intensely *luxurious* mattress seemed to beckon with an overpoweringly seductive appeal.

For a moment, I simply stood in the threshold of the chamber and gazed longingly at this alluring article of furniture. Even in my somewhat fuddled state, I was cognizant that—for a guest to uninvitedly enter his hostess's *boudoir* and avail himself of her bed—represented an egregious violation of every known standard of propriety. Still, I silently argued, what harm could there be in reposing for a moment on so inviting a surface—particularly when there was no one about to witness this entirely innocent transgression of etiquette?

Having thus settled the matter to my satisfaction, I softly closed the door behind me, staggered towards the enormous bed, and, with a great sigh of contentment, threw myself backwards onto the mattress, my arms and legs extended in a "spread-eagle" position. No sooner had I settled onto the bed, however, than I became conscious of the heavy tread of approaching footsteps—the door flew open to its fullest extent—and there, in the threshold, loomed Mrs. Nicodemus, her features wrought into an expression of shocked incomprehension.

"Mr. Poe!" she exclaimed in a tone in which outrage and reproach were equally commingled. "I saw you walk—or, rather, *stagger*—from the party and followed you to ask what was the matter. Little did I suspect that I would discover you stretched out upon my bed! What is the meaning of this extraordinary breach of decorum?"

Head swimming, I hurriedly pushed myself into an upright attitude and began to stammer out an explanation. Before I had managed to complete a single sentence, however, I was rendered utterly speechless by an intensely startling circumstance.

Directly to the rear of Mrs. Nicodemus, another presence had suddenly materialized in the doorway—a masquerader whom I had not previously noticed at the party. This figure was made up to resemble the hideous spectre of Death, as it is commonly depicted in the medieval *danse macabre.* Of medium height—and dreadfully *gaunt*—it was shrouded from head to foot in the *habillements* of the grave. The mask which concealed the visage was made so nearly to resemble the grisly countenance of a fleshless human skull that the very sight of it caused the marrow to freeze in my bones.

In its hands it grasped a long-handled scythe, the razor-like edge of whose great, crescent blade glittered in the light from the gas-jets.

At the sight of this wan—this *hideous*—apparition, my own countenance must have grown deathly pale; for Mrs. Nicodemus—who continued to scrutinize me from her vantage point in the threshold—suddenly exclaimed: "Are you ill, Mr. Poe? Your face has gone white as chalk."

My organs of vocalization still paralyzed by fright, I lifted my trembling right hand and pointed wildly in the direction of the doorway. Responding to my frantic gesticulations, Mrs. Nicodemus—her brow contracted in perplexity—turned to look behind her. At that instant, the gruesome spectre raised the scythe high over its left shoulder and—bringing it down in one fierce, sweeping motion—struck the elderly matron directly across the throat!

Had Mrs. Nicodemus been a woman of more slender constitution—or had her attacker been of more formidable strength—the poor widow's head would certainly have come flying off. As it was, a great spray of blood issued from her severed throat, and her head tilted sideways at a ghastly angle. Raising the lethal implement high above its head—like a hooded executioner, poised to deliver the *coup de grâce* to a condemned prisoner—the implacable fiend brought the gleaming blade down upon the widow's neck once again. This time, Mrs. Nicodemus' entire head—eyes bulging, mouth agape—fell from the shoulders; while the decapitated body—after remaining grotesquely upright for a brief but unspeakable moment—tottered and collapsed to the floor.

The sheer overwhelming horror of this atrocity—occurring so close to the bed that a shower of arterial blood gushed from the stump of the poor victim's neck and bespattered my costume—caused a shriek of the purest terror to erupt from my fear-constricted throat. As I cringed—and quailed—and cowered on the mattress, the hideous spectre dropped its scythe upon the floor, stepped over the prone and headless body of the butchered widow, and drew close to my side. Reaching up one slender, white hand, it plucked the death-mask from its visage, causing a shudder of absolute dread to course through my frame as I gazed upward at the same appalling countenance I had witnessed on two prior occasions: a countenance whose features, though possessed of a distinctly feminine cast, bore an uncanny resemblance to . . . *my own!*

The room swam—a swirling fog of inky blackness began to becloud my vision—my consciousness commenced to dim. In the instant before I lapsed into utter insensibility, the spectre bent towards me, and—placing its pallid lips in exceptionally close proximity to my right ear—whispered a single, portentous, and ineffably *sinister* word.

Quoth my double: "Nevermore!"

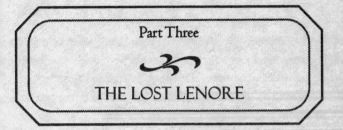

Part Three

THE LOST LENORE

CHAPTER 24

The intrinsic *duality* of human nature—our intense and perpetually antagonistic desires for, on the one hand, experiences of a sublime, elevated, purely *spiritual* variety and, on the other, for sensations that appeal sheerly to our earthly and even *prurient* selves— is a phenomenon that has posed a profound moral dilemma to philosophers throughout the ages. Christian dogma has ever rested on a staunch and unambiguous principle: to wit, that the sensual strivings in man must be utterly subdued and, if possible, extirpated entirely from our bosoms. Notwithstanding nearly two thousand years of this teaching, however, society persists in contriving the means by which our basest impulses can be continuously gratified, along with our most exalted.

Thus, the theatregoer of Elizabethan days might— after devoting several hours to viewing the incomparable Burbage perform *King Lear* at the Globe—cap his afternoon of leisure by attending the protracted public torture, evisceration, and dismemberment of a condemned

traitor. An educated Frenchman of the Jacobin era
might take a respite from his perusal of Voltaire's *Essai
sur les moeurs* to watch a dozen gruesome beheadings at
the Place de la Révolution. And even in our own, more
enlightened and ostensibly less barbarous time and
place, the Sunday churchgoer might return directly to
his home after his weekly worship and—previous to
partaking of his Sabbath dinner—spend a diverting
hour by poring over the latest edition of one of those
increasingly prevalent "penny" publications whose contents are replete with the most graphic imaginable
accounts of appalling calamities, unspeakable atrocities, and grisly crimes.

To the individual whose mind is unfettered by the
unreflecting prejudices of mere *conventional* wisdom, the
co-existence within the human bosom of these seemingly irreconcilable impulses suggests a novel, perhaps
even *heretical*, idea: *viz.* that the cultivation of one's fullest humanity depends, not upon the suppression of
either one's spiritual or sensational desires, but rather
on the judicious indulgence of them both—that these
two predilections, far from being mutually exclusive, are,
on the contrary, complementary and inter-dependent:
inextricably bound together in ways that neither science
nor theology has taken into consideration. In short
(and *contra* the orthodoxies of our religious tradition),
it may well be the case that, for the higher self to
achieve its full fruition, the lower must be permitted its
own gross, if stimulating, nourishment—in precisely
the same way that, to produce a perfect rose, the plant

must be rooted in soil that is fertilized by the richest (and often rankest) ordure.

Certainly there are men of exceptional endowments—beings whose intellectual and spiritual faculties have been developed to the highest degree—who, when not pursuing more elevated pleasures, find inordinate delight in the morbid—the macabre—the violent—and the grotesque. For the sake of convenience, I shall use myself as an *exemplar*. That pleasure which is the most purely stimulating to my soul is derived from the prolonged contemplation of Ideal Beauty, as it is embodied in the sublimities of great music, in supreme works of painting, and in the poetry of a handful of authors, whose number includes Tennyson, Keats, Shelley, and (with certain significant caveats which I shall refrain, for the sake of concision, from enumerating at this juncture) Coleridge.

And yet there are other, almost equally cherished, moments when nothing affords me deeper pleasure than to meditate on the most dire and abominable of calamities: on the Earthquake at Lisbon—the Plague of London—the Massacre of St. Bartholomew—the stifling of the hundred and twenty-three prisoners in the Black Hole at Calcutta—the unspeakable depredations of the Spanish Inquisition. In short, while acutely, if not *painfully*, sensitive to the excitation of what may be termed the *Poetic Sentiment*, I have ever derived an altogether different, though scarcely less extreme, satisfaction from themes having to do with atrocity, bloodshed, and horror.

It must not be supposed, however, that—in confessing to a fascination with such dark and gruesome matters—I intend to portray myself as a man of vicious and depraved temperament. For—even while *printed* accounts of unspeakable enormities and unpardonable crimes can suffuse my soul with a dreadful, if delicious, excitation—the actual *sight* of human suffering in any of its manifold forms is and has ever been a source of the most unmitigated dismay and revulsion. Oh, gigantic paradox, too utterly mysterious for solution! To read—to think—to dream—about the torments of Christian martyrs, the *autos-da-fé* of Toledo, the fiendish ingenuities of the medieval torture-dungeons has, since the days of my earliest boyhood, constituted a cherished and beguiling pastime. But to *witness*, at first hand, an act of extreme physical cruelty or violence is a horror from which my soul utterly and instinctively recoils.

In light of the foregoing observations, it will come as no surprise to the reader that the appalling murder of Henrietta Nicodemus—taking place only several feet away from my horror-struck eyes—affected me so adversely that I was plunged into a state of profound insensibility. Although I had frequently pondered the subject of decapitation—perusing various gruesome accounts, for example, of the executions of Charles I and other notables who had been dispatched by this time-honored means—nothing had prepared me for the hideous actuality of seeing a fellow-human beheaded.

How long I remained thus unconscious I cannot state with precision. Amid subsequent, earnest efforts to remember—amid determined struggles to regather some token of the condition of seeming nothingness into which my soul had lapsed—there have been brief, very brief periods when I have conjured up vague recollections of droning voices—of milling figures—of urgent efforts to rouse me from my oblivion. But all attempts to restore my mind to consciousness proved fruitless, as though my anguished soul were willfully resisting the painful return to life, perception, and knowledge.

At length, by slow degrees, I *did* recover. But even *then*, my harrowed mind clung with a fierce, tenacious hold to the sweet anodyne of utter incomprehension. I perceived but did not *understand* the details of my surroundings—the brilliantly illuminated bedchamber, now crowded with other people, among whom I recognized Crockett, Count Languedoc, and a number of police officers, including Captain Russell. I *heard* but could not account for the strange admixture of sounds—the hushed, urgent consultations of the policemen—the sobs of grief and dismayed exclamations emanating from the group of horror-stricken partygoers gathered just outside the doorway of the room.

It was not until I glanced down at the floor and noticed the ponderous and prostrate human form—mercifully shrouded with a white sheet—and, beside it, the discarded, blood-stained sickle, that the truth came rushing back upon me. Bolting into an upright position on the mattress, I emitted a gasp of sheer, inexpressible terror, which immediately brought the frontiersman rushing to my side.

"Rest easy, ol' hoss," said Crockett in a kindly, solicitous tone, as he bestowed several reassuring pats upon my shoulder. "You are amongst friends now."

Trembling convulsively in every limb, I stared wildly about the blood-spattered room. Only then did I notice a second, shrouded form lying prone upon the floor, not far from the threshold. Utterly bewildered as to what had transpired in the interval since I lapsed into oblivion, I parted my lips and attempted to frame a question. My powers of speech, however, had been rendered so feeble by the dreadful experience I had so lately endured that I was unable to utter more than a quavering "B-but wh-hat . . . ?"

"McGrath!" commanded Captain Russell, addressing one of his subordinates. "Fetch Mr. Poe some water." In response to this directive, the young officer in question immediately swivelled on his heels and hurried from the room, forcing his way through the crowd of distraught onlookers clustered around the doorway.

In the meantime, Crockett—as though intuiting the question I had attempted to ask—sombrely declared: "It don't surprise me none that your voice is plumb wore out, Poe. That howl you let out was loud enough to raise the dead. It brought a whole passel of us running."

Here, the frontiersman emitted a sigh so profound that it appeared to originate in the uttermost depths of his bosom. Indicating, with a tilt of his head, the shrouded figure near the threshold, he said: "Miz Nicodemus' man, Toby, was first through the door. When he set eyes on the horrificacious sight, why the poor feller went down like the Philistine temple when ol' Samson give it a shove. We done our best to bring him to, but it wasn't no use, for his heart had plumb give out, and the life was already extinctified in him."

Captain Russell had, by this point, joined Crockett at the bedside. From his presence, and that of his subordinates, I deduced that I must have been unconscious for a considerable period of time—long enough, at any rate, for the police to have received word of the atrocity and make their way to the locale of the crime. This supposition was confirmed by Russell, who—scrutinizing me with a singular and somewhat disconcerting *intensity*—explained that he and his men had already been on the scene for nearly twenty minutes.

"I need hardly say," remarked the stout, moustachioed police captain, "that—in addition to my distress at the appalling sight which greeted us upon our arrival—I experienced no small degree of surprise at finding yourself and Colonel Crockett here."

At this moment, the young policeman whom Russell had addressed as "McGrath" returned to the room, holding a large tumbler of water, which I gratefully took from his hands and drained in a single, greedy swallow. Then—clearing my now-moistened throat—I began to explain to Captain Russell how we had come to be present at the ill-fated *masque.*

Before I could complete more than a few sentences, however, Russell interrupted me with a dismissive wave of the hand and declared: "Colonel Crockett has already informed me about the contents of the newspaper article that aroused your concerns over Mrs. Nicodemus' safety—concerns that have now been all-too-fearfully realized. I must confess, Mr. Poe, that I am dismayed at your having withheld such vital information from me."

"There were compelling reasons to do so," I softly replied.

"Be that as it may," he declared, "I must request— no, *demand*—that, in the future, you apprise me of any discovery that may have bearing on this case."

Arranging my features into an expression of sincere compliance, I gave a nod of assent.

"Now, Mr. Poe," said Russell grimly. "Since you have fully regained both your conscious faculties and powers of speech, please tell us in as much detail as possible precisely what transpired in this room."

The mere prospect of recollecting the abomination I had witnessed, of reliving the terror—the enormity—the sheer, indescribable *hideousness*—of Mrs. Nicodemus' death caused my heart to sicken. Inhaling a deep breath, I proceeded to recount the ghastly narrative, beginning with my decision to retire temporarily from the ballroom, and concluding with the murder itself. Notwithstanding Captain Russell's recent admonition, however, I refrained from describing the terrible revelation which had been vouchsafed me in the instant before I fainted.

Following the conclusion of my recitation, a moment of silence ensued, during which Captain Russell—his lips pursed, his eyes narrowed—continued to regard me with an inscrutable, though distinctly *appraising*, look. "So the perpetrator of this ghastly deed was costumed as the Angel of Death?"

"That is correct," I replied.

"And the killing occurred so near to your vantage point on the bed that your own costume became embrued with the blood issuing from the poor woman's neck."

"Yes," I replied.

"I take it that the same phenomenon accounts for the blood on your *hands*, as well."

Taken aback by this observation, I instantly lifted my hands and scrutinized my palms. To my surprise—for I had not, until that moment, been cognizant of the fact—they were indeed mottled with blood. "When the atrocity occurred," I said musingly, "I must have raised my hands before my face in an instinctive, *shielding* motion."

Slowly stroking one end of his extravagant moustache, Russell subjected me to a prolonged and intensely *discomfitting* period of inspection. At length, and in a voice whose tone possessed a strangely *insinuating* undercurrent, he declared: "You appear to have a peculiar habit of being present whenever disaster strikes, Mr. Poe. I first set eyes upon you over the ghastly remains of Elmira Macready. You were a guest at Roger Asher's when he and his sister perished in the dreadful conflagration. It was you who discovered Alexander Montague's horribly mutilated corpse. And now this."

"There's a right smart chance of funerals whenever Poe is around, for a fact," Crockett said, casting a quizzical look at the police captain. "But you ain't suggesting that he—?"

"I am suggesting nothing," said Russell. "I am merely offering a detached observation."

Despite the latter's protestation, it was now unmistakably clear that Russell had begun to perceive *me* as a suspect in the series of unparalleled atrocities that had commenced with the slaying of Elmira Macready. An icy chill coursed through my spine—my heart began to palpitate uncontrollably—my mouth grew parched with fear. At that instant, Count Languedoc—who had been hovering several paces to the rear of Captain Russell—stepped forward and declared: "*Excusez-moi*, Monsieur le Prefect. I could not help but overhear. While I am reluctant to cast doubt on the testimony of Monsieur Poe, I must in good conscience declare that I myself saw no one at poor Mrs. Nicodemus' ball who was costumed as *La Mort*."

Swiftly turning on the Frenchman, Crockett—his handsome visage wrought into an irate scowl—said: "Are you calling my pard a liar, *mon-sewer?*"

"*Pas du tout*," replied the other indignantly. "I am

merely stating that—though present from the very commencement of the ball—I observed no such masquerader." With a haughty elevation of one eyebrow, he inquired: "Did *you?*"

This query appeared to catch the frontiersman off guard. "Why, no," he replied in a somewhat flustered manner. "I can't rightly say as I did." Turning quickly to Russell, he proclaimed: "But that ain't nothing. The keenest-eyed injun scout in the whole blamed world wouldn't of noticed *every*one. Why, there was as many folks at that shindig as piss-ants in a holler log."

For a moment, Captain Russell stood in silent rumination, pinching his lower lip while casting a speculative gaze at Crockett. At length, he turned towards his young subordinates and declared: "McGrath. You and Blair go into the ballroom and interview the other witnesses. See if you can ascertain whether anyone observed a guest who was attired in the manner Mr. Poe has described."

At this reference to the remaining partygoers, I was seized with a spasm of sudden and overpowering *alarm.* So distraught—so *disoriented*—had I been rendered by the catastrophic events of the evening that I had entirely forgotten about Virginia!

Reaching out a hand, I clutched at the fringed right sleeve of Crockett's deerskin shirt and, in a tremulous voice, anxiously inquired as to my darling Sissy's whereabouts.

"Don't you fret none, ol' hoss," replied the frontiersman consolingly. "Maryanne Mullany has fetched her back home. I figgered this scene of infernal butchery wasn't no place for the gals."

Relinquishing my hold on the frontiersman's garment, I emitted a heartfelt sigh of gratitude and relief. All at once, I grew cognizant of a peculiar commotion emanating from the direction of the doorway. Casting my gaze thitherward, I perceived that this disturbance was occasioned by a new arrival, who was attempting to make—or rather to *force*—his way through the press of onlookers congregated outside the room. A moment later, the crowd gave way, and a singular personage strode across the threshold. His identity was quickly established when—noticing his entrance—Captain Russell took a step in his direction and declared: "Welcome, Mr. Bedloe. I have been expecting you."

This name was immediately recognizable to me from various newspaper accounts I had perused over the years, involving manifold crimes, accidents, and fatalities. It was none other than the Coroner's Physician of the City of Baltimore, Mr. Augustus Bedloe. Never having set eyes on this individual before, I took a moment to study his appearance. Clad entirely in black, he was inordinately tall and thin. He stooped much. His limbs were exceedingly long and emaciated. His forehead was broad and low. His complexion was absolutely bloodless. His mouth was large, pale, and arranged in a perpetual frown. His eyes, though abnormally large, were so totally vapid, filmy, and dull as to suggest the idea of a long-interred corpse. Altogether, he conveyed an impression of profound melancholy—of phaseless and unceasing gloom.

Speaking not a word, nor pausing in his stride, Bedloe swiftly crossed the room and, bending to the bulkier of the two shrouded forms, reached down one long, bony hand and swiftly drew aside the blood-stained sheet. So sudden was this motion that—before I could avert my eyes—I found myself staring directly at a sight that chilled the very marrow in my bones.

The mutilated corpse of Mrs. Nicodemus lay flat on its back, legs extended and slightly apart, arms outstretched, palms turned upward. Not merely the head but the entire neck was severed from the body, the death-blow having been delivered at the level of the shoulders. The ghastly condition of the maimed, truncated cadaver, its upper torsal region embrued in gore, was in itself profoundly appalling. Adding to the horror, however, was the sight of the severed head. Situated directly above the left shoulder, it sat upright on its neck-stump, its glassy eyes wide open, its bow-shaped mouth forming a perfect O, as though it were issuing a small exclamation of surprise at finding itself thus detached from the trunk.

At the first glimpse of these grisly remains, I could feel the blood drain completely from my countenance. A wave of nausea rose up in my bosom, which I struggled in vain to subdue. Perceiving the intensity of my distress, the frontiersman tapped a forefinger on Captain Russell's shoulder and addressed him thusly: "Cap'n, I reckon I'd best take Poe back home, for he is looking mighty poorly."

"Very well," said Russell. "I see no reason why he

should not return to his domicile." Then, turning to me, he inquired: "You are quite certain that you have told us *everything* that transpired here tonight, Mr. Poe?" As before, the tone of his voice conveyed a sense of the liveliest suspicion.

Assuring him—with all the sincerity I could muster—that I had omitted nothing from my testimony, I set my feet upon the floor, placed my hands against the edge of the mattress, and pushed myself into a standing position. So debilitating, however, had been the effects of that evening of madness that—when I endeavored to walk—my knees immediately buckled, and I nearly collapsed to the floor. I was rescued from this mishap by Crockett, who—swiftly grabbing me by the upper portion of my right arm—prevented me from falling.

"Let me give you a hand, ol' hoss," he said, as—with his stabilizing assistance—I slowly made way across the room. "I'll be hanged if you ain't as unsteady as a steamboat with one wheel."

CHAPTER 25

The barouche which bore us to the party having been employed to transport Sissy and Miss Mullany back to Amity Street, it fell to Crockett to secure another conveyance for our use. How this was accomplished, I cannot say. My mental condition was one of extreme stupefaction. Though my limbs retained their power of locomotion, my conscious mind had ceased to operate with any degree of autonomy. I can compare this state to no phenomenon more properly than to a waking dream—or, rather, *nightmare*. Even with my eyes fully open, I saw nothing but the all-too-vivid image of Henrietta Nicodemus' savaged body—severed neck—and sundered head. The awful spectacle I had witnessed continued to possess me with a fierce and unrelenting hold.

At some point, Crockett *must* have succeeded in obtaining a carriage. He *must* have led me to the passenger's side and helped me to clamber on board. Then—assuming the driver's position and taking hold of the reins—the steadfast backwoodsman *must* have maneuvered the vehicle through the dark, cold, and empty streets, while I sat shivering beside him.

I know these things, not because I possess any positive memory of them, but rather by *inference*; for—following the lapse of an indefinite period of time—I found myself standing before the doorway of my modest domicile on Amity Street, with Crockett's steadying hand grasping one of my elbows. Of the circumstances which ensued I retain only the vaguest and most fragmentary of impressions: ill-defined recollections of the door being flung open by Muddy; of the good woman's cries of alarm as she perceived my blank eyes, pallid countenance, and blood-spattered attire; of Crockett's warm reunion with Maryanne Mullany, who—after escorting Virginia back to our abode—had awaited the arrival of the frontiersman; of Muddy's welcome tidings that Sissy, although deeply distressed by the events of the evening, was now soundly asleep; of Crockett's prompt and considerate leavetaking, after assuring me that he would return on the morrow for a "pow-wow"; and of Muddy's strong and indescribably consoling arm wrapped about my shoulders as she assisted me into my bedroom, where—without bothering to exchange my garments for a nightgown—I staggered towards my bed and fell face forward upon my mattress. Instantly, I found myself submerged in a long, profoundly unsettling, and uncannily vivid dream in which the condemned queen Marie Antoinette sat keening in a great wooden-wheeled tumbrel as it clattered through the serpentine streets of Paris on its way to her dread appointment with the "Nation's Razor."

Awakening with a groan, I found my chamber suffused with sunlight. For several moments, I was incapable of coherent thought. Though possessed of a dim, yet intensely *disquieting*, sense that events of a highly anomalous nature had occurred the evening before, I could conjure up no definite recollection of them. What precisely had transpired? How had I come to be reposing on *top* of my bedclothes, instead of comfortably beneath my blankets? And why was I garbed in such extraordinary attire?

All at once, I became aware of an odd and wholly unpleasant sensation on the palms of my hands. Raising them to the level of my eyes, I saw that they were dabbled with reddish-brown stains. At that instant, the truth came rushing back upon me. Leaping from my bed, I hurried to my washstand and vigorously scrubbed away the sanguinary vestiges of the awful atrocity. Then, divesting myself of my blood-soiled costume, I rapidly changed into my customary attire and strode from the room.

Muddy was not in the kitchen. Repairing to Virginia's chamber, I discovered the good woman at her dear daughter's bedside. Only Sissy's empillowed head was visible, the remainder of her body being concealed beneath her quilt. Her eyes were closed—her features were utterly immobile—and her complexion was exceptionally pallid. In all, she resembled nothing so much as a recently deceased corpse—an appearance which, I could not help but observe, endowed her with a strange, supernal beauty. A tremulous gasp escaped my lips, at the sound of which Muddy became aware of my presence. Perceiving the distressed look upon my face, she quickly assured me that—though the intensely trying events of the *fête*, as well as an excessive indulgence in its many culinary delights, had left Sissy somewhat indisposed—there was nothing seriously amiss with the angelic creature.

After inquiring as to my own state of physical and emotional health—and learning that I was as well as could be expected—Muddy declared: "There is some nice porridge for you on the stove, Eddie. Go and help yourself to some. It will do you good. I will stay here with Virginia a bit longer."

Obeying the good woman's injunction, I proceeded to the kitchen and quickly fortified myself with a large portion of the bracing substance. I had just finished scraping the last remnants from my bowl when a vigorous rapping upon the front door signalled Crockett's arrival.

Within moments, I had admitted the frontiersman to our domicile and escorted him into my study, where we took our accustomed places—I in the seat behind my writing table, he in the facing chair. Having exchanged his backwoods raiment for his ordinary attire, he looked much the same as I had grown used to seeing him. There was, however, a peculiarly *troubled* expression upon his rugged, sun-browned countenance.

"I am right happy to see you back on your feet, Poe," he said, scrutinizing me with a gaze of singular intensity. "You was looking mighty poorly when I fetched you home last night. How's Miz Virginny faring?"

"She is resting comfortably in her chamber, attended by our ever-faithful Muddy, who has assured me that the dear child is expected to achieve a complete and rapid recuperation. In view of the extreme fragility of Sissy's youthful constitution, it is a wonder that she has not been rendered even more severely incapacitated by the shocking events of last evening."

"*Shocking* is right," exclaimed Crockett. "Why, I ain't seen such deviltry since the bloody massacre at Fort Mimms, when that infernal varmint Red Eagle and his band of cutthroats carried out the work of death as a butcher would in a slaughter pen."

"Indeed," I said. "I can perceive by the lineaments of distress engraved upon your visage just how deeply you have been affected by the appalling tragedy whose occurrence we foresaw, but were helpless to prevent."

"I reckon so," the frontiersman grimly replied. "Why, there wasn't but one thing you and me was supposed to be doing at that shindig—an' that was making sure no harm come to poor Miz Nicodemus. I don't know about you, Poe—but failing is mighty bitter medicine for Davy Crockett to swallow."

"I am entirely sympathetic to your feelings," I said gravely. "And yet, I cannot help but wonder whether any efforts on our part would have sufficed. I have begun to conceive"—and here, I could not keep my voice from betraying a slight, though noticeable, *quaver*——"that the adversary with whom we are faced is a being possessed of no ordinary human powers."

For a moment, Crockett merely stared at me in silence. Then, shifting uneasily in his seat, he declared: "There is something else that's got me a mite discombobillated, Poe."

There was, in his voice, a strangely *hesitant* quality, as though the matter he felt obliged to broach were fraught with the most acute embarrassment. An irrepressible tremor of premonitory alarm pervaded my bosom.

"Has anything else transpired since we parted last night?" I nervously inquired.

"I'll be shot if there ain't," Crocket confirmed. "Something mighty troubling."

With their digits so tightly interwoven that the knuckles showed white, I placed my folded hands upon the surface of the writing table and leaned forward in my seat. "Please apprise me of this matter at once," I urged.

Several tense and discomforting moments elapsed while the frontiersman continued to scrutinize me in silence. "Dagnab it, Poe," he ejaculated at last. "It's Cap'n Russell. He came to see me at the hotel this morning while I was eating breakfast. Sat himself right down at the table and begun asking me all sorts of questions."

"And what was the subject of his inquiries?" I barely managed to utter, my organ of vocalization having been seized with a sudden onset of extreme nervous constriction.

"Why," exclaimed Crockett, "they was all about you!"

Far from being unexpected, Crockett's reply only confirmed the foreboding conviction that had been mounting within my bosom for the past several moments. The *predictability* of his remark, however, in no way mitigated its singularly *unnerving* impact. Uncoupling my hands, I extended my arms sideways and tightly grasped the edge of the writing table. "And what were his reasons for propounding these queries?" I asked in a tremulous voice.

"Why it's the most jackass notion I ever struck," Crockett declared with a snort of incredulity. "I'll be chewed to death by tree-squirrels if he don't suspect that you had something to do with killing Miz Nicodemus—and all them other folks, too!"

No sooner had these syllables passed the frontiersman's lips than my entire frame was seized with an uncontrollable shudder. My limbs trembled—my heart quaked—my brain swam. I leapt from my seat and—in a voice that quickly rose to a shriek of wild desperation—cried out: "But he is *correct!* It is all *true!* Oh, do you not see, Colonel Crockett? It is I—and I *alone*—who am the murderer!"

The effect of these words upon Crockett may be easily imagined. He appeared absolutely dumbstruck. For some minutes he remained speechless and motionless, regarding me with an open mouth and eyes that seemed to start from their sockets. Before he could recover from this state of tongue-tied stupefaction, the heavy tread of approaching footsteps could be heard outside my room—the door to my chamber flew open—and in burst Muddy, her plain yet endearing countenance contorted into an expression of intense anxiety.

"Is something the matter, Eddie?" she worriedly exclaimed, her large, work-chapped hands clasped before her bosom. "I thought I heard the most fearful scream!"

Through an exertion of will-power that fell nothing short of the *heroic*, I managed to arrange my trembling lips into a reassuring (if somewhat thin and sickly) smile. "Everything is perfectly fine, Muddy dear," I replied in what I hoped was a convincingly *earnest* tone. "Colonel Crockett and I were merely rehearsing the tragic events of last evening."

For several moments, Muddy continued to study my visage with a look of the deepest concern. At length—as though vanquishing whatever lingering doubts she possessed as to the absolute veracity of my assertion—she emitted a sigh of relief and cast her gaze downward at our visitor. "And how are *you* this morning, Colonel Crockett?"

"Fair to middling," came the frontiersman's dispirited reply. He shook his head slowly from side to side several times, then looked up at Muddy and inquired: "What about Miz Virginny? Is the gal feeling better?"

"She is much improved, having just re-awakened from a long and restful nap," replied Muddy. "I really *must* get back to her. May I bring you boys something to eat before I go?"

"No thank you, ma'am," said Crockett. "All these pestiferous doings has put me a mite off my feed."

Having only recently partaken of her excellent porridge, I, too, declined Muddy's considerate offer—at which point she excused herself and departed from the room. No sooner had the door closed behind her than Crockett turned to me and, fixing me with a stern and penetrating gaze, declared: "Now, Poe. I reckon you'd best tell me just what in the blue blazes you meant by that outlandish speech of yours, for I'll be shot if it ain't hit me like a clap of thunder on a bright, sunshiny day."

Sinking back into my chair, I propped my elbows on the tabletop and buried my face in my hands. At length—having regained a measure of control over my turbulent emotions—I looked up at Crockett and said: "I can well appreciate the disconcerting effects of my extraordinary confession, Colonel Crockett. Be assured, however, that your own sense of dismay—no matter how intense, unmitigated, or *profound*—cannot possibly exceed my own."

My lips feeling dry to the point of desiccation, I took a moment to moisten them with the tip of my tongue before inquiring: "Are you familiar with the term *doppelgänger*, Colonel?"

"I don't reckon I am."

"It is a German word, meaning, in effect, a walk-ing—or *living*—double."

"I don't take much stock in German notions," came the frontiersman's reply. "Nor them of any other furriners, neither."

"Be that as it may," I said, "the term in question refers to a phenomenon whose reality, however seemingly *fantastic,* is acknowledged by societies throughout the world. Indeed, I have recently been perusing a most fascinating volume which treats of the subject as it pertains to the beliefs of the native inhabitants of Melanesia."

"I ain't entirely following your line of thinking, Poe."

I paused to consider how best to approach the subject so as to render it accessible to the frontiersman's comprehension. "You will grant," I said at last, "that there are two distinct conditions of mental existence. On the one hand are those faculties belonging to the realm of lucid *reason.* On the other are those features that partake of the purely *irrational.* This latter class comprises all those impulses, urges, desires, and phantasies that civilization decries as violent, immoral, and even insane. It must not be supposed, however, that—as abhorrent as they appear to our more refined and enlightened conceptions—these dark and lawless characteristics are peculiar only to those who lead lives of active criminality. On the contrary, a resolute and impartial process of self-scrutiny unmistakably reveals that they exist as a living, if deeply hidden, portion of every human being, residing in the nethermost recesses of even the most loving and law-abiding soul."

"Drat it all, Poe," interjected Crockett at this juncture. "I'm damned if I got the smallest notion of what you're saying."

Regarding the frontiersman with a firm—an *unflinching*—gaze, I drew a deep breath and declared: "I am speaking, Colonel Crockett, of the ancient and ubiquitous belief that each of us possesses an evil *alter ego:* a dark, daemonic spirit that, under certain exceptional conditions, may spring to life and enact—entirely without the complicity of our conscious minds—our most secret dreams and wishes!"

In response to this statement, Crockett's eyebrows leapt upwards in an involuntary gesture of surprise. "You mean what my grandpappy Crockett knowed as a *fetch?*" he said after a moment. "Well, I'll be jiggered! I have heard of such-like notions being common amongst the old-timers, especially folks that never had no schooling. But I am plumb bamfoozled to hear that an educated feller like yourself believes in them."

"But I do. Absolutely. Indeed, I have direct and unimpeachable evidence that the phenomenon to which I allude is *real.*"

"An' just what in the nation makes you so all-fired certain?"

"Because," I grimly declared, "on three distinct occasions I have now come face to face with the living incarnation of my own secret self. I have scrutinized—at a distance no greater than that by which we two are presently separated—her wan, her implacable, her utterly *uncanny* features."

"*Her?*" Crockett exclaimed in surprise.

Unable to remain seated in my overwrought state, I sprang to my feet and—striding to the center of the chamber—began pacing wildly about the floor, while Crockett turned his chair in my direction and continued to regard me with a sharp, interrogatory gaze.

"For reasons that I cannot conceive, the phantasmic apparition has taken a feminine form. Indeed, I have described her to you on several previous occasions."

For several moments, Crockett merely stared at me in puzzled silence. All at once, his countenance assumed an expression of startled realization. "You ain't speaking of that same mysterious she-male you said you spied in Asher's house, and then again in the bedroom of that Montague feller?"

"I am indeed referring to that dark and sinister being," I replied. "It was *she* who—garbed in the ghastly cerements of the tomb—materialized last night within Mrs. Nicodemus' *boudoir! She* who wielded the fearful weapon that so horribly struck down our poor hostess!"

"And just how in thunderation do you reckon *that*, when you never even set eyes on her face?" demanded Crockett.

Pausing in my agitated circumambulation of the room, I cast a penitent gaze at the frontiersman. "Colonel Crockett," I ruefully declared, "I must beg your forgiveness; for—in an utter violation of the bond of mutual trust upon which even the most transitory partnership must be founded—I have withheld from you a vital piece of knowledge. My sole excuse for this egregious lapse was my own conviction that the information in question was of such a highly anomalous—if not *incredible*—character that your faith in my veracity would have been taxed to the breaking point by a complete and uncensored disclosure of the facts. I see now, however, that I should have shared this intelligence with you at once."

"You mean there's something you ain't told me?" the frontiersman demanded.

Deeply abashed, I lowered my head and answered with an affirmative nod. "In each of the foregoing instances to which I have referred," said I in a tremulous voice, "I have directly beheld the visage of the sinister female intruder. This was true of last night's atrocity as well, when—immediately following the appalling murder of Mrs. Nicodemus—the heartless assassin plucked off her mask in my presence. And I tell you, Colonel Crockett, that—while the countenance I beheld may not have constituted a *precise* mirror image of my own—nevertheless, in its overall mold, lineaments, and cast, the resemblance was so startling as to leave not the slightest doubt of her—or rather *its*—identity.

"Oh, Colonel Crockett!" I cried out. "I am sure of it! This inhuman killer is nothing less than the incarnated agent of my own darkest, most diabolical wishes, directed against those upon whom I wish to exact a fierce and bloody revenge!"

Having thus divulged the terrible secret with which my bosom had been fraught for so long, I buried my face in my hands and emitted an agonized sob that seemed to emanate from the bottommost depths of my being.

This wrenching outburst brought Crockett to his feet. Stepping directly before me, he extended his arms and clasped each of my shoulders with a firm and steadying hand. "Easy there, pard," he exclaimed. "You are getting yourself all in a lather over nothing. Why, it don't make a lick of sense. Why in the nation would you want to do harm to all them folks?"

"About this," I moaned, "I can offer no more than the merest speculation, since my motives remain shrouded in obscurity, even to myself. It is evident, however, that the series of murders that commenced with the slaying of Mrs. Macready are in some still-unknown manner intertwined with the fate of my mother, Eliza. As you know, the sainted creature perished in the most wretched circumstances conceivable—friendless, alone, abandoned by all who professed to care about her. It may well be the case that these crimes were acts of long-overdue vengeance, perpetrated against those erstwhile admirers who—while deriving unparalleled pleasure from her histrionic genius—made no effort to assist her in her hour of direst need."

His mouth wrought into a grimace of intense skepticism, Crockett shook his head and declared: "Poe, I don't aim to be contrary—but I'm blessed if that ain't the *consarndest* notion I ever struck! C'mon back to your chair and let's study on this for a spell. I'll wager dollars to doughnuts that there's some other way of explaining what you seen."

Acceding to the frontiersman's proposal, I returned to the writing table and lowered myself into my seat. "But what other explanation can there possibly be?" I asked as Crockett resumed his place across from me.

"Liquor, for one," he replied. "You was plumb absquottleated at Asher's place. And you was hitting that punch bowl mighty hard again last night. Hell, Poe, there've been times I stowed away so much whisky I was seeing two-headed grizzly bears doing the fandango, and pink-striped rattlesnakes climbing over the walls."

I took a moment to consider this apparently plausible explanation before answering thusly: "I confess that, in spite of my determination to lead a life of rigorously *abstemious* habits, I may well have succumbed, in each of the two instances you speak of, to the temptations of the moment. Nevertheless, while my resulting mental condition may fairly be described as one of intoxication, it fell far short of the sort of extreme *inebriation* that would have produced such intense and lifelike hallucinations.

"Moreover," I continued, "on the evening I confronted the sinister female spectre in the gloomy precints of Alexander Montague's dwelling, I had indulged in no drink stronger than water. No, Colonel Crockett," I concluded with an emphatic shake of my head. "Mere intemperance alone cannot possibly account for the ghastly feminine horror I have now witnessed no less than three separate times."

"Maybe liquor *ain't* the whole story," Crockett

conceded. "But you mix it together with that pesky queer imagination of yours, and I'll be blowed if that don't serve as all the explaining you need. Hell, just look at these-here pestiferous books you spend your whole blessed life reading." Here, he turned his gaze upon the myriad volumes lining my bookshelves and laboriously began to enunciate their titles: "*The True History of Satan Worship; Devils, Demons, and Witches; The Art of Dying; Burial Practices in Ancient Europe; Torments and Tortures of the Spanish Inquisition*—"

Abandoning his efforts with an exaggerated sigh, Crockett shook his head—fixed me with a sharp, sardonic look—and wryly declared: "My souls, Poe. If *my* days was spent readin' such-like ornery truck, *I'd* be seeing double, too!"

Recalling the several recent occasions when I had been the recipient of strange, nocturnal visitations (such as the radiant apparition that materialized in my chamber on the very night of Crockett's advent in my life), I was forced to conclude that there might be a modicum of truth to the frontiersman's observation. "It is undeniably the case," said I, "that I am constitutionally *nervous* to an unusual degree, and thus prone, under conditions of extreme anxiety and duress, to visions of a wild and phantasmagoric nature. In short, your hypothesis is not entirely without an element of validity.

"Still," I continued, "even if I have been mistaken in the *precise* facial appearance of the dark and unsettling female presence I have thrice encountered, there is no doubt whatsoever that the figure itself was literally and palpably *there* on each of these occasions."

"Poe," Crockett responded, "I just cain't credit that such savagerous killings could've been done by a she-male."

"We err, Colonel Crockett," said I, "in attributing an utter incapacity for violent behavior to the fairer sex. The history of humankind is replete with instances of the most savage atrocities committed by women."

With deeply knitted brow, Crockett ruminated on this statement for several moments before replying: "I reckon you ain't wholly mistook there, Poe, for I have heard of injun squaws doing things to captives that'd make a body's blood run cold." Throwing up his hands in a gesture of impatience, he added: "Anyways, whosomever done this, man or woman, the main thing is for us to track down the eternal varmint—*fast!*"

"I concur absolutely," I replied. "Indeed, our mission has achieved a new and dramatic level of urgency, since there is now the additional motivation of allaying Captain Russell's suspicions of my own direct involvement in these horrific crimes."

"Well sir," said Crockett, slapping both hands against his thighs, "how do you reckon we'd best proceed?"

"I have given this matter some thought and have arrived, I believe, at a reasonable course of action. As you are aware, the mystery that confronts us is related, in some still-unknown fashion, to the theatrical world of which my late mother was such a shining adornment. This fact, as I have previously indicated to you, is attested by *this*."

Here, I reached for my casket-shaped "treasure box" and—opening the lid—extracted the yellowed newspaper clipping and held it aloft. "You will recall that this review was composed by Alexander Montague. In view of the latter's *rôle* as a drama critic, it appears likely—or at any rate *feasible*—that further clues to the mystery might well be contained in other of his writings."

"But where in thunderation will we find them?" Crockett demanded.

"I have already determined," I answered, restoring the clipping to its receptacle, "that they are contained in the collection of moldering newspapers with which his apartment is *crammed* to overflowing. I propose, therefore, that you and I repair at once to his dwelling and conduct a thoroughgoing search of these time-worn publications."

For a moment, Crockett sat in silent rumination. "Damned if that don't sound like mighty tiresome work," he said at last. "Still," he added with a sigh of resignation, "I reckon it *is* a level-headed idea."

"Then let us proceed without delay," I declared.

As Crockett got to his feet, I rose from my chair, stepped around the writing table, and—positioning myself before the frontiersman—extended my right hand. "Before we depart, Colonel Crockett," I solemnly declared, "I must convey to you my heartfelt sense of gratitude for the unwavering faith you have shown in me, at a time when others—and indeed, even

I myself—have been beset by the gravest doubts as to my innocence."

Grinning broadly, Crockett enveloped my hand with his own and gave it a vigorous shake. "There ain't no need for thanks, Poe. That's what friends is for. You and me is pards to the end, ol' hoss—and until this plaguesome business is all took care of, I will cling to you as tight as a snapping turtle to a fisherman's toe!"

CHAPTER 26

Before embarking on our mission, I strode down the hallway to Virginia's bedchamber and tapped lightly on the door. From within, Muddy's voice beckoned me to enter. Proceeding inside, I was overjoyed to find Sissy fully alert and reposing in a half-upright position in bed, her back supported by a voluminous pillow.

Beside her sat Muddy, an open book resting upon her lap. To beguile her daughter's time, the good woman had plainly been reading aloud from this volume, which—I was startled to discover—turned out to be the very copy of Colonel Crockett's life story that Mr. Timothy White had sent me for review. Unbeknownst to me, Muddy had rescued it from the ever-replenished pile of discarded books that accumulated in my study and that I periodically transported to a local bookseller, who paid me a small remuneration for each volume.

"Oh, Eddie," exclaimed Sissy, after I had expressed my delight in seeing her thus recuperated. "Colonel

Crockett has had the most *thrilling* life! And what a *wonderful* book he has written about it!"

"I am pleased that you find it so," I replied somewhat stiffly, "and will be sure to convey your compliments to its author who is, even now, awaiting my appearance." I next turned to Muddy and informed her that, along with Colonel Crockett, I was involved in an undertaking that would keep me occupied until dinnertime at the very earliest—and, quite possibly, even later.

Then—after bestowing a fond farewell kiss upon the brow of each of my darling ones—I rejoined my companion, who had already repaired to the street and taken his place in the driver's seat of his borrowed chaise.

Twenty minutes later—after a trip during which my companion drew the usual measure of excited recognition from his adoring public—we arrived at our destination. It was a surpassingly lovely spring day. In contrast to the climatic conditions prevailing at the time of my first visit to Montague's dwelling—when the skies had been ashen and sober—the weather was exceedingly balmy and bright. Far from mitigating the dismal atmosphere suffusing the neighborhood, however, the brilliant sunshine only served to exacerbate the pervasive sense of *bleakness*.

The street, so crowded with curious onlookers during my initial visit, was now all but deserted—its sole visible occupant being a small, towheaded lad who was in the process of tying a tin can to the tail of an emaciated mongrel pup as our carriage drew to a halt before the dilapidated edifice. As Crockett dismounted and affixed the reins of our vehicle to the warped and weather-beaten hitching post, the kneeling boy cast an intense, quizzical gaze at the frontiersman. All at once, his visage assumed a look of almost comically exaggerated astonishment. Releasing the struggling dog from his hold, the young boy leapt to his feet—dashed to the end of the street—and disappeared around the corner.

Climbing down from the carriage, I mounted the stoop of the squat, red-brick building with Crockett at my side and tried the door. As anticipated, it was unlocked. Stepping inside, we paused for a moment in the malodorous entranceway, allowing our eyes to adapt to the extreme gloominess of the interior.

At length, with Crockett in the lead, we proceeded down the cramped and murky hallway to the bedroom. At my first glimpse of this insufferably squalid chamber—a site now forever linked in my mind with the unspeakable horrors I had encountered there—my frame was seized by a paroxysm of dread. Apart from the yawning hole in the floorboards, where Montague's horribly mutilated corpse had once lain, the room looked much the same as it had when I had previously entered it—which is to say, in a state of the most complete and chaotic disorder. The countless, brittle copies of the *Baltimore Daily Advertiser*—the newspaper to which Montague had been such a frequent contributor—lay scattered all across the floor, having evidently been completely undisturbed since my last visit. As Crockett made a brief, exploratory circuit of the room, I reached into my pants pocket and extracted a large, freshly laundered handkerchief that I had made certain to bring. Folding it in half, so that it formed a large, isosceles triangle, I raised it to my face, brought the corners around the back of my head, and affixed them into a knot. I then adjusted the front of the handkerchief so that it hung down from the bridge of my nose and entirely covered the lower portion of my face, its pointed end depending to the bottom of my chin.

No sooner had I completed this operation than Crockett—whose back had been turned to me for the past several moments—looked my way and gave a start of surprise.

"Good land, Poe! Are you fixing to rob a bank?"

In a voice somewhat muffled by the double layer of fabric overhanging my mouth, I replied thusly: "I am merely taking a precautionary measure against the noxious conditions which precipitated such a violent respiratory outburst during our earlier investigation."

"You mean that thunderacious sneezing you done?" Crockett said. "That was a window-rattler, for a certainty." Then—after gazing about the room with a somewhat baffled expression—he turned back to me and asked, "How do you figure we ought to commence?"

"Given the state of utter confusion in which the newspapers are strewn across the floor," I replied, "a systematic examination of Montague's collection is plainly impossible. My suggestion, therefore, is this. Let each of us occupy one of the chairs at the dining table and, selecting a newspaper at random, carefully peruse its pages. Once finished, the reader will discard his paper *beneath* the table, thus ensuring that each man does not inadvertently re-examine an issue that has already been scrutinized by the other."

"That makes good sense," said Crockett. "And just what exactly are we supposed to be looking for?"

"Each of these publications," said I, gesturing towards the newspapers that blanketed the floor, "should contain an article composed by Alexander Montague. Most of these writings will, of course, have no bearing whatsoever on the matter which concerns us. The ones we must look out for are, in the first place, those relating to any theatrical performances involving my late mother, Eliza Poe; second, those containing references to any of the individuals who have already fallen victim to the unknown killer; and, last but by no means least in importance, any that might illuminate the signification of the mysterious word, 'Nevermore.' "

"All right," said Crockett.

"Then let us proceed without delay," I said.

After stooping to pick up the papers that lay nearest to our feet, Crockett and I settled ourselves on opposite sides of the dining table, and—carefully unfolding the brittle yellow pages—bent ourselves to our task.

For the following hour, we pursued this occupation with silent intensity, the quiet of the room broken only by the dry, crepitant rustle of the turning pages, and the occasional muttered complaint from my companion, who periodically avowed that he would "sooner be wrassling a passel of wildcats than wading through all this infernal writing."

And indeed, the perusal of the crumbling yellowed pages, with their endless columns of badly faded print, was an exceedingly laborious task. Still, it was not (at least from my own point of view) entirely devoid of certain pleasures. I discovered that Montague, though far from the most fluent—adroit—or *felicitous*—of writers, had been a man of considerable cultivation, erudition, and taste. That the entire latter portion of his life had been passed in circumstances of such extreme, such *oppressive* squalor struck me as almost unbearably sad. Laying aside my paper, I emitted a deep and tremulous sigh.

At this sound, Crockett lowered his own paper and—gazing across the table with a sympathetic expression—declared: "I know just how you're feeling, ol' hoss. This here is monstrously tiresome work, and no mistake."

"The sigh that issued from my bosom was not one of fatigue," I replied, "but of profound, nearly *insupportable* melancholy."

"Concerning *what?*"

"I had been ruminating on the exceedingly harsh and bitter life led by poor Montague. Here was an individual possessed of a high intelligence and an unusually literate sensibility. And yet, for much of his life, he appears to have existed in a state of the most excruciating poverty and deprivation imaginable." Shaking my head, I ruefully declared: "In a country such as this, to be a man of letters is a grim—if not indeed a *tragic*—fate."

"Why, that ain't necessarily the case," exclaimed the frontiersman. "Take a gander at *me*. I'll be pecked to death by humming birds if I don't stand to make a whole bundle of money off of *my* book!"

That a work of such staggering ineptitude as Crockett's crudely written *memoir* could meet with resounding commercial success was, of course, a precise confirmation of my point. Only in a nation whose citizens were possessed of the most primitive, if not actively *debased*, literary sensibility could such a phenomenon occur. Not wishing to insult my companion, however—nor to engage in a protracted debate about the deplorable reading tastes of the American public—I merely said, with subtly calibrated irony: "Clearly, Colonel Crockett, you have discovered the secret of successful writing."

"Danged right I have," he replied, oblivious as ever of the nuances of my tone. "Know what it is?"

"I confess to my ignorance in this matter."

"Write about things that common folks can understand! Take a look at this-here Montague feller," he exclaimed, indicating the paper in his hands. "Here he is, a-rattling on and on about some writing by ol' Shakespeare—some blame foolishness about a midsummer dream, all full of fairies and whatnot." His features wrought into a look of the purest disdain, he dropped the newspaper onto the tabletop and continued: "No sir, Poe. That kind of flapdoodle just ain't got no *meaning* for folks nowadays. They want to read about the *real* world. If you want folks to buy your writing, give 'em the plain facts of life—tell them what you *done*—what you *lived* through—what you *seen* with your own two eyes!"

In spite of my resolve to avoid a dispute with the frontiersman, I could scarcely refrain from offering a response to this exceedingly *callow* aesthetic pronouncement. Before I was able to speak, however, my attention was arrested by a peculiar noise emanating from a spot directly to my rear.

Swivelling in my seat, I was startled to perceive a quartet of young male faces, eagerly gathered at the partially open window. Among this group I immediately recognized the towheaded lad who had been kneeling in the street at the time of our arrival, and whose act of casual childhood cruelty we had unwittingly interrupted.

"What the devil are you looking at, Poe?" asked Crockett, leaning far to one side so as to peer around my body, which occupied an intervening position between the window and himself. The instant his face became visible to the small band of juvenile observers, they immediately burst into a chorus of excited ejaculations.

"It *is* him!" cried one of the boys, his round, somewhat porcine countenance suffused with wonder. "You were right, Jesse!"

"Didn't I *say* so!" crowed the towheaded lad, who— I now perceived—suffered from that unfortunate ocular affliction commonly known as *walleyes*. "You *are* Davy Crockett, ain't you?" he asked, addressing the frontiersman while keeping his gaze riveted firmly on me.

"Blamed if I ain't, young 'un," said Crockett with an amiable chuckle. By this point, he had risen from his seat and was standing, arms akimbo, in the center of the floor.

"I *knew* it was you the minute I saw you!" exclaimed the walleyed youth named Jesse. Gesturing at me with a tilt of his chin, he asked: "And who's *that?*"

"My pard," said Crockett. "Mr. Edgar Poe."

"Why's he wearing that snotrag around his face?" asked the boy.

Though this crudely phrased question was addressed to my companion, I thought it only proper to reply to it myself. Accordingly, I explained that the handkerchief affixed to my countenance was intended as a prophylactic measure to protect my somewhat delicate respiratory organs from the insalubrious atmosphere of the chamber.

"As you are perhaps unaware," I elaborated, "the pleural membranes of the human lung are, in many cases, unusually susceptible to certain varieties of airborne mold commonly found in houses which——"

Before I could elucidate further, the walleyed youth——whose upbringing had clearly been sadly deficient in matters of rudimentary etiquette——abruptly turned to Crockett and asked: "What are you doing here, Davy?"

"Me and Poe is searching for clues as to the nefarious murder of the feller what used to live here."

"Old Mr. Montague!" cried the lad. "We heard all about it. How his eyes were stabbed out, and his throat was cut from ear to ear, and his body was buried under the floorboards!"

"That is the sorry truth of it, all right," Crockett said gravely. "Any of you fellers hear anything else that might help us out?"

"No sir," said Jesse, shaking his head. Then, pointing a thumb at the moonfaced lad at his side, he added: "Tommy here *saw* something, though."

"Yes?" I said, looking intently at the youth denominated as Tommy. "And what precisely was the 'thing' that you observed?"

"A woman," he replied.

"A *woman!*" Crockett and I exclaimed in unison.

"Yes sir," said the boy. "The day old Mr. Montague disappeared. It was real early in the morning. I was just coming back from the privy, when I saw this strange woman sort of snooping around the street."

"And what did she look like?" I eagerly inquired in a voice that quavered slightly with excitement. "Were you able to attain an unimpeded view of her visage?"

"Was I *what?*" asked the boy.

"Did you see her *face?*" I asked.

"No sir," said the lad. "I only saw her from the back. She was about middling height, and there didn't appear to be much meat on her, and she was dressed all in black. Her hair was black, too. *Real* black. As black as"—and here, he slowly raised his right hand and, extending his stubby forefinger in my direction, said—"as *yours*, mister."

At this astonishing pronouncement my heart

began to beat wildly within my bosom. Here at last was persuasive testimony—if not incontestable *proof*—that the ominous female being I had thrice encountered was something more than a mere *phantasm*.

Pensively stroking his clean-shaven chin, Crockett ruminated on this intelligence for a moment before saying: "Well, young 'uns, you've been a power of help. Now, you'd best skedaddle on out of here, and let me and my pard get on with our business."

"Aww," sighed young Jesse. "Can't we stay here and help you some more, Davy?"

"Tell you what," Crockett said. Approaching the window, he inserted a hand into the pocket of his gray-striped trousers, extracted a coin, and proffered it to the walleyed youth. "If there's one thing Davy Crockett holds to, it's showing thanks to his friends. So here's a shiny new five-cent piece—and if that ain't enough to buy peppermint sticks for the whole lot of you, I wish I may be tromped to death by centipedes. Now you just make for the nighest candy shop—and if me and Poe need you, why, we'll just give a hoot and a holler!"

Snatching the coin from the frontiersman's hand, the walleyed lad emitted an exultant *whoop*, turned on his heels, and darted out of sight, his companions following directly behind.

"Well, Poe," Crockett said gravely as he resumed his place at the table. "I reckon I was mistook. Looks like that mysterious she-male you seen wasn't just a figger o' your imagination after all."

It is a feature of our all-too-human nature that few emotions are sweeter—more purely *delicious*—than a feeling of vindication. In this instance, however, my pleasure was entirely eclipsed by a sense of the deepest foreboding—by the dreadful certainty that, should the frontiersman and I fail in our present undertaking, another innocent person would soon fall victim to the sinister, raven-haired female whose existence had just been corroborated by the testimony of the corpulent youth, Tommy. I therefore replied:

"So it would appear. And unless we succeed in discovering both the motives and identity of this mysterious assassin, another tragedy—I am firmly convinced—will shortly ensue."

"Let's get cracking, then," said the frontiersman.

Without further delay, we returned to our labors. For the following hour—or possibly even longer (for I did not take note of the time)—my companion and I perused one newspaper after another in perfect silence. I read—with eyes that grew increasingly bleary as the afternoon progressed—a seemingly endless succession of theatrical reviews, a few concerning such legendary performances as the elder Booth's interpretation of Richard the Third, which created an unusual sensation at the Holliday Street Theatre on the evening of November 2, 1821, and Edmund Kean's stirring portrayal of the doomed protagonist of *Macbeth*. The majority of Montague's essays, however, dealt with actors and plays wholly (and no doubt justifiably) obscure: a Mr. George Boniface as Captain Bleinheim in *Diamond in the Rough*; a Miss Effie Germon as Sally Scraggs in *Sketches of India*; a Mr. Charles Matthews, Sr., as Bob Tyke in *The Trip to Paris*, and many others of this inconsequential ilk.

But in none of these articles did I discover even the slightest clue that might help us resolve the terrible mystery of the ominous word "Nevermore," or shed light on the identity of the shadowy female assassin.

Gradually, the act of reading became very nearly impossible, partly owing to the sustained ocular exertion demanded by the task, and partly to the inexorable dwindling of the daylight filtering in through the window. Laying down my paper, I closed my aching eyes and gently massaged them with the tips of my fingers; while Crockett—taking note of my discomfort—attempted to ignite the lamp that stood at the center of the table. The oil reservoir proving utterly depleted, however, he extinguished his match and declared: "I reckon we might as well call it quits, ol' hoss. The light in here don't amount to shucks."

"Indeed, the illumination afforded by the rapidly fading daylight is entirely inadequate to our needs," I replied. "Moreover, while the tightly woven fabric of my handkerchief has succeeded in shielding me from the many pulmonary irritants suffusing the air, it has also rendered the simple act of respiration exceedingly strenuous.

"At the same time," I added after a brief pause, "I am loath to abandon our efforts, while so much remains to be accomplished."

"What do you reckon we ought to do?"

I ruminated on this question for several moments before replying: "Perhaps we can transport the remaining publications back to Amity Street, where I can continue to persue them in the more congenial environment of my study."

Glancing dubiously at the floor, Crockett said: "There's a monstrous sight of papers here, Poe. Why, just toting them all out to the carriage would be a mighty drearisome job."

"It would be difficult indeed," I agreed. All at once, I was struck by a thought. "Do you not recall," I asked, "how eager young Jesse and his friends were to assist us? Perhaps now is the time to avail ourselves of their offer."

"That ain't no slouch of an idea," Crockett conceded. "Let me see if I can round them up."

Rising from his seat, he hurried from the room. In the meanwhile, I took the opportunity to undo the handkerchief, emitting a deep sigh of relief as I removed it from my face. Some ten or fifteen minutes later, the frontiersman reappeared with the youthful quartet in tow. The four boys then happily assisted us in conveying the newspapers out to the chaise, while Crockett regaled them with a protracted and wholly improbable anecdote about his ostensible encounter with a prodigious member of the species *Amiurus lacustris*—or, as he put it in his crude backwoods vernacular, his "rip-roarious scrape with a monstracious great cat-fish."

At length, the task was completed and—bidding

farewell to young Jesse and his companions—we set out for Amity Street, arriving at my dwelling some twenty minutes later. Dismounting from the vehicle, I gathered up an armload of papers and carried them to my doorway. With my arms thus occupied, I found it necessary to announce my arrival by drawing back my right boot and delivering a single, emphatic kick with the toe. An instant later, the door swung open and there stood Muddy, wearing an expression of such extreme dismay that—my thoughts immediately turning to Virginia—I felt my heart seize up with fear.

"What is the matter, dearest Muddy?" I cried. "Has something happened to Sissy?"

"Oh, Eddie, I am so relieved to see you! No, no—Virginia is perfectly well. But only minutes ago, I received an urgent visit from a young police officer named Carlton, who was seeking you and Colonel Crockett."

"Why, what is the matter?" I inquired. By this point, Crockett, whose arms were also laden with a quantity of Montague's papers, had materialized at my side.

"Something dreadful has happened," said Muddy. "The two of you are to go to Calvert Street at once."

"Calvert Street?" I repeated.

"Yes," said Muddy. "To the Baltimore Museum."

CHAPTER 27

The Baltimore Museum and Gallery of Fine Arts was the offspring of the redoubtable Mr. Charles Willson Peale, a personage of seemingly inexhaustible energies and spectacularly variegated talents. Silversmith, saddler, watchmaker, wood-carver, violinist, inventor, and painter——as well as the creator of the first set of enamel teeth ever made in America——this remarkably *protean* genius (who had also done distinguished service in the Revolutionary War) aspired to establish a great public institution dedicated to the cultivation of aesthetic taste and the diffusion of scientific knowledge. In 1786, this dream was realized when Mr. Peale opened his first museum at Philadelphia——"an elegant establishment," as he advertised it, "for the rational enjoyment of Natural History & the leisurely contemplation of Art." In 1801, following the discovery of two mastodon skeletons in Orange County, New York, he undertook——largely at his own expense and with the assistance of his sons Raphaelle, Rembrandt, Titian, and Rubens——the painstaking excavation of these remarkable specimens, one of which eventually became the centerpiece of his imposing collection.

The second of these magnificent fossils became the property of his son, Rembrandt, who took up permanent residence in Baltimore in 1813. In August of the following year—impelled by the same worthy ambitions that had inspired his father—the younger Peale opened his own branch of the museum in a three-story edifice on the west side of Holliday Street, just north of Lexington. For a modest admission fee (twenty-five cents for gentlemen and ladies, half price for children), the public gained access to a succession of bright and spacious galleries, each housing a vast—not to say, wildly *eclectic*—assemblage of artifacts.

In candor, it must be stated that the scientific—aesthetic—and pedagogical—value of these *objets* was irregular in the extreme, ranging from the truly sublime to the merely *bizarre*. Here, visitors might see an authentic Egyptian mummy in its ornate sarcophagus, displayed alongside the stuffed remains of a tropical boa constrictor measuring eighteen feet in length; or view an electrostatic generator, arranged next to a hideously shrunken human head from the isle of Borneo; or contemplate a surpassingly graceful brass statuette from Herculaneum, exhibited beside a Barlow knife with ninety-eight blades; or marvel at a working model of Charles Readhjefer's perpetual-motion machine, situated close beside an armless young woman named "Madame Helene," who—by wielding a pair of scisssors with the toes of her right foot—

could transform a square sheet of white paper into an elaborate snowflake pattern.

The art galleries featured an equally heterogeneous collection of works, many of them painted by various members of the prodigiously gifted Peale family itself. These latter comprised over forty portraits of Revolutionary War heroes by Charles Willson Peale; historical and allegorical paintings by Rembrandt Peale, including *The Roman Daughter*, *The Death of Virginius*, and his colossal (if somewhat overly portentous) *The Court of Death*; Sarah Miriam Peale's portraits of such Baltimore notables as Mayor John Montgomery and Mr. Hugh Birckhead; Raphaelle Peale's *Still-Life with Herring*; and Rubens Peale's depiction of his family's original establishment in Philadelphia.

In spite of—or, perhaps, *owing to*—the exceptionally miscellaneous nature of its offerings (some of which were hardly distinguishable from the grotesque specimens of human malformation to be found in the tawdriest curiosity-shows), Peale's Baltimore Museum rapidly became one of the city's leading attractions. Its great success, along with its ever-multiplying acquisitions, eventually necessitated a move to larger quarters; and in 1830, the entire collection was relocated to a handsome building on the northwest corner of Calvert and Baltimore streets. In early 1833, however, disaster struck in the form of a terrible conflagration, which severely damaged the building and consumed many irreplaceable artifacts. It was yet another tribute to the prodigious energies of this remarkable clan that,

a mere seven months later—on July 4, 1833—the
museum was able to reopen its doors in a newly reno-
vated, exceedingly handsome, marble-faced edifice.

It was to this vast repository of science, art, and
novelty—this singular combination of painting gallery, natural history museum, live menagerie, and collection of human oddities—that Crockett and I had
now been summoned. After hurriedly unpacking the
remaining newspapers from the chaise (a task greatly
expedited by the assistance we received from my ever-
dependable Muddy), we immediately set off for this
destination.

That something of great urgency had occurred at
the museum was an unavoidable supposition; and, as
our vehicle rumbled through the darkening streets, I
clung to the hope that we were not journeying to the site
of still another gruesome murder. The instant our carriage turned the corner of Calvert Street, however, that
hope was utterly dashed; for I immediately observed a
sight that filled my soul with dread. Congregated outside the imposing, three-story building was one of those
milling crowds of morbidly curious individuals who
invariably materialize at the scene of any atrocity, and
whose presence—like the slow, ominous circling of
those avian scavengers denominated as *buzzards*—signi-
fies the proximate occurrence of sudden, ghastly *death*.

Hurriedly dismounting from our vehicle, Crockett
and I made for the entrance. Awed ejaculations arose
from the crowd, as its members became cognizant of
the frontiersman's presence. Co-mingled with these

exclamations were several audible expressions of perplexity as to my own identity. "See how melancholy he looks—and how drearily he is attired!" I heard one elderly woman loudly whisper to her companion. "Surely, he must be the undertaker!"

Entering the building, we passed through the *foyer* and found ourselves inside a cavernous gallery, brilliantly illuminated by gas-jets and filled with several hundred mounted specimens of birds, beasts, amphibians, fishes, and insects. As we hurried down the center of this imposing collection—past glass-fronted cases replete with every imaginable variety of carefully preserved *invertebrata*—Crockett shook his head and muttered: "I can't cipher it nohow, Poe. Why would folks pay good money just to see whole rows of little bugs and other such varmints stuck up with pins?"

In more leisurely circumstances, I would have replied to this exceedingly naive query with a concise discussion of the vitally important science of biological taxonomy, as pioneered by the great Lamarck in his magisterial (if not *wholly* original) work, *Histoire naturelle des animaux sans vertèbres*. There was, however, no opportunity for such a disquisition; for, as we reached the far end of the gallery, I perceived a trio of policemen conferring at the opposite end of the adjacent room.

One of these, I saw as we drew nearer, was Officer Carlton. Along with his two colleagues, he was standing beside a display of preternaturally lifelike wax mannikins, representing such immortal literary figures as Shylock, Falstaff, and Tam O'Shanter. Noticing our approach, Carlton turned from his companions and, after welcoming each of us by name, declared: "I am glad that you have come. Captain Russell is most eager to see you."

"What precisely has transpired here?" I inquired. "Not—I fervently hope—another ghastly murder?"

"I am afraid, Mr. Poe, that the implacable fiend has indeed struck once again," the young man acknowledged grimly.

"Well, I'll be a sheep-killing dog," Crockett exclaimed. "Where in the nation is the cap'n?"

"With the victim," said Carlton. "Come. I will show you the way."

Instructing his companions to await his return, the young officer motioned for us to follow, then turned on his heels and conducted us through an arched passageway and into an adjoining gallery. In the middle of this lofty and capacious hall loomed the reconstructed fossil of the towering, great-tusked mastodon whose bones had been exhumed from their primordial resting place in rural New York by the elder Mr. Peale.

Passing this monstrous skeleton in awestruck silence, we came at length to a latched wooden door, situated in the extreme northeast corner of the hallway. This door was of the sort that might conceal a small storage area or closet. Upon its being opened by Carlton, however, there stood revealed—not, as I had anticipated, a storeroom—but rather a steep, exceedingly narrow wooden staircase that descended into the subterranean reaches of the building.

On the wall beside the door, at approximately shoulder-level, a lantern hung from a wooden peg. Carlton now took hold of this appliance and—after lighting it by means of a phosphorous match—turned to us and said: "Follow me, gentlemen. And please be careful where you step."

Then, with the young man preceding us, the frontiersman and I cautiously made our way down the cold—dark—and exceptionally *musty*—stairwell, until we came at length to the foot of the descent and stood upon the damp floor of the catacomb-like basement.

By the glow of the lantern, I now perceived that the extensive collection of cultural artifacts, biological specimens, and scientific curiosities that filled the three main floors of the museum constituted only a portion of its contents; for here, stretching in every direction, was a vast accumulation of items that had been consigned to the basement for the purpose of storage. As Carlton raised his lantern and surveyed our surroundings, I could see in its beam a seemingly endless medley of rare and remarkable *objets:* several mummified cats, the jawbones of a spermacetti whale, an entire stuffed rhinoceros, a Chinese opium pipe, a life-sized wax figurine of Julius Caesar, a precise replica of the famed Liberty Bell that hangs in Philadelphia's Independence Hall—and much, *much* more.

"This way, gentlemen," said Carlton, directing the beam of his lantern approximately thirty degrees to the left, where I now perceived the mouth of what appeared to be a narrow, low-arched tunnel. Stooping our heads, we made our way through this cramped and labyrinthine passage—whose damp walls gleamed with a white web-work of nitre—and proceeded, by slow degrees, into the furthermost recesses of the basement.

At length—after innumerable windings—we emerged into a large, high-ceilinged chamber, or rather *vault*, illuminated by the flames of several oil lamps that had been placed atop some of the myriad storage crates, puncheons, and barrels that were piled everywhere about us. I immediately spied Captain Russell, who—along with three other police officers and a gray-haired gentleman I could not immediately identify—was standing several yards away, beside an upturned, iron-hooped cask at the remote end of the vault.

"Ah," said the captain, as we approached. "I had almost despaired of your coming."

"Having been engaged on an errand of some moment," I replied, coming up beside him, "we did not receive your message until a short while ago, at which point we set out at once for the museum."

"I assume," said Russell, "that Officer Carlton has already apprised you of the reason for my summons."

Acknowledging the accuracy of this observation with an affirmative nod, I gazed about the area and grimly inquired: "Where is the body?"

Without a word, Russell extended a hand toward the upright cask. Casting my gaze at this receptacle, I now saw that its lid had been removed. Its interior, however, was entirely cloaked in shadow. Bending closer, I peered inside, while Officer Carlton—to facilitate my inspection—extended his lantern over my left shoulder, so that its beam fell directly on the contents of the cask.

In consideration of the reader's sensibilities, I shall withhold a description of the ghastly—the hideous—the utterly *unspeakable*—sight which smote my eyes at that instant. Suffice it to say that I found myself staring at the remains of an elderly gentleman, whose body—in order to make it fit within the narrow confines of the cask—had been subjected to the most fearful mutilation and dismemberment. Gasping in horror, I staggered backward from this awful spectacle; while Crockett—who had stepped up to the cask so as to view its contents for himself—loudly exclaimed: "Why I'll be shot if that ain't the horriblest outrage I ever struck!"

For several moments, dizziness overwhelmed me. Closing my eyes, I leaned my weight against a large, iron-bound crate, clutching at one edge for support. At length, the vertiginous sensation subsided. Upon re-opening my eyes, I saw that Captain Russell was regarding me narrowly.

"This atrocity," I said hoarsely, "can only be the handiwork of the fiend we are pursuing."

"Of that there can be no question," Russell answered, "for the killer has left his customary signature." Then, turning to Officer Carlton, he commanded: "Show him."

In response to this directive, the young police officer dropped to one knee and held his lantern close to the cask. The light revealed the enigmatic word "Nevermore," crudely inscribed across the middle portion of the cask in daubs of dried blood that possessed the texture and appearance of thickly applied, rust-brown paint.

"The murder weapon was discovered there," said Russell, pointing to a place on the floor several feet away. Following his gesture, I saw an antique headsman's ax lying on the ground, its formidable, razor-edged blade darkly stained with gore.

"It is a precise replica of the one used in the execution of Mary, Queen of Scots," remarked the gray-haired gentleman who stood at Russell's side. "One of several hundred items in our collection of rare, historical armaments."

Turning my gaze upon this speaker, I scrutinized him narrowly for several moments. His features seemed strangely familiar, although I felt absolutely certain that I had never before set eyes on him. He was a middle-aged man of singularly distinguished mien, with a countenance remarkable for its harmonious admixture of masculine force and feminine sensitivity. His eyes were bright and penetrating to the highest degree; his forehead pale and lofty; his nose of a delicate Hebrew model, but with a breadth of nostril surpassing similar formations. His chin was prominent, cleanly chiselled, and remarkably square, bespeaking both physical vigor and moral fortitude. In striking contrast to the manifest strength of his jawline, however, was the surpassing delicacy of his mouth, whose soft, almost voluptuous shape suggested that contour which the god Apollo revealed but in a dream to Cleomenes, the son of the Athenian.

All at once, I realized with an inward start that this exceedingly noble-looking gentleman was none other than Mr. Rembrandt Peale himself, whose visage was familiar to me from the handsome self-portrait displayed in the *foyer* of the museum, where I had contemplated it on earlier visits. After introducing myself to this eminent personage with a deferential bow, I gently inquired as to the identity of the victim.

"His name is Joshua Hutchins," Mr. Peale sorrowfully replied. "He served for many years as my trusted caretaker." Then, in a voice fraught with both outrage and grief, he added: "Why this atrocity has befallen the old fellow I cannot, for the life of me, conceive, for—so far as I know—he was without an enemy in the world."

"When was the last time you saw him?" I inquired.

"At around noon today. I had come to the museum in search of a certain item—a tricornered hat originally belonging to the great Dr. Franklin, which I had promised to loan to the governor, who wished to put it on temporary display at his mansion. Unable to locate it—and prevented from conducting a more extensive search by a pressing lunchtime engagement— I asked Mr. Hutchins if he would, at the earliest opportunity, see if he could uncover it among the miscellaneous items kept down here in the basement."

"This dreadful act of butchery, then," I mused aloud, "occurred sometime during this very afternoon."

It was Captain Russell who replied to my observation. "That is correct," said he, peering at me intently. Then, after pausing briefly—as though reluctant to broach a matter that must, of necessity, prove deeply unpleasant—he said: "Forgive me, Mr. Poe, but I am obliged to inquire as to your own whereabouts earlier today."

Having been fully apprised by Colonel Crockett of the police captain's suspicions regarding my involvement in the crimes, this query scarcely came as a surprise. Before I could formulate a reply, however, the frontiersman—who had, by this point, stepped up beside me—turned to Russell and declared: "He was within spitting distance of me the whole time. I *told* you you was barking up the wrong tree! Why, ol' Poe here ain't got no more harm to him than a hornet with a busted tail."

Visibly abashed at the frontiersman's testimony, Captain Russell regarded me with a chastened expression and addressed me thusly: "I beg your forgiveness, Mr. Poe. It is true, as Colonel Crockett suggests, that I had come to regard you as a possible suspect. I see now that I have been utterly mistaken."

This apology, delivered in a tone of heartfelt contrition, demanded a commensurately *gracious* reply. Accordingly, I gave a little bow and declared: "Captain Russell, please do not castigate yourself unnecessarily. All of us, even those endowed with unusual powers of discernment, are liable, on certain occasions, to be mistaken in their assumptions. Indeed," I continued, exhaling a heavy sigh, "I myself—as it now appears—have been guilty of just such an error."

"How so?" Russell asked, lifting his eyebrows inquiringly.

"For reasons that, at the present moment, are far too complicated to delineate, I had come to suspect that the victims of these dreadful crimes were all affiliated with the theatrical realm. But this appears not to have been the case with the present victim, who was employed—not in any capacity related to the stage—but as a museum caretaker."

"But poor Hutchins *was* involved with the dramatic arts!" exclaimed Mr. Peale.

"What!" I cried, turning towards the speaker with a look of undisguised *amazement.*

"Many years ago," Mr. Peale continued, "long before he entered my employ, he trod the boards under the stage name of Thorowgood J. Kemble."

At the mere pronouncement of this singular cognomen, I immediately recalled having encountered it that very afternoon while perusing Alexander Montague's old theatrical reviews, a number of which had praised the dramatic performances of this minor, if much-admired, player, who had excelled in such subsidiary roles as Shakespeare's Bottom, Webster's Ambitioso, and Jonson's Sir Politic Wouldbe.

"Well, boil me for a sea-horse if ol' Poe ain't hit the mark again," exclaimed Crockett, delivering an enthusiastic *smack* to my shoulder, which—owing primarily to the sheer *unexpectedness* of this gesture, as well as to the exceedingly irregular surface of the cellar floor—caused my knees to buckle slightly. I quickly regained my equilibrium, however, and turned to face Captain Russell.

It was evident from the dark look suffusing the latter's visage that he did not share the frontiersman's appreciatory view of my achievement. "Mr. Poe," said he with a frown, "I am deeply chagrined to find that—despite your promise to the contrary—you have concealed *another* piece of knowledge from me. You have said nothing to me about these suspicions regarding the theatre."

"In my own defense," I replied, "I can say only that—my suspicions being of such an *indefinite* nature—I deemed it best to withhold them until I had managed to arrive at a positive conclusion."

"And have you succeeded in doing so?" demanded Russell.

"At present—no," I conceded with a dispirited sigh.

"I see," Russell said, stroking his luxuriant moustache while he continued to regard me narrowly. "But you are persuaded that these heinous crimes are in some way connected to the theatrical profession?"

"That is correct," I replied.

"Perhaps, then," said Russell, "my officers and I should undertake to interview the sundry individuals—play-actors, stage-managers, and so forth—connected to the various dramatic companies currently sojourning in Baltimore."

"The course of action you propose might indeed

be productive of important *clues*," I answered. "And now, I must ask your forbearance. The strains of this long and arduous day—combined with the intensely *oppressive* air of these surroundings and the shocking spectacle of the disarticulated victim—have had a severely enervating effect upon my frame."

"Looky here, Cap'n," the frontiersman declared, "I'm feeling a mite tuckered out myself. I'm all for calling it quits for tonight. Us three can pow-wow again tomorrow if you've a mind to."

This proposal was readily accepted by Russell; whereupon, we bid farewell to Mr. Peale and—with Officer Carlton once more in the lead—proceeded through the dank, labyrinthine passages of the cellar and up the narrow, twisting staircase. Emerging once again into the hall of the great mastodon, we took our leave of the young officer and made our way out of the museum.

By this point, the crowd of curiosity seekers had entirely dispersed. We mounted the carriage in silence and drove away through the dark, largely deserted streets. Little conversation passed between us as we went. At length we arrived at my domicile.

"Reckon I'll head on back to the hotel," Crockett said with a great yawn as I climbed down from the carriage. "It's been a poison long and tiresome day. I'm fixing to get me some shut-eye, and I suggest you do likewise. I'll come by before lunch tomorrow, and we'll finish plowing through them damn newspapers."

So saying, he bid me good-night and, maneuvering

the chaise about, disappeared down Amity Street, while I approached the door of my abode.

The hour was sufficiently late that I did not expect to find either Sissy or Muddy awake. And indeed, as I entered the house, the pervading stillness led me to deduce that my loved ones had retired for the night. This supposition was confirmed when, stepping into the kitchen, I found a note on the table from Muddy, informing me that she and Virginia had gone to bed, and urging me to eat some of the Bologna sausage she had prepared for supper, which I would find on a platter near the stove.

Though I had consumed virtually nothing all day, I did not feel hungry in the slightest degree. Nor—in spite of my physical fatigue—was I inclined to repair to my bedroom, my overstimulated nerves having reached that pitch of excitation at which slumber becomes an impossibility. As a result, after extinguishing the oil lamp in the kitchen, I proceeded to my study.

The multitudinous newspapers we had transported from Montague's residence were piled, helter-skelter, on the floor of my study. Taking a large bundle of these publications in my arms, I carried them to my desk, settled into my chair, and began to read. Soon, I was wholly absorbed in this undertaking, poring over innumerable accounts of long-ago theatrical productions. I read about Mrs. Broadhurst's winning depiction of Constance Macintosh in Cumberland's charming comedy *Everyone Has His Fault*. About Clifton Tayleure's riveting interpretaton of the titular *rôle* in Gilmore's *Gustavus Vasa*. About Edward Sinclair Tarr's somewhat disappointing début performance in Wignell's *The Busy-Body*. Thus did the hours speed by.

It was not until the sky outside my uncurtained window was already beginning to manifest the first, faint gleams of daylight that—with bleary eyes and pounding heart—I rose from my chair, clutching in my trembling hands an issue of the *Baltimore Daily Advertiser* from the year 1810—an issue in which I had discovered, only moments before, the significance of the fateful word "Nevermore."

CHAPTER 28

Twenty-four years earlier, almost precisely to the day—on Saturday, May 3, 1810—a troupe of itinerant thespians appeared on the stage of the New Theatre on East Baltimore Street. For several years, this company had made its home in Boston; but with the completion of that city's theatrical season in early April, its members—impelled by the precarious financial circumstances inherent to the artistic life—had embarked on a tour of the southern states.

The play performed on that occasion (an evening which—though seemingly unremarkable at the time—eventually proved to have consequences that were nothing short of *momentous*) was a then-popular, now wholly forgotten, farce entitled *Sebastian Barnwell, or the Brazen Lover.* In the leading female *rôle*—as the desirable young noblewoman, Lady Amelia, whose hand is sought in marriage by a variety of suitors, including the Duke of Cornwall—was the gifted and much-beloved actress Eliza Poe, who, less than four months earlier, had served as the dear, maternal agent of my own nativity.

In a minor, if not entirely negligible *rôle*, as a courtier named Belmore who functions as the Duke's intermediary, was the being whom I am compelled, much to my own chagrin, to acknowledge as my father: the vain, ambitious, but hopelessly inept play-actor David Poe the younger.

I knew these facts from the dramatic review I had just discovered during my long, laborious perusal of Alexander Montague's collection of old newspapers. This review, published on the Monday after the evening in question, contained a vivid description not only of the production itself but of the audience's reaction to it.

My mother's portrayal was greeted with the intense, the *unbridled* enthusiasm characteristic of the responses that her acting invariably evoked. My father, too, in his exceptionally *fleeting* appearance, elicited a reaction that typified his effect on theatrical audiences. In his case, however, this reaction was not one of approbation but of its diametrical opposite—a fervent outpouring of the most vociferous and heartfelt *disdain* for the utter incompetence of his acting. I shall quote from the relevant portions of the review. After perusing this passage, the reader will readily understand why—upon my discovery of this document—I leapt from my chair in a veritable *frenzy* of astonishment, excitement, and awe. Here is what Montague wrote:

> It must be reported that—while Mrs.
> Poe performed the part of Amelia with

her customary authority and grace—her husband's exceedingly brief appearance in the *rôle* of a foppish courtier in the service of the Duke was painful both to witness and to hear. In addition to his physical shortcomings—his muffin face and excessively slender frame—Mr. Poe seems inordinately susceptible to that debilitating nervous condition which occasionally afflicts even the most experienced stage-actor but which, in *his* case, operates so acutely as to deprive him of nearly all his powers of speech and exertion.

On Saturday evening, Mr. Poe's part in the production required him to deliver but a single line. The Duke of Cornwall—his marital proposal having been rejected by the beauteous Amelia—dispatches his man, Belmore (Mr. Poe), to convey his sense of extreme disappointment. The line in question went thusly: "I am bid to say: Your 'nay' hath made my lord so sad that he shall nevermore be glad."

This speech comprises fewer than twenty words, all but one of them consisting of a single syllable. And yet, the hapless Mr. Poe managed to deliver it in so faltering, so *egregious* a manner, that he could scarcely be comprehended by the audience, among whom were some of our city's most eminent citizens: Mr. Samuel Ogden Asher, Mr. and Mrs. Junius Macready, Mrs. Josiah Nicodemus, and others. His stammering attempt to enunciate the polysyllabic word "Nevermore" would have been positively comedic, had it not occasioned such intense *embarrassment* in both the actor and his audience. (Indeed, at least one member of Mr. Poe's own company troupe could be seen snickering openly at the poor man's bungling efforts. This was the ever-amusing Mr. Thorowgood J. Kemble, in the *rôle* of Amelia's clownish servant, Tom Crackskull.)

At the conclusion of the play, the audience rewarded Mrs. Poe with a loud, prolonged, and richly deserved outburst of applause. Upon Mr. Poe, however, it lavished nothing but a veritable torrent of catcalls, hoots, and insults. "Nevermore return to Baltimore!" shouted one incensed theatregoer, and soon the jeering cry of "Nevermore!" echoed throughout the auditorium.

With this severe but not-unmerited verdict the present reviewer is wholly in

accord. Mrs. Poe will always be a welcome sight on the theatrical stages of
our city. But as for her husband, we
would feel intensely grateful if we were
to see him perform—*nevermore!*

Still shaking violently in every limb, I sank back
into my chair, while a crowd of tumultuous thoughts
rushed hurriedly through my mind. Precisely how long
I remained seated at my writing table, I cannot, with
any degree of certainty, state. There was a mad disorder in my brain—a tumult unappeasable. I had managed to resolve one crucial element of the puzzle. But
the mystery as a whole remained as bewildering—as
maddeningly *elusive*—as ever.

Of my principal deduction—that the ghastly
series of murders was somehow related to long-ago
theatrical events involving my own family—there
could no longer be the slightest doubt. But in another
vital respect, my speculations had proven to be wholly
erroneous. The gruesome string of killings was not—
as I had supposed—related to my *mother.* Rather, as
was sufficiently clear from the above-quoted review,
they were in some way connected to a severe public
humiliation suffered—nearly a quarter-century before!
—by my *father.*

About this deplorable being I possessed relatively
little information. Whatever curiosity I may once have
felt in his regard had long since been expunged by my
overwhelming sense of bitterness—by my utter dis-

dain for a man so lost to honor and decency that he had abandoned his young wife and babes to the cruel buffets of the world. The few facts I *did* know were these:

The namesake of that celebrated personage who had served his country so ably during the Revolutionary War, the younger David Poe had, in his early manhood, trained to be a lawyer. Even then, however, he apparently harbored dreams of becoming an actor—dreams excited to an even greater pitch when, at the age of twenty-five, he attended a performance of Richard Gilmore's then-popular comedy *The Market Lass*, and was struck with the charms of its leading actress, Miss Elizabeth Arnold. By the following year, he had abandoned his legal studies to pursue the histrionic calling. Endowed with a strong, melodious voice, a supple physique, and a burning ambition, the young man possessed attributes well suited for the stage. Unfortunately, he was also prone to a paralyzing fear that often rendered him entirely incapacitated while performing.

Hoping that this severe liability would dissipate over time, he joined the Virginia Players, appearing in a variety of minor *rôles*: as "Falliero" in *Abaellinor, or The Great Bandit;* "Allan-a-Dale" in *Robin Hood;* "Harry Thunder" in *The Tale of Mystery;* "Young Woodland" in *Cheap Living;* and more. By 1805, he had married another member of the troupe, the aforementioned Miss Arnold—my future mother. For the next several years, the couple performed together in countless productions. But—while his beautiful young wife gained increasing renown with each passing season—his own reputation underwent a corresponding *decline*, until he had become a virtual laughing-stock. The *coup de grâce* to his career had evidently been delivered on the fateful evening I had just read about; for, shortly thereafter, in July 1810, he vanished abruptly, leaving no clue as to his whereabouts.

These meagre facts were all I knew of the man. What had become of him—where he had gone, how he had supported himself, and indeed whether he was living or dead—were matters of the purest speculation. Now, more than two decades following my father's disappearance, the spectre of this cruel, this *deplorable* being had intruded once more into my life.

That the bloody word "Nevermore" scrawled at the various murder sites was an allusion to that long-ago evening of mortification seemed incontrovertible. But if such were the case, then who was the perpetrator of these terrible crimes? Could it be the man himself, still living after so many years and returned to take vengeance on the surviving agents of his humiliation? Though such a circumstance was not wholly inconceivable (assuming that he were yet alive, my father would be fifty-seven years of age, still physically capable of working harm), this theory failed to account for the sinister female apparition I had confronted on numerous occasions.

With these and other conundrums preoccupying my mind, I was oblivious of the passage of time. All at once, from the opposite side of the wall that divided my study from the kitchen, I became cognizant of certain noises—muffled footsteps, creaking floorboards, the clattering of dishes. Glancing up at my clock, I saw that it was almost 6 A.M. The sounds from the kitchen were now fully explained, for I quickly deduced that my ever-devoted Muddy had already arisen and was embarked upon her early-morning chores.

Leaping from my chair, I hurried from my room and burst into the kitchen, the *abruptness* of my entrance causing Muddy—who was situated before the stove, attempting to ignite it—to emit a little yelp of surprise.

"Oh, Eddie!" she panted, one hand clutching her capacious bosom. "You nearly frightened me to *death!*" Pausing momentarily until her breathing had resumed its normal rhythm, she inquired: "How long have you been awake?"

"Yesterday's events sent my soul into such turmoil," I replied, "that—to paraphrase the Immortal Bard—Nature's soft nurse would not weigh my eyelids down and steep my senses in forgetfulness."

"My goodness!" she exclaimed. "Do I take that to mean you have gotten no sleep?"

"Such, indeed, was the purport of my statement," I replied.

"My poor boy!" she cried. "You must be exhausted. Sit down at the table and I will fix you a nice cup of tea."

Obeying her directive, I settled into my customary place, while—setting a pot of water upon the now-enkindled stove—the good woman inquired as to the nature of the crisis that had occurred at the museum.

"Someone was killed," I grimly replied. "And in a manner so savage, so sheerly *atrocious*, that to recount it in any detail would serve no other purpose than to fill your soul with revulsion."

"How awful," she said. "But what have all of these dreadful crimes to do with *you?*"

"As of yet, that mystery remains unresolved," I replied. "Through my indefatigable exertions, however, I have at last discovered a clue which may lead to an answer."

"What sort of clue, dear?" she inquired.

"One whose significance you yourself may prove instrumental in helping me to discover."

"Me?" she exclaimed.

"Yes," said I. "And now, dear Muddy, if you will join me at the table, I wish to ask you some questions regarding a person of whom we have rarely, if ever, spoken. I refer to your elder brother—my long-vanished father—David Poe."

In response to this statement, Muddy's visage assumed an expression of the purest surprise. "Why, what do you wish to know about him?" she said at last.

"All that you can tell me of the circumstances which impelled him to violate the most sacred, the most *primal* bonds of both conjugal and parental devotion, and to abscond from his young wife and babes."

The startled look on Muddy's countenance was now replaced by one of intense chagrin. Very plainly, her brother's perfidious behavior remained, even after the passage of so many years, an acutely painful subject for the good-hearted woman. A sympathetic pang coursed through my bosom at the sight of my dear Muddy's distress. Nevertheless—though loath to occasion her even a modicum of unhappiness—the urgency of the situation demanded that I persist in my interrogation.

Accordingly, I again requested that she seat herself beside me and tell me what she knew of my father's disappearance. Before she could comply, however, the unmistakable sound of bubbling water could be heard issuing from the pot on the stovetop. Turning from me with a sigh of relief—as though having been granted a welcome reprieve—Muddy proceeded to prepare two mugs of tea in a conspicuously dilatory fashion. After an inordinately protracted interval, she carried the cups to the table, set one down in front of me, then lowered herself onto the facing chair. Several additional delays ensued, while she blew on the steaming beverage—took a few tentative sips—and commented on the potency and flavor of the brew.

At length, perceiving that further procrastination was impossible, she gazed at me with mournful eyes and declared: "Oh, Eddie, it seems so wicked to speak ill of my family—and particularly of my own older brother, whom I idolized so as a child. He was so dashing—so handsome! Like you, dearest boy!"

Here, she extended her right hand towards my countenance, and—gently placing the fingertips upon my left cheek—patted it lovingly before continuing thusly:

"In my eyes, even his flaws became virtues. For he

was terribly headstrong. When he announced his intention to abandon his legal studies, our father was heartbroken. But to me, his determination seemed so admirable, so *heroic*. David was convinced, you see, that he had been born for the stage, that he was destined to achieve immortality as an actor."

"Did you ever see him perform?" I inquired.

"Once," said the good woman with a heavy sigh. "Here in Baltimore, at the New Theatre, in a production of a very amusing play."

"Sebastian Barnwell, or The Brazen Lover?" I asked.

"Perhaps," replied Muddy. "I no longer remember the title. But I recall your father's performance as though it happened yesterday. I was so excited when he strode onto the stage, dressed as an English gentleman. He seemed the very incarnation of manly nobility. He spoke only a few words that, to my ears, sounded like the sweetest poetry imaginable. But the audience! They hooted and hissed and called out such terrible insults! Poor David! I could see him flush and cringe in mortification. Oh, how savage I felt at that moment. Truly, Eddie, had I been armed with a weapon, I believe I would have silenced his tormentors for all eternity. For you see, at that time, my brother could do no wrong."

Gazing intently upon Muddy's visage, I took note of a singular phenomenon. Her demeanor—which I had rarely observed in anything other than a state of perfect composure or extreme, maternal solicitude—had grown incensed to the point of lividity. Her complexion, normally of a uniform ruddy hue, was now mottled with deep, crimson patches—her small eyes blazed with indignation—her mouth was contorted into an angry grimace. It was very evident that the memory of her brother's humiliation remained a source of the most painful, the most *galling* emotions.

It was nearly a minute before she was capable of resuming her speech. After imbibing several soothing mouthfuls of tea, she declared: "It was shortly after that horrid occasion that I saw my brother for the last time."

"When was that?" I eagerly inquired, leaning forward in my seat.

"A rainy night in early June. I was home by myself, reading one of Mr. Dickens' novels, when I heard somebody pounding on the front door. Opening it, I was startled to see my brother. Without speaking a word, he strode into the parlor and seated himself on a chair. His clothing was so thoroughly soaked that a puddle quickly formed itself at his feet. And the look on his face! It was so wild—so fierce—that I felt positively *alarmed*. The moment he opened his mouth, I could tell that he was terribly inebriated. Oh, Eddie, it broke my poor heart to see him in such a state."

"And what did he say?"

"He began to rant and rave about his life—how wretched it was, how everyone was against him, how the whole world was to blame for his failure. All at once, he asked me for money. Of course I had none to give him, my circumstances being what they were. When I gently explained this to him, he leapt to his feet and shouted: 'Then my destruction will be on your head, too!'

"'Why, whatever can you mean, David?' I gasped.

"'I am done with this life! I will no longer suffer such brutal mistreatment. Farewell forever!' And with that, he turned and fled into the night, never to be seen by myself—or any other member of his family—again."

These last words were uttered by Muddy in a tone of the most heartfelt sorrow. Her voice faltered—her eyes brimmed with tears. Raising the hem of her apron to her countenance, she dabbed at the twin rivulets of moisture that now trickled down her cheeks, while I reached out and administered a comforting pat to her shoulder.

"And from that time until the present you have heard nothing about his fate?" I inquired after a moment.

Shaking her head sadly, she replied: "Only rumors. That he died of yellow fever in Norfolk, Virginia. That he was murdered in a tavern brawl in Savannah, Georgia. That he ran off with a Scottish hussy and went to live with her abroad. But which—if *any*—of these stories is true, it is impossible to say."

For some moments, the two of us sat in absolute silence, while a crowd of wild speculations rushed tumultuously through my mind. At length, I could remain inactive no longer. Leaping to my feet, I announced: "Muddy, I am, as always, deeply in your debt for the assistance you have rendered, and beg your forgiveness for whatever distress my questions have occasioned you."

"But where are you going, Eddie?"

"To apprise Colonel Crockett of all that has transpired since we parted last evening. Though he has promised to return here at noon, I am too impatient to await his coming hither."

"But you have not had your breakfast," exclaimed Muddy.

"At present, I am not at all afflicted with the gnawing pangs of hunger, though—should such discomforting sensations assail me at a later period—I can readily avail myself of the dining facilities at Colonel Crockett's hostelry. In the meanwhile, please convey my deepest love to Sissy upon her awakening."

Then, after placing a grateful osculation upon Muddy's expansive brow, I hurried to the door and emerged onto the street.

Despite the earliness of the hour, the day was already unusually warm and humid, the sky being entirely overcast with gray, lowering masses of cloud. Though the streets would soon be teeming with humanity, they were, at present, largely deserted—a circumstance that allowed me to proceed in the direction of Fayette Street at full, unimpeded stride. As I bent my steps towards the Barnum Hotel, my mind was deeply occupied with the intelligence so recently imparted to me by Muddy. Her description of the intensely humiliating experience suffered by my father on the stage of the New Theatre accorded entirely with the newspaper article I had discovered earlier that morning. I was struck, moreover, by her account of the infuriated state into which she herself had been driven by the cruel, the *caustic* gibes of the audience. That a creature as gentle— as loving—as intrinsically soft-hearted—as Muddy should have been thus provoked only served to confirm what I had already surmised: that the recent spate of murders was the poisonous outgrowth of that long-ago evening of torment and mortification.

But then who was responsible for these hideous crimes? The identity of the perpetrator remained as enigmatic as ever. In this connection, I was intrigued by Muddy's reference to a rumor I had never before heard: that my feckless father had not merely abandoned his wife and children but had done so in order to abscond with another woman: a "Scottish hussy," in Muddy's uncharacteristically harsh phraseology. Was it possible that this rumor had some basis in fact—and that the savage, spectral female I had observed on three separate occasions was in some way related to this circumstance?

My attention was completely engaged by these reflections as I hurried towards my rendezvous with Crockett. All at once, a sudden gust of wind, arising from the northeast, blew a particle of dust into my left eye, causing it to shed copious tears. Pausing in my stride, I extracted my pocket handkerchief and attempted to remove the offending mote. As I stood there on the deserted street, dabbing at my ocular organ and blinking repeatedly, I became vaguely aware that another pedestrian had materialized directly in front of me and—for an unknown reason—come to a complete halt. At length, my vision cleared, permitting me to scrutinize the strange figure looming before me. The reader may readily imagine my astonishment—shock—and utter dismay—when I found myself staring into the singularly odious visage of . . . *Hans Neuendorf!*

"Morning, Mr. Poe," he said, his inordinately wide and *lipless* mouth contorted in a sneer of the utmost contempt. Having come face to face with this terrifying figure on only one previous occasion, I had somewhat forgotten the unnerving effect of his intensely ill-favored appearance: of his grotesquely oversized head, his porcine eyes, his thick and flattened nose. His left ear, which had been partially detached during his "rough-and-tumble" with Crockett, had evidently been sewn back on by a particularly unskillful police surgeon and protruded from his head at a bizarre angle—a feature that only added to the sheer ghastliness of his demeanor.

Gazing at me with an expression of utter malice, this appalling figure declared: "You've been slipperier to catch than a soaped eel, you damn whey-faced runt. But I reckon I got you now." And so saying, he took a step in my direction.

There arrives a moment in the existence of every man—even the least pugnacious—when circumstances compel him to unleash those wild, indeed *feral*, energies that Nature has implanted within the male bosom. Thus it was that when Neuendorf came at me, I instinctively assumed the fighting posture familiar to me from my days as student at the University of Virginia, when my skills as an amateur pugilist won the admiration of the entire student body. Turning in a sideways position, I bent my legs slightly at the knees and—after curling my hands into tightly compacted balls—raised each of my arms at a precise ninety-degree angle, keeping the left somewhat more elevated than the right in accordance with the time-honored tradition of fisticuffs.

I then cleared my throat and declared (in a voice that quavered slightly from the intensity of my emotions): "I am obliged to warn you, Neuendorf, that—though normally averse to violent behavior—I am viewed, by those familiar with my athletic achievements, as a master of the pugilistic arts. Should you rashly persist in this course of action, I shall not hesitate to direct the full, destructive force of my combative abilities upon you."

The immense monitory impact of this statement—to say nothing of the *ferocity* of my aspect—brought the ruffian to a sudden, startled halt. Placing his hands upon his hips, he fixed me with a look of sheer malevolence before exclaiming: "Why, you jabbering little bastard. When I get done with you, you'll wish you was in hell with your back broke."

In spite of this vicious pronouncement, the villain made no further effort to advance upon me. Very plainly (or so I assumed) he had expected to meet with no resistance and was now reconsidering the prudence of engaging with an adversary so proficient in the pugilistic realm.

All at once, however, I realized—or rather *sensed*—

that Neuendorf and I were no longer alone: someone else had crept up behind me. I began to turn around, but before I could move, a sack-like article with the rough, abrasive texture of burlap was thrust over my head, while—almost simultaneously—I received a sharp blow to the top of my cranium with a heavy, solid object. An explosion of brilliant white light flared within the confines of my skull, accompanied by a paroxysm of the most intense pain. Then the blinding light faded—the pain was mercifully cut short—and all was darkness—and silence—and utter oblivion.

CHAPTER 29

Among the many harrowing anecdotes recounted by Dr. Valdemar in his remarkable volume *The Recrudescence of Leprosy and Its Causation*, one in particular had left a deep and lasting impression upon my imagination. This was the case of a young Trinidadian gentleman who—while seated on the portico of his plantation house one afternoon, enjoying a panatela cigar—had suddenly become aware of the distinctive aroma of roasting meat. The scent appeared to be originating from somewhere nearby; and yet, when he cast his gaze about, the young man was unable to detect its source.

With a dismissive shrug, he returned to his contemplations. After an interval of several moments, he raised his cigar to his lips with the intention of taking another draw. It was only then that he perceived—to his inexpressible astonishment and consternation—that the panatela had burnt itself down to a hot, glowing stub, clamped between the first and middle fingers of his right hand. The smell he had detected was his own smoldering flesh!

Leaping to his feet, he dashed to the nearest pump and doused his hand in water. His injured fingers were so severely charred that the topmost knuckle of each digit ultimately required surgical amputation. And yet, he had felt not the slightest glimmering of pain, his fingertips having become utterly deadened to any sensation whatsoever—the first sign of that dreadful affliction which would ultimately infect his entire body and condemn him to the hellish existence of the leper.

It was not merely the grotesque details of this story that made it so compelling to me when I had first encountered it in Valdemar's book, but also the profound—and paradoxically *reassuring*—lesson it conveyed. It is customary to regard acute physical suffering as an absolute evil—an experience to be avoided at all costs. But as the above-related incident suggests, there are times when pain, even of the most excruciating sort, may—and indeed *ought*—to be perceived as a vital and even beneficial impulse, equivalent to the brazen clamor of an alarum bell: a protective device which Nature has built into our systems in order to alert us to a hazardous condition and to rouse us to those measures necessary for the maintenance of our health.

And suffering may perform another salutary function as well, by assuring us that we are still susceptible of *feeling*—for it is only those who have ceased to exist (or, as in the case of the unfortunate young Trinidadian, who have been reduced to a state of living death) that are incapable of experiencing pain.

* * *

Very gradually, I awakened to a powerful, insistent *throbbing* deep within my head. But—in spite of the almost sickening nature of this sensation—I experienced it with a rush of gratitude and relief; for its very intensity informed me that I was still among the living.

That knowledge, however, was all that I could claim, for in every other respect my conceptions were in a state of the greatest indistinctness and confusion. By slow degrees, however, my mental faculties regained their normal acuity and my present situation became clearer.

I was lying prone on the ground, my hands tightly secured behind my back, my head still swathed by the burlap sack, into which an aperture had been torn around the area of my mouth to permit respiration. My vision was, of course, entirely obscured, while my hearing—though not wholly obstructed—was greatly muffled by the fabric. Even so, I was able to deduce— by the feel of grass and stones and twigs beneath my body—that I had somehow been transported from the city to the countryside.

For many moments, I lay absolutely motionless while attempting to ascertain the precise nature of my predicament. I could hear, even through the barrier of the burlap sack, a strange, methodical *thudding* sound, as though someone were digging in the ground nearby. All at once, this shovelling noise ceased and an exceedingly gruff male voice exclaimed:

"Shit, I ain't digging another inch."

In response to this coarse and querulous pronouncement, a second male voice—belonging, as I immediately recognized, to my nemesis, Hans Neuendorf—harshly inquired: "How deep's the damn hole?"

"Three feet down. Maybe four," replied the first speaker.

"A mite shallow for a grave," growled Neuendorf. "But I suppose it'll do for the scrawny little bastard."

The reason for my abduction was now perfectly— if not *hair-raisingly*—plain. I was to be cruelly murdered, then buried in an unmarked grave far out in the countryside, where the grisly evidence of the crime would remain forever undetected! The reader may easily imagine my reaction to this dire, this *dastardly* plan. My nerves—already strained to the breaking point— became thoroughly unstrung, and a groan of the uttermost horror escaped from my trembling lips.

"Well, lookee here." This observation was uttered by yet another person, in a voice every bit as menacing as—if somewhat less guttural than—the others. It was now alarmingly evident that I had fallen into the clutches of Neuendorf and at least two of his barbarous henchmen.

"C'mon, you sorry-assed sumbitch," exclaimed this third ruffian, administering a sharp, painful kick to the region of my upper rib cage. "On your feet."

All at once, rough hands seized me by the left elbow—violently pulled me to a standing position— and tore the burlap hood from my head.

The day—as it had been when I first left home that morning—was heavily overcast; but even in the gray, dismal light, my eyes required several moments to adjust, having been deprived of any retinal stimulation for so many hours. Gradually, I was able to take stock of my surroundings. My deductions, I now perceived, had been correct. I had been conveyed somewhere out into the countryside. I was standing in a small, roughly quadrangular clearing, surrounded on three sides by a thick forest of deciduous trees. On the fourth side rose a small hill, upon whose gently ascending slope a trio of saddled horses—obviously belonging to my abductors—grazed serenely.

Several yards to my right—leaning upon the long wooden handle of a shovel whose blade was plunged into a substantial mound of dirt—stood a figure I recognized at once as the unsavory, shaggy-browed wretch with whom I had exchanged such acrimonious words on the day of Crockett's battle with Neuendorf. At his feet stretched a freshly excavated hole whose dimensions left no doubt as to its intended purpose as a makeshift human grave.

Neuendorf himself sat directly before me, coolly observing me from his vantage point atop a large, oblong rock. The third member of the gang—the wretch who had pulled me so unceremoniously to my feet—was positioned to my rear, his visage being entirely concealed from my view. All at once, he released his grip on my elbow, walked over to Neuendorf, and turned towards me with a smile of fiendish delight—thus disclosing a set of gruesomely discolored teeth from which the two upper incisors were missing. At my first glimpse of his repellent dentition, I recognized him as the second of the two ill-bred louts I had encountered at the time of Crockett's wharfside battle.

"He's wide awake now, Hansie," said the toothless one. "Let's get down to business." His countenance, as he uttered this statement, was suffused with a singular excitement—his small eyes gleaming with anticipation, his pale tongue avidly moistening his lips.

For a moment, Neuendorf continued to scrutinize me in silence. Then he slowly slid from the rock, took several lumbering steps in my direction, and growled: "Why not?"

That my death was imminent seemed certain. That my interment would be ignominious in the extreme was incontrovertible. To be horribly murdered and left to molder underground somewhere deep in the wilderness—surely, this was a most appalling, a most unimaginable fate. And yet, I was powerless to prevent it. With my hands tightly bound behind my back and three implacable brutes surrounding me, resistance and flight appeared equally impossible.

Still—I silently vowed—*if I am destined to die in such a manner, I can at least do so in a manner befitting a Poe!* Putting this bold resolution into action, I drew myself up to my fullest height, threw back my shoulders, and—as Neuendorf planted himself directly before me—spoke thusly:

"You may shoot, stab, strangle, or dispatch me in any other manner which your diabolical ingenuity may contrive, Hans Neuendorf. But never shall you see me quail—or cower—or cry out for mercy, for the noble, the valiant, the *indomitable* spirit of my heroic grandfather, General David Poe, continues to live and breathe within my own bosom!"

Stung to the quick by the penetrating force of this bold declamation, the villain grabbed me by the shirt-front and exclaimed: "Who said anything about stabbing or shooting or strangling? You need *live* bait for fishing. And that's all you are, you jabbering little shit-ass. Live bait."

Though conveyed with his characteristic savagery, this statement could not fail to have a reassuring effect upon me. So I was not to be slain, after all! My sense of relief quickly faded, however, when—emitting a maniacal cackle—the repellent-looking creature who stood leaning upon his shovel gazed at me and said: "Live *buried* bait!"

The appalling implication of this latter observation caused the blood to congeal within my veins. "Why, wh-whatever do you mean?" I asked in a hoarse, stammering voice.

"Real simple," replied Neuendorf, his simian features contorted into a look of sheer, gloating malice. "I want that Tennessee bastard out here where I can deal with him myself—no coppers, no crowds. And you're the bait that's gonna lure him. You're going down into the ground, my friend. I got a man, Charlie Dawson, on his way to the Barnum Hotel right now, to tell that shit-heel Crockett he better haul his ass out here in a hurry if he hopes to dig you up alive, you damn quivering little worm."

So inconceivably dreadful was the purport of this statement that, for several moments, I could scarely breathe, let alone speak. My breast heaved—my brain swam—the very hairs stood erect upon my head. At length, through sheer effort of will, I managed to gasp: "But surely you do not mean to subject me to the ghastly, the *unspeakable* horror of premature inhumation!"

Wrinkling his brow in apparent befuddlement, Neuendorf replied: "I'll show you what I mean." Locking the upper portion of my left arm in an iron grip, he nodded brusquely to his toothless associate, who immediately stepped to my opposite side and applied a corresponding hold to my *right* limb. Thus flanked by the two ruffians, I was hauled unceremoniously to the edge of the freshly excavated hole, while the third member of the unutterably repellent trio looked on in diabolical merriment.

That our ordinary physical capacities represent only a fraction of our *latent* powers becomes strikingly evident in moments of extreme crisis. Faced with the prospect of such a fearfully, such an inconceivably *hideous* death, I summoned up every ounce of my strength and began to struggle against my captors with the fierceness of a tiger. But my exertions were in vain. At the first sign of resistance, Neuendorf and his cohort simply redoubled their hold upon my arms. Shouting, writhing, kicking, I was thus dragged inexorably toward the edge of the yawning pit.

For a moment, I stood tottering at its brink, my arms still tightly clamped in the unbreakable grip of my captors, my bulging eyes fixed in an extremity of horror upon the gaping hole at my feet.

"Breathe deep, you son-of-a-bitch," growled Neuendorf. Then, with one sharp, vicious motion, he and his loathsome assistant released their grip and hurled me downward into the grave.

I landed with a thud upon my back, the impact of the fall driving the air from my lungs. Gasping for breath, I gazed upwards in an agony of terror and perceived my three tormentors staring down at me with a single, shared expression of demonic glee. As I attempted—unsuccessfully—to emit a shriek of horrified protest from my fear-constricted throat, Neuendorf glanced over at his shovel-wielding henchman and spoke two words whose dreadful import froze the very marrow in my bones:

"Bury him."

CHAPTER 30

To be buried while alive is, beyond question, the most harrowing—the most ghastly—the most sheerly *calamitous*—ordeal that has ever fallen to the lot of mere mortality. Indeed, it may be asserted without hesitation that no event is so terribly well adapted to inspire the supremeness of bodily and mental distress as is premature inhumation. The mere thought of this appalling fatality carries into the heart a degree of exquisite and intolerable horror from which the most daring imagination must recoil. We know of nothing so agonizing upon Earth—we can dream of nothing half so hideous in the realms of the nethermost Hell.

I hasten to add that there is nothing merely *speculative* about the foregoing assertions; rather, they are solidly founded upon my own actual experience—upon my own direct and personal knowledge.

No sooner had Neuendorf issued his dreadful command than his shovel-wielding henchman thrust the blade of his implement into the mound of freshly excavated dirt and began, with fiendish deliberation, to re-fill the hole at whose bottom I lay helplessly prone. The first load of soil landed at my feet—the second upon my upper legs—the third squarely upon my chest. As the full, awful awareness of my predicament forced itself into the innermost chambers of my soul, I once again endeavored to cry aloud. My lips parted—my fear-parched tongue moved convulsively in my mouth—but before the slightest sound could issue from my lungs, another mass of dirt struck me square on the face, filling my nostrils with the peculiar odor of moist earth and causing me to spit—and choke—and cough uncontrollably. Despair—such as no other species of wretchedness ever calls into being—flooded through my bosom and drove the blood in torrents upon my heart.

And then, amid all my infinite miseries, came suddenly the blesséd cherub *Hope,* arriving in the guise of a loud, reverberant, and inexpressibly beautiful *sound.* It was the sound of a booming male voice, calling out in tones so strong and commanding that—even with my ears partially obstructed by the dirt which had just landed about my head—I could clearly apprehend each separate word:

"Throw down that shovel, you low-down, yellow-bellied varmint, or I will make daylight shine through you faster than God's wrath!"

The voice was none other than that of my remarkable companion, Colonel Crockett, who had arrived—by what mysterious, providential agency I could not begin to conceive—in the very nick of time! The intensity of my emotions at this propitious intervention can scarcely be conveyed in mere words. Those who have been condemned to a ghastly, unspeakable doom, only to be delivered at the penultimate moment by a sudden and wholly unforeseen reprieve, can alone appreciate the feelings which suffused my bosom at this seemingly *miraculous* occurrence.

Frantically shaking the soil from my face and head, I blinked my eyes rapidly and cast my gaze upward. Directly above me, poised on the brink of the open grave, stood the shovel-wielding lout, his implement still clutched in his hands, his eyes fixed in the direction from which the frontiersman's menacing words had emanated. All at once, the sonorous voice called out again:

"Drop that digger right now, you no-account serpent, or I will perforate your ugly carcass for a certainty. Blamed if I ain't feeling fiercer than the latter end of an earthquake!"

Hearing the unmistakable note of savage resolve in Crockett's warning, the ruffian wisely relinquished his implement, plunging the blade into the soft earth at his feet. As he did so, Neuendorf—who was standing out of the range of my vision—spoke up in a crudely sarcastic tone:

"Ain't you the brave one, with a gun in your hands." A momentary pause ensued. "Shit, that-there looks like Charlie Dawson's rifle."

"I relieved him of it," came Crockett's reply. "He won't be needing it no more, for I have dispatched the varmint to a place where they give away brimstone and the fire to burn it."

By this point, I had managed, by dint of much athletic *wriggling*, to work myself around onto my belly. From this attitude, I was able to move onto my knees and from thence to a standing posture, the topmost portion of my body from the shoulders upward protruding from the mouth of the grave.

With my head thus elevated, I glanced rapidly about the clearing. The scene that presented itself to my eyes was dramatic in the extreme. Several yards off to my right stood Crockett, a somewhat battered-looking flintlock rifle held at waist level in his hands. The muzzle of this well-worn, though still-formidable, piece was aimed directly at the breast of Hans Neuendorf, who faced Crockett with a look of absolute, overpowering *malice*. Flanking Neuendorf were his two detestable henchmen, their visages similarly contorted with expressions of sheer antipathy and loathing.

The look on Crockett's own countenance was one of cool but deadly determination. Keeping his weapon levelled at Neuendorf's chest, he flicked his eyes in my direction, then——returning his gaze to the reprobate crew before him——addressed me thusly:

"How're you faring, Poe? Blamed if you don't look like a gol-danged groundhog with his head poking out of his burrow."

"Though somewhat unsettled by my recent ordeal," I replied, "I am, in all essential respects, perfectly well, owing to your timely arrival. Lacking the use of my hands, however—which remain securely bound behind my back—I am incapable of climbing from this hole and offering you my assistance."

"Don't you fret none about helping me, Poe, for I can deal with this pack of rapscallions easier than swallowing a mouthful of huckleberry pie."

"You think you're the pig's whiskers, Crockett," growled Neuendorf. "But to me, you ain't nothin' but a fart in a windstorm. Lay down that firearm and we'll see just how big you are."

This insolent remark brought no immediate response from Crockett, who merely glared at his opponent, his dark eyes blazing. Slowly, however, a smile of the purest *disdain* spread across the frontiersman's rugged countenance. In one rapid, fluent motion, he lowered his rifle—leaned it against the trunk of a nearby tree—stripped off his high-collared coat—and, planting his hands upon his hips, threw back his head and proclaimed:

"Why, you damned, impudacious varmint! I'll persuade you that I'm pluck and grit united in one individual. My gizzard's so all-fired hot that I'm fixing to breathe fireballs! I will double you up like a spare shirt—twist you into the shape of a corkscrew—and chaw you as small as cut tobacco."

"Crockett," Neuendorf muttered in reply, "you talk too damn much." Even as he spoke these words, his right hand was inching towards the handle of a long-bladed dagger hanging from the side of his belt in a faded leather scabbard. All at once—in a movement swift as thought—he plucked the knife from its sheath, and—grasping it by the very tip of its blade—raised it high above his head and flung it through the air directly at Crockett's bosom.

So great was the dexterity with which this projectile was thrown, and so deadly the intent, that it would surely have pierced the very heart of the frontiersman, had he not—with a rapidity quite as remarkable as that with which the weapon was hurled—dropped into a crouching position. Even so, the revolving blade passed alarmingly close to his body, missing his left shoulder by mere inches before burying itself in the tree trunk against which he had rested his firearm.

Eyes flashing, Crockett sprang from his crouch and threw himself at Neuendorf, driving his head into the midsection of his brutish adversary, who expelled a loud, agonized grunt as the enraged frontiersman fell upon him like a panther. Rolling upon the ground, the two combatants began to punch—bite—gouge—and kick—with such extreme, such *uncontained* fury that a cloud of dust rose up around them and obscured their struggling figures. The very earth seemed to shudder from the force of their battle, and the stillness of the forest was shattered by the savage oaths that issued from their throats as they fought.

In the meanwhile, Neuendorf's two associates leapt into action, the bushy-browed shoveller snatching up his implement; while his toothless companion—after glancing about for a suitable weapon—seized a large, gnarled branch that lay on the grass nearby.

Raising these objects above their heads, these two miscreants arranged themselves on either side of the grappling pair, their evident intention being to deal the frontiersman a deadly blow with their makeshift clubs. This nefarious plan, however, could not immediately be put into action, since the two combatants were so completely intertwined that it was impossible to strike at Crockett without risking a lethal blow to Neuendorf.

Seeing my companion outnumbered by a ratio of three to one, I felt desperate to assist him by some means. Without the use of my hands, however, I was powerless to remove myself from the hole. All at once, a solution occurred to me. Leaning the upper part of my back against one wall of the excavation, I raised my feet, one at a time, and pressed the soles against the opposite wall. I thus found myself suspended several feet above—and approximately parallel to—the bottom of the grave. Very slowly and cautiously, I then proceeded—by an alternating, precisely coordinated movement of my shoulders and feet—to inch myself up the sides of the excavation until I had reached the surface; whereupon, with one firm, decisive thrust of my legs, I propelled myself out of the excavation and onto the ground!

Struggling to my feet, I quickly took stock of the situation. By dint of his unparalleled fighting skills, the frontiersman had by now achieved a superior position, kneeling above the supine figure of his opponent and delivering a succession of blows to the villain's face. Crockett's ascendancy, however, had placed him in an exceptionally vulnerable situation, exposing him to the murderous designs of Neuendorf's henchmen. Indeed, at that very moment, the shovel-wielding villain was standing directly above the frontiersman, poised to bring his implement crashing down upon the latter's skull!

I parted my lips, intending to shout a warning. Before I could produce a sound, however, Crockett—evincing an instinctive, almost *preternatural* alertness and agility—flung himself away from the body of his opponent and rolled to one side, just as the shovel descended. At that instant, Neuendorf groggily raised his head. Completely missing its intended target, the heavy blade struck Neuendorf on the left temple with a sickening thud.

Bounding to his feet, Crockett sprang at the shovel-wielding henchman and—drawing back his tightly balled right hand—delivered a staggering blow to the scoundrel's jaw. Dropping his implement, the villain let out a quivering moan and fell crossways over Neuendorf's unconscious body.

At that instant, the second of Neuendorf's minions leapt to the attack. Wielding the gnarled branch like an aborigine's warclub, he charged madly at Crockett, who stooped—snatched up the fallen shovel—and, as the enraged attacker came at him with a roar—drove the rounded end of the wooden handle into the latter's abdomen. With an agonized expulsion of breath, the ruffian doubled over at the waist; whereupon Crockett elevated the shovel high over his head and, in one savage, sweeping motion, brought the edge of the blade crashing down upon his antagonist's neck, causing the cervi-

cal vertebrae to break with an awful—an appalling—
snap. As heavily as an overstuffed sack of feed, the toothless villain dropped lifelessly to the ground.

For a moment, Crockett stood panting over his
vanquished foes, eyes still enkindled, clothing dishevelled, hair hanging wildly about his flushed and
weather-creased countenance. His shovel was poised to
deliver another blow—if needed—to the prostrate
figure sprawled at his feet. At length—perceiving that
his antagonist would never rise again—Crockett
dropped his heavy implement to the ground and
stepped in my direction, pausing momentarily to
extract Neuendorf's long-bladed dagger from the tree
trunk in which it was lodged.

"I am happy as a soaped eel to see you alive and
kicking, Poe," he declared as he came up beside me.
"Here. Swivel around, and I will have you free quicker
than winking."

Obeying, I turned my back to the frontiersman
and—tilting my body forward from the waist up—
extended my tethered wrists in his direction. "But
how," I inquired as he proceeded to saw at the rope
with his blade, "did you manage to arrive so expeditiously—even before Neuendorf and his minions
could put their unspeakable design into action and
entomb me, while still living, in the earth?"

"Why, that's easily told," answered Crockett. "I
woke a mite earlier than I figured, had me a thumping
big breakfast, and headed off for your home. But when
I showed up, your Aunty Clemm told me that *you* had

set out to find *me*. Well, that struck me as rather queer, since I hadn't seen hide nor hair of you. So I back-tracked, and soon come across a feller who said he'd seen something almighty peculiar a while afore. It appears he was out on a stroll earlier that morning when he spied a couple of ornery-looking varmints slinging a big heavy sack onto the back of a hoss. Only the sack had two legs poking out of it!

"Well, I suspicioned the truth right off. So I bor-rowed a mount and lit out after the varmints like the devil on a gambler's trail. Before I'd gone too far out of the city, I run into that rapscallion named Dawson, who was sent to fetch me. After exchanging a few words, I pitched into him like a streak of forked light-ning, and sent him straight to kingdom come. Then I took his firearm and followed his trail back here as easy as falling off a log."

By this point, Crockett had succeeded in severing the rope. Massaging the sorely chafed wrists of my now-liberated hands, I turned to face my comrade, whose back was to the tree against which he had leaned Dawson's flintlock.

"Well, Colonel Crockett," I began in a tone of the warmest gratitude, "owing to the frontier skills of which you are so supremely possessed, I have once again been saved from——" I did not, however, manage to complete this heartfelt declaration; for——glancing over Crockett's right shoulder——I was startled into silence by a paralyzing sight.

There, standing several yards away, was the

shaggy-browed reprobate who had been felled by Crockett's punch. This ruffian had evidently regained consciousness while Crockett was in the process of freeing my wrists, and—making his way stealthily towards the tree—had taken hold of the rifle, the muzzle of which was now aimed squarely at Crockett's back!

Even before I could utter a warning, Crockett— perceiving the expression of utmost *alarm* on my countenance—quickly spun around, facing the cowardly villain just as the latter drew back the hammer of his weapon.

"No!" I shouted. With one determined stride, I stepped directly in front of the frontiersman. "I shall not permit you to slay my companion in so craven, so ignominious a fashion!"

"Step aside, ol' hoss," Crockett muttered grimly into my ear. "I will extinctify this reptile quicker than hell can scorch a feather."

Shaking my head decisively, I declared: "Colonel Crockett, I owe you my life, which you have saved on several separate occasions. To shield you now from certain destruction is an obligation that I will not—that I *cannot*—shirk."

"Why you damn blabbering pip-squeak," snarled the shaggy-browed villain. "At this range, one ball'll do for the both of you!" And so saying, he took careful aim at my bosom. I saw at once that his assessment of the situation was all-too-disconcertingly accurate. From so near a distance, a single bullet would pass directly through my heart and enter the body of my companion, who was positioned directly to my rear.

I squeezed my eyes shut and waited for the fatal roar of the firearm. In that instant, several things occurred in swift succession. First, I felt a firm hand grab me by the shoulder and fling me so violently to one side that I went crashing to the ground. Almost simultaneously, I heard a *whooshing* in the air directly above me. This was immediately followed by an anguished cry of pain from the would-be assassin and, an instant later, by the explosive discharge of the rifle.

Glancing up, I saw an astonishing sight: the shaggy-browed assailant leaning heavily against the tree trunk, his smoking rifle aimed directly into the air. He was staring down with a look of utter incredulity at the center of his chest, from which the handle alone of Neuendorf's dagger protruded, the blade itself being entirely embedded in his body. A moment later, his knees buckled—he emitted a fluttering moan—his pupils rolled back—and he slid lifelessly onto the ground.

I saw at once what had happened. Even as our would-be executioner had begun to squeeze the trigger, Crockett had shoved me aside and, with unerring accuracy and lightning speed, hurled the dagger into the breast of the villain, who, recoiling from the impact of the blade, had discharged his rifle harmlessly into the air!

The danger was past. My life had again been spared. A feeling of profound, of *overpowering,*. relief flooded through my bosom. As I attempted to rise from the ground, however, I became cognizant of an altogether different—and infinitely less pleasurable—sensation: an intense, if not excruciating, pain in the area of my right wrist, upon which I had fallen with the full weight of my body when hurled to safety by my companion.

"Are you all right, Poe?" Crockett solicitously inquired as he stepped to my side and, reaching down to grasp my left arm, assisted me to my feet.

"I am still among the living," I replied, "a condition I owe entirely to the extraordinary prowess for which you are so universally—and, I have come to perceive, so *justly*—renowned." Indicating my right wrist, which had begun to assume a most unnatural coloration, I added: "I fear, however, that I have badly sprained, or perhaps even broken, my arm."

Closely examining the limb in question, Crockett clucked his tongue and declared: "She's swole up mighty bad, for a certainty." Tearing off his striped cravat, he quickly draped it about my neck—arranged it into a makeshift *sling*—and tenderly slipped my wounded arm inside.

As he performed this deft maneuver, I took the occasion to articulate a concern that had been gathering force within my bosom. "Perhaps," I suggested, "it would be prudent to make a closer inspection of the main instigator of this entire catastrophe, Hans Neuendorf. It would be most inconvenient if he, too, should suddenly surprise us by unexpectedly emerging from his seemingly inanimate state."

"That ain't no slouch of an idea," Crockett said. Stepping over to the prostrate body of Neuendorf, he extended the toe of his boot and nudged the fallen man's head. From the utter *limpness* with which it lolled to one side—as well as from the sheer quantity of blood that had issued from his nostrils, ears, and mouth—I perceived that our nemesis was in fact absolutely deceased: slain by the unintended blow from his henchman's shovel.

"Deader than a herring," Crockett said as he returned to my side. "Killed by his own pard."

No sooner had these words issued from Crockett's lips than the black, roiling clouds above the horizon released a jagged bolt of lightning. This was followed, seconds later, by a booming peal of thunder. Then heavy droplets of rain began to fall from the sky, pattering on the grass around us.

"Poe," said Crockett, casting an appraising glance at the heavens. "I reckon you and me best find us a place to hole up for a spell. We don't stand a Chinaman's chance of getting back home afore that storm lets rip—especially since there ain't but one mount for the two of us."

"One?" I exclaimed. "But what about the steeds belonging to our vanquished opponents?"

"Why, ain't you noticed?" said Crockett. "Them nags has took off like drunks to a barbecue."

Gazing towards the hillside upon which the three beasts had been grazing, I observed that Crockett was right: the untethered horses had indeed bolted—

frightened off, perhaps, by the booming discharge of the rifle.

"But where shall we find shelter in this godforsaken expanse of countryside?" I inquired, wincing from a sudden *throb* of pain in my injured right wrist.

"Why, there's a place not a half-mile from here that'll serve just fine," said Crockett. "C'mon, pard. You can ride my hoss, and I will lead the way."

CHAPTER 31

Before stealing up on Neuendorf and his minions, Crockett had taken the precaution of concealing his horse in the woods. He now hurried off to retrieve the animal. While he was gone, I tested the condition of my damaged wrist by gingerly moving it to and fro, while alternately contracting and extending my fingers. I was pleased to discover that, however painful the effort, I could operate my hand with little difficulty: a reassuring sign that my right *carpus*, though badly sprained, had not sustained anything so severe as a fracture.

Moments later, my companion emerged from the trees, leading a handsome sorrel. Supporting me by the arm, he assisted me onto the saddle. Then—walking beside the horse with the reins in one hand and his rifle in the other—the frontiersman led us from the clearing and onto a narrow trail that ran through the forest in a westerly direction.

The trying events of that long and singularly *unnerving* day—which had begun with my violent abduction and culminated with the savage, if wholly justified, slaying of the trio of cutthroats—had left me in a state of extreme physical and emotional depletion: so much so that, in spite of my aching arm and the added discomfort of the steady, drizzling precipitation, I was unable to keep my eyelids from sagging. How long we travelled, I am thus unable to state. All at once, however, I was startled from my doze by the frontiersman's voice, announcing that we had arrived at our destination.

Shaking my head to clear it, I found myself confronted by a sight that, for several moments, was a source of the deepest perplexity. Directly ahead loomed the charred walls and blackened beams of a great, derelict mansion that had evidently been destroyed by a catastrophic fire. Only gradually did I realize that I was staring at the ruins of the once-proud house of Asher.

"But how in Heaven's name," I exclaimed in astonishment, "have we ended up *here?*"

"We have got Neuendorf and his gang to thank for that," replied Crockett, pausing at the foot of the causeway that led to the shattered manse. "Them no-account miscreants hauled you clear out here into the country to work their infernal mischief. I knowed we wasn't no more than spitting distance from the Asher place just as soon as I clapped eyes on that clearing. So I reckoned we'd find a place to hole up here 'til the weather clears."

Owing to the intense *gloominess* of the weather—as

well as to the lateness of the rapidly dying day—the visibility of the manse was greatly reduced. Even so, I could clearly perceive the utter devastation that had been wrought upon the once-fair and stately edifice. The great, carved portal was now a gaping void. The imposing *façade* was merely a shell-like wall, perforated with vacant, paneless windows. The vast, sloping roof had almost entirely collapsed, leaving little but a series of dark, skeletal beams silhouetted against the clouds. The towering battlements had likewise been reduced to rubble—though a section of one still reared jaggedly into the sky.

"C'mon, ol' hoss," said Crockett, rain trickling steadily from his broad-brimmed black hat. "Let's get out of this drencher."

Quickening his pace, the frontiersman led the sorrel over the causeway—through the gaping portal—and into the grim, hollow shell of the manse. Helping me to dismount, he glanced about the wreckage; then—spotting a relatively sheltered area where a portion of the shattered roof remained intact overhead—he tethered the horse's reins to a fallen rafter and motioned for me to follow.

By this point, my clothing was thoroughly saturated, and I had begun to shiver violently from the cold. Sinking to my haunches, I huddled with my back against a pile of bricks from a great, tumbled chimney, while Crockett scavenged for material with which to ignite a fire. At length, he returned with an armful of fuel—pieces of wood, fragments of furniture, a portion of black velvet tapestry which had somehow escaped the blaze. Perceiving my distress, he quickly built and enkindled a fire, then turned to me and declared:

"Scrouch up closer to this campfire, Poe. Before you know it, you'll be feeling snugger than a tick on a cow's belly."

Obeying his directive, I situated myself in greater proximity to the flames, adopting the cross-legged posture of an Indian brave participating in a tribal "pow-wow." Crockett—after removing his dripping hat and setting it beside him upon the blackened floor—followed suit. Ten or more minutes of silence elapsed while we thus warmed ourselves by the blaze.

"Poe, this is nice," Crockett commented at length, extending his hands, palms outward, toward the flames.

"Indeed," said I, savoring the deep, revitalizing warmth that had begun to suffuse my entire frame, "few things are more conducive to a sense of both physical and spiritual well-being than a hospitable fire on an intemperate night."

"Seeing as how we got us some time to kill," said my companion, "whyn't you tell me what put you in such a sweat to see me this morning."

The enormity of what I had endured that afternoon was so extreme that, for a moment, I could not respond to the frontiersman, having no immediate recollection of the matter to which he was referring. The horrifying ordeals—wild adventures—and unparalleled excitements of that extraordinary day had utterly supplanted all other thoughts in my mind.

At length, after several minutes of intense and highly concentrated effort, I managed to cast my memory back to the events of the early morning. Clearing my throat, I proceeded to tell Crockett of my discovery of the newspaper story that had cast such unexpected light on the portentous word "Nevermore." I also recounted my subsequent conversation with Muddy regarding the hypothetical fate of the man who had been the source of so much unhappiness to us both.

A minute elapsed following the completion of my tale, during which the frontiersman merely stared at me in ruminative silence. At length, he drew a deep breath, exhaled a sigh, and said: "Well, I'll be shot for a jackrabbit. How do you cipher it all, Poe?"

"I regret to say," I humorously replied, "that I have been somewhat too preoccupied for the past several hours to have given the matter much thought. There are, however, a number of points upon which certain deductions may be reasonably based. First, there is my firmly rooted belief that—however much the notion contravenes our commonly held conception of the so-called weaker sex—the perpetrator of these grisly deeds is a *woman*. Second, the bloody inscription—whose signification, by dint of long, assiduous effort, I have at last succeeded in uncovering—unmistakably indicates that the killer is someone intimately acquainted with the life history of the deplorable being who sired me. The choice of victims, moreover, strongly suggests that the motive for these atrocities is nothing less than revenge against those who participated in the public humiliation that finally ended my father's ignominious career. Add to these facts the rumor conveyed to me by my Aunt Maria—namely, that her brother reportedly absconded to Europe in the company of an illicit lover—and I believe only one inference is possible."

Regarding me narrowly, the frontiersman said: "Are you suggesting that the savagerous killer is the no-account she-male your daddy run off with?"

"By no means," I answered. "The figure I encountered was far too youthful in appearance. Even if my father had eloped with a female barely past the age of nubility, she would, at present, be significantly older than the person I saw."

"Then what in tarnation do you mean?"

"Let us suppose," I said, "that after fleeing to another country where his connubial status was unknown, David Poe had married his paramour and, with her, had sired another child—a *girl*. Given our close consanguinity, it would not be surprising if this daughter and I bore a striking resemblance to each other; for indeed, our relationship would be that of half-brother and -sister. Assume, moreover, that—like most daughters—this one grew up with an unquestioning devotion to her father: a father who, given what we know of the man's profoundly *embittered* nature, might well have filled her heart and soul with his own implacable hatred of the people he blamed for his failure. Is it so unlikely that, having been infused with such poisonous sentiments throughout her young life, this daughter would, at maturity, embark on a mission to take vengeance on those who had inflicted such pain and humiliation upon her adored parent?"

"Why, I reckon there's some sense to all that," Crockett said after a brief, reflective pause. "It's a mighty worrisome proposition, too—for any sister of yours is bound to be monstrous clever. How in the nation are we going to track the hell cat down before she works even more deviltry?"

"The urgency of that problem," I replied with a sigh, "is exceeded only by the maddening difficulty of its solution."

By now, the rain had ceased falling. Through a large gap in the shattered roof, I observed a parting in the clouds, through which a bright, gibbous moon was clearly visible. Glancing at my comrade, I perceived a troubled look upon his countenance.

"Is something the matter, Colonel Crockett?"

Nodding his head slowly, he replied: "I'm feeling powerful uneasy."

"And what, precisely, is the source of your discomfort?"

"It's them fellers lying dead in the woods. Now that the rain's stopped, it won't be three shakes of a sheep's tail before the coyotes and other such critters come along and chaw them up for dinner. I know they ain't nothing but the lowest kind of rapscallions, but it just don't sit right with me to leave them unburied in the forest."

"Your qualms do you credit, Colonel Crockett," I said. "For indeed, it is a terrible fate for any Christian soul to be denied the sacred rite of sepulture. But what can be done?"

Donning his hat, the frontiersman rose from the ground with a sigh and declared: "Reckon I'll take a ride back to that clearing and plant them reptiles in the ground. Can you do all right on your own for a spell?"

"Most certainly," said I. And indeed, though my injured wrist continued to suffer from an inordinate degree of *stiffness*, the pain had largely subsided.

Pointing toward his firearm, which stood leaning against a pile of rubble, several yards from where I sat, Crockett said: "I'll leave you my rifle, in case any varmints come nosing around—though I reckon the fire'll keep them away." Then—after assuring me that he would return as soon as he had accomplished his mission—he strode to his horse, undid the reins from their makeshift hitching post, and—mounting the steed—disappeared into the darkness.

The circumstances in which I now found myself were of a sort that might easily have induced a state of extreme nervous agitation in even the most steadfast of souls. I was seated by myself in the cavernous ruins of the great, fallen manse, while—in the spectral moonlight overhead—a swirling mass of windblown clouds careered through the sky like a bevy of demons on their way to a witches' Sabbath.

And yet—far from feeling in any way unsettled by my situation—my entire frame was suffused with a sense of the deepest calm and relaxation: a symptom, no doubt, of my extreme physical and emotional *fatigue*. Repositioning myself before the fire, I lay on my side with my knees drawn up and my uninjured left hand cushioning my face from the ground. Then, with the companionable crackle of the burning wood filling my ears, I closed my eyes and drifted off into a peaceful slumber.

In my dreams, I was a sailor on board the ship that bore the wily Odysseus past the isle of Anthemoëssa—the dwelling-place of the Sirens—as recounted in George Chapman's magisterial (if intermittently laborious) translation of the great Homeric epic. Following our captain's bidding, I—along with the other members of the crew—had obstructed my auditory canals with plugs of melted wax to shield myself from the fatal spell of the Sirens' intoxicating song. Even with this precaution, however, faint, faraway strains of the unearthly music seemed to filter into my ears. Suddenly, I awoke with a start, prodded from my dream by the deep, unsettling conviction that the singing I had heard was *real*.

Sitting erect, I glanced all about me. It was evident that I had not slumbered for very long. The fire, though somewhat reduced in intensity, continued to burn. The crystalline moon still floated more or less directly overhead. Straining my auditory faculties to the utmost, I listened in vain for a repetition of the uncanny music. All at once, I heard it—the dim, barely audible but nevertheless unmistakable echo of human vocalization. The feeling of serenity that had so recently possessed me vanished in an instant, replaced by a sense of profound shock—dismay—and wonder.

Whence arose this bizarre—this utterly inexplicable—sound? Rising hastily to my feet, I endeavored to ascertain its origin. From its intensely *muffled* quality, it appeared to be emanating from some subterranean source, deep within the interior of the devastated manse. By now, the clouds had thoroughly dispersed, and the moon cast an unobstructed glow on my surroundings. Proceeding by its light, I picked my way cautiously through the rubble and debris of the incinerated building, guided by the low, scarcely audible melody. All at once, the singing ceased! I paused in my steps, expecting it to resume at any moment. After the lapse of several moments—the silence having persisted—I slowly moved forward, keeping my ears fully open for the sound.

I had not taken more than a few steps when I halted abruptly. Several yards ahead of me, a large rectangular hole gaped in the blackened flooring-stones. By the luminous moonlight, I could perceive a series of well-worn steps leading downward into utter darkness. Clearly, I had stumbled upon the head of a staircase that descended into the basement of the manse. Cautiously approaching this opening, I stood at its brink and, bending an ear toward the stairwell, listened attentively. I could detect nothing, however, but a complete and tomb-like *silence*. Had the vague, uncanny singing been a mere figment of my tired and overwrought imagination? No! I had heard the noise, however faint. I was convinced, moreover, that I had discovered its ultimate source: it had issued from the very bowels of the hollow, ruined manse.

For several minutes, I remained in a state of paralyzed indecision. What course of action should I now pursue? My prudent self urged me to await the return of my comrade before undertaking any further explorations. But a contrary impulse—born of both intense curiosity and an overpowering sense of inescapable necessity or *fate*—seemed to urge me to proceed without delay. It was to this latter impulse that—after a brief period of intense inward struggle and debate—I ultimately yielded.

Making my way back to the campfire, I hastily contrived a torch from a stick of wood and a piece of the black velvet tapestry that Crockett had managed to procure. I enkindled the fabric-wrapped end by dipping it into the flames. Then, with the blazing flambeau held aloft in my uninjured hand, I returned to the head of the stairwell.

Steeling my resolve, I carefully made my way down the winding stone steps until I arrived at the foot of the descent. In the intensely oppressive atmosphere of the cellar, my torch gave off only a feeble glow. Pausing for a moment, I waited until my vision had grown accustomed to the enveloping gloom of my surroundings. All at once, I emitted a sharp, involuntary gasp. Never shall I forget the sensations of awe, horror, and confusion that overwhelmed me as I stood and gazed about.

In the dim and lurid glow of the torch, the cavernous cellar had all the appearance of a *medieval* torture dungeon!

Several feet away, propped against one wall, loomed an object that I recognized at once as a precise replica of the infamous "Iron Maiden of Nuremburg"—a great, anthropomorphized casket whose wide-flung double lids were lined with a series of razor-sharp dagger blades. Directly to the left of this monstrous implement stood an antique wooden rack, the mere sight of whose enormous, four-handled winch—by means of which the unfortunate victim was stretched until every joint in his body was completely dislocated—sent a sickening tremor through my frame. A massive interrogation chair—its seat, arms, and back bristling with iron spikes—hulked in the shadows; while the walls were hung with infernal devices of every imaginable description: branding irons, punishment collars, scourges, thumbscrews, pincers, and more.

Was it conceivable, I wondered as I gaped at this assemblage of ghastly equipment, that the late owner of this mansion, Roger Asher, had, in reality, been a latter-day Torquemada—a being who, unbeknownst to the world at large, had spent years performing the most unspeakable atrocities on a host of unknown victims? But no! Having passed an evening in his company, I could not believe this to be the case. To engage in sustained acts of torture, a man must possess certain singular attributes, a cruel—passionate—and furious *energy* being foremost among them. By contrast, the pale and melancholic master of the Asher house had struck me as so hopelessly enervated and filled with *ennui* that the mere operation of these fiendish mechanisms would have proven beyond his capacities. It was far more probable that these diabolical artifacts—whose location in the depths of the damp and cavernous cellar had saved them from a fiery destruction—were merely a part of his collection of bizarre antiques, a portion of which Crockett and I had viewed in his drawing room on the night of our ill-fated visit.

Having resolved this issue to my satisfaction, I felt somewhat reassured. My sense of relief, however, was exceptionally short-lived; for no sooner had my initial shock subsided than I was startled anew by a resumption of the uncanny singing—only much louder, closer, and *clearer* than it had been heretofore!

As I stood frozen in place—my auditory faculties fully alert—I could clearly perceive that the voice was that of a woman. For the first time, I could also ascertain the *words* of the song, which I instantly recognized as the lamentation of the poor, grief-crazed Ophelia, following Hamlet's uncharacteristically *impetuous* stabbing of her father:

> "He is dead and gone, lady,
> He is dead and gone,
> At his head, a grass-green turf,
> At his heels a stone.
>
> "And will a' not come again?
> And will a' not come again?

No, no, he is dead.
Go to thy deathbed,
He will never come again."

Trembling in every fibre of my being, I proceeded in the direction of the singing, exercising the utmost caution as I made my way past the innumerable, bizarre objects for which the cellar served as a repository. At length, I turned a corner and found myself within a vaulted passageway, at the far end of which a massive iron door stood partly ajar. The singing was emanating from the opposite side—as was a sickly yellow light that spilled out into the passageway.

The intensity of the agitation which then possessed me it is folly to attempt describing. Shaking from head to foot—as if I had been seized with the most violent fit of the ague—I crept down the corridor and paused behind the partially open door. Then, mustering every bit of courage I possessed, I stealthily peered around its copper-sheathed edge.

The sight that smote my eyes nearly caused me to swoon. There, perched on a packing crate, her back toward me, was a dark-haired female clad entirely in black, an oil lamp burning dully at her side. From the hunched position of her upper body, the occasional movement of her right arm, and the accompanying sound of rustling paper, I surmised that she was perusing a volume that lay open on her lap. The chamber, or *vault*, in which she was seated had evidently been employed by Asher as a place of storage for the supernumerary pieces of his extensive art collection. Stacks of framed canvases leaned against the walls, while positioned all around the floor and atop the numerous wooden boxes were a host of precious objects: Italian statues, marble busts, and ancient urns and vases.

What made the scene especially unnerving—in addition to the presence of the crooning, black-clad female—was the unmistakable evidence that this gloomy, subterranean enclosure had recently been employed as her dwelling-place; for, scattered among the many *objets d'art* were a number of wildly incongruous, domestic articles: a washbasin, a water jug, a blanket-covered pallet, as well as a pile of female garments.

Suddenly overcome with a sickening, vertiginous sensation, I leaned heavily against the iron door, causing it to grate harshly as it moved on its hinges. At this strident sound, the female figure stiffened—clapped her book shut—slowly rose from her perch—and swivelled to face me.

My eyes bulged with terror as I stared at the all-too-familiar countenance of the ghastly female being, whose own eyes seemed to glow with a preternatural intensity.

"So," said she, as her pale lips stretched into a cold, triumphant smile. "Fate has brought you here to me. I bid you welcome—*brother.*"

CHAPTER 32

The fraternal designation by which the bizarre, sable-clad female had addressed me—combined with the close, if not *uncanny*, resemblance between her features and my own—served to confirm the hypothesis I had so recently set forth to Crockett: *viz.* that the killer we were seeking was none other than a long-unknown sibling, sired by my own reprobate father. Having set out to demonstrate the superiority of pure, deductive reasoning over mere brute strength, I would—under ordinary circumstances—have felt a keen sense of vindication at this confirmation of my theories.

Owing to a variety of factors, however—the dreadful ordeals of the day, the unnerving atmosphere of the subterranean vault in which I now stood, the sheer indescribable *strangeness* of finding myself face to face with my sinister female double—my reaction was substantially different. Emitting a gasp of dismay, I staggered backwards several steps while loosening my grip upon the blazing torch, which fell from my hand, struck the uneven stone floor, and—rolling beside a large oil painting of a moonlit landscape that leaned against one wall—immediately ignited the wooden frame.

With a sharp intake of breath, my distaff counterpart snatched up the water jug and—striding swiftly to the enkindled oil painting—doused the incipient fire. Then, turning to me with a look of solemn reproach, she declared:

"One conflagration has already ravaged this house. Surely that is sufficient."

"A conflagration," I replied in a tremulous voice, "ignited by *yourself.*"

"Yes," she replied, her pallid lips forming themselves into a smile of grim satisfaction. "It was I who brought down this proud and stately dwelling!"

"But why?" I asked, although I had already surmised the answer.

As if endowed with a preternatural faculty that permitted her to read my very thoughts, she replied: "But have you not already guessed?"

"Yes," I acknowledged after a momentary pause. "Vengeance."

"Even so," said she. "Vengeance on those who brought ruin upon *him.*"

For a moment, I merely stared in awe-struck silence at the wan—slender—and seemingly *delicate* creature who had wrought such mayhem on so many. Making allowances for the differences in our respective *genders*—and the presence, in my own case, of the neatly trimmed moustache that adorned my upper lip—our two visages were remarkably alike. She was a singularly handsome young woman, endowed with a smooth and lofty forehead—luxuriant tresses of jetty hair—a nose of graceful, Grecian mold—and a pale, voluptuous mouth behind whose slightly parted lips I could clearly perceive her small, narrow, and excessively white teeth.

Only one intensely unnerving feature detracted from the placid loveliness of her appearance—the strange, unnatural luminosity of her enormous, dark eyes, which glinted with the hysterical brilliancy of barely suppressed *madness!*

"So it is true," I observed at length. "You are indeed his child."

"I am," she smilingly replied, taking another step in my direction. "And your own dear half-sister."

At this unequivocal confirmation of our kinship, I was overcome with an acute sense of vertigo. My knees tottered—my vision swam—and it was only by a violent effort of will that I prevented myself from sinking to the floor in a swoon.

Quickly darting out a hand, my black-clad counterpart seized me by my uninjured arm and led me to the crate upon which she herself had been perched prior to my arrival. "Come, brother," said she. "Seat yourself here, while we converse. I cannot, I am afraid, offer you much in the way of hospitality—though perhaps there is still enough water in the jug for you to drink."

"But h-how is it that you are dwelling in this sombre, this *dismal* place?" I stammered as she passed me the water jug. Grasping it by its handle, I raised it to my parched and trembling lips and greedily quaffed the small, remaining quantity of the revivifying fluid.

"Dismal?" she replied. "No, brother. *Desolate*, perhaps—but is there not something *sublime* in such sepulchred ruins? These catacombs—which I discovered while exploring the still-smoldering ashes of the great, fallen house—are well suited to my temperament. And to my *purpose*. Here, I can dwell in undisturbed solitude, emerging only at night to pursue my retributive mission. A mission that is now nearly *complete*."

The tone and content of this utterance—as well as the maniacal expression of its speaker's countenance—made it sufficiently plain that she was in the grip of a particularly dangerous form of lunacy. My mind raced as I sat there and considered what course of action to pursue. With Crockett to assist me, it would be a simple matter to take the murderous madwoman captive. My goal, then, was to keep her attention diverted until such time as the frontiersman returned from his undertaking. To this end—as well as to satisfy my natural curiosity about my father's ultimate fate—I inquired:

"And why have you felt it necessary to devote yourself to such a dire and implacable mission? What precisely was the nature of the 'ruin' that befell our common progenitor?"

"Too terrible for words!" wailed my maddened half-sibling, clutching at the bosom of her long, sable gown. "Insulted beyond endurance—vilely taunted by those with no ability to appreciate his genius—he,

with his new wife at his side, fled this benighted land
for London. My poor mother perished while bringing
me into the world. He alone raised me—educated
me—inspired me with his love of poetry, philosophy,
and the arts. By twelve years of age, I could recite the
entirety of *Lear!*"

I smiled thinly. "No doubt. And I assume that you
imagined yourself in the *rôle* of Cordelia!"

Her great, dark eyes grew even rounder. "Yes! Yes!
So you *do* understand! That was what our father fondly
called me: his 'little Cordelia.' I alone—his all-devoted
daughter—could assuage the dreadful injustices he
had suffered at the hands of a cruel and uncompre-
hending world." Here, her countenance underwent a
singular transformation—her eyes narrowing to fierce,
glittering *slits*—her mouth contorted into a savage
snarl. "And I alone," she added, "could make that
world pay for the terrible mistreatment it had inflicted
on my father."

"And is that then your name," I softly inquired.
"Cordelia?"

She shook her head emphatically, causing the
ringlets of her long, jetty tresses to dance about her
face. "No. It was merely his affectionate *sobriquet.* My
true name is . . . Lenore."

"Lenore," I repeated. "Indeed, I have always felt
that there is a strange—sonorous—singularly *melancholy*—beauty which inheres in that particular appellation." I paused momentarily before inquiring: "And
what, in the end, became of the man?"

"The terrible humiliation he had suffered in America left an incurable wound upon his soul. Seeking to salve his pain with drink, he sank, by gradual but inevitable degrees, into hopeless degradation. Before his death from a terminal *phthisis*, he had taken to the street as an *Abraham-man*."

"An Abraham-man!" I gasped. I had heard rumors of these odious creatures—wretchedly debased beggars who roamed the thoroughfares of London in the guise of raving Bedlamites, hoping for alms from pitying passersby. Even the intense and life-long antipathy I bore for my father could not prevent me from shuddering with pity at the thought of this abominable—if not entirely undeserved—fate.

"And so," I said, "you made your way back to these shores, resolved to wreak vengeance on those you held responsible for his destruction."

"Yes," she hissingly replied. "He told me the tale many times—of that fateful evening on the stage of the New Theatre, and of those jeering, mocking beings who had driven him into a shameful exile. But they will jeer and mock no more! My work here is nearly done. And nothing can prevent me from completing it."

As of yet, Crockett had still not reappeared. Seeking to distract my new-found sibling for as long as possible, I remarked: "I perceive that you are an inordinately *strong-willed* young woman."

"Even so," she replied with a cold smile. "Look—lying there beside you. The book I was reading when you first appeared. It was one of our father's dearest possessions."

The volume to which she was alluding lay open on top of the crate. Placing it upon my lap, I quickly perused the text and immediately recognized the work as Joseph Glanvill's celebrated *Treatise on the Will*. One particular passage, which had been underscored in pencil, caught my eye: "And the will therein lieth, which dieth not. Who knoweth the mysteries of the will, with its vigor? Man doth not yield him to the angels, nor unto death utterly, save only through the weakness of his feeble will."

Raising my eyes from the book, I inquired: "I am curious as to the exact signification of a comment you rendered a moment ago—namely, that what you denominate as your 'work' is almost, but not quite, completed."

"That is correct," she replied. "There is one remaining person on whom I have vowed to exact a bloody, if richly merited, revenge."

A sudden chill coursed through my frame at this assertion. "And whom do you mean?" I asked, my voice quaking slightly with premonitory dread.

"Why his sister, Maria, of course," answered Lenore. "The same unpitying being who so cruelly rebuffed my poor father in his hour of crisis."

"Villainess!" I cried as I sprang to my feet, sending Glanvill's treatise flying from my lap and onto the stone floor. "Never shall I permit you to work evil on that sainted woman. You are mad!"

"What you call evil, I call *justice*," said she. "And nothing will stop me from administering it. Certainly," she added, her upper lip curled into a sneer of the purest disdain, "not you, dear brother!"

Drawing myself up to my full height, I declared: "You err in your judgment. Though loath to employ physical violence against a member of the gentler sex, I shall use every means at my disposal—not excluding brute force—to prevent your insane, your *nefarious* design!"

A burst of maniacal laughter emanated from her throat as she exclaimed: "We shall see who has misjudged!" And so saying, she launched herself in my direction.

In regard to such considerations as martial prowess, physical agility, and sheer muscular strength, the advantages I enjoyed over my maddened attacker were nothing less than *extreme*. Even today, there is no question in my mind that—under ordinary conditions—I could have subdued her with the greatest of ease.

Owing to a singular combination of circumstances, however—the incapacitated state of my arm, an instinctive reluctance to injure a female, and the highly uneven surface of the stone cellar floor, which rendered me somewhat off-balance—I immediately found myself sprawled upon my back, my demoniacal half-sibling kneeling upon my chest and assaulting me with the ferocity of a *hell-cat*. While I vainly attempted to fend her off with my flailing left arm, she scratched at my face with her long, claw-like fingernails, then grabbed me by the hair and viciously pounded my head against the floor. As an involuntary moan of capitulation escaped from my lips, she sprang to her feet—snatched the oil lamp from its place atop the wooden crate—and dashed from the chamber.

Struggling groggily to my feet, I stumbled through the partially open doorway and staggered off in pursuit of my sister, following the receding glow of her lamp as she hurried through the labyrinthine passageways towards the stairwell.

"Stay!" I yelled as I made my way half-blindly through the subterranean gloom.

All at once—as if in obedience to my command—she stopped, swivelled, and slowly glided back in my direction.

Somewhat startled by this unexpected turn, I froze in place and waited until she had come to a halt several yards in front of me. The lurid glow of her lamp, shining upward upon her countenance, endowed her features with a ghastly, mask-like quality.

"Sister," I declared. "I urge you to abandon your implacable scheme and consign yourself to the merciful judgment of the law, which may well see fit—in view of your youth, sex, and manifestly deranged frame of mind—to spare your life for the atrocities you have already committed."

Emitting a sharp, disdainful *snort*, my half-sibling replied: "I might have slain you before this—on the evening I struck the head off the fat cow, Nicodemus, or encountered you in old Montague's sty. I spared you, however, because we share the same blood. But I shall not allow such foolish sentimentality to deter me now."

"You are unarmed," I coolly replied, feigning a bravado I did not entirely feel. "You cannot do me harm."

"No?" she sneered, elevating her eyebrows. Then—extending the lamp in my direction—she said: "Look down at your feet, dear brother."

I did as she commanded—and my heart instantly grew clammy with fear. I was standing upon a wooden trapdoor!

"Look there, brother," said Lenore. "Over your head."

I glanced upward and emitted a gasp of sheer, thunderstricken horror. Depending from the ceiling was a long, metal chain, terminating in an iron hook that dangled just inches above my head.

"Do you understand?" said she, as she took a step to one side and placed her hand upon a long wooden lever that had been concealed by the gloom but that now stood revealed in the dull glimmer of her lamp.

"I do," I said hoarsely, as the awful realization drove the blood in torrents upon my heart. The doom that awaited me was dreadful indeed.

I had been lured onto the trapdoor of a diabolical mechanism whose existence was known to me from certain authoritative accounts I had read of the Spanish Inquisition. This was a singularly ingenious variation of the *strappado*, a common form of torture in which the poor victim's arms, bound behind his back, are hooked by the wrist to an overhanging chain. The victim is then either drawn into the air by means of a winch or sent plummeting through a trapdoor on a scaffold. In either case, the weight of his own body causes his shoulder joints to tear loose from their sockets, resulting in the most agonizing pain.

In their diabolical refinement of every known method of torture, the black-robed judges of Toledo had added to the horrors of this torment by positioning the victim, not upon a scaffold, but over a bottomless *pit*, into whose prodigious depths he would dangle for what felt like an eternity. Only after being subjected to both the direst physical agonies and most hideous emotional horrors would he finally be sent plummeting into the awful abyss.

I could only surmise that—in his evident obsession with antique devices of torture—the late, eccentric master of the Asher house had constructed a precise replica of this fiendish mechanism in the depths of his own cellar.

"Farewell, brother," said Lenore, as I vainly attempted to emit a desperate cry of entreaty from my fear-constricted throat. With one swift, unhesitating motion, she drew the lever towards her—and the trapdoor crashed open beneath my feet!

A long, echoing shriek exploded from my lips, as my left hand reflexively shot upwards and clutched at the great iron hook. I was saved!—but only for the moment. Hanging by my very fingertips, I remained in the most perilous imaginable situation. I could smell the vapor of decayed fungus wafting up from the pit—feel the chill of the bottomless abyss—hear the subsiding reverberations of a small, dislodged fragment of masonry as it dashed upon the sides of the chasm in its descent.

"You are harder to kill than I would have thought, dear brother," said the pitiless, the *maleficent* female. "But it will afford me some amusement to watch you struggle."

That struggle, I perceived, was destined to be exceedingly short-lived; for the muscular strain involved in holding onto the chain by my one operative hand was already unendurable. The intensity of my fear had also caused my entire body—including the undersides of my fingers and palms—to perspire freely, adding to the extreme precariousness of my situation.

All at once, I heard a sound—very faint but nonetheless unmistakable. It was the distant whinny of a horse. Drifting through the stillness of the undisturbed night, it carried down the open stairwell and—faint as it was—filled my ears like the trumpeting of an angelic herald.

"Someone approaches!" muttered Lenore to herself. "But who—? Of course, it must be that meddling backwoodsman. I should have guessed he would be near." Addressing me directly, she continued thusly: "Brother, do not think me rude for departing so abruptly, but I must leave you to your fate. There is a matter of the utmost urgency which requires my immediate attention." Then, turning briskly on her heels, she hurried away in the direction of the stairwell and quickly vanished from my sight.

I was now left in total darkness—a condition that rendered my situation even more seemingly hopeless than before. Unless I could contrive a way to reach the edge of the pit, I would—in a matter of mere seconds—plunge into the bottomless chasm. But how to save myself? I could accomplish nothing with my hands, the left being engaged in clinging to the hook, the right remaining more or less totally incapacitated. Only my legs were free to move.

All at once, I was struck with an inspiration. Slowly at first, then with ever-increasing velocity, I began to swing my lower limbs back and forth, causing my entire body to move over the pit with the smooth, rhythmic oscillation of a clock pendulum. Back and forth I swayed in an ever-widening arc, until—having reached the farthest extension that the chain would permit—I silently uttered a brief, desperate prayer— let go of the hook—flew through the darkness—and landed with a thud upon solid ground!

For several moments, I lay face forward on the cold, rough stonework of the cellar floor, the breath having been knocked out of me. At length—impelled by the knowledge that I had not a moment to waste— I pushed myself to my feet and groped my way blindly through the black, subterranean passage until I perceived, directly ahead of me, the spectral glow of moonlight filtering down the stairwell. Picking up my speed, I stumbled forward, staggered up the steps, and found myself once again on the surface!

Immediately, the clopping sound of Crockett's approaching horse reached my ears. Dashing towards the nearest casement, I thrust my head through the opening and observed the frontiersman riding over the causeway towards the house. But where was Lenore?

In that instant, I heard an unmistakable sound, emanating from above. Someone had cocked a rifle! Casting my gaze upward, I saw a sight that caused the blood to congeal in my veins. Poised atop one of the ruined battlements, a wild-haired female figure stood silhouetted against the moon. In her hands she held a Kentucky long rifle. Evidently, this was the same firearm that Crockett had left for my protection, and that my demented half-sister must have stumbled upon as she emerged from her lair. The muzzle of this fearsome weapon was now aimed directly at my oncoming companion!

My reaction was instantaneous. Cupping my one good hand to my mouth, I shouted:

"Davy! Look out!"

This warning was scarcely out of my mouth when the thunderous report of the firearm shattered the stillness of the night—and my companion tumbled from his horse!

I gasped in horror as a shout of sheer malignant *triumph* echoed from above. But my sibling's exultation was destined to be exceedingly short-lived. As I turned my eyes in her direction, I saw the fire-damaged stones beneath her feet suddenly give way. She let go of the rifle and flailed her arms wildly for a moment, before losing her footing. Emitting a shrill cry of protest, she plummeted downward like a great, black-winged bird of night and struck the ground with a terrible—a *sickening*—thud.

A feeble moan issued from her throat as she lay crumpled at the base of the ruined house. To my astonishment, she had survived the terrible fall—though not, I inferred, without having suffered grievous, if not mortal, injuries. At the moment, however, my concern was entirely for my companion's well-being. Dashing through the vacant main portal of the house, I ran towards the frontiersman's supine form, my heart filled with an indescribable feeling of dread. Even before I reached him, however, he stirred, shook his head, and— to my inexpressible relief—rose to his feet.

"Davy," I cried. "You are all right!"

"I got you to thank for that, ol' hoss," he said, brushing particles of dirt from his jacket sleeve. "When you let out that holler, I give my head a jerk, and that bullet just hardly grazed my skull. Didn't do no more harm than pebbles bouncing off a gator's hide."

Gazing at his brow, I could see a trickle of blood—black in the moonlight—issuing from a small laceration just below his hairline.

"Who in blue blazes was taking potshots at me?" Crockett demanded.

"Come," said I. "I will show you."

Taking him by the arm, I led him towards the seemingly frail but fiercely *implacable* being who had wrought so much havoc, and whose broken body now lay amid the rubble of the devastated house. She was spread-eagled on her back, her eyes closed, her breathing harsh and intensely labored. A substantial quantity of blood had issued from her partially opened mouth and was oozing down her chin.

After silently gazing upon her visage—bathed in the ghostly luminosity of the moon—Crockett gasped: "Well, I'll be hornswoggled! Is that . . . *her?*"

"Yes," I solemnly replied. "The analysis that I set forth prior to your departure this evening has proven to be entirely accurate. You see before you the pitiless and intensely *prolific* multi-murderer we have been seeking. Nevertheless, in spite of the numerous atrocities for which she is responsible—not least of which were her foiled attempts to slay both you and myself only minutes ago—I cannot help but feel an oppressive sense of sadness at her imminent demise. For this wretched, unappeasable being is none other than my own long-lost and previously unsuspected half-sister—*Lenore.*"

"I wish I may be shot if she ain't the spitting image of you," Crockett marvelled. "But how in the nation did she come to be *here?*"

Before I could reply to this query, the fatally injured young woman stirred slightly at our feet—opened her eyes—fixed her dying gaze upon me—and endeavored to speak. Her voice being barely audible, I crouched at her side and bent an ear close to her lips—

whereupon she murmured a statement I immediately recognized as the concluding words of the underscored passage in Joseph Glanvill's treatise:

"Man doth not yield himself to the angels, nor unto death utterly, save only through the weakness of his feeble will!"

Then, as if overcome with an unbearable exhaustion, she closed her eyes, exhaled a long, tremulous sigh—and ceased to respire!

"I reckon she is a goner, ol' hoss," said Crockett consolingly, as I rose unsteadily to my feet. "What was them words she mumbled before she croaked?"

Shaking violently in every limb, I repeated Glanvill's observation to the frontiersman.

"Why, what in the nation does it *mean?*" he asked, his brow knit in puzzlement.

The terrible stresses—overwhelming anxieties—and fearful ordeals of that long, harrowing day had, by that point, taken a severe toll upon my emotional equilibrium. Indeed, my nerves had at last become thoroughly unstrung. Clutching at the bosom of my shirt with the trembling digits of both hands, I replied—in a voice that quickly ascended from a harsh, desperate whisper to a hysterical shriek: "Oh, do you not see? It means that the fierce, the *monstrous* will-power of which she was possessed shall not permit even *Death* to restrain her! It means that she will one day return from the tomb—a grim and ghastly revenant, shrouded in her blood-dabbled cerements—to complete her dreadful mission of revenge!"

"Eddie," the frontiersman replied, "you do have

the beatenest notions in the whole dad-blamed world. That varminous sister of yours is as dead as a bedpost. Don't you fret none—she won't be coming back before the final trumpet blasts, no more than anybody else."

Encircling my shoulder with his powerful right arm, he added: "Come along, ol' hoss. I don't know about you, but I am rotten glad this ornery business is over and done with."

So saying, he led me away from the motionless form and towards the scintillant embers of the stillglowing campfire. There, I would huddle unsleepingly at his side, recounting the bizarre, blood-chilling events that had transpired during his absence.

With the coming of the dawn, we prepared to bear the pallid corpse of my mad, monomaniacal sibling back to the police. In the clear light of the newborn day—as we arranged the cadaver across the saddle of Crockett's steed—I perceived that he had been both right *and* wrong. It was not Lenore herself that I had to fear; for, indeed, she was utterly and irrevocably *dead*. But the memory of her brief—anguished—and wildly destructive existence was another matter entirely. Even then, I knew it would remain with me always: a grim and sorrowful shadow that would cease to haunt me— *nevermore!*

EPILOGUE

I have said that—however justly deserved—the death of my demented half-sister cast a deep and sorrowful shadow upon my soul. For the citizens of Baltimore, however—whose wonted tranquillity had been severely disrupted by the string of savage killings—the resolution of the case meant that a fearful pall had been *lifted*.

My own invaluable contributions to the affair did not fail to make the deepest impression upon the police. Captain Russell in particular was profuse in his praise—as well as in his apologies for those suspicions that had caused him, however briefly, to perceive me as the culprit. The analytical means by which I had disentangled the mystery struck him as little short of miraculous, and—among the emissaries of the law—my inductive abilities quickly assumed the status of *legend*.

In the popular mind, however, it was not myself but rather the heroic figure of Crockett who loomed most prominently in the drama—an impression that the inveterately self-aggrandizing frontiersman did little to modify. In his statements to the press following our return to the city, he evinced little shyness in attributing the successful termination of the case to his own unshrinking efforts—though he never failed to acknowledge the "splendiferous help" he had received from his "little chum, Eddie Poe."

Under the circumstances, I could not begrudge my friend these outrageous overstatements of his own *rôle* in the affair. He had, after all, saved my life on several occasions and—following my abduction by Hans Neuendorf and his gang—rescued me from a fate of unspeakable *ghastliness*. Moreover, the crude acclamation of the *mob*—so desperately courted by Crockett—was infinitely less consequential to me than the profound respect—if not outright *awe*—that I had earned from the *cognoscenti* of the law.

In the end, whatever political benefit Crockett had hoped to accrue from our triumphant resolution of the case failed to materialize. Sadly—and much to my own surprise, in light of the great esteem in which the public clearly held him—he lost his attempt to regain his congressional seat in the 1835 elections and found himself exiled from political life.

By then, my own circumstances had undergone a radical alteration. In August of 1835—slightly more than one year following the extraordinary events recounted in the foregoing pages—I moved back to Richmond, the city of my youth, having been offered a remunerative position as editorial assistant on Mr. Thomas White's journal, the *Southern Literary*

Messenger. One month later, my deepest prayers were answered when my darling little Sissy and I were joined as husband and bride. By the middle of October, the two of us—along with our dear, all-devoted Muddy—were settled in a handsome brick boarding house on the southeast corner of Bank and Eleventh Streets, belonging to a kindly widow named Mrs. Yarrington.

In addition to these vast improvements in my financial and domestic arrangements, I had also undergone a period of remarkable creative inspiration. Having concluded that there was unsuspected merit in Crockett's literary advice (to wit, that the surest way to achieve commercial success was for an author to write about his own experiences), I had embarked on a series of tales based upon those incidents and situations to which I myself had been so recently exposed: the savage butchery of the landlady—the masked ball visited by the dread figure of Death—the torture dungeon equipped with a bottomless pit—the mutilated old man concealed beneath the floorboards—and so on. Having altered certain details of the actual events to accord with the rigorous requirements of the short-story *form*, I had succeeded in producing a handful of tales that were, I devoutly believed, among my finest fictional efforts to date.

By way of acknowledging the assistance he had thus afforded me, I had mailed a handwritten copy of one of these tales to the frontiersman, along with a letter informing him of my recent nuptials. I had not received an answer, however, and assumed either that he had not received my package, or that his recent political defeat had left him too dispirited to reply.

It was a brisk, brilliantly sunny afternoon at the very end of October—more than a year since I had last set eyes on the frontiersman. Seated at my writing table in front of the second-story window that overlooked Capitol Square, I was so deeply absorbed in my latest endeavor—the composition of a story about a man haunted by a mysterious *doppelgänger*—that only by slow degrees did I became aware of a strange commotion on the street outside my boarding house.

Glancing out the window, I gave a start of surprise. There, mounted on a handsome black steed, was a singularly imposing figure, garbed in the colorful, buckskin attire of the backwoods huntsman. I saw at once that it was none other than my erstwhile companion, Davy Crockett, whose presence had already attracted a large, excited crowd of neighborhood children.

Leaping from my place, I dashed down the stairs and into the parlor, where Muddy, seated upon a chair before the dormer window, was thoroughly engrossed in her needlework. Stretched out, face downwards, in the center of the floor was my darling little wife, who—crayon in hand—was busily drawing a delightful sketch of a frolicking puppy, while humming softly to herself.

"Muddy! Sissy!" I cried. "You must come at once!

We have a most unexpected, if inordinately *welcome*, visitor."

Accompanying their actions with many expressions of curiosity and wonder, my loved ones immediately suspended their occupations, rose to their feet, and followed me out the front door. Excited ejaculations burst from their lips at their first glimpse of the frontiersman. Making our way through the chattering crowd of children, we hurried toward our visitor—myself in the lead, Muddy and Sissy following closely at my heels.

"Howdy there, pard!" Crockett declared with a broad grin as he saw me approach. "I am mighty tickled to see you again." Swiftly dismounting from his horse, he gave my hand a powerful shake before turning his attention to the women.

"Why, I'll be hanged if you two gals ain't got even purtier since I last clapped eyes on you!" Enveloping Muddy in his arms, he hugged her warmly, then turned to Sissy and—placing his hands upon her slender waist—raised her high in the air for a moment before setting her back down upon her feet.

"Miz Virginny, I reckon that marriage plumb agrees with you, for you are lit up just as bright as a glow-worm on a summer night!"

As Virginia giggled with pleasure, Crockett turned back towards his steed, reached into his saddlebag, and extracted a large, oddly shaped bundle, crudely wrapped in brown paper and twine. Thrusting this object towards Sissy, he said: "This here's a wedding present for you and Eddie."

Squealing with excitement, Sissy quickly tore off the wrapping, then emitted a sharp gasp of astonishment as she found herself holding a medium-sized, taxidermically preserved member of the species *Procyon lotor*—more generally known as the common *raccoon*.

"I shot, skinned, and stuffed her myself," proudly declared Crockett, who was wearing a hat that closely resembled our wedding gift. "Why, she's as fine a varmint as any you'll find in Mr. Peale's museum."

"Indeed," I said, "it is a most handsome specimen." Removing the creature from Sissy's hands, which had begun to tremble slightly, I continued: "But to what circumstance do we owe the pleasure of this wholly unanticipated visit?"

"Why, I had to take care of some unfinished business in Washington City. So I reckoned I'd stop by and say howdy on my way back."

"Did you receive the package I mailed you some weeks ago?"

"Yes sir, I did. I read over your story concerning that ol' Asher house, too, and it war a humdinger— though I will say there are considerable many stretchers in it."

"But that," I replied, "is the very essence of the fictional prose tale. The skillful literary artist does not fashion his thoughts to accommodate his *incidents*, but having deliberately conceived a certain single effect to be wrought, he then *invents* such incidents, he then combines such events, and discusses them in such tone as may best serve him in establishing this preconceived effect."

For a moment, Davy merely stared at me in silence. Then, chuckling softly, he said: "I'll be kicked to death by grasshoppers if I ain't missed hearing that highfalutin palaver of yours, Eddie. Why don't you come along with me?"

"Come along?" I said. "To where?"

"Why, to Texas," he replied.

"Texas!" I exclaimed.

"Yes sir," declared the frontiersman. "I have made up my mind to head out West and give the Texians a helping hand on the high road to freedom. Davy Crockett has always been fond of having his spoon in a mess of that kind—for if there is anything in the world that is worth living and dying for, it is freedom."

A reverential silence had, by this point, descended upon Crockett's juvenile audience, who gaped up at him with undisguised wonder as—hands on hips and chest thrust forward—he continued thusly:

"When the folks back home chose to throw me out of Congress and elect a timber-toed rascal in my place, I told them that they might all go to hell, and I would go to Texas. There is a world of country to be settled out there, and a man may make a fortune for himself and his family quicker than it would take lightning to run around a potato patch."

"I wish you well, Davy," said I. "But the boundless and untamed expanse of the great Western frontier—

rich though it may be in material opportunity—possesses little, if any, allure to me."

"No," Crockett said fondly, "I reckon you ain't the wilderness type, Eddie."

At that moment, as though to recall his attention to more pressing obligations, Crockett's magnificent black stallion shook his great head and emitted a snort.

"Reckon I'd best be on my way," said Crockett, patting the creature on the neck.

"Won't you stay and have dinner with us, Colonel?" exclaimed Muddy.

"No thank you, ma'am," said the frontiersman. "I have a heap of travelling to do before the sun goes down. But seeing you all again has made me feel happier than a soaped eel."

"Thank you for the lovely gift," Virginia said sweetly, if not (to my ears) with entirely *wholehearted* conviction.

Crockett, however, merely beamed with delight. "You are almighty welcome, Miz Virginny," he said.

All at once, a young, freckle-faced boy at the front of the crowd exclaimed: "But Davy, ain't you going to tell us a story?"

"Ain't got time, young 'un," replied the frontiersman. "But Mr. Poe here is a mighty splendiferous storyteller—and if you ask him real polite, I am tolerable certain that he will tell you all about the rip-roarious times him and me had together."

He inserted a foot in the stirrup of his saddle and

swung himself onto his steed. "Farewell, friends!" he cried, doffing his coonskin cap and waving it high in the air.

Then he wheeled his horse around and, sitting erect in the saddle, trotted off in a westerly direction—towards the wild, majestic territory where Immortality awaited.

LOOK FOR THESE TRUE-CRIME
SCHECHTER SHOCKERS

**"Deserves to be...pored over by
the hard crime enthusiast."**
—The Boston Book Review

"Top-drawer true-crime." *—Booklist*

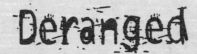

"Horrifying." *—American Libraries*

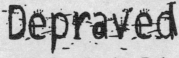

"Shocking." *—Ann Rule*

POCKET BOOKS   2372

The A to Z Encyclopedia of Serial Killers

by Harold Schechter
and David Everitt

"The scholarship is both genuine
and fascinating."
—*The Boston Book Review*

POCKET BOOKS

2373